BARRACUDA 945

Patrick Robinson is the author of five previous bestselling novels, including, most recently, *The Shark Mutiny*. He is also the author of several non-fiction bestsellers including *True Blue* (with Dan Topolski) and *Born to Win*. He is the co-author with Admiral Sir Sandy Woodward of *One Hundred Days*.

Also by Patrick Robinson

Nimitz Class
Kilo Class
H.M.S. Unseen
Seawolf
The Shark Mutiny

Non-fiction
Classic Lines
Decade of Champions
The Golden Post
Born to Win
True Blue
One Hundred Days
Horsetrader

BARRACUDA 945

Patrick Robinson

Century · London

Published by Century in 2003

1 3 5 7 9 10 8 6 4 2

First published in the United Kingdom in 2003 by Century
The Random House Group Limited
20 Vauxhall Bridge Road, London SW1V 2SA

Random House Australia (Pty) Limited
20 Alfred Street, Milsons Point, Sydney,
New South Wales 2061, Australia

Random House New Zealand Limited
18 Poland Road, Glenfield
Auckland 10, New Zealand

Random House (Pty) Limited
Endulini, 5a Jubilee Road, Parktown 2193, South Africa

The Random House Group Limited Reg. No. 954009

www.randomhouse.co.uk

A CIP catalogue record for this book is available from the British Library

Typeset by SX Composing DTP, Rayleigh, Essex
Printed and bound in Great Britain by
Clays Ltd, St Ives Plc

ISBN 0 7126 2176 8

ACKNOWLEDGEMENTS

For this, my sixth techno-thriller, I drew on much of the experience and learning of the past. However, I continued to require long and careful advice from my regular tutor, Admiral Sir Sandy Woodward.

When you are trying to con a big nuclear submarine through dangerous, electronically-surveilled Arctic waters, I find it helpful to sit next to a man who has actually done it. The Admiral is not only a former SSN Commanding Officer, he was also the Royal Navy's Flag Officer (Submarines), and, of course, the Forward Commander of the Royal Navy Task Force which defeated Argentina in the Falklands War.

I am further obliged to admit it was he who declared the world's next really severe terrorist problem might be when a Middle East group acquires a nuclear submarine.

He regards all of my books as warnings to the West to stay alert, to stay on top of the game, and to stay out in front, essentially because someone might be gaining on you.

I also owe thanks to at least three Special Forces officers who were so generous with their time and expertise. In particular, *Barracuda 945* owes much to the enormous detail provided by one of them, a high-explosives expert who grappled with my complicated demolition problem for several weeks, before solving it.

Finally I would like to thank my friend Hitesh Shah who steered me, with his customary good humor, through some of the intricacies of the Muslim faith.

CAST OF PRINCIPAL CHARACTERS

Senior Command

The President of the United States (Commander-in-Chief US Armed Forces)

Vice Admiral Arnold Morgan (National Security Advisor)

General Tim Scannell (Chairman of the Joint Chiefs)

Harcourt Travis (Secretary of State)

Robert MacPherson (Defense Secretary)

Jack Smith (Energy Secretary)

National Security Agency

Rear Admiral George R. Morris (Director)

Lt. Commander James Ramshawe (Assistant to the Director)

Captain Scott Wade (Military Intelligence Division)

US Navy Senior Command

Admiral Alan Dickson (Chief of Naval Operations)

Rear Admiral John Bergstrom (Commander Special War Command [SPECWARCOM])

Rear Admiral Freddie Curran (Commander, Submarine Force, Pacific Fleet [COMSUBPAC])

British SAS

Lt. Colonel Russell Makin (Commanding Officer 22 SAS)

Major Ray Kerman (Commanding Officer Israeli Garrison)

Sergeant Fred O'Hara (Advisor Israeli Defence Force)

Sergeant Charlie Morgan (Advisor IDF)

HAMAS Terrorists

General Ravi Rashood (C-in-C Military Assault Division)

Lt. Commander Shakira Rashood (Precision Targeting, Special Navigation Officer, Barracuda 945)

Captain Ben Badr (Commanding Officer, Barracuda 945)

Lt. Commander Ali Akbar Mohtaj (Commanding Officer, Barracuda II)
Lt. Commander Abbas Shafii (Senior Submariner Iranian Navy)
Chief Petty Officer Ali Zahedi (Propulsion)
Chief Petty Officer Ardeshir Tikku (Auxiliary)
Major Ahmed Sabah (Freedom Fighter)

International Strategists
Admiral Zhang Yushu (Senior Vice-Chairman, Peoples' Liberation Army/Navy Council, China)
Admiral Vitaly Rankov (C-in-C Russian Navy)
Admiral Mohammed Badr (Iranian Navy)
Senior Ayatollahs and Hojjats (Iran)

US Navy SEALs
Lt. Commander Bill Peavey (Team Leader Operation, Main Assault Group)
Lt. Patrick Hogan Rougeau (2 I/C Operation, Team Leader Recce Group)
Lt. Brantley Jordan (Bomb-lashing Chief)
Lt. Zane Green (Overall Command Group)
Lt. Brian Slocum (Overall Command Group)
Chief Petty Officer Chris O'Riordan (Diver and Combat SEAL)
Petty Officer 2nd Class Brian Ingram (Combat SEAL and bodyguard to Lt. Rougeau)
Petty Officer Mich Stetter (High Explosives Expert and assistant to Lt. Commander Peavey)
Petty Officers Joe Little and Tony McQuade (Landing Area and Materiel Security)

Navy Air Wing
Lt. Commander Steve Ghutzman (Senior COD [Carrier On Delivery] Pilot)

Close Connections
Kathy O'Brien (Fiancée and Personal Assistant to Admiral Morgan)
Mr and Mrs Richard Kerman (Parents of Major Ray Kerman)
Rupert Studley-Bryce MP (School friend of Major Kerman)

PROLOGUE

Sunday, February 19, 1995

Captain Ray Kerman was shivering. Frozen half to death, he was shaking uncontrollably, lying down on the frigid concrete floor of his cell. At least he thought he was lying down, but in fact he had assumed the fetal position, curled up tightly, striving for warmth, his backside resting in a three-inch deep puddle of cold water, or worse.

They had taken off the hood, but the Captain wore no boots, just ripped, bloodstained socks. His pants and shirt were coated in mud. His warm military jacket had been confiscated. And now the hallucinations were growing worse, and he was drifting along in a no man's land, somewhere between reality and mirage. He could no longer ascertain whether his eyes were open or closed in the sullen, icy darkness of the cell.

There was a jug of water somewhere, but he was too afraid to grope in the darkness to find it, in case he knocked it over. And so he remained tightly coiled, his mouth parched, his entire body racked by cold so painful he thought it might freeze his heart and cause it to stop beating.

They came for him at 2 a.m., dragging him up, shoving him down a corridor, and throwing him into a room. Both of his captors wore the uniform of some eastern European army, and now they aimed an arc-light into his eyes. Two young officers marched in, wearing similar foreign uniform, and one of them cupped his hand under Ray's chin and said in heavily accented English, 'You will tell us your mission and that will save you being beaten half to death . . . that's my speciality. I beat snivelling little spies . . . *What were you doing out there on the moor . . .?*

'*I'm 538624 Captain Ray Kerman . . .*' Number, rank, and name.

The officer moved to the back of the room and returned with

a wooden truncheon. 'You see this . . . I'm going to deliver one blow with this . . . straight across your mouth and you're never going to look the same again.'

He raised it high across his body and screamed '*Tell me . . . or I'll rearrange your ugly face . . .*'

'*I'm 538624 Captain Ray Kerman.*'

They kept him there for three hours, alternately threatening and bargaining. Threatening to execute his companions, threatening to jail him for twenty years. Bargaining for his knowledge about the Abbey.

After one hour they dragged him back to his cell, bound him again, and placed the hood over his head. At midnight, he heard the sound of marching feet, then the unmistakable sounds of a man being punched, beaten, the sound of a fist smacking against the flesh of a face. Then thumps of boots slamming into a human body. Moans, then screams, terrible screams, a pleading voice, '*Please no . . . please no . . . please no.*'

And then someone booted his cell door open. And hands grabbed him, and the hood was removed and someone took him firmly by the hair. 'Right, and now we try something different.'

And the screams along the corridor grew louder. And now the unseen man was begging, begging for them not to beat him again.

'*I'm 538624 Captain Ray Kerman . . .*'

All through the night, they kept him awake, firing questions, demanding, threatening, always threatening. The same officer marched about with the truncheon. Another swished a riding crop. They gave him water, but nothing else.

They threatened to torture Andy. They told him it hardly mattered anyway because Charlie had broken down and told them everything. They just wanted his confirmation as the officer. Just the details of the mission on the moor.

'*I'm 538624 Captain Kerman . . .*'

They took him back to his cell at 0700. Gave him stale bread. And then awakened him every half-hour until midnight, making thirty-four different entries into his cell. Then at midnight, they piped earth-shattering music into the cell, cheap rock 'n roll. Ray had to sit with his fingers pressed into his ears to lock out the sound.

They changed his cell, pushed and shoved him down into a cellar with deeper puddles of freezing water. They left him to his misery, and short fitful sleep, for two more hours, then hauled him out again, and poured a bucket of ice-cold water over him, and dragged him back to the interrogation room. And now Ray was trembling uncontrollably.

And this time there were four lights aimed at his eyes. And two men, one obsequious, reasonable, bargaining. The other, an unshaven brute, threatening violence and torture. He kept hold of Ray's chin, staring at him, insulting him, yelling at him.

And Ray just kept saying over and over, '*I'm 538624 Captain Kerman . . .*'

Now he had no idea whether it was night or day. He no longer had a grip on time. He had no idea what day it was, where he was, whether he was. Stripped of his dignity and most of his clothes, starving hungry, shaking with the cold, no longer with any grip on his words or actions, he knew he was on the verge of breakdown.

All he had left was defiance. Obdurate, hard-nosed, stubborn defiance. They could not get that out of him. But they kept trying, marching him to the interrogation room. Shouting and screaming, taking him back to the cellar, throwing him down in the water, which seemed unaccountably deeper. There was nowhere dry to sit, and he just lay there, shivering, trying to sleep, trying to ignore the screams of the tortured men, the ones that now ventured into his dreams.

He thought it was dark when the two interrogators came clumping down the stairs and booted the door open. But he could not tell, and they manhandled him to his feet, dragged him up the stairs, and stripped off his hood. He found himself facing the senior officer, crisp in a different uniform.

Hallucinating quite badly now, he answered instinctively, unaware of whether he was in a dream or reality, muttering, '*I'm 538624 Captain Kerman . . .*'

And to his amazement, the officer held out his hand. 'Hello, Ray,' he said. 'Welcome to the SAS . . . and will someone turn off those bloody recordings out there . . .?

'Now, Ray. Come on down to the officers' mess. It's five o'clock in the morning. You can have a bath, and some breakfast, and then sleep for the day. We have a clean uniform ready for you, and I thought we'd fly back to Hereford around 4.30 this afternoon.

'You've done very well . . . very well indeed . . . but I regret it was not a vintage intake . . . of the eighty men who applied only five made it.'

'Anyone I know?'

'Yes. That young Paratroop Officer you started with, Lieutenant James, stuck it out. So did that Corporal you were on the moor with, Charlie Rider . . . we lost a lot of chaps towing them across the moor behind the jeep. Your other pal, the Sergeant, Bob, I think cracked about two hours ago under interrogation.'

'Jesus, you guys know how to put someone through hell . . .'

'We also know what we're looking for. And no-one pretends that courage on this scale is all that common.'

'No, sir . . . I suppose not.'

1000 Monday, February 20, 1995
CO's office, Stirling Lines, Hereford
Captain Ray Kerman stood to attending in front of Lieutenant Colonel Russell Makin, the Commanding Officer of 22 SAS. 'It is my very great pleasure to welcome you to this Regiment, Captain Kerman. I see from your record that you won The Sword at Sandhurst a few years back, so you are used to excelling. And I am sure you will find ample outlets for your undoubted talents here in the Special Air Service.'

'Thank you, sir.'

'You have seen from your training and indoctrination process what we demand. And I hope it will be of some reassurance that every single man here has passed the courses which you have just undergone. We are not like other Regiments, but when the bugle sounds for our style of warfare, I think you will find your-self working among the supreme practitioners of our profession.'

'Yessir. I am sure that is so.'

The Colonel then stepped forward, and handed to Captain Ray Kerman the distinctive, coveted beige beret of the SAS. On the front was the cloth badge of the Regiment, the upright winged dagger. Beneath it were the words, '*Who Dares Wins.*'

Thus at four minutes after 10 o'clock on that Monday morning, Captain Raymond Kerman was accepted into one of the two top fighting military units in the world, the other being the US Navy SEALs, four members of which were in residence at Hereford when Ray wore the beret for the first time.

He saluted the Colonel, made an about turn, and left the room.

No-one else had been present to see the little ceremony, and only those who had served in the SAS would have understood its significance – but a soldier's own soul is an iron taskmaster, and there was a smile on the face of Ray Kerman.

CHAPTER ONE

1900, Wednesday, May 12, 2004
SAS Training Camp (Counter Terrorist)
Southern Israel (Location: CLASSIFIED)

Major Ray Kerman, on his second tour of duty with the Regiment, stared westward out towards the desert city of Beersheba. In the setting sun, the heat still rose shimmering along the foothills of the Dimona Mountains, despite the eternal wind. A long line of Bedouin camels heading for the last oasis north of the river, moved symmetrically across the sandy wastes, not 100 yards from the SAS stronghold.

Ray Kerman stood almost in the long shadows of the caravan. And he watched the black-hooded men, swaying to the tireless rhythm of the camels, their wide hooves making no sound on the soft desert floor. The nomads of the Negev desert turned neither right nor left, acknowledging nothing, especially a swarthy broad-shouldered Army officer in Israeli uniform. But Ray could feel their hard, dark eyes upon him, and he understood he would be forever an intruder to the West Bank Bedou.

He usually found the tribesmen were different, trading at the Bedouin market in Beersheba, where the hand of friendship was frequently offered to any prospective buyer. But as his Sergeant, Fred O'Hara had mentioned, 'These blokes would rush up and french-kiss Moyshe Dayan if they thought they could sell him a second-hand carrot.'

Ray however saw them differently. Before making this first tour of duty to the near east he had read the works of the important Arabist, Wilfred Thesiger. And he had arrived in the Israeli desert filled with an unspoken admiration for the noble savages of the wide, hot, near-empty Negev desert . . . men who could, if necessary, go without food or water for seven days, who could not be burned by the pitiless sun, nor frozen by the harsh winter nights. Men who could suffer the most shocking deprivations, yet still stand unbowed. They were men who accepted certain death only upon the collapse of their camels.

The English officer had not forgotten the first tribesman he had met in Beersheba, a tall robed nomad, trading goats and sheep in the market. The man had been introduced, and he had stared hard, without speaking, into Ray's eyes, the traditional mark of contact in the desert.

Finally he had touched his forehead and gracefully arched his hand downwards in the Muslim greeting. Softly, he had said, '*As salam Alaikum*, Major. Peace be upon you. I am Rasheed. I am a Bedouin.'

In that split second, Ray Kerman knew what Wilfred Thesiger had meant when he had written about the Bedouin's courtesy, his courage and endurance, his patience and light-hearted gallantry. 'Among no other people,' Thesiger once wrote, 'have I felt the same sense of personal inferiority.'

Ray recognized that as high praise. Not only had Thesiger been one of only two white men ever to make the murderous journey across the burning wastes of the 'Empty Quarter' in the south-east of the Arabian Peninsula, he had won a boxing Blue at Oxford University, and served in the SAS during the war. More telling yet, the craggy, teak-tough Thesiger had been educated at Eton, England's school for its highborn, a place which in 560 years had never produced a pupil who felt personally inferior to anyone, never mind a camel driver. Ray knew about Etonians. He had attended Eton's 'upstart' rival public school, Harrow, alma mater of Sir Winston Churchill, founded as recently as 1571 as a Protestant school in the reign of England's first Protestant Queen, Elizabeth I.

And now Ray stood watching the camel train head westward, into the shifting sands, into the silence. He knew they would remain at the oasis overnight, before heading into the market at first light. He held his Heckler and Koch machine-gun lightly in his right hand, the barrel downwards, and he shook his head as he contemplated tonight's mission.

And he muttered inaudibly to himself, 'I really do not want to end up shooting these people. I wonder if I ever should have accepted this command?'

The truth was Major Kerman, with his immaculate SAS record, and inescapably Jewish surname, was not precisely what he seemed. Major Kerman's parents had both been Iranian, brought up as Muslims, and descended from nomadic Arabs in the southern city of Kerman, on the edge of Iran's vast southern desert, Dasht-e Lut.

But when the downfall of the ruling Shah appeared to be inevitable, back in the early seventies, the wealthy couple had emigrated with their infant son, Ravi, to London. And there they began importing from the family's carpet manufacturing business in their home city.

The booming British economy during the premiership of Margaret Thatcher was perfect for the family. Mr. and Mrs Reza Sharood quickly became Mr. and Mrs Richard Kerman, taking a new name from an old place in the manner of many Middle Eastern families far from home.

While dozens of tribesmen stitched and wove the elegant patterns in the hilly regions north of Bandar Abbas, Richard Kerman opened a string of warehouses in southern England, and then invested in a small shipping line to transport the costly wool and silk floor coverings up through the Suez Canal and on through the Mediterranean to Southampton.

Richard's sea-going freighters led him to oil tankers, and to the gigantic profits which were commonplace during the 1980s. His Iranian carpets led him to expand his importing empire. But he stuck to what he knew, shipping superb Iranian dates out of Bandar Abbas . . . tons and tons of them, all grown in another town in the province of Kerman, the tree-lined twelfth-century citadel of Bam. Most of the dates were cultivated by his Rashood relatives.

Soon the Kermans owned an expansive gabled house on North London's fabled Millionaire's Row, The Bishop's Avenue, next to the old Cambodian Embassy.

Twin Rolls Royce Silver Ghosts occupied the garages. And, not so far away, fifty-five miles west down the M4 motorway in the Berkshire village of Lambourn, six highly-bred thoroughbred flat horses were expensively in training, doing battle during the summer months under Richard Kerman's jet-black and scarlet-sashed silks.

And young Ravi, whose first sight of the world had been the hot, dusty streets of the depressed urban sprawl of his hometown in the desert, was renamed Raymond.

Raymond Kerman, after a six-year junior education in one of the most expensive preparatory schools in London, now owned a British passport and at the age of thirteen, would enter Harrow, admitted, even by Etonians, as probably the second best fee-paying school in the country, and a long established haven for the sons of Middle Eastern ruling families.

On the entry form, Richard Kerman had declared the boy's religion as *Church of England*. In the space for birthplace, he had filled out *Hampstead, London*. No formal birth certificate had been required. Nothing to reveal that Raymond Kerman was really Ravi Rashood, born Iranian from the south-east of that country. It was Richard Kerman's view that in England it was unwise to be different from the majority. The more patrician tribes of London society found it disquieting.

Indeed by the time young Ray entered Harrow it was assumed he had more or less forgotten anything he ever knew about the religion of Islam. And he had. More or less. But his mother, the former Naz Allam, was a great deal more devout than her husband, and she had, when Ravi was aged around seven, sent him to a series of private tutorials with a senior Imam at a North London Mosque. She would sit quietly with him while he learned simplified rudiments of the Koran, God's revelations to the Prophet Mohammed, detailed over 114 chapters.

When those lessons had concluded, shortly before Ray began prep school in Knightsbridge, his Muslim groundings came to an end. And Richard Kerman took care they did not begin again. Later on, his son Ray attended all church services at Harrow with the vast majority of the school in the Church of England faith. Never once was he a part of the small group of separatists, whose parents, Roman Catholics, Muslim or Jewish, insisted they remain exclusively within their denominations.

It was widely assumed, within the confines of the great school, that Ray Kerman probably had a Jewish grandfather, or some-thing like that. But Harrow is a bastion of racial equality, and no-one ever asked him. In any event, Ray was one of the toughest boys in the history of the school, a thunderous fast-bowler in the school cricket team, and a brutally-strong front-row forward on the rugby team, which he captained. Those kind of kids *never* had to answer questions.

His entry forms for a scholarship to England's Royal Military Academy, Sandhurst, were prepared by his headmaster, utilizing school records. And Ray entered the British Army without a trace of his very early background in the official records. So impressive was his school record, written and signed personally by the Headmaster of Harrow, they never even asked for a formal birth certificate.

He was 2nd Lieutenant Raymond Kerman, first in his year at the Academy, a top sportsman at Harrow School, the son of wealthy, well-known North London parents, heir to the Kerman shipping line. Religion: Church of England.

His first Regiment was the Devon and Dorsets, an infantry outfit whose soldiers were historically drawn from south-west England. And it was from there he had first entered the SAS, fighting his way through the brutal, soul-searching indoctrination process, before serving for four years, with immense distinction, in the Kosovo Campaign, and then earning the coveted Queen's Gallantry Medal during an SAS rescue mission in Sierre Leone the following year.

He'd returned to his Regiment as Captain Kerman, an acknowledged SAS 'hard man', expert in unarmed combat, skilled in the use of explosives and demolition, an efficient satellite communications operator. He was trained in Close Quarter Battle (CQB), short-range missiles, navigation, strategy and specialized SAS transport over all terrains. Break-ins to enemy compounds were his speciality. The Regiment had him taught Arabic at the secret Army language school in Bucking-hamshire. At thirty-four, he had not yet married.

Recalled to the SAS for a second tour of duty in 2002, Ray Kerman had been personally selected to command a small highly-trained SAS team, training members of the Israeli Defence Force (IDF) in counter-terrorism procedures. The operation, highly classified, was funded by the Israeli Gervernment. Ray's team contained six senior non-commissioned officers, each of them vastly experienced in a wide range of military skills and techniques.

One week before they left Hereford, bound for an unidenti-fied Army base in the Negev, Captain Kerman had been summoned to see the SAS Commanding Officer. There he was told the Ministry of Defence had issued a special authorization for his promotion to Major. 'I may say, we are all delighted,' the CO had told him. 'You've earned it.'

Ray Kerman was already a very special man in a very special Regiment. And now he had been in the desert for several weeks, mostly confined to the wire-surrounded, camouflaged SAS compound, with its custom-built urban area, designed to prepare the Israelis for house-to-house combat in city streets.

The SAS enjoys a towering reputation in the Israeli Army and Major Kerman, a stern and uncompromising officer, was deadly serious about the ruthless nature of his business. He was not particularly liked, but he quickly earned a full measure of respect. Like his father, he had little humor, and he possessed the same ruthless streak in his chosen occupation, and this he endlessly tried to drill into the Israeli recruits. He worked them right out on the edge, forcing a supreme fitness upon them, urging them on, driving and cajoling them, hammering home the SAS creed, 'Train hard, fight easy.'

Only rarely did he venture into the nearby desert towns, Beersheba to the east and a few miles further north to Hebron, the volatile flashpoint of so many murderous Arab-Israeli clashes, intensified always by the city's sacred place in the scriptures of Jews, Muslims and Christians alike. This is the burial place of Abraham, Isaac and Jacob.

The city's holiness has always added fuel to the incendiary atmosphere between its Palestinian and Israeli populations. As long ago as 1929 Muslim extremists massacred the entire Jewish minority in Hebron. And ever since then, both sides have initiated endless bloodshed. In 1994, a Jewish extremist gunned down thirty Muslim worshippers. And nothing much improved after 1997 when the western part of the city (H-1) became a Palestinian autonomous zone. Riots and hard military restrictions continue to dominate the last resting place of Abraham.

Ray's first visit to ancient Hebron was in fact his first close encounter with an Arab populace. With his tall red-haired Irish Sergeant Fred O'Hara he had wandered through the criss-cross alleyways of the *casbah*, watching the Palestinian traders, robed men sculpting olivewood, heating and blowing the city's famous colored glass, selling fruit and vegetables. Ray and Fred both wore civilian clothes, trying hard to blend in as strolling tourists, each of them eating from a bag of pale, sweet Hebron peaches, reputed to be the finest in the world.

The trip was essentially business. The two SAS men were trying to familiarize themselves with the layout of the city, because as ever there were rumors around that the Palestinians were once more stockpiling weapons and bomb-making materials. Ray carried with him a tourist guide and throughout the afternoon he made careful notes inside the little book.

The Major of course realized that he too had been born in a similar town, not so steeped in culture, but nonetheless on the edge of a vast desert, among people who wore robes, of the Muslim faith. Like these Hebron Arabs, his own people must have toiled for little in a similar hot, dusty urban trading center. And he wondered whether, deep in his subconscious, there was a remembrance of another place, like this, where the infant Ravi Rashood had eaten peaches and walked with his mother Naz, wearing her long black *chador*.

But the years in London, in English schools, in the officers' mess, in exclusive Western civilization, had driven any vestige of his birthright deep into the past. He was Major Ray Kerman, and these Arabs were foreign to him, though their closeness did jolt a certain recall of stories told to him by the bearded Saudi in the North London Mosque a quarter of a century ago. He could remember some of them clearly, but one stuck in his mind, a quotation from the Koran which the Imam had asked him to learn:

> *Cling one and all to the rope of God's faith*
> *And do not separate.*
> *Remember God's blessings,*
> *For you were enemies*
> *And He joined your hearts together*
> *And now you are brothers . . .*

He supposed that all these robed and bearded men around him knew the same words. And he found that strange. And, in addition, there was another difference Ray experienced in Hebron − different, that is, by the standards of other visiting Englishmen. He had a distinct feeling of *déjà-vu* among the buildings of the city. He could not remember ever having seen houses like this, not the flat-roof symmetry, nor the archways, nor the sheer narrowness of the streets. And yet it seemed familiar to him, the yellow brick and stonework of the buildings, some of it exposed by a crumbling cement outer shell.

Ray was only faintly aware of this curious sense of having visited before, and he pushed it to the back of his mind. Meanwhile he and Fred compared observations about the possible locations of snipers who would undoubtedly show up when the Israelis began any cordon-and-search mission in the Palestinian areas of the town.

Ray and Fred both spent time chatting to Arabs, and in particular Ray fell into conversation with a youngish man in his twenties, trying to trade goats. He was an obvious Bedouin, and Ray liked him, his soft, polite voice, the natural acceptance in his voice that soon he must take his camels and his herds back to the desert, which lay to the east, simmering in the oncoming summer heat. Ray thought the Bedouin might have made a halfway decent SAS trooper.

Late in the afternoon he and Fred crossed from the large Palestinian section (H-1), over Al-Shuhada Street near the old bus station and into the Israeli occupied section (H-2). From there they made their way through the market, south of the small Israeli settlement on the edge of the Old City, and on to the great edifice of the Tomb of the Patriots, the burial ground of Abraham and his family.

Ray's guide book told him that here God had bestowed upon Abraham his father-role of the Jewish people. And it might not just be Abraham, Isaac and Jacob buried here. There could also be all twelve sons of Jacob, not to mention Adam and Eve.

It was on the rough, sandy lower ground, below the great and sacred place, that Ray felt an uneasy stirring in his mind. He was standing next to a group of seven Arabs in black robes, and he was staring, like them, at the ramparts of the massive Tomb, and he felt utterly certain he had seen it before, or at least something very like it.

His heart beat faster as he struggled to recall when, where and how. Because he knew he had never been within a thousand miles of Hebron in his life. And yet there were distant images, and he fought to summon them. He found in the recesses of his memory a long, covered bazaar filled with traders, lines of them, in a faraway land. And there was a building, a huge building, a great yellow stone edifice. He could see it from the bazaar. He remembered that.

But the details escaped him – his memory simply could not find accurate pictures of his first neighborhood, the Bazar-e Vakil, and its vaulted underground teahouse where he had so often tasted sweet pastries with his parents. The Tomb of the Patriots was jolting his brain, trying to force the image of the lofty *Mosque-e*

Jame into focus. But the greatest building in Kerman's memory remained shrouded in mist. Ray's mother had carried him around it so many times, just along the street where they lived. But that part had also vanished, along with his name, and his past.

'Penny for your thoughts, sir,' said Sergeant. O'Hara. 'You thinking of going inside?'

Major Kerman shook his head. 'I don't think so, Fred,' he said. 'We ought to be getting back. Whistle up the driver, will you? Tell him we're on the south side of the Tomb just near the main entrance.' And Fred immediately took a few steps away from the Arabs, and dialed up the number, issuing curt instructions to the Israeli corporal.

Which left Major Kerman once more alone with his thoughts, saying nothing, his secrets safe. Which was just as well, because right now he was posing questions to himself which would not have been greeted with wild enthusiasm among his SAS colleagues. Nor indeed at number 86, The Bishop's Avenue.

Why do I like and admire these people so much? Is it just the influence of Wilfred Thesiger? Or is there something in my blood which I cannot understand? Why do I feel at home here in the desert?

And he wondered, somewhat dangerously, for the first time in his life, *Who the hell am I? Am I really among my own people, right here standing next to the last remaining Bedouins of the Negev?*

By 10 p.m. that evening Major Kerman was issuing his final briefing to the SAS team which would shortly embark the Israeli Army helicopter and take off for several different locations.

He stood before his men and told them, 'As you know, the situation here in Israel remains very tense. The government is under considerable pressure from the USA, the UN and the European nations to revive the peace process with the Palestinian leadership, and to commit Israel to a lasting truce with the Arab world.

'We all know it's been damned difficult. I think the Israeli Government has being trying to exercise restraint despite frequent acts of violence from terror groups like HAMAS and Islamic Jihad. The recent acts of aggression and indiscriminate suicide-murder against the Israeli people in both Jerusalem and Tel Aviv have been committed by groups whose strategic aim is the wholesale destruction of the nation of Israel. That's where we come in. That's why we're here.'

Ray paused. And he paced across the front of a large map of the immediate area around Hebron.

'Tonight,' he said. 'At the specific request of the Israeli Government, the IDF are mounting a co-ordinated military intervention, a large scale cordon-and-search operation against several Palestinian occupied towns on the West Bank and Gaza . . . the "A Territories," which we have discussed before. Our objectives are simple: to flush out the terrorist leaders and seize their arsenals of weapons and bomb-making equipment.

'Don't let's pretend this is going to be a neatly achieved operation, because it won't be. In fact it will almost cerainly be extremely untidy. Maybe even messy. Nonetheless, given the relative balance of forces in our favor, it will ultimately be successful. Futhermore, the Israeli Government is certain no other Arab force will come to the aid of the Palestinians, particularly in the short time frame envisaged for the operation.

'You must remember, we are here in a very specialized role, to help and advise the Israelis. Most of their Commanders have been trained here by us, so they know what they're doing. Nevertheless, we must be watchful and ready to move in with on-the-spot advice, probably up front, wherever it may be needed. All SAS staff will be wearing IDF combat clothing and helmets, but without insignia. You will carry a personal weapon, your H & K MP-5 sub-machine gun, strictly for your own protection. Only in extreme circumstances will you use it.'

Ray Kerman was keenly aware that this operation would be conducted under hair-trigger stress. Hebron was nothing short of superheated these days. The slightest incident could spark off an eruption of gunfire and explosive. He did not want to lose some of his best men in a senseless shoot-out in the dusty streets of the West Bank. And he had cautioned them over and over.

'If we get through this without someone going berserk, it will be a bloody miracle,' he said. 'But it won't be one of us. We will each be attached to individual attacking Israeli forces. So try to keep it down, guys. Be careful with your advice, but try to stop anyone doing anything really stupid.'

He outlined the Israeli strategy, explaining that on the following night the IDF would attack several parts of Gaza, as well as the key Palestinian enclaves in the West Bank, at Jenin, Nablus, Ramalla, Bethlehem and Hebron. They had already conducted a mass of intelligence gathering, even some minor maneuvers

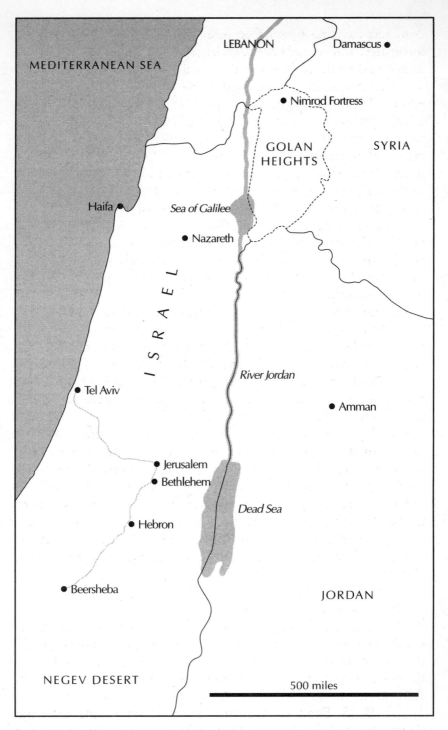

ISRAEL - A PLACE OF DIVIDED LOYALTIES

designed to identify suitable points of entry into the targeted territories. IDF Reservists had already been called up, and were armed and ready at their parent unit depots.

'I will personally be attached to the force attacking Hebron,' said the Major. 'I will be in company with Sergeants O'Hara and Charlie Morgan. And we will be conducting ourselves in precisely the same way as everyone else. Remember also, this little war is unlikely to end tomorrow night, so let's make the most of the opportunity to observe at first-hand precisely how the Israelis conduct themselves on a volatile operation like this.'

Thirty minutes later the Israeli helicopter took off bearing the SAS men to their destinations, flying over the Holy Land, bound first for the grim headquarters of Northern Command, where Ray Kerman, Fred and Charlie would disembark prior to joining the Golani Brigade, the tight IDF force which would provide the main cordon in Hebron.

Ray knew the drill. He'd masterminded the drill. The Golanis, backed by a squadron of tanks for extra firepower and protection, would send in Special Forces familiar with the area to conduct the search-and-sweep operation within the perimeter of the town. They would be additionally supported by a battalion of Israeli paratroopers. Search-trained military engineers were scheduled to go after the Palestinian arms caches.

Ray had stressed to all levels of the Israeli Command, the success of the operation depended entirely on the spearhead of the force inserting a steel-rimmed cordon around the target without being detected. Stealth and secrecy were paramount, and there would be a full twelve-hour briefing in Northern Command throughout the following day.

Major Kerman would officially assist in the execution of the operation from the Golani Brigade field headquarters in western Hebron.

0100 Friday, May 14
By now, the IDF battalions were fanning out over the West Bank, zeroing in on their targets. Around Hebron there was dark, quiet efficiency from the Israeli troops who made up the Golani Brigade, now approaching the city from three different directions.

The Barak Battalion, moving north along Route 60 from Beersheba, had already halted two miles from Hebron, just south of the tiny village of Beit Khagal, dismounted their vehicles and were moving silently forward through the darkness on foot.

From the west on Route 35, the Gideon Battalion had stopped near the village of Beit Kahil, and they too were walking down the deserted road, weapons raised, every sense on high alert in the pitch black of the moonless Negev Desert.

Major Kerman was with the third battalion, the Golani Buds (newest recruits) combined with men from the Egoz Reconnaissance Unit. With headlights on low beam, they skirted around the outskirts of Bethlehem on minor roads to the west, rejoining Route 60 coming in from the North at El Arub.

The Commander of the IDF force permanently stationed in the Jewish section of Hebron, had trebled his covert patrols up close to the dividing line, and throughout the Old City. And now his colleagues in the three armed battalions of the Golani Brigade advanced upon his territory.

By 0430 they were inside the perimeter. The Barak group deployed immediately from Jabal Abu Sneina, placing its cordon just south of the Old City in a line running hard down the dividing frontier between H-1 and H-2. The Gideons moved west to the Bir Al-Saba Road, and then north up to the Hebron bypass. The third battalion deployed along the whole span of the north end of the town, with the Egoz Unit moving south to occupy the inner city dividing line, then west along Al-Qarantina Street.

In the Brigade headquarters west of the city, the troops constructed a wire-rimmed holding area for arrested Palestinians. There was also a tented section both for conducting the inter-rogation of prisoners, and for first-aid and help for the wounded.

The Israeli Tank Squadron now deployed to troop positions astride the Hebron bypass, covering the western and northern approaches to the city. A separate unit guarded the southern approaches.

At 0530, with the city and its perimeters secure, the specialist teams were ready to go.

In Brigade headquarters, Major Kerman watched carefully, and at first light on that sultry Friday morning, the sky blazing scarlet along the eastern horizon, the Golani Commanding Officer let loose the dogs of war into the sleeping city of Hebron.

They started in the north, the specialist Israeli search teams moving through the area, entering warehouses, workshops and some residences where known extremists resided. There were a very few arrests, and there was little interference from local people. The cordon held, no outsiders were permitted into the area, and anyway no-one felt like arguing with the heavily-armed paratroopers who stood menacingly in the rear.

The Ras al Jura section, a 100-percent enclave of Palestinian streets, was dealt with in less than two hours. A half dozen Arabs were arrested and just a handful of weapons was found. From there the search teams began moving south, working swiftly down either side of the Jerusalem Road, banging on doors, forcing locks, kicking their way into secure premises, setting off the occasional alarm and then silencing it with with a burst of gunfire.

Steadily they elbowed their way towards the center of town, where there were increasingly shuttered stores, and the troops did not hesitate to smash their way inside. There was no question of looting, just searching, and the Israelis maintained the iron discipline, upon which the SAS Major, Ray Kerman, had insisted in their training.

Behind them everything was quiet, since no Arab, terrorist, craftsman nor goatherd, wanted to follow in the wake of the legendarily-tough Israeli paras. But up front, by 0930, unrest was beginning to develop. Mobs of Arab youths were gathering east of the Jerusalem Road, between the wide commercial street and the dividing line between the zones of H-1 and H-2.

They were starting to position themselves upstream of the search parties in the Haarat Al-Sheik area, right on the edge of the Old City. They were yelling and taunting the armed troops, and at 0940, the first stones were thrown; initially just a few stray missiles. But by 10 a.m. the stones were streaming through the air in a lethal hail of resentment. And, as the minutes wore on, the stones were growing larger, fist-sized rocks mingled with slabs of concrete picked up from the ruins of buildings.

The gangs of youths were now combining into a full scale mob, bent on humiliating the Israeli troops. They had, of course, no conception of the strength and depth of the IDF force, and they ran forward hurling rocks and screaming abuse.

The paratroopers immediately raced forward and began firing rubber bullets into the crowd, which had now swung right to face the oncoming Israeli battalion. And the paras instantly raised the stakes, hurling a volley of CS gas grenades, which reduced the front line of the rock-throwers to a retreating, eye-streaming confusion. But it increased the tension, as others ran forward to replace their comrades.

Again and again, the paras fired rubber bullets into the crowd. And now there were adults joining the youths, the entire scenario becoming more frenzied and vociferous by the minute. Then, suddenly, the rocks were being accompanied by petrol bombs, which landed right at the feet of the Israelis, and blasted fire straight at them. But through it all, the search teams kept going, beating down doors, demanding access, ransacking small businesses.

They were covered by the fire and fearsome reputation of their paras, but the conflict was now beginning to look serious. At 1015 the troops fired three more volleys of rubber bullets, and several Arab youths, hurling rocks in the middle of the melee, hit the ground. Their colleagues, not knowing whether they were dead or just stunned, thronged forward to pick them up. The paras instantly unleashed CS gas grenades straight into the middle of the Arab rescue parties.

There was a brief pause, but in that time, the Israeli searchers started to swarm through an old workshop in a notorious area just to the north of the crossroads at Bab Al-Zawiye. Moments went by, while the Palestinian mob was in temporary disarray, and then the Israelis came bursting out of the workshop calling up transport to confiscate one of the biggest caches of weapons and bomb-making materials they had ever seen. All hidden in the workshop and in a neighboring shed.

And as a dozen Arabs trudged out with their hands high, folded across their heads, a group of Israeli paras rushed forward to carry out the arrests and to remove the bomb-makers to military custody. So far, even under heavy attack, the IDF personnel had exercised rigid discipline.

But even as the first Arab prisoners were loaded onto trucks, the first real live bullets were being fired. Not by the Israelis, but by Palestinian snipers, now ensconced on wasteland on the Haarat Al-Sheik. And they were firing from various vantage points on the edge of Haarat Al-Sheik, east of the crossroads with the sun behind them.

The Israeli paras, now crouching and running forward, hurled gas grenades into the wasteland and opened up a fusillade of covering fire while the searching troops raced for the safety of the only open building – the workshop where the arms and bomb-making materials were stored.

The paras, having temporarily silenced the snipers around the wasteland, headed for the same cover, and quite suddenly the building was full of Israeli troops, all massing in the stairwell, attempting to reach firing positions on the top two floors of the four-story building.

Immediately the air was filled with machine-gun fire, then the blast of real hand grenades as more Israeli paras came up to clear the wasteland positions.

No-one saw the HAMAS terrorist leader, the one who had been trying to co-ordinate resistance to the methodical Israeli sweep through these most sensitive desert streets. Dressed in denim jeans and jacket, with the black and white chequered headdress of his nation slung over his shoulders, the young warrior, no more than twenty-five years old, seized a hand-held anti-tank rocket-launcher and fired one round, at 100 yards range, straight through a downstairs window of the workshop.

The rocket exploded with a mind-blowing roar in the confined space, instantly blasting through the ceiling, and the one above it, before bringing down the entire building in a choking fireball of dust, sand and rubble.

Fourteen Israelis were killed, seventeen injured. Only twelve of them managed to climb out of the wreckage, all with their eardrums shattered by the blast, their clothing in shreds, blood everywhere, faces blackened. Some of them were appallingly disfigured, unable hardly to walk; four of them had lost arms or legs.

Within seconds the atrocity was reported to the paratroop company headquarters, and reinforcements were immediately on their way into the Haarat Al Sheik area; the Israelis were hell-bent on seeking out the perpetrators. They were desperate for revenge, never mind the rule book. Never mind Major Kerman's advice.

Israeli drivers gunned six ambulances crammed with nurses and medics down route 35 right in the rear of the convoy of seething paratroopers. Sirens screamed as they raced along Al Qarantina Street, and within ten minutes of the blast the Israelis were leaping from the trucks, stunned at the sight which greeted them. Surrounded by the terribly wounded and dying men, their colleagues were helpless, and the snipers were beginning to open fire from the wasteland again, straight at the ground immediately in front of the devastated workshop where the grisly scenario was taking place.

Rarely had an Israeli brigade reacted with such speed and ferocity. The younger paratroopers formed up and stormed the wasteland from both flanks, hurling in grenades, firing from the hip. The Palestinians turned to run but were cut down in their tracks, women and children in the sidestreets were caught in the crossfire.

HAMAS leaders were blasting away from behind low walls with three machine-guns, but they were silenced by the grenades of the Israeli stormtroopers. This was developing into a truly major confrontation, and there was nothing anyone could do about it. The Israeli troops had decided to wipe out the Palestinian fighters, and they were well on the way to doing it, driving dozens of Arab 'freedom fighters' back across the Jerusalem Road, many of them wounded.

By now Ray Kerman, in company with Sergeant O'Hara and Sergeant Morgan, was on his way into the city in an Israeli armored car, currently speeding along Al Qarantina Street towards the carnage at Haarat Al-Sheik. And out to the left they could hear the battle raging fiercely on the western side of the Jerusalem Road.

The Major knew there was nothing he could do at the scene of the catastrophe, but there must be something he could achieve at the scene of the fighting. And when finally he swung into the fray, he was appalled by what he saw. Because he could see a highly disciplined Army almost completely out of control; soldiers going berserk, charging forward in blind fury, killing anything or anyone that moved.

'Jesus Christ!' said Major Kerman, realizing immediately the Israeli troops had unwittingly been drawn into a HAMAS stronghold, which the Palestinians would try to defend to the last. On the radio he could already hear the Golani commanders summoning more ambulances. God alone knew the state of the Arab fighters.

And now he was literally watching the battle, the Israeli troops moving into the streets of H-2, still hurling grenades, still enraged by the massacre in the workshop, their machine-guns raking buildings to the west of the Jerusalem Road.

Ray Kerman could see at least three Israelis priming hand-held rocket-launchers similar to the one which had blown up their colleagues. When the first one fired, the damage was terrible, knocking down three houses, and causing certain 'civilian' casualties.

For the first time in his life Ray Kerman was close to a feeling of shock. This had to be stopped. It was already out of hand, but it could still get a whole lot worse. And there was always the danger of another Arab nation joining the Palestinians, who would undoubtedly claim the Israeli Army had swooped on them in the small hours of an innocent Friday morning, and attacked innocent, law-abiding Arab citizens.

Ray could see the paratroopers' Forward Commander tucked into a doorway beyond the wasteland. Twenty feet away there were two of his men ripping out pins and flinging the hand grenades into the Arab street beyond the wall. No-one was doing anything to prevent this battle, and Ray assessed two glaring problems:

1) This was not winnable. Nothing good could come out of it for either side, only world headlines, more blood, sorrow and tears.

2) The Israeli troops were now too widely scattered, and too full of fury to give up their hot pursuit of the Arabs who had blasted their colleagues to pieces.

As for the narrow street beyond the wall, it would be filled with women and children, all of whom were going to die if this firefight could not be halted. Major Kerman knew he stood an excellent chance of getting the blame for this personally. After all, a principal part of his job was to prevent this kind of thing. Any damned fool could cause chaos. The SAS were in the Negev, on behalf of the Government, to bring an element of clinical efficiency to the Israeli Defence Force.

This was a nightmare, and Ray seized his MP-5 machine-gun and helmet, and belted across the wasteland, to see the paras' Forward Commander. Already he could hear the rumble of Israeli tanks moving up to the front line of this sudden, unexpected conflict.

The IDF officer shrugged, and told Ray he could do nothing. 'Well, we could start off by withdrawing the rocket-launchers and the grenades,' said Ray. 'That way we can begin to withdraw east to the dividing line. It's not as if we'll be pursued. It's up to us to stop this. No-one is going to thank us for continuing. The Knesset will be furious.'

23

'Too late,' said the Commander. 'I'm not going over the wall – just leave it to the guys.'

'Then I'll go,' said the English Major. 'Gunfire's one thing, blowing up Arab civilians in their homes is another.'

Ray made his way to the end of the wall and rounded it, crossed the street, and gained the cover of the houses on the right-hand side of the street. Crouching, he made his way forward to the gap in the row where two buildings had been blown sky high. The next house was perfect. The top floor was gone, but there was cover on the street floor and he would be in yelling distance of the paras with the grenades and rockets.

He made the entrance, crashing through the door, and splintering the lock. Inside was rubble and the body of a man half hanging through the ceiling, plainly dead. Outside, the battle had, if anything, intensified, and the smell of cordite permeated everything. The gunfire was unceasing, and periodic explosions shook the entire street.

Ray exercised the SAS man's natural caution, kicking open a door to another empty but more or less intact room. There was only one more door, and Ray booted that open, and found himself standing at the top of a flight of stone stairs.

Just then a tremendous crash shook the remains of the building, showering plaster from the ceiling. The noise died away, and once more there was just the rattle of the gunfire, and the eerie crackling of burning, very close. In a split second Ray guessed the Palestinians had got hold of some grenades of their own.

But then, he heard another noise, coming from deep in the cellar, somewhere near the bottom of the stone stairs. He fired a short volley into the gap, and roared a command in Arabic, '*Come out right now, hands high . . . or I'll blow you to hell.*'

Nothing. Every battle-instinct Ray had told him this was trouble. For all he knew there were a half-dozen fully armed Arabs down there, and there was no way he was going to test the theory.

Again he yelled for the surrender of all cellar dwellers. Again there was nothing. And another diabolical explosion, not thirty yards away, once more shook the building to its sandy foundations. But then, as the rumble died away, there was a lull in the gunfire, and Ray could hear distinctly the sound of sobbing, female sobbing.

'Jesus,' he muttered. 'I'm not really ready for this.' But he began to walk down the stairs, pressed against the left-hand wall. When he reached the bottom, the sobbing was louder, as if a child was also crying.

Ray groped for a light switch, and to his amazement found one, and switched on a bare bulb on the low ceiling. He was still not in the room, and he inched forward, the machine-gun he held in front of him, ready to spit instant death at any foe.

But there was no foe. Just three terrified figures covered in dust, huddled in a corner, two of them children, neither of them more than six or seven years old. Their mother was dressed in a black *chador*, but the hood was pushed back. She was bareheaded, and her face was tear-stained, and she was trembling helplessly, trying to hold her two children close to her.

The older, a little boy, had blood on his face from a cut deep in his hairline. The mother, a very beautiful Palestinian girl, aged about twenty-three, stared at Ray through wide-set brown eyes, saying over and over . . . *'Please don't kill us . . . please don't kill us . . .'*

Ray had no intention of killing anyone, unless his life was threatened. And he spoke in Arabic . . . 'I am a British officer, here to advise the military . . . you have no need to be afraid – at least not of me. You may stand up and we'll see about getting you out of here, somewhere safe.'

Ray Kerman had a better chance of stopping the battle than the girl's tears. And she sobbed uncontrollably, still clinging to the children . . . *'But the Israelis will kill us . . . my husband is dead . . . we have nowhere to go . . .'*

'The first place we must go is out of this cellar,' he said, 'Before the whole place caves in . . . come on . . . up these stairs . . .'

But they were all too frightened to move, and another thunderous explosion, outside in the street, again shook the house.

The girl tried to regain control, but she was shaking with fear, and she spoke again with difficulty, in Arabic . . . 'Please, please they will kill us if we go outside . . . we want to stay here . . .'

'What's your name?' asked Ray Kerman.

'Shakira.'

'Well, listen, Shakira. If we hang around down here, we just might get buried alive . . .'

'Well, we may not have long to live, before we go I must pray with my children it's almost midday . . . we must pray for my husband . . .' And then she stared at him, observing his dark eyes and complexion, and she asked, 'Are you a Muslim?'

'Not really,' he replied. Then he blurted out, 'But my parents both were.' It was a phrase he had never uttered to anyone.

'Then you should pray with us, sir. Allah is great.'

Ray stared back at her. He could see she was slim and even more beautiful now she was standing. She had long dark hair, and an almost perfect oval face, with the full lips of so many Arab women. Her little boy clung to her hand, the daughter, aged around five, was trying to wrap herself in her mother's robe.

Ray smiled. 'What are their names?'

'This is Irena. My son is Ravi.'

Ray's heart missed about three beats. And he was glad of the noise of the battle, because it gave him time to gather his thoughts.

'Okay, Shakira. You stay here for a few moments and pray with the children. I'll go up and find a way to get us all out of here . . .'

And with that, Major Kerman evacuated the cellar and bolted back up the stairs. Through the open door to the street, he could see running figures, Israeli troops heading back towards the wasteground. Then there was another mighty explosion, maybe forty or fifty yards away, deeper into Palestinian territory.

'Christ,' he thought. 'These crazy bastards will knock down the whole city if we don't do something.'

And he headed back to the cellar door, and yelled, '*Shakira! Get up here!* You have to get out. This place could get hit again, any moment.'

And now he could hear them climbing the stairs, both children crying, Shakira trying hopelessly to comfort them. The body of their father, still holding his sub-machine gun, hung grotesquely from the ceiling, the unseeing eyes gazing upwards. And Ray shepherded them into a corner, from where they would not see the corpse.

He knew the Israelis were now systematically clearing the buildings along the main streets, throwing grenades before entering.

'Is there a rear entrance to the house?' he asked Shakira.

'Yes, there is a small yard, then an alley which leads into a new street. There's a way out into the city from there, and it will be quieter. There's no way from that street to the waste-ground.'

Ray nodded. 'Where will you go?'

'I don't know. My parents are both in Saudi Arabia, but Mohammed's parents are in Bethlehem. 'We might be able to get there. We have a car parked out in the alley.'

'That sounds good . . . but I want you to hide for the rest of the day, away from the fighting. There's an army cordon around Hebron and Bethlehem . . .'

Before she could reply, there was a tremendous flurry of gunfire outside, two men screamed, and then the massive figure of Sergeant Fred O'Hara came barreling through the open door, followed by Sergeant Charlie Morgan.

Both SAS men looked up in astonishment at Ray.

'Christ, sir,' said Fred. 'We've been looking all over for you. I was beginning to think some fucking towelhead had shot you.'

'Not me, Fred,' said Ray. 'I'm supposed to be in charge.'

'You're telling me, sir. Things have been getting right out of hand. These bastards want to kill each other. I've never seen anything like it. Officers, men, maniacs. They're all at it. Fucking guns, bombs, grenades and Christ knows what. If we don't get the hell outta here they'll be wheeling up heavy artillery. This is no place for us, sir. We have to get the fuck out. There's no rhyme nor reason in this place.'

Fred's own reasoning was close to flawless. But Ray now had the added responsibility of Shakira and the children. There was of course no reason why he should have that responsibility. He and the two SAS NCOs could have left and no-one would have been any the wiser.

But there are times in the life of almost every soldier when there is a summons to obey the heart, not the brain, nor the training, nor the experience. And Ray Kerman knew he faced one of those, right now.

He gestured to the little Arab family, and Sergeant O'Hara swung around, reacting instantly to the movement. Little Ravi held up his toy spaceship and stepped forward, and the big SAS man, who had been shot at too many times in the past hour, flinched away from the sudden move and hit the trigger of his MP-5. In about one hundredth of a second there was a line of five neat holes clean across the forehead of Ray Kerman's namesake.

Irena screamed and ran towards her brother holding in her right hand a stuffed bear. Charlie could see only hand grenades in his mind right now, and he gunned her down in cold blood, fearing yet another explosion.

For a split second there was silence in the room, and then Shakira screamed and ran at Fred O'Hara, her hands raised like claws at his face. Charlie swung to his right. In a lightning movement he whipped his machine gun towards her face. And at that precise moment Major Ray Kerman blew the entire front of Charlie's head off with a savage burst of fire. No-one could kill an SAS men quite like that. Except for another one.

Charlie's MP-5 had fired two shells in the instant of his death. And a measure of Ray's speed was that both bullets headed downwards, one of them cutting a deep groove on the outside of Ray's left thigh, which immediately started to bleed like hell.

For a few heartbeats, nothing happened. Then Sergeant O'Hara turned incredulously to his CO. 'Sir . . . did you just kill Charlie . . .?' he asked, blankly.

Ray's brain raced. The word 'murder' flew through his mind. Then 'court martial'. Then 'jail'. Then 'firing squad.'

Then he looked again at the two lifeless bodies on the floor, Shakira, whimpering, cradling Ravi's head while the blood spilled down her robe, reaching out with her right hand to try to reach Irena. But the little girl was unreachable.

Fred stepped forward, anxious to ensure she carried no weapons. '*Get up!*' he shouted. And those two rough and heart-less words ended his life.

Ray Kerman wheeled left, picked up a small rock and slammed it into the space between Fred's eyes, breaking that part of the skull like a walnut. Then he crashed the butt of his gloved right hand with all of his strength right into the nostril end of Fred's big Irish nose. The force rammed the nose-bone deep into Fred's brain, and he was dead before he hit the floor, felled by the SAS classic unarmed-combat blow.

Two dead children. Two dead SAS men. It was a biblical conclusion, in a biblical city, to a vicious two minutes. An eye for an eye, and a tooth for a tooth.

Ray turned to Shakira, who was plainly in shock. Her tears had stopped, as if she had nothing left, except a broken heart.

'Did you just save my life, sir?' she asked, softly.

'I think so,' replied Ray.

'Then I just wish you hadn't.'

Nonetheless Shakira appreciated the situation with near-military coldness. With her family dead, in the dust and rubble of her home, her own situation remained desperate, especially with the bodies of two SAS men both in Israeli uniform lying on the floor of her living room.

She had been a fleeting second away from death herself, and, through her devastation, she knew somehow she had to save herself. She had to get away, and she had to get this British officer away for several obvious reasons.

But first she went to a cupboard and pulled out a soft rug, and laid it over her two children.

And Ray found himself saying, so naturally, it seemed as if the words must be someone else's: 'It is fine to grieve, but you must not worry. They are both in the arms of Allah now.'

The words of the North London mullah came rushing back, and he remembered the stories of paradise, and the promises to the martyrs who die in the name of Allah.

Finally Shakira stood up and faced him. 'Where will you go?' she asked, as if aware of the impossibility of his position.

'Well,' he said. 'Ten minutes ago I'd have escorted you to the back door, and then got out of the front door, turned left, and fought my way back to my colleagues.' He glanced down at the dead bodies of Sergeant O'Hara and Corporal Morgan, before adding, 'I'm not quite sure what to do right now. But I plainly cannot return to the IDF having just killed my two bodyguards.'

'Would they find out it was you?'

'I don't know. They might. But my problem is greater than that. Ever since I arrived here I have felt for the Palestinians, and how they are treated. That's common to a lot of people, but I have deep roots in the Middle East, and there is something in me that has changed. I cannot be a part of a military force which thinks it can rampage among innocent people, killing and destroying families.

'Look at little Irena and Ravi, just children, gunned down by my soldiers . . . inside I feel you are my own people, all three of you, and your tears are mine, and I can't do this anymore. Not here. Not in the desert.'

Shakira could see his tears now, streaming down the Major's face, this stranger who had saved her life. And she walked across to him, and put her arms around his neck, and held him closely.

And the blood of little Ravi stained his uniform, and the blood from his own thigh ran on to her *chador*, and their tears mingled together.

Outside the blasts continued, and Ray sensed the Israeli tanks were finding their range, shelling the street. Shakira went to another downstairs cupboard and came back with a long white robe, a full length *thobe,* and a white-and-black patterned *ghutra* headdress, complete with the double headcord, the *aghal*.

Ray ripped off his Israeli combat jacket and pulled the *thobe* over his head. Shakira fitted the headdress, and arranged the cloth around his neck in such a way he could cover the lower half of his face if necessary.

Then she found a clean robe for herself, and bandages to bind Ray's cut thigh. Finally she said quietly, 'We must go now, before the Israelis come.' And she took his hand, murmuring '*Insh'Allah*,' as God wills, leading him to the back door of her devastated home.

And they ran through the yard, leaving behind them five bodies in the house. They could see smoke and rising dust in the street to the rear, but in front it was all clear.

'Will we take the car?' asked Ray.

'I don't think so. We must get to the headquarters of HAMAS. My brother Ahmed will be there. And they will take care of you.'

'You sure they won't kill me?' said Ray, tightening his grip on his MP-5, and running hard on his wounded leg, to keep up with Shakira.

'Yes, I'm sure,' she said.

'How do you know?'

'Because I don't want you to die, and that will be good enough.'

Tuesday, May 18
A steel cordon of Israeli tanks now surrounded the entire area where the battle of Jerusalem Road had been fought the previous Friday. With hard-eyed efficiency the IDF troops had evacuated the area, moving Arab families temporarily further to the west while they searched the rubble for casualties and bodies.

They brought in heavy lifting equipment and bulldozers, and avoided another flare-up by announcing they were also searching for Palestinians and would provide medical treatment for anyone found alive.

This of course gave them ample opportunity to conduct a search for more weapons and bomb-making facilities. In three days the area would be as 'clean' as it could ever be; even though everyone knew the wily Arabs had been moving military materiel to safe houses on the edge of the city ever since Saturday morning.

Shakira's house had finally caved in after dark on Friday, burying all five bodies under several tons of debris. They were all unearthed on the following Tuesday afternoon and taken to the morgue in the Israeli section of the city, where thirty-eight IDF troops already lay.

The Palestinian dead, more than sixty-two men, women and children, were later removed to a converted schoolhouse just west of Bir Al-Saba Road.

The bodies of Sergeant O'Hara and Sergeant Morgan were the only known casualties among the SAS troops, though Major Ray Kerman was currently listed as 'missing in action'.

Since he was the Commanding Officer of the SAS force garrisoned in the Negev, this was regarded as a most serious matter, as indeed were the deaths of two top NCOs from the Regiment. Hereford Headquarters was immediately informed, and the response was fast.

'*Transport Sergeant O'Hara Sergeant Morgan bodies immediately to Israeli Army HQ in Jerusalem, for initial post-mortem. Inform soonest any ransom demand for Major Kerman.*' The latter order was routine. Members of the Regiment rarely, if ever, are taken prisoner.

Two days later, there was still neither sight nor sound of Major Kerman, but the new SAS Commander in Israel, Acting Major Roger Hill, wore an extremely quizzical look as he read the report of the IDF pathologist.

'*Sergeant Charles Morgan died as a result of five bullet wounds, fired from point-blank range into the right side of the head, a straight line of hits, stretching from a point two inches above the temple directly downwards to the lower jaw which was shattered. All five bullets penetrated right through the brain, the upper four exiting the skull on the left side. The lower bullet was lodged in the jawbone on the left. It was consistent with a shell fired from a Heckler and Koch sub-machine gun, and has been sent for examination to the Israeli Army forensic laboratory in Tel Aviv.*'

Major Hill knew that it would be rare for an Arab freedom fighter to aim a sub-machine gun so steadily and so accurately.

But the report on Sergeant O'Hara was even more perplexing. Big Fred had not been shot, and neither was the cause of death attributable to the collapsed ceiling in the ruins of the house in which he was found.

Sergeant O'Hara had died after receiving a crushing blow with an uneven object to the central skull area between his eyes. The nose-bone was lodged three inches into the brain, consistent with a headlong fall into the edge of a table, or an encounter with an unarmed combat expert in the Special Forces of either Great Britain or the USA. The fall possibility was of doubtful merit, since there were no other injuries to the SAS Sergeant's face.

Major Hill realized very quickly that both men could have been killed by a member, or at least a former member, of one of the world's Special Forces. And these days there were many such men. No-one perhaps quite as efficient as the SAS or the US Navy SEALs. But the Israelis were very good, and so were the Iraqis. The fact was, it looked as if one or more of such trained killers had turned on the two dead SAS men from Hereford . . . even though they were both still holding their sub-machine guns under the rubble.

Meanwhile the search continued for the missing SAS Commander. Israeli investigators were in the area, examining wreckage, questioning known personnel from HAMAS. No-one knew anything, no-one had even seen him, never mind killed him, or taken him prisoner.

The best information available was from the Israeli Forward Commander who confirmed he and Major Kerman had spoken at the height of the battle, and that he had seen the British officer reach the wall and disappear around it. He had glimpsed the Major running in a crouch, up the right-hand side of the street, next to the now-shattered row of Palestinian houses. Israeli troops, however, had found no trace of his body.

And one week later the situation was unchanged. Ray Kerman, an officer many believed was destined for the highest command in the SAS Regiment, had essentially disappeared. Into hot, dusty, but very thin air.

CHAPTER TWO

Eight Months Later
Monday, February 14, 2005

Lieutenant Colonel Russell Makin, Commanding Officer 22 SAS, strode through the cold Hereford rain towards his office, carrying beneath his right arm a heavy black plastic file of classified documents, hundreds of pages. The Colonel, a tall, powerful ex-combat officer in the Falkland Islands war, had, in his time, carried anti-tank guided missile launchers (loaded) which weighed a darned sight less.

The file had grown weekly since midsummer. On its jacket it just contained the word 'SECRET.' On the first page were the words 'Major Raymond Kerman.' On the remaining 560 pages was a highly detailed account of how one of the most extensive and secretive investigations of recent years had failed to find one single trace of the missing Major.

Colonel Makin reached his office, removed his rain-cape, asked someone to bring him some coffee, and placed the file on the table. He'd been up for four hours, since 0500, mostly talking to the investigating chief in the ultra-secret Shin Bet Intelligence Office, in faraway, sunlit Tel Aviv, two time zones and several light years east of rainswept, foggy Hereford.

The two men spoke often these days, drawn together by the consuming military mystery of the SAS Commanding Officer, who had run, crouching through an embattled street in the middle of Hebron, and never been seen again.

The one single fact which Colonel Makin knew for certain was that the Shin Bet team, Israel's ruthless interior Intelligence equivalent of London's MI5, and Washington's FBI, had conducted the most painstaking and thorough search of the area west of the Jerusalem Road. They'd used everything from bulldozers and mechanical diggers, to microscopes and forensic laboratories. The result being precisely nothing.

They had turned up evidence, compelling evidence. But nothing led to where it was supposed to go. The most important fact was that Sergeant O'Hara had been killed by a member of someone's Special Forces, professionally and deliberately. Sergeant Morgan had been blown away by an MP-5 sub-machine gun, of the precise type carried by Major Kerman, and every combat soldier in the IDF, plus God knows how many Palestinians with smuggled weapons.

They had found the bodies of two children in the same house, one boy, one girl, both killed by bursts of fire from an MP-5, though the rounds were not fired by the same gun that eliminated Sergeant Morgan. The times of death of all four were approximately identical. Another body in the house had been killed by the blast of a shell which had crashed right through the top floor of the house. The man had been the father of both children.

The wife, Shakira Sabah, was discovered living with her brother, a deeply suspected, but unproven member of HAMAS, and his family, a half-mile south-east of her former home, still in deep H-1 territory. She had been at a neighbor's house when her own home was hit, and she was unable to regain entry through the rubble. She knew nothing of any British officer, had seen nothing, cared nothing and was too upset at the slaughter of her family to be of any further help to anyone. Shin Bet did not believe her.

Which was encouraging but brought no-one any nearer to the whereabouts of Ray Kerman. In point of fact, Shin Bet thought they may have found his combat jacket buried in the debris of the house, but it contained nothing, and was unmarked, and, of course, Israeli. It was also ruined, under the dust and cement of the building.

It had much in common with the other evidence. The Major *could* have killed both his colleagues, he *could* have killed the children, and it *could* have been his jacket, and he *could* be on the run. But from what? And where?

This was no ordinary SAS soldier, this was Ray Kerman, a decorated officer of impeccable character, training and background. If he had been killed in the battle, where was his body? If HAMAS had him prisoner, or hostage, why had they not contacted anyone, either for reward or hostage exchange? Like they always did.

No answers. No Major.

Russ Makin, at the age of thirty-eight, a career officer since Sandhurst, had never encountered anything quite like it. In his twenty years as a serving officer he had never even heard of anyone going missing from the SAS. And there was no doubt, Major Kerman was a very important person, privy to many, many secrets in Great Britain's most secretive combat regiment.

In a quiet, irritated way, the Ministry of Defence had been pressurizing him for months. He had been obliged to deal with the Legal Department, the Public Relations Department, the Pensions Department. There had been endless questions from the Next-of-Kin officials, from the Compensation Department. Did he consider the file should be closed under the heading '*Missing in Action*'?

But was the Major really missing? And above all, was there anything about Major Kerman that no-one knew?

This last question, Colonel Makin understood, may be answered in the next hour. At 1030, a special courier was due to arrive from the MOD in Whitehall, bringing with him a classified report, the result of an exhaustive investigation conducted in tandem by the Ministry and by MI5.

The SAS chief knew there would be no courier if there was nothing of any interest. And when the document finally arrived, on time, he read it with a sense of real disquiet.

The parents of Ray Kerman, Mr and Mrs Richard Kerman of North London, revealed, with very little prompting, that they were formerly, Mr and Mrs Reza Sharood, lately of the city of Kerman in the south-east of Iran, where Ravi Rashood had been born.

'Ravi Rashood! Holy Shit!' Colonel Makin muttered. 'I had no idea.'

Of course there was nothing illegal about any of it. Thousands of Middle Eastern families had emigrated to England and changed their names to fit in better with the locals. And certainly, neither Richard Kerman, nor his wife, wished to hide anything. They produced Ray's birth certificate, and the family's immigration documents, including the official change-of-name papers issued just before Ray's fourth birthday. This included the boy's British citizenship conferred upon him when he was five.

They produced his school records, and even made arrangements, through Harrow's headmaster, for the men from the Ministry to go to the school and conduct whatever further investigations they wished.

The result of these further interviews were contained in a secondary document, which demonstrated how thoroughly concerned Whitehall was at the loss of the SAS Major. They had located two Old Harrovians who had shared studies with Ray during their school years. One of them, now a practising barrister in London, recalled nothing of note.

The other, a struggling poet in North Wales, recalled that he had once seen a copy of the Koran on Ray's bookshelf. He remembered having asked his room-mate about it, and he even remembered the reply. Ray said it had belonged to his mother and that there were some very beautiful passages in its pages. The poet, named Reggie Carrington, had been interested and in later years purchased a copy he found in a secondhand bookshop. He was pleased to show it to the man from MI5.

Like the headmaster at Harrow, the Chaplain at the Royal Military Academy at Sandhurst confirmed there had been no instance, to his knowledge, when Raymond Kerman had attended any other service, or Church Parade, other than those of the regular Church of England denomination.

A Muslim by birth, of Muslim parents, Ray Kerman had vanished in Muslim territory. Of that there was no doubt. However, there was not one shred of evidence to suggest he had not quietly converted to the Protestant Faith, long before his tenth birthday, and become totally westernized, before embarking on a career in the British Army which would see him valiantly follow the creeds of fighting, *for God, Queen and Country.*

The Ministry of Defence had taken every possible step to insure secrecy in their investigation, but they had spread their net widely. They had plainly been obliged to involve their Israeli colleagues, who had taken it upon themselves to repatriate the bodies of the two NCOs.

The British Embassy in Tel Aviv had also undertaken a great deal of investigation, but had advanced no further than the men from Shin Bet. The CIA in Langley, Virginia, had found out for themselves that '*the Goddamned Brits have lost a high ranking SAS officer,*' which was regarded as very bad news indeed.

Using a variety of Arab contacts, the CIA had done as much as they could to assist in the investigation but had succeeded only in finding an Arab member of HAMAS who claimed to know the Major was dead. Since there was no body to be found, no-one had the remotest idea if he was telling the truth or not.

36

Colonel Makin sat alone on this rainy day, and read large parts of the report, new stuff and old stuff. Like all senior officers involved in the case, he smelled a gigantic rat. It did not add up. If the Major was dead, they'd have found him. Even if he was a hostage, they would have heard. If he was merely hiding in Hebron with a new lover or something absolutely ridiculous, someone would have either shopped him, or seen him.

For the past few months he had dismissed any thoughts that Ray Kerman could have gone over to the other side, as ridiculous. But Ravi Rashood? That was different. And all of the Kermans' apparent respectability could not remove from the CO's mind, the chilling thought that for the first time in its history, the SAS had harbored a traitor . . . a traitor he himself had essentially hired and nurtured.

'Holy shit!' said the Colonel, for the second time that morning. He sipped his coffee amd waited not terribly enthusiastically for the inevitable call from MI5 asking what he made of the latest information.

Meanwhile that morning, there had been two, possibly three enquiries from journalists, direct to SAS headquarters in Hereford. As ever, the SAS said nothing, referring all enquiries to the Ministry of Defence, whose Press Department immediately claimed to know even less than nothing, if that were possible.

The cordon of secrecy which surrounded the matter was about as secure as a ring of IDF tanks in Hebron. But when an inquiry goes on this long, with more and more people finding things out, it's just a matter of time before a credible leak interests a reporter, or, more likely, a senior defence correspondent with Whitehall contacts.

In this case, it happened at a cocktail party at London's Indian Embassy, a great, gray, granite building on the south side of London's Aldwych, up the street from the Law Courts. Anton Zilber, the tall, long-serving French-born editor of the Diplomatic Corps' magazine, *Court Circular,* was chatting to a slightly drunk Whitehall mandarin he had known for years.

'Busy week, Colin?'

'Matter of fact, it has been, Anton. Damned busy. The bloody Special Forces have mislaid one of their commanding officers. Bloody careless of 'em, eh?'

Anton was not a newshound. The *Court Circular* meticulously recorded all the diplomatic events around town . . . who was at which party, with photographs and captions. It recorded promotions, and farewells to departing ambassadors, with articles about any new arrival to London. In a sense, it was something of a vanity mag for the Diplomatic Corps. Even its title suggested something of the grandeur of the ancient Court of St. James, the official title for all London ambassadors. Each one of them is an Ambassador to the Court of St. James, not just London, England.

Never a breath of scandal appeared in the *Court Circular*, nor indeed any news story which might embarrass anyone. Anton Zilber was handsomely paid, with an exclusive 'beat' among lavish parties and dinners. And every embassy in London sent its glossy copies home to let their ministers know they were not idling around.

What no-one knew, was that Anton had a very prosperous little sideline. He never printed a hot story himself, but he had a web of contacts on national newspapers, especially in the society diaries, where ill-connected journalists could hardly wait to hear that Anton had seen a member of the Royal Family or the Government misbehave badly at an embassy party.

Anton Zilber could stop a busy newspaper diary in its tracks with the conspiratorial opening he always affected . . . 'Hello, Geoff. Not a word about me of course, but something happened at the Belgium Embassy last night I thought might amuse you . . .'

At $300 a time, this was a profitable little sideline.

'Yes,' he replied, carefully, to the jovial but incredible revelation about the SAS officer from the man from Whitehall. 'That does sound a bit careless. No-one we know, I suppose?'

'No-one I know, old boy,' chuckled the mandarin. 'Some bloody SAS killer I think. Just a Major, nothing big. But it happened in Hebron during that nasty battle last spring. A lot of people are very exercised about the whole thing . . . I say, shall we try another glass of that excellent champagne . . . say one thing for the Indians . . . they always push the boat out, eh?'

And that was all it took. The following morning Anton Zilber was on the telephone to one of the very senior defence correspondents of London's *Daily Telegraph*, a former military man who would have no need of the press office at the MOD.

He phoned his oldest friend in the Ministry of Defence, a brigadier, who had helped him over the years with a variety of difficult stories. But today was different. There was not a semblance of help. John Dwyer, himself a former colonel in the

38

Gloucestershire Regiment ran into a brick wall for a full ten minutes of conversation. The brigadier claimed to know absolutely nothing about any disappeared SAS major.

But just before he terminated the conversation, he offered one sentence of assistance. 'Tell you what, Johnny. You mentioned Hebron, battle of Jerusalem Road. I did hear we lost a couple of our chaps in that. I expect they were SAS and that will be in the public records. Have a look there.' It was a classic backside-covering sentence from a senior official.

John Dwyer replaced the receiver thoughtfully. 'Don't know how the hell to do that,' he thought. 'Since I don't even know their bloody names. And no-one's going to tell me.'

He decided the story was beyond his expertise in the field of newspaper sleuthing. But he called his editor with the scant information he had, and the editor, who was equally inept at such down-and-dirty investigations, tipped off his news editor, a bellicose, ex-crime reporter named Tom Howard, from Liverpool, who probably should have been a policeman.

Tom put six men on it. Two at the Public Record Office, checking the death certificates of all serving military personnel from May to July. One at the Hereford County Records Office checking deaths, burials and funerals. One at Whitehall, to try and pressure the Press Office into revealing all in the public interest, and another in the town of Hereford, checking pubs, garages and supermarkets for rumors of SAS men who had recently been killed.

They did not succeed in nailing the story down. But they turned up some detail, and produced a slightly half-baked, but nonetheless intriguing story for those interested in such matters:

BRITISH SAS TROOPS MAY
HAVE FOUGHT HEBRON BATTLE

The Ministry of Defence last night refused to confirm there had been an official squad of SAS troops serving with the Israeli Defence Force during the Battle of Jerusalem Road in Hebron last May.

An MoD spokesman said: 'We have had close ties with the Israeli Army for many years, and have assisted them with training since the country's start in 1948. However the MoD never reveals details of SAS operations. So I am afraid I cannot help.'

Nonetheless, there is a deep mystery surrounding that battle. Two SAS NCOs are believed to have been killed in the Jerusalem Road

39

action. They were Sergeant Frederick O'Hara and Sergeant Charles Morgan, both of Hereford.

Their deaths are recorded in the official British ROD, and the place of death is listed as Hebron, Israel, on May 14th. Both men were cremated, though the Army declines to say when and where, confirming only that the formalities took place in England.

A far greater mystery concerns the unnamed Commanding Officer of the SAS in that conflict during which 100 people are known to have lost their lives.

SAS personnel stationed in the area have all been recalled, but there is no record of any senior officer accompanying them. A Whitehall spokesman would not confirm or deny, that Major Raymond Kerman was the officer in charge, or that he was officially listed 'missing in action'.

However, sources close to the SAS garrison in Hereford insist he has not returned from the Holy Land.

The military attache at the Israeli Embassy in London would only say, 'We are occasionally requested to provide information on missing service personnel in the Middle East. I have no information on any Major Kerman.'

Four days later, a team of London *Daily Mail* reporters, following up the *Telegraph* report, cracked the story. The headline announced:

MYSTERY OF THE MISSING SAS MAJOR
North London Shipping Tycoon
Accuses MOD of 'Lying about my son'

There followed a detailed interview with a 'devastated' Richard Kerman and his wife Naz. Without a qualm, Major Kerman's father outlined every last inquiry by commanders of his son's Regiment, and investigators from the Ministry.

'Our son is missing,' he said. 'We have heard absolutely nothing from him since he left England last February. The mission was of course classified, and they did not even tell us he had been in Israel until August – three months after he disappeared.'

Mr Kerman pointed out that his wife was 'broken-hearted,' and it was obvious there was a great deal not being told to them or anyone else. 'We don't know if Ray is alive or dead,' he said. 'That's a terrible burden for any parent to cope with. At the moment we are just living from day to day, hoping for news of our son.'

And in that, Mr and Mrs Kerman were not alone. British military Intelligence did not believe him dead. And they very much wanted to know where he was. But for rather different reasons.

Major Ray Kerman knew a great deal too much about British Special Forces in the Holy Land – enough to cause a public outcry if the truth should ever come out. He was also, in his own right, a military treasure to any other government or even a group of dissidents.

Major Kerman was a lethal exponent of unarmed combat, a polished operator in every form of military activity, a man who could turn an armed disorganized rabble into a smooth, efficient force against the West. Ray Kerman, Harrow-educated, star of his year at Sandhurst? That was one thing. Ravi Sharood, former reader of the Koran, missing somewhere off the Palestine-Road in Hebron? That was entirely another. And Britain's innately suspicious Ministry of Defence understood the problem, all too well.

No-one in Whitehall, or Hereford, would ever comment on the newspaper stories, but they found their way around the world in short order. Within two hours of publication, the *Mystery of Ray Kerman, the Missing SAS Major* was on the Internet.

Shortly after 2200 (Eastern Standard Time), the CIA's Middle Eastern desk in Langley, Virginia, electronically fired the *Daily Mail*'s story into the middle of the duty officer's desk in the Military Intelligence Division of the National Security Agency, Fort Meade, Maryland.

The calculated speed with which the CIA moved on this was revealing. All Western Intelligence agencies, and their natural allies, Special Forces and Special Agents, are apt to react with horror at the possible defection of one of their own. And the CIA had been tracking the situation for several weeks.

But this new development in the British press, disclosing the Muslim past of the vanished officer, had ratcheted up the entire scenario, by several notches. The midnight electronic communication, from Langley to Fort Meade, was a clear signal the CIA wanted the world's largest, most secretive, most powerful Intelligence agency to go to work.

The National Security Agency employs almost 39,000 people. It is more a city than a government agency, a vast complex of glassed modern buildings, glowering behind razor-wire fences, patrolled by hundreds of armed police, and bomb-sniffing dogs. Generally speaking it makes Beijing's old Forbidden City look like open house. The NSA is known as Crypto City.

Behind those gleaming bulletproof walls stand battalions of supercomputers, tended by sensational mathematicians, on keyboards controlling databases of septillion operations per second (that's a '1' followed by twenty-four zeroes and eight evenly-spaced commas). They don't do regular time in here. They do femtoseconds (one million billionth of a second). This is military micro-management gone berserk. Fort Meade sits at the center of a gigantic global listening network, connected to the satellites, intercepting, eavesdropping, hearing all, saying nothing beyond its prohibited ramparts.

To amuse each other, operators have occasionally played back audio tapes of phone calls from Osama Bin Laden, direct from his cave to his mother, on his INMARSAT cell phone. The National Security Agency provides training for its linguists in ninetey-five different languages, plus every possible dialect of Arabic, including Iraqi, Libyan, Syrian, Saudi, Jordanian and Modern Standard Arabic.

Translating Bin Laden in the NSA represented the work of moments. In this world it is virtually impossible to communicate cross-border from one military operation to another without being heard, with immense clarity and understanding by the electronic interceptors at Fort Meade, Maryland.

The vast compound covers 325 acres, with thirty-two miles of roads. There are more than 37,000 cars registered in Crypto City. Its own private Post Office delivers 70,000 pieces of mail per day. Its annual budget runs into billions of dollars, making it probably the largest municipality in the state of Maryland. Crypto City has never appeared as a city on any map.

The National Security Agency, with 700 active armed cops, has a twenty-four-hour command, control and communications center. Under any kind of threat, it activates immediately a machine-gun toting Emergency Reaction Team to 'battle stations' covering all gates. A million to one fluke might allow an intruder inside the compound, but the chances of such a person ever being seen, or heard from, again are remote.

The Executive Protection Unit mounts a twenty-four-hour armed bodyguard on the NSA's Director. And up on the eighth floor of the massive one-way glass walls of the OPS-2B Building,

Admiral George Morris was still at his desk when the duty officer from the Military Intelligence Division, US Army Captain Scott Wade, nodding cheerfully to the two policemen on duty outside the door, tapped softly and let himself in.

''Evening, sir,' he said. 'We just got a communication in from Langley. About that British SAS officer gone missing in Israel. I thought you might want to see it right away.'

The two men were very familiar to each other, and the Admiral looked up from his desk. 'Hello, Scotty,' he said. 'Did they find him?'

'Nossir. No, they did not. And there's been no hostage demand. They seem to have written that off as a possibility.'

'Hmmmmm,' replied Admiral Morris, reading the *Daily Mail*'s account with interest. 'They sure as hell didn't find him. Jesus Christ! The guy's a Muslim.'

'Well, at least he used to be, sir. I'm not sure about that changing-religions bullshit. I always thought once a Muslim always a Muslim.'

'I guess that was the intention of the Prophet, Scotty,' said the Admiral, smiling. 'But lemme ask you something. You spend most of your life looking at situations like this. And I guess we've suspected Major Kerman may have gone over to the other side, even if the Brits have confirmed nothing. But have you seen any evidence, or any signs at all, in the hundreds of pages of reports, that Major Kerman has defected to some Islamic fundamentalist group?'

'Not really, sir. And no-one's ever actually *said* he did. At least not for sure. It's only been speculation.'

'Yeah. I know. But just take a look at the treatment this big national newspaper in London has given this story. It's cross-referenced on the front page, and inside they run this damn great tabloid spread, big headlines, pictures of Ray Kerman at school in Harrow, pictures of his parents, pictures of this Iranian dust-hole he was born in . . . Christ, they got about five guys covering this.

'I'm telling you, Scotty, someone over in England thinks this really matters. Not someone on the newspaper, they're just guessing, hoping to be right. But someone in Whitehall has alerted them, let 'em know the Defence Ministry is very concerned.

'Jesus, look at this coverage. There's a clear implication this Kerman character gunned down two of his colleagues, SAS

NCOs. Professionals. That makes him very dangerous indeeed.'

'I agree with you, sir. I just wonder what group could have recruited him. I mean, this story implies he was in line possibly to command the entire SAS. Everyone thought so highly of him, and he had no money worries. Looks like his dad was going to give him a dozen ocean-going freighters when he finished with the Army.'

'People do some goddamned weird things, Scotty,' replied the Admiral thoughtfully. 'Goddamned weird things.'

George Morris was a deceptive character, a big man, with a kind of lugubrious manner, deliberately slow in his responses, deliberately ponderous in his thinking, but rock steady in his judgements, and wryly amused at his ability to convey the impression he was a bit slow-witted.

Vice Admiral George Morris was in fact lightning-witted, a former Commanding Officer of the massive *John C. Stennis* Carrier Battle Group, he had ruled his flotilla of twelve warships, eighty-four fighter-bomber aircraft, and thousands of men with a quiet certainty which was admired throughout the US Navy. No-one gets to command a modern CVBG without an intellect hovering close to genius level.

And at the conclusion of his seagoing days he had been hand-picked by the Big Man himself to move into the National Security Agency. Then, one year ago, Admiral Arnold Morgan had announced that George Morris would succeed him as Director, when he Arnold moved to the White House.

Most new National Security Advisers to the President *recommended* things. Arnold Morgan did not recommend. He ordered. And when he ordered, people jumped. Sometimes on all five Continents.

And now Admiral Morris sat comfortably in the Big Chair in Fort Meade, and everyone knew he was in it for as long as he wanted to be. Except, of course, when the Big Man from the White House came visiting and automatically walked straight in and sat right down at his old desk. It was as if Arnold considered he held both top jobs in National Security, rather than just the one at the right hand of the President.

'Scotty,' said Admiral Morris. 'This is a goddamned interesting piece of journalism. Full of facts. And some of 'em may even be true.'

'Yes. I thought so, sir'

44

'But I think enough of this is obviously true for us to make a pretty simple worst-case judgement.'

'Sir?'

'I think we got a fucking tiger out there. And he's not on our side. This Kerman bastard has gone over the wall. No doubt in my mind.'

'Er, actually I think he went around the wall, Admiral.'

Big George paused, smiled. 'Exactly so, Scotty,' he said at length. 'Around the goddamned wall, right in the middle of Hebron. Right now it's only a very uncomfortable possibility. But in my opinion, that's where he's gone. And that requires some action. Just in case it's true.

'Scotty, I want you to tell someone to bring us some coffee. I need to think. And I think better when I'm awake . . . and when I have someone to talk to. How long you got?'

'I'm here 'til 0400, sir,' said Captain Wade making for the door.

'That's good. We'll arrive at some good conclusions. Nice and steady.'

Ten minutes later, sipping black coffee in the relative calm of OPS-2B in the dead of night, the two men took a serious run at the problem Whitehall had so far not dared to name.

'If this guy is on the loose,' the Admiral said slowly, 'what's the worst thing that could happen, from our point of view?'

'I guess he could train a group of Arab terrorists to hit at the Israelis with the same kind of efficiency the SAS use against their enemies.'

'Correct. That's what he *could* do. And I guess we have to ask ourselves, first, for whom would he be likely to do this?'

'I would say, sir, we are almost certainly looking at HAMAS, the old Islamic Resistance Movement. Even now it's still the main Palestinian fundamentalist political movement out there. The whole organization grew out of that Muslim Brothers outfit down on the Gaza Strip – every time we conduct a search for terrorist action in Israel it always leads to HAMAS.'

'Remind me, Scotty. Who runs it?'

'That's hard to know. The main leader was old Sheik Ahmed Yassin, but the Israelis popped him in the slammer ten years ago. Since then they've been responsible for building a lot of Palestinian schools and hospitals, but every now and then they break cover and do something diabolical.

45

'My department thinks that since the various peace initiatives have broken down, HAMAS has become a bigger and bigger player, challenging the PLO for pole position. Just about every big bang in downtown Jerusalem and Tel Aviv in the last few years has been directly down to HAMAS.'

'Who funds them?'

'Dunno, sir. They seem to be pretty damn good at funding themselves . . . and in my view they better be . . . HAMAS is committed to the total liberation of Palestine, including the entire State of Israel, then to the creation of an Islamic State.'

Admiral Morris was pensive for almost a minute. Then he said carefully, 'If this Major Kerman hopped around the wall in Hebron, there must have been an element of impulsiveness to his actions. Because the Palestinians had not staged, or even caused, a riot. It was the Israelis on the attack, the Arabs were kind of defending. They had planned nothing.'

'That's true, sir. But the military documents were very clear. Once the fight broke out, the Palestinians organized themselves very quickly. They brought up rockets and grenades and several machine-guns. That's HAMAS, trust me. No-one else could have pulled that off.'

'They got any known strength in Hebron?'

'Hell, yes, Admiral. They have, all through the Negev desert, every town from Beersheba to Bethlehem and Jerusalem. The whole place is a tinder box of HAMAS armaments and enclaves. The Gaza Strip is worse. I'm telling you, the ole Hebrews have got their goddamned hands full down there.'

'Look, Scotty, it's been several months since Major Kerman made an apparent rush for the desert. Has anything happened in that time to suggest HAMAS has come under some inspired front-line leadership?'

'I don't think so, sir. Just the usual rash of bombs and stuff. No firm evidence of anything unusual.'

'Well, I'll tell you what. Someone is supplying these guys with heavy cash. Can you run a quick check and see if there's been any big robberies in any of the Israeli cities. You know, HAMAS may not even have been suspected. But these terror groups often turn to regular crime for funds, and the SAS are probably the best break-in guys in the world.'

'Sir, I'll have to go check that in Security Ops. They got a very bright young Navy guy in there called Jimmy Ramshawe. He's new, and he's on duty tonight. I'll get him buzzing on it. You know, there's very few robberies in urban Israel. But if anything's happened, Jimmy'll pick it up.'

'See you back here in a half-hour.'

'You got it, sir.'

One hour later, the two men were still waiting, up there in the quiet of the eighth floor for the appearance of Lieutenant Ramshawe, when the guard on duty outside tapped on the door, opened it, and said, 'Lt. Ramshawe would like Captain Wade to go down to his office.'

'Guess I'll get another cup of coffee, Scotty. Keep me awake if we're going to be another hour.'

'Sir, I won't be long. Fifteen, max.'

Admiral Morris already knew all about Lt. Ramshawe. In fact he'd known his father, an Admiral from New South Wales who had ended up Military Attache at the Australian Embassy on Massachusetts Avenue, right here in Washington.

Young Jimmy had been born in America, but, surrounded by Aussies all his life, he still carried a distinct inflection of Australia in his speech. He could hardly have been more American, schooled in Connecticut, he was an outstanding baseball pitcher, and had attended the Naval Academy at Annapolis, thus following his father into a career in dark blue.

At the Academy, he had excelled, demonstrating a brilliant IQ, and a capacity for infinitesimal detail. A tall, lanky, athletic boy, he also showed many of the qualities necessary to command a warship. He was tough, shrewd, and relentless in achieving his objectives.

It was his brain that set him apart, and his brain which tied him up. One of his instructors once expostulated, 'Ramshawe! Jesus Christ, he could end up a second Captain Queeg, counting the fucking strawberries when all hell was breaking loose.'

But the United States Navy is expert at channeling talented people. And they quickly spotted the meticulous and tireless Ramshawe as, possibly, a natural-born Intelligence Officer. Which, unhappily was the last thing on Jimmy's mind.

'Christ,' he said. 'You mean all these bloody jokers in my class are going off to join warships, and leaving me behind in an office somewhere in that bloody Kremlin in the middle of Maryland? Get outta here.'

47

But the Navy was not joking. And the selection boards got their way, offering the Lieutenant a rare, three-year tour of duty in the National Security Agency, with a gilt-edged promise that if he really did not fit in, his career would be reviewed, with the intention of sending him to sea.

Lt. Ramshawe, urged by his father, agreed, and duly reported to Fort Meade, where he instantly made an impression for his watchfulness, and ability to become accomplished at many tasks, all of which required weeks and weeks of study. He had been in the Security Ops center just a few weeks, but already officers like Captain Wade knew all about him, and his ability to pull up truly obscure information and make sense of it.

Fifteen minutes later, Captain Wade returned to the office of the Director. It was now well after midnight, and Admiral Morris was surprised to hear a real edge to Scotty's voice.

'Ramshawe's on to something,' he said. 'Right now you can't even open the door to his office because he's working in the middle of about four tons of paper. But he's located a couple of bank robberies in Israel, totally different in character, totally separate dates, separate cities, separate methods of entry and completely different circumstances. He says they're the same, and he'll be here to explain himself in the next ten minutes.'

Admiral Morris smiled, slowly, and nodded. 'Guess he sees something we might miss, eh, Scotty? I look forward to this . . . did you tell him what we were looking for?'

'Nossir. That's why it's interesting, right?'

'Precisely so. Tell him to hurry up.'

Right on cue, the door opened and the duty guard ushered Lt. Ramshawe inside.

'G'day, Admiral,' he said, issuing the perennial Aussie greeting, and heaving a pile of maps and papers onto a big table.

George Morris chuckled. 'Hello, Lieutenant. They working you so hard you can no longer tell the difference between day and night?' he said.

'Matter of fact, yes,' said Jimmy. 'But I can't walk around saying "G'night, Admiral," can I?'

'Well, I guess not. How about "G'd evening?"'

'Nah. I'd sound like a bloody pooftah.'

All three of them laughed at this interlude from the outback. And George Morris found that lopsided Aussie directness engaging in the extreme, political correctness being hurled to the four winds, in the renowned idiom of Arnold Morgan himself.

'Okay, sir. I expect Scotty here has told you I've found two bank robberies committed in Israel during the last six days of this past year. I'd prefer to go through them one at a time, that way you can see the similarities when they arise while I'm going through the next one.'

Admiral Morris nodded. And Jimmy spread before him a map of Jerusalem. In red pen he had marked off an area off Jaffa Road, a half-mile north-east of the Old City Gate. 'Right here, Admiral, in this high-rise, is the biggest US bank in Israel, the New York and Beirut Savings. It acts as a dollar clearing house.

'I'm not dead sure how it works, but every day millions and millions of US dollars come into the country via the tourists, and somehow or another they all end up in the New York and Beirut. I imagine this huge dollar amount is then wire transferred back to the NY and B headquarters in Manhattan. Then they systematically destroy the old currency bills. Anyhow, at various times of the month there's a bloody great stack of cash hanging around Jaffa Road.'

Captain Wade and the Admiral were silent, as Lt. Ramshawe outlined the robbery.

'Okay, it's Christmas Day, a Saturday, the holiday being observed by most people but not everyone. Even in the Holy Land where Christ is regarded only as a prophet, there's nothing open on the Sabbath in Jaffa Road.

'At around 1530, would you believe, a bloody riot breaks out over a car accident. It quickly escalates and before anyone knows it there's twenty police cars and the IDF moving in to try and stop it. Right now we're talking petrol bombs and Christ knows what.

'By six o'clock, it's over. But it's not until Monday morning they discover that sometime during the weekend, a gang hit the bank and got away with all the dollar bills, mostly old, all unmarked. Streuth! That caused a major investigation.

'And the upshot of that was as follows.' Ramshawe read from handwritten notes:

'*1) The gang got in through the roof, blowing off the lock to the fire stairs.*

'*2) They knew where the alarm system was located, because they* silenced it with a burst from an MP-5 sub machine gun. Put the bastard right out of action.

'3) They knew where to find the strongroom, where the vault was, because there was no further sign of strife. They located the security system, which was not timed, dismantled it, then blew the vault open and took all the bread. Conclusion: an inside job.

'4) They got away off the roof, because none of the downstairs doors or windows had been opened. No doors or windows anywhere in the building had been opened.

'5) A large military-type helicopter, probably a Sikorsky, and probably unmarked, was seen by several onlookers, taking off from the roof in the middle of the bloody riot, and everyone assumed it was to do with the bloody riot. But it wasn't. And it was five days before anyone realized that.

'I think anyone would agree, there's distinct overtones of a brilliantly planned heist. Military in its nature. Almost.'

'Where'd you get all this stuff, Lieutenant?' asked George Morris.

'Well, some of it was reported in the Israeli press. But I filled in a lot of details from a guy at Shin Bet. We got a pretty good *quid pro quo* with them.

'But you know, Admiral, it was never a big story, and I think the reason for that was because the bank never let on how much cash was stolen. They played it all down, because, of course, the bank notes were being destroyed so they did not really have a big value to the bank itself. But bloody oath! They'd be real handy for a bloke who wanted to do some heavy spending.'

'Sure would,' mused the Admiral. 'Any take on how much cash was actually removed?'

'Not accurately. The police announced the sum stolen may have been six figures. Which sounds like not much for a bank robbery. But our guy in Shin Bet thinks it could have been $50 million, in used dollar bills.'

'Jesus,' said Scotty.

'Anyway, that story appeared in the *Jerusalem Post* on Tuesday morning, December 28; small, inside page, six paragraphs, no photograph of the bank. No mention of $50 million, or of the helicopter. I also thought it was significant that the pro-Palestinian *Jerusalem Times* never did carry the story . . . and that brings us to robbery number two, which took place in Tel Aviv, thirty-eight miles away along the Sorek Valley.'

Lieutenant Ramshawe changed over the map in front of the Admiral, and pointed up an area of the urban sprawl of Tel Aviv-Jaffa, specifically around King Saul and Weizmann streets, where the most dazzling modern edifices rise up from the sandy foundations of the city.

'Right here, sir, is the New York and Beirut Bank, in a big building. It's the main branch on the coast, bigger than the one in Jerusalem, and again a place where the dollars on the West Coast end up, before being transported to Jaffa Road.

'Now, sir, according to the police, this place was robbed on Saturday night December 26 – just a few hours after the bank in Jerusalem. This robbery was discovered by cleaning staff on Sunday, because they did not work on Christmas night. This story was also played down, and appeared in Monday morning's *Jerusalem Post*, the day *before* news of the Jerusalem robbery was printed . . . I've put together some more notes which I'll read because they're just handwritten, and then I'll get 'em printed up:

'*1) This operation took a long time. The thieves had rented a much smaller building next door, four months previously, and then tunnelled their way through into the unused lower basement of the bank. They actually cut through a couple of steel pillars in order to get in.*

'*2) They used ladders and scaffold to reach the ceiling and battered their way through a cement floor, the police say using drills and sledgehammers.*

'*3) Once inside, they went straight to the electronic surveillance and alarm system and hit it with just one bullet from an MP-5, right in the side so you could hardly notice it. That gave them one hour, because this place had a timed security system override, and it would be that long before an alarm was raised. And that bloody hour was all they needed.*

'*4) They reached the Tel Aviv vault, identical in every way to the one in Jerusalem, and blew open the gate and the safe, with the minimum of explosive, much less than they had used in Jerusalem.*

'*5) Then they closed the vault, and the gate, dropped all the bags of dollar bills through the floor into the basement, placed a thin piece of plywood, around four foot by four foot, over the hole under the carpet, somehow flipped the carpet back into place, and dropped through the hole to safety.*

'*6) When the bank security guys answered the call to come in to see why the alarm system was down, they never even noticed the break-in, just called in electricians to come and fix the system. Wasn't until some poor bastard with a bucket and mop stood on the bloody carpet that Sunday afternoon they realized what the bloody hell was going on.'*

'How many of the security guys kept their jobs?' asked Admiral Morris.

'None, I shouldn't think,' said Lt. Ramshawe. 'Anyway, there you have two highly-professional break-ins, into very secure modern buildings. There was plainly inside information for both the layout and locations of security systems and the vaults. One was carried out in the middle of a staged riot, with a big rooftop getaway in a helicopter. The other took months and months to plan and then execute quietly in the middle of the night, with the aid of heavy machinery. And that second one was more efficient than the first, in terms of time and the amount of explosive required.

'In my opinion there were a lot of guys involved, but they were the same guys, same calibre of bullet, same kind of explosive, same objective – used US dollars – same banking corporation. Same holiday weekend.'

Admiral Morris looked up from his sketch pad. 'One question, Lieutenant,' he said. 'I can see the heavy vault door was just swung back shut in Tel Aviv. But how come the security guys did not notice the *gate* to the vault was blown.'

'Sir, according to the police, they used a high-powered electric drill, probably portable, to penetrate the cold steel locking bar. They inserted the charge and blew that bar to pieces, but hardly damaged the wrought iron framework to the gate. After the grab, they just shoved it closed and left it, looking locked, but not locked. The police reckon that door was blown by a real expert.'

Captain Scott Wade spoke for the first time. 'I'll tell you one really clever thing,' he said. 'They guessed, correctly, no-one would discover the Jerusalem robbery until the Monday morning, because there was no timed security system to sound the alarm automatically if it was deactivated. However, they were pretty damned sure someone would discover the Tel Aviv robbery sometime during the weekend. And that put the robberies on different days, newspaper-wise. No editor got the chance to link the two break-ins on the same weekend.'

'Damn smart,' said the Admiral. 'And perhaps even smarter to work out the Bank of New York and Beirut would never want to announce precisely how many used notes were stolen.'

'And that means one thing,' said Jimmy Ramshawe, pushing

his thick dark hair off his forehead. 'Right here we're looking at one of the great robberies in history. Maybe $100 million. Snatched with unbelievable precision. And the bastards pulled it off damn nearly in secret. And no-one's got a clue who did it. Bloody oath, that's some operation.'

Admiral Morris stood up, and walked over to the Lieutenant. 'Thanks, Jimmy,' he said. 'That's brilliantly done. And it's time I went home to bed.'

He showed the Navy Lieutenant to the door and then turned back to Captain Wade.

'Well, Scotty,' he said. 'I think we may just have located a career-change for Mr Raymond Kerman, don't you?'

'It sure looks like it. Those robberies were never committed by simple freedom fighters. And it's got some classic signs of Special Forces about it . . . you know, sir . . . weeks and weeks of planning . . . total secrecy before and after . . . faultless execution . . . no mistakes . . . no surprises. Even a diversionary uproar, right in the middle of Jaffa Road.'

'Absolutely. This wasn't pulled off by some Arab rabble. These robberies were masterminded, and carried out, by a real professional.'

'For the moment I think we will say nothing. Meanwhile try to locate some detail on Major Kerman's military career, will you? We'll have a chat in the morning. For the moment, this better be a need-to-know operation. And that means just us.'

'Okay, sir. I'll start some enquiries right now. It's almost 0800 in London.'

The following morning
Director's Office Fort Meade
Captain Wade stood before the Admiral bearing a sheaf of papers and two maps. The first showed the Republic of Sierre Leone, which sits on the Atlantic coast in the bottom left-hand corner of Africa's top half. To the north and east lies Guinea, to the south-east is Liberia.

Sierre Leone is substantially smaller than South Carolina, but it has more intense revolutions, the most recent and most persistent being the relentless, bloodthirsty forces of the Revolutionary United Front against the ruling President Kabbah.

This truly ghastly African war saw 50,000 people lose their lives, generally because the forces of the RUF, led by the savage

Foday Sankoh, conducted years of terror against civilians, raping, pillaging and mutilating.

Back in the year 2000, Sankoh's brutal hordes actually managed to capture 500 United Nations troops in the towns of Maskeni and Kailahun. They stole their vehicles and weapons, adding them to their own formidable arsenal, purchased with income from diamond mines they controlled deep in the western interior of the country.

This was too much for the Brits, the old Commonwealth masters. They sent in a force of 700, 1st Battalion Parachute Regiment, to begin evacuating British and European citizens. The paras captured a large hunk of the capital, the coastal city of Freetown, including the airport.

But there was fierce fighting. The British paras forced the release of most of the hostages, and hammered away at Sankoh's jungle fighters, utilizing helicopter gunships, driving the RUF back into the hinterlands.

But Sankoh would not let go. They attacked again, and suddenly siezed six soldiers of the Royal Irish Rangers, holding them hostage deep in the interior. These characters called themselves the West Side Boys, and they held the British troops captive in a very strong position either side of the Rokel Creek.

Whitehall considered there was an obvious risk the men would end up with their throats cut, or worse, unless the British Army moved very quickly indeed.

And the map Captain Wade was now showing to Admiral Morris showed a detailed plan of this grotesque little theatre of war, around the village of Gberi Bana, north of the Creek, and Forodugu, to the south.

'The Brits sent in the SAS right away, sir,' he said. 'D-Squadron. And they infiltrated this area right here, high above the river, five observation posts, brilliantly camouflaged in the brush, while the Special Forces made their assessment of the problem.

'Their Commander masterminded the entire operation. He talked in five helicopters loaded with British paras, who landed downstream along the creek and attacked on either bank, knocking out the machine-gun positions.'

Captain Wade adjusted the map and pointed out the direction of the onrushing British paras. 'These guys right here, sir. They drew the West Side Boys' fire . . . then at the correct moment, the SAS commander gave the order, called up the gunships, and led his men into the attack . . .

'Right here, sir,' said Scotty. 'SAS D-Squadron stormed out of their hides at first light, and rampaged down the north bank of Rokel Creek. They swept into the village, gunning down anything in their way, and freed the men. They blasted a path back to the waiting helicopters, leaving twenty-five dead RUF rebels behind them, eighteen wounded and captured. Only one SAS man died in the action.

'Admiral, I've really checked this one out. We're looking at a classic Special Forces operation right here. I guess I don't need to tell you the SAS Commander was Raymond Kerman . . .'

'Jesus . . . !' breathed George Morris. And without a word, he picked up his telephone, and dialed the White House, secure line direct from Crypto City.

'Get me Admiral Morgan,' he said.

Kathy O'Brien, the stunning red-haired secretary to the National Security Advisor, picked up the telephone and heard the familiar voice of George Morris, the one voice in the entire country Arnold Morgan would always answer.

At the time, she was standing between her desk and the big wooden door to her boss, and, knowing he was alone, she walked across and pushed it open.

'George is on the phone,' she said. 'Shall I put him through?'

'George who?' grunted the Admiral absent-mindedly, staring at a pile of documents. 'George Washington? George Patton? George III?'

'Christ!' said Kathy, knowing full well he knew precisely who she meant. 'Vice Admiral George Morris, Director of the National Security Agency, located in Fort Meade, Maryland, five miles north of the Beltway, latitude 39 spot one zero.'

'Vague,' he grunted. 'Too vague.' Then Admiral Morgan sprang to his feet, chuckling, walked across the room and hugged her, told her he loved her, and, 'To put that clever old bastard through right away,' and could he have some coffee, and where the hell was the *Washington Post*, and, 'Tell that lunatic in the Kremlin to get off his ass and send the answers we want in the next hour . . . goddamned nuclear boats in the Baltic . . .'

'I can't tell him that . . .' said the future Mrs Arnold Morgan. 'I'm not even a communist . . .' she added, absurdly. But she refrained from continuing, because conversations like that merely played into the Admiral's hands, allowing him full latitude for what he believed to be humor.

Kathy headed for the door, resolved to e-mail Moscow and inform them that Admiral Morgan regarded the matter with some urgency and an early response would be appreciated. Then she connected Admiral Morris on the secure line.

''Morning George.' Arnold greeted his old buddy with equanimity, knowing he would *never* have called if it was umimportant.

'Hello, sir,' responded Admiral Morris, granting the President's right-hand man full respect, before lapsing into 'Arnie', which thirty years of friendship, most of it in the US Navy, plainly permitted.

'Can I come over and see you?'

'Sure, is it urgent?'

'No. But my team has turned up a situation I don't like and neither will you. Can you give me an hour early afternoon?'

'Come for lunch, George. White House. About 1300.'

'Perfect,' said Admiral Morris. 'I'll be there.'

Right on time, the staff car from Fort Meade pulled up outside the West Wing, and the agents escorted the NSA chief to the office of Admiral Morgan. The two men chatted for a few moments and then went directly to a small private dining room, the table set for two.

Admiral Morgan poured them each a glass of fizzy mineral water, and hit a button to alert the waiter.

'Okay, George. Lay it on me.'

'Right. I'll start with a question. Did you know the Brits lost an important SAS commander in that battle in Hebron last spring?'

'Can't say I did. You mean dead?'

'I thought I did a few days ago, although there was no evidence of his death. He just disappeared, and there's been no hostage demand. But I don't think he's dead anymore. I think he's alive, and he may have a) deserted, and b) joined HAMAS.'

'He's *what*! An SAS commander joined a terrorist group? Christ. That's bad. But at least in HAMAS they pretty well restrict themselves to the Middle East. So it's not life threatening.'

'No. Not yet. But this character is unusual. He's called Ray Kerman, which sounds Jewish. But he's not. He was born in Iran, and his parents were Muslims. He used to read the Koran.'

'What's his rank?'

'Major. He was the SAS Commander who rescued everyone in that action in Sierre Leone three or four years ago.'

'Was he? I remember that. Hell of an operation. Didn't the Brits charge across the river and blow the place apart?'

'That's the one, and Ray Kerman was in charge. You'll remember they hit suddenly, at dawn, got everyone out, killed or wounded around forty people, and escaped. Lost only one man. Textbook Special Forces.'

'Yeah. Big surprise. Big stick. That's the way to do it,' replied the Admiral, approvingly.

At this moment the waiter came in with two bowls of lobster bisque, and placed one in front of each Admiral.

'You remember to put a splash of dry sherry in each bowl?' asked the NSA.

'Yessir.'

'That's good. Don't want my guest to think my standards are slipping.

'Now, George, lemme ask a key question – why do you think this guy's still alive?'

'Mostly because no-one can find his body. Not the Brits, not the Israelis, not the Mossad. Even Shin Bet have turned up nothing. And right here, there's a most unusual clue. Two other SAS men, both senior NCOs, were found dead in the precise area Kerman was last seen. One had been killed by bullets from an MP-5, the other by an obvious Special Forces punch to the front of the face. The Brits seem to think Kerman may have killed them both, and then made a run for it.'

'But why, George? Why would he do that?'

'Beats me. He was a career officer, outstanding at Sandhurst, and destined, possibly, to command the entire Regiment. Also his family are loaded, sent him to school at Harrow. It's a real mystery.'

'Well, George. I've known you a lot of years, and what you have told me is damned interesting. But not interesting enough for you to want to talk to me, specifically, in private. The Brits have mislaid a top guy in Israel. But that's not really our problem, is it?'

'No. Not yet. But this gets better. Or, at least worse.'

And Admiral Morris proceeded to entertain Arnold Morgan

with the full story of the two bank robberies, chapter and verse, from Jerusalem to Tel Aviv.

And at the end of this, the Big Man in the White House just said, 'Holy shit! These guys ran off with $100 million in old bank notes, and no-one's even made it public? That's amazing. But more amazing is the fact that two crimes in Israel, that brilliant, must have been planned and executed by professionals. Someone in there has serious military training – and the officer who did it must be a very talented man.'

'My thoughts exactly, sir. We got a goddamned tiger out there, in charge of a very organized group. And we must surely not discount the fact they may not restrict their enemy to just Israel.'

Just then the waiter returned to clear the soup bowls. 'Everything okay, sir?'

'Nectar,' replied the Admiral.

The two medium-rare sirloin steaks which followed were also perfect. And between luxurious bites, Admiral Morgan assessed the situation, trying to judge firstly, whether Ray Kerman was in fact a spy of the very worst type, who had somehow infiltrated the British Army.

He was inclined to dismiss that, on account of the known wealth of the Kerman family, still living in London, still highly respectable. 'Sounds more likely, Ray had a sudden fit of conscience. Were there any suggestions to that effect?'

'Not really. But the house the dead SAS guys were in,was in the middle of the battle zone, and it did previously contain a family. The Israelis found two quite young children, under nine, both shot dead. The father was also dead. The mother escaped, and has been found. She says she knows nothing of any SAS officer. For what it's worth, the Brits don't believe her.'

'Do we know Major Kerman's religion?'

'Church of England. School, and military. No suggestions otherwise.'

'Well, the only thing I can imagine is that Ray Kerman did have a sudden attack of conscience, and in that battle, appalled by the savagery of the IDF attacks on the Arabs, decided to change sides.'

'Arnie, I understand that is a possibility. What brings me here is to discuss what we should do in the event he moves on from the HAMAS groups fighting in the Holy Land, and decides to have a bang at the rest of the Western world.'

'Christ. I guess we better find him before he gets that far. But those groups have been pretty quiet for a while now. And I don't think anyone's planning a mass murder of civilians anymore. Not after 2001. There's no doubt, the US military scared the hell out of the entire Muslim world when they pulverized Bin Laden's forces . . . but we gotta keep our guard right up. Because this Kerman character is, in my view, about ten times more dangerous than al-Qaeda. And right now he's only practising. And I think he might already have grabbed $100 million of our money.'

'That's what we think. But we don't know where he's put it, and we don't know where he is. So far as I can see, we can only keep a sharp eye on big crimes and bombs in the Holy Land.'

'Well, George, I think we should alert the Mossad and Shin Bet as to our suspicions and fears for the future. They're pretty good at finding people. Right now I'd be ninety percent certain those robberies were carried out by a military professional of Major Kerman's calibre. And talking of calibre, I would not be surprised if the bullets which hit the SAS Sergeant were from the same MP-5 as the one which hit the alarm system in the Tel Aviv bank. Maybe they could check.'

'I'll do that this afternoon, Arnie. Meanwhile do we let the Brits know we are onto something?'

'Might as well. But they'll be on the leading edge of this inquiry. The Brits only sound stupid. It's part of their weird upbringing. But they always know a lot more than you think.'

The two Admirals sat in silence for a few moments. Then George Morris asked, 'How do you think a new recruit like Major Kerman would get from a back street in Hebron into HAMAS and then into the very front line of Middle Eastern politics, fundamentalist politics?'

'Well, you know they'd be extremely suspicious, right from the get-go. He's probably on a trial right now, but I guess those robberies proved a point real quick. Kerman's probably already in touch with the Palestinian Islamic Jihad, which is strong down in the Gaza Strip and has a very moderate agenda, centering on the total destruction of Israel and the immediate creation of a Palestinian State.'

'Nothing serious?' chuckled Admiral Morris.

'Hell, no. Just the brink of World War III . . . and remember the Jihad is pretty ruthless in its fight against Israel. They were the guys who killed or injured 100 people in the shopping mall in Tel

Aviv a few years back. It has four main Palestinian factions, and one of them operates up near the Lebanon border with Hezbollah.

'The key, George, may be a guy called Sheik Biud Altmimi. He's from Hebron, and is known to be supported by Iran, Kerman's homeland. But none of it's easy. An awful lot of those fundamentalist military leaders are already in jail in various countries like Egypt, but especially in Israel.

'A man like Major Kerman would be the best thing that could ever happen to those kind of terrorists. Not you understand, to go around committing mass murder. I think those days are gone, at least for the moment. But with a leader like this SAS Commander, they could still launch very destructive attacks on the West, even without killing people.'

'Well, right now we can't do much except to alert everyone to keep a very careful watch on the situation in Israel.'

'Yeah,' said Admiral Morgan. 'And stand by for the unexpected. I doubt Major Kerman's $100 million is sitting idle.'

CHAPTER THREE

Wednesday, April 27, 2005
The Golan Heights
(Five miles inside the
Syrian Disengagement Line)

There's tension up here, even in the quietest hollows. Even five miles behind the Syrian border patrols, there is always that simmering Arab resentment along the ridges of the looming natural fortress of Golan.

The greatest tank battle the world has ever seen was fought here, in the 1973 Yom Kippur War. Israel won it, leaving behind 1,200 blasted Syrian steel hulks. And amid the debris of war, there was the rage of an ancient nation, the custodians of Damascus, the oldest continuously-inhabited city on this earth.

The Golan Heights are a dark and formidable range, a green and granite landscape, strewn about with black basalt boulders, possibly placed by the Devil himself, on this centuries-old battleground of the religious faiths.

Doves become hawks up here. For just a very few miles to the west lies Syria's disengagement line. And then, five miles on, across No Man's Land, there is carved in the mountains, another line, along which the hated Israeli conquerors guard the spoils of war, vast lands which were once as Arabian as the towering Citadel of Damascus.

Today there were almost 100 armed warriors up there, gathered in an old Syrian military camp. Their fifty-foot-long open-sided tent was new, and it was set beneath new camouflage, netting and brushwood, in a remote vale between two granite rises, through which the snow-capped crown of Mount Herman could clearly be seen. The old compound was ringed with its original sandbag walls four-feet high. Four manned machine-gun nests punctuated those walls. There were lookouts in the surrounding hills. Each man had a mobile phone and a loaded

MP-5 carbine at the ready. The place was on a strict war-footing, in the tradition of the Golan Heights.

Three unmarked military trucks were parked outside. Beyond them was a rough, wooden building, with a tin chimney jutting from its roof. Outside the rear entrance was a broken-down tanker truck, filled with fresh water. But it was still obvious there were more men here today than those actually living in the compound.

Inside the tent there was a long, trestle table, behind which, supported by two easels, was a large scale cork board, almost covered by three wide maps and two charts. The assembled armed men sat on ammunition crates, making notes, listening to two Syrian officers who were lecturing them on the least visible point of entry into no man's land, and into Israel.

Between the two instructors sat the Commanding Officer of the 1st Battalion, HAMAS Assault Force – General Ravi Rashood, formerly of D-Squadron SAS, Sandhurst and Harrow. Promotion had proved to be swift for the best Western officer ever to offer his services to a third-world terrorist group. Major Ray Kerman no longer existed.

Today he wore battle fatigues, and around his head and shoulders was the black and white *ghutra*, complete with the two stranded cord *aghal*. He looked what he now was, a battle-hardened desert fighter, descended from Bedouins, operating on behalf of an Islamic nation. In his pocket he carried a handwritten note which read in Arabic: '*Dearest Ravi, Please take care of Ahmed. You and he are all I have left now. Allah go with you both. I love you, Shakira.*'

The girl who had saved his life running through those blasted Palestinian streets almost a year ago was now his only personal relationship. She and her brother had hidden him, and then smuggled him north to the isolated little Druze village of Mas'ada, just a few miles from the HAMAS compound.

Weeks later, after Ray Kerman had been accepted into the terrorist high command, it was Shakira who had befriended a senior clerk in the Jerusalem bank, and mapped out the floor plan and security system; Shakira who had somehow penetrated A.M. Shwartz National Locksmiths of Hebron, and drawn up the diagrams of their most secure gate and door systems.

After that Ray had made his position clear. He would either take complete command of the operation or it would not happen.

With some reluctance, and a little suspicion, the HAMAS commanders decided they had nothing to lose by agreeing. They could always shoot him. But by the evening of December 26, they knew they had a brand new military leader. And in a dusty cellar hideaway, on the outskirts of Bethlehem, Ray was commissioned in the field, appointed General Rashood, C-in-C First Batallion, HAMAS Assault Force.

Shakira had been there, and they had sat the night out, huddled together against the stone wall, sharing a blanket, talking through an adrenalin-high with the sixteen other HAMAS freedom fighters who had hoisted $100 million out of the two banks. Ray found the conversation unusually agreeable. He liked his companions, and he was falling in love with the beautiful Shakira, whose life he had saved, as she had saved his.

And, when they had all prayed together the following morning, he had felt at home, here in this sandy dungeon. And he remembered the words of the Koran, spoken to him long ago by the North London Imam:

> For you were enemies
> And He joined your hearts together
> And now you are brothers . . .

Removed now from the responsibility of two young children, and the innate strain of an arranged Muslim marriage to a nice man she had never loved, Shakira now devoted her time to the planning of HAMAS attacks on the Israelis. She still wore traditional Arab dress, and she remained a devout Muslim. However, she had taken to arriving for work among the HAMAS military wearing boots, jeans, and combat jacket. Such was her reputation, and so sharp was her mind, no-one ever questioned this break with tradition. Shakira of the Desert had become a law unto herself. And she truly worshipped General Rashood, whose word had now become everyone's law.

On two or three of the less dangerous missions she had insisted on joining the front-line force, once successfully blowing up an empty Israeli tank. And she now assumed she could take part in any mission she wished. And the General mostly shrugged and agreed. However Shakira was not permitted to join this gathering on the Golan Heights, and she was currently sulking back in Damascus, while the former Major Kerman briefed his troops for tonight's insertion into Israel.

He was only just back himself from a third mission inside the Israeli border. The operations had been spread over one and a half months, each one lasting seven days and seven nights. Each time Ravi had taken just four men to the observation post he had established on the slopes of the mountain which rises up to the ruined battlements of Nimrod Castle. This thirteenth-century Syrian fortress, which they had once defended against the marauding Crusaders, occupies a select place in the folklore of the nation.

It was a devasting blow when it fell into Israeli hands in the Yom Kippur War. But that's what happened, and borders were constructed to its east, and there it stood high on the Golan plain, surrounded by the wreckage of a thousand tanks, and several hundred ghosts of Syria's fighting men.

Nimrod Fortress, located now in Israel, has one of the most commanding views in all of the Middle East, spectacular vistas of the lush farmland of the Northern Galilee. It was from this high garrison in the 1967 war that Syrian forces launched attack after attack on the Israelis below, blasting shells into the Kibbutz communities of Dan, Ashmura and Shi'ar Yashuv.

On that occasion the Israelis outflanked them, counter-attacking behind the defences, forcing the total surrender or abject retreat of all Syrian units on the Golan. It was, if anything, worse in 1973, after the Israelis struggled up to the Heights, the odds stacked against them, and with stupendous courage, hurled the attackers back, driving on towards Damascus before the United Nations demand for peace was heeded.

No Syrian can even think about the Golan Heights, and the annexing of the ancient Nimrod Fortress without a rising sense of rage, frustration, and, in the Arab ethic, an obdurate, unending desire for revenge.

If that awareness was powerful in 1973, it became obsessive after the end of 2004, because in the final months of that year the Israelis committed the unthinkable. They bulldozed the entire interior of the ancient fortress, and turned it into a high-security prison, constructed with massive granite blocks, inside the old castle ramparts. And behind its towering, gray, five-foot thick walls, were incarcerated fifty of the most important political prisoners the Israelis had ever captured. It was packed with personnel from HAMAS and its sister organization Hezbollah, along with various other highly-influential members of the Islamic Jihad.

Nimrod Jail thus stood as a terrible symbol of Israeli power, constructed, perhaps, in anger at a violent rash of terrorist attacks at the end of 2001, but as inflammatory, in its way, as the division of Jerusalem itself.

On their most recent mission, Ravi Rashood and his team had again watched the place ceaselessly for one week, observing the jail, noting the comings and goings of the guards, observing the change of shifts, counting the minutes of the four-man outside patrols, measuring the distance from the main gate to the lower level of the old rock-built foundation, gauging the precise time it took one guard to walk down there, and then assessing the time which would be needed for other men to make the short journey, some of whom might be weak, or even ill.

Trying to log the timing of the lights in the main courtyard had proved to be almost impossible from the vantage point of the HAMAS recce group, huddled in their hide, close to the top of the escarpment, but still forty feet below the ground level of the jail. After days of observation, General Ravi had finally said, in his now impeccable Arabic, 'If it's not accurate, we don't need it. We'll attack in the daylight.'

This last remark had sent a tremor of concern through the four-man team which accompanied the General . . . *What! Try to storm this Israeli stronghold in broad daylight? No covering darkness? No element of surprise? Risk being seen and obliterated on the steep upward slopes of Nimrod, probably by heavy artillery? Sir! We could all die out here . . . we wouldn't have a chance.*

Above them they could see the evidence of Israel's defenses on an encircling ridge outside the jail walls. There was obvious artillery, plus machine-gun nests, and rocket launchers. The Israelis, whatever else, were not stupid, and they understood the possibility of 'some lunatic terrorist group taking a shot at the jail'. But they'd made provisions for that, ensuring that no attacking battalion would have a prayer of survival.

General Ravi was thoughtful. He dictated on a slim micro-phone, directly into his computer, the strength and direction of the fixed artillery positions. He assessed the time it would take for the Israelis, caught unaware only briefly, to turn those killer weapons on to their enemy.

For an hour he had said nothing, listening patiently to the apprehension of his men. But he never stopped making his notes, using his calculator, dictating his responses.

Finally, he had said, quietly, 'We'll attack in the daylight. I have not yet decided time and date.'

And now, back in the Golan compound, direct from the jaws of the Israeli Lion for the third time, he rose to speak to his warriors. And there was not a sound in the long tent as he raised a long polished stick and pointed it at the first map, tapping it on the Syrian Disengagement Line east of the tiny village of Hadar.

'We leave Syrian territory right here,' he said. 'And begin our crossing of No Man's Land, south of the village. It's about five miles across, and we can safely take the big truck in for a little over a mile without attracting Israeli attention, maybe a little further, depending on the weather.

'I have marked our entry point into Israel right here, 33.18 North, 35.40 East. You will find it is 1,000 yards upstream of the nearest Israeli observation post, and we expect a patrol to come by, heading north, every thirty-two minutes, and then returning south, eight minutes later. That gives us a clear insertion window of twenty-four minutes. We will cross the border under cover of darkness, in four-man groups.

'There's thirty-six of us, which means nine short dashes across the line, one after the other, with two minutes between each start. We regroup, right here, one mile inside Israeli territory, east nor'east of Mas'ada. We will all wear dark combat gear, with black hoods. Each man will carry in addition to his water canteen, a carbine pistol, his MP-5 sub-machine gun, and a combat knife. Team leaders will in addition have a compass, a cell phone, a GPS, and two hand grenades to distribute among his team. These will only be used in dire circumstances . . . questions?'

Sir, any details on the holding area before we make the dash across the line?

'Yes,' replied the General. 'The Israeli Disengagement Line runs between two sloping hills. But the ground is flat between them for about sixty yards on their side. On our side, there is a hillside, kind of scooped out like the inside of a spoon. It's very rocky and provides outstanding cover for all of us until the Israeli patrol comes by heading south. I'm hoping it's not too dark, because I found the terrain very awkward on the recce. If there's no moon you'll walk as swiftly as you can without colliding with the rocks, but once you reach the Israel line, the ground flattens right out, and if it's dark you can run like hell, due west to the RV Point.'

Any details about the RV, sir?

'Yes,' said Ravi. 'I was there with the second recce team. That means four of us have first-hand knowledge. I will lead the first team across the line, and one man from my original group will run with Groups Three, Six and Nine. That means everyone will be within two minutes of a little local expertise.

'The RV Point itself is close to the top of an escarpment, way off any road or track. It's uninhabited, no livestock to speak of, and I do not expect to see anyone. Should someone stumble into our path, you will take them out instantly and silently, man, woman or child, preferably with the knife. Then hide the body.'

He stopped for reaction. But there was none. He had trained them well, and each man understood his responsibility, and above all, the high stakes involved.

'Once we reach the RV Point,' the General continued, 'we are five and a half miles from the lower hills below the Fortress. If we cross the Israeli line at around 2300 hours, we should be on our way by 0100, in four groups of nine men, moving cross-country, in the darkest part of the night.

'I have personally completed this journey three times. I was not trying to break any record, just moving easily, through farmland, and it takes under two hours. But we do have to cross a shallow river.'

The General pointed to a thin blue line on the map. 'Sometimes,' he added, 'this is just a muddy puddle. But right now it's a river. Thigh-high. Keep your arms up, weapons dry. Okay?'

Everyone nodded. The General sipped from a glass of water, and then pointed again with his baton. 'This, right here, is the road up to the Fortress. It's a mountain road, but it has only one hairpin bend. The rest are gentle, but steep slopes. The castle is hundreds of feet above the flatland around it. I have marked a spot with this 'X', right here. And I want you to look at this much larger scale map here, which shows the road, from its lower levels, and then the two miles up to the Fortress itself . . . here's the 'X' . . . okay?'

The entire assembly moved forward, each man holding his own map, and watching the General's pointer.

'Right here,' he said, 'fifty feet below the road, is an overhang of rocks, about one hundred yards long, with a lot of under-growth. It's about one third of the way to the top, a mile below

67

the castle and less than that from the point the road rises. That overhang provides complete cover from the road. We'll be in there by 0300 which gives us time to cut and improve the cover of the brushwood. I will personally carry in the two pairs of pruning shears we'll want for this phase of the operation. There'll be two shovels waiting for us. By 0600 we'll have our communications straight, and by first light we'll be invisible from the road. Anyone strays near us, he dies. Is that clear?'

At this point, Shakira's brother, Ahmed Sabah, to whom Ray Kerman almost certainly owed his life, said quietly, 'General, I think I may have missed something. But I have absolutely no idea what we are going to do at this jail . . .'

'That's because I have not yet told anyone,' replied the CO. 'I am just coming to that.'

'I think my comrades would feel better if you were able to tell us right now,' replied the young Palestinian. 'I feel as if we are all somehow in the dark . . .'

General Rashood smiled. 'Well, since we're leaving tomorrow night, and no-one's leaving here before then, you may as well know now . . . as you wish.'

He replaced his baton on the table, and sat down, once more between the two Syrian officers. He consulted his notebook and told them, 'This jail, with its fifty prisoners, and approximately thirty-six guards, is resupplied with food only once a week. Every Friday morning, a huge twenty-eight-wheel truck, from the military garrison on Route 90, fourteen miles north of the Sea of Galilee, arrives at the main gates of the jail at 1100 sharp. I've logged it in three times, and it's never been late. Its delivery *this* Friday morning, however, will contain a surprise. There will be no bread, flour, frozen meat, milk and eggs on board. There will be thirty-six HAMAS warriors. Us.'

The gathering was utterly stunned, like the home crowd at a soccer game when one their own players accidentally bangs the ball into his own net. No-one spoke, and they struggled not to betray fear, nor even surprise. But the collective gasp, a kind of stifled, '*wow!*', could still be heard, even though it was nearly soundless.

No-one wanted to be the first to raise a thousand questions. Instead they just waited for their new warlord to clarify the situation.

General Rashood was inordinately serious. He stared out at his men. And then he spoke again. 'The supply truck contains a driver and an assistant, both of them soldiers wearing the uniform of the IDF. The road is lonely. I counted the traffic for the hour prior to the truck's arrival and again for the hour after its departure at 1300 hours.

'My conclusions were simple. No vehicle climbed the hill before the truck. And the only vehicle which went down the hill after the truck was the prison van itself, transporting guards down to civilian living quarters six miles away, at the change of the shift. Since the Israelis closed the road to tourists and civilian traffic, that road has been practically deserted.'

But how do we get in the truck instead of the meat and eggs?

Suddenly everyone wanted to know that. And General Rashood carefully answered. 'At 1050, a car driven by two Arabs in traditional dress will drive up the road and stop thirty yards before our hide. It will pull up in the middle of the road, and its driver and passenger will walk around the front and lift up the hood.

'At this point, Ahmed and I will move up from the hide, and station ourselves on either side of the road. When the supply truck is forced to stop, ten minutes later, for the apparent breakdown blocking the road, the two IDF men will most certainly disembark, and we will kill them both, using the knife. Plainly, we do not want gunshots within a mile of the jail.

'At that moment the road will be deserted, except for us, and the stretch we will occupy cannot be seen from the jail. All of you will rush up the escarpment and unload that truck, drag out the cases and throw 'em over the edge. It's a massive vehicle; really a ship's freight container being hauled by a powerful front end. And it carries a ton of stuff. It may even be going on to deliver in other locations. But there's thirty-six of us, and we're going to empty it. Meanwhile the breakdown car will head back down the hill where it will break down again, sideways, once more blocking the road. In the unlikely event any other vehicle arrives, the occupants will be killed instantly.

'By now everyone will be in the truck. You guys in the container, which will be open at the rear, covered only by tarpaulin. Ahmed and myself will be in the cab, wearing the Israelis' uniforms. I'm driving.'

But what happens then, sir? How do we get in the jail? What if there's a password? What if they want to search the truck before they open the gates?

The General explained, again with care, how he had lain in wait for the truck, crouching on the escarpment the previous Friday, listening in the quiet of the morning, way up there on the ridge of the Nimrod.

'There was no password,' he said. 'The delivery was obviously expected. And the driver gave two light beeps on the truck's horn. The guards on the outside flanks of the jail, in charge of the artillery, did not even walk around. The gates opened and the truck drove directly inside.

'Two days from now, that precise moment represents our H-Hour, the instant we hit. When the truck has moved into the jail, through the gates, out of sight of the outside patrols, but not far enough inside for anyone to close the gates. That's our H-Hour. That's when I hit the brakes, and you guys hit the ground.'

General Ravi, still every inch the SAS commander, stood up once more, and moved back towards the third map. 'Gentlemen,' he said. 'This is the map of the jail, constructed from satellite pictures we have obtained, and refined for us by our staff in Damascus. For the next three hours we will work on the detail of our attack, each man reporting to me for complete instructions of his personal duties. Like all highly-briefed Special Forces, we want no surprises, no confusion, and as little opposition as possible.'

The General knew he was putting his foot-soldiers through a crash course of preparation, which would not have been good enough for the SAS. Only his twelve most trusted men had been party to the infinite detail of the operation – the ones who had accompanied him to Nimrod.

Ravi was torn between the SAS method of briefing, practising, rehearsing and more, and the need for secrecy. He could have staged a dummy run somewhere in Syria, but he was uncertain about security leaks, of the Israelis finding out something was going on, and he elected to play his cards close to his chest.

'It's 1600 now,' he said. 'We'll be through by 1900. We'll break for dinner, and sleep as long as possible. There'll be a two-hour meeting tomorrow at midday, then rest in the afternoon. We'll eat early, final short briefing at 2200, trucks away at 2300 sharp.'

HAMAS Compound, Golan Heights
2300, Thursday, April 28
The two unmarked army trucks growled as softly as possible into

the night, heading west, trying to stay out of the howling low gears, trying to keep their headlights down yet still miss the rocks, trying to navigate a more or less straight line to the Syrian Disengagement Line.

General Rashood, who had traversed the route a dozen times with Ahmed, sat next to the driver of the lead truck, watching the compass, peering through his night goggles, doing his best to translate familiar landmarks, from the granite-strewn sunlit land-scape of his memory, into the spooky, greenish glow of the Russian-made night glasses.

They bumped and bounced their way forward, driving up small, rough tracks, cutting across flat areas, glad to be on smoother, quieter ground, but anxious to regain the cover of the rocks. They were literally 'between a rock and the hard place,' and, on reflection, the bumping, lurching tracks between the jutting granite, had the edge. Uncomfortably safe, as opposed to more comfortably exposed. To the Israeli satellites, that is.

They reached the Syrian Line, and Ravi signaled to the patrol which awaited them, all was well. They drove on into no man's Land, beginning to come down off the Heights, moving over a gentle downward slope almost all the way.

Ray Kerman ordered the headlights doused at the border, and the little convoy was now dependent on the night goggles through which Ray was staring. They kept going for a mile and a half, and then Ray could see lights way up ahead, magnified by his glasses, and unmistakably those of vehicles, lower down the slopes, maybe three and a half miles away. He took off the goggles but could see nothing through the dark with the naked eye.

'Okay, guys, this is it. This is the end of our ride. Trucks return to base, everyone else split into team formation. I'll lead, the rest of you stay in your "fours" and follow tight behind. Any problem, no shooting . . . the knife, always the knife. Stay alert.'

The men from HAMAS jumped lightly down onto the damp winter grass, and zipped their jackets aginst the cool night air. They wore standard molded-rubber, desert boots, supple, expen-sive equipment, calf-high, tight fastened. Even if they crossed the river, minimal water would leak in.

And now they set off across the desolate night acres of the Buffer Zone on the Heights, moving swiftly, at the jog, following the ex-SAS Major who had recced this very path several times before. After twenty minutes they saw the lights of the Israeli patrol moving north up the westward Disengagement Line. And each man flung himself flat on the ground, heeding General Rashood's warning, that high-powered night binoculars could pick up running men at two miles.

When the lights disappeared, they picked themselves up, and ran on west some more, until the lights returned, this time heading south, back down the Line. Again they all hit the deck, and then powered forward when the coast was clear, running hard now, going for the hide under the spoon-shaped rock, just short of the Line itself.

The General led them safely into the shelter of the rock, and they fanned out in the formations they had practiced, unseen from the path of the Israeli patrol. Each man was supremely fit, but breathing heavily after the run in. They huddled together, between their own guards, front, rear and up on the granite cliff face.

Ray Kerman watched the jeep driving towards them, and there was not a sound as it came by at around 30 m.p.h. They waited until it returned, exactly eight minutes later, and Ray watched it go south. Two minutes more, and he called softly, 'This is it, guys . . . form up and let's go . . . see you at the RV point . . . groups of four . . . two minute intervals . . . fast and quiet . . . watch the GPS now . . .'

And with that, he and his three-man team set off, again running hard, straight across the Israeli Line, pounding over the ground, right on the heels of the General, who still wore the night goggles, peering in front of him through the deserted landscape. They ran strongly for eight minutes, when Ray stopped to check the GPS.

On course, he reduced speed to a steady jog, and within a few moments they hit the rising ground, breasted a low hill, and then climbed again for fifty yards, before striding easily into a natural rock fortress, around seventy-five feet across. They'd have to climb the west wall and slide down to level ground, before the next stage of the journey. But Ray had selected this desolate place carefully, and he had buried six containers of water on his last visit. He'd also hidden a shovel which he now found and began prising the earth away.

One minute later, Team Two arrived, then Team Three, and Team Four. In forty-five minutes they were all there, gulping water, and preparing for the five-and-a-half mile walk in, across rich, brilliantly-created Israeli agricultural land, just now beginning to yield superb crops of apples, pears and almonds, peaches, plums and cherries.

So far they had covered only a few miles from the compound, but the landscape was changing before their eyes. At least it would have been if it had not been pitch black, from the arid, rocky wastes of the Syrian side of the Golan, to the lush, irrigated triumph of Israeli farming policy.

It was exactly 0115 when the HAMAS General led his lead team of nine up over the granite 'wall' and began the fifty-foot grassy slide to the ground. They achieved this in near-silence, and when the group was all present and correct, Ravi Rashood checked the GPS and whispered, '*Okay, guys. Here we go. Follow me.*'

Behind them Group Two was high on the ridge preparing to slide down as soon as the leaders were under way. Within twenty minutes all thirty-six of the armed, hooded figures were walking softly through the fields approaching Highway 91, north of Mas'ada, heading west.

Ever cautious, and acutely aware of the possibility of radar, patrols, and intense Israeli surveillance, General Ravi ordered his men back into four-man groups for the highway crossing. And his caution was well-founded. There was bristling danger on that highway, because on Ravi's last sortie to Nimrod, an Israeli security detail had indeed picked up shadowy, furtive movement. It was, in fact, a fluke. The driver had been parked on a high ridge, peering through long range night glasses about a mile south to the shallow, narrow valley the HAMAS warriors now occupied.

Through the pale green landscape shown in the lenses of the glasses, the guard had been only half-focused. But up here, observation was hair-trigger sensitive. The guard had no idea what he had seen, but everyone at Northern Command knew that no big animals lurked on the Golan. It did not really matter what the guard had seen, anything was enough. And for the past week a four-man Israeli foot patrol had been sweeping a five-mile strip of Highway 91, operating in pairs, each armed man wearing black camouflage cream, and soft desert boots.

Right now, the south moving pair of Israeli guards was heading near-silently down the middle of the deserted highway, not twenty-five yards from where Ravi and his three men were about to make the first dash across the blacktop, into the safety of the dark, verdant farmland.

Ravi's four was already split into pairs, the first two men poised to bound up the bank, and rush across the highway, half-crouched, weapons poised. Ravi and his bodyguard would provide them with covering fire if necessary.

'Now!' hissed Ravi, and the two HAMAS fighters broke cover, heading for the center of the highway. But they never got there. The first Israeli guard saw them, bang in front of his astonished eyes. And he had his weapon leveled, a short-barrelled MP-5 machine-gun.

'Halt!' he yelled in Hebrew. 'Freeze! Right there. Hands high!'

The HAMAS warriors froze, and raised their hands, their machine-guns still dangling around their necks. The guard, standing only four yards from them, but ten yards in advance of his colleague, began to move forward, gripping his MP-5 tightly.

But as he did so, Ravi's bodyguard came off the bank with a bound which would have made a jungle leopard gasp, and plunged his combat knife clean through the second Israeli's back, ramming the life-ending blade through the center of the heart.

The only sound was the scuffing of the Israeli's boots as he fell backwards into the HAMAS killer's arms. The lead guard turned, swinging around almost involuntarily, calling sharply, 'Izak?'

Big mistake. Ravi Rashood was up the bank and on him. With his left hand, he clamped an iron grip on the barrel of the Israeli's MP-5, wrenching it sideways. And then he brought his gloved right hand down in a murderous chopping arc, hammering the handle-end of his combat knife into the space between the guard's eyes, smashing the central forehead bone.

Back came Ravi's lethal right hand, and, still holding the knife, he rammed the butt of his fist with stupendous upward force into the nose of the guard, driving the bone deep into his brain. In the hundredth of a second before he died, the Israeli could probably have guessed how SAS Sergeant Fred O'Hara had felt a few months before in a Palestinian house in Hebron.

The situation was now critical. General Rashood and his three-man team were stranded in the middle of a highway, in Israel, with a couple of members of the IDF laying dead on the highway, murdered in cold blood. But the night was dark, and silent, and his HAMAS fighters were superbly trained for any eventuality which might compromise their mission.

Groups Two and Three were already on the highway, grabbing the two inert bodies and dragging them across into the fields beyond.

'Everyone cross, as fast as possible, and make for the river,' Ravi ordered. 'Four men on each body. Drag or carry, whatever's easiest. Keep going. Try to stay in fours, and be ready if anything else happens.'

They reached the bank of the river which ran through a mile or so of swamps, and there they dumped the bodies out of sight in marshy wetland, deep in the bullrushes. No-one missed a beat. Ray guessed correctly it would be a couple of weeks at least before anyone found anything. And even then the Israelis would never admit two of their guards had been murdered.

The men from HAMAS moved away from the burial area, swiftly and silently, moving through the lush farmland at such a pace, they never even heard the Israeli Army jeeps roaring back and forth along the highway looking for two missing personnel.

Ray picked up a path used mostly by visiting observers of nature and the rich bird population which has found a home in these northern wetlands.

In fact he had acquired a map from the Galilee International Bird Watching Society, after enrolling Shakira as a member. She thought he must have gone out of his mind, but he would not tell even her why he needed a detailed knowledge of the secret paths of the 'twitchers' through this peaceful Israeli wildlife reservation.

She still did not know, but the thirty-five men who tracked him through the night of April 28/29, were astounded at his navigational expertise in the pitch dark. So, incidentally, had Shakira been, but for different reasons.

By 0230, they were officially off the foothills of the Golan Heights, and across the river. Before him Ray could pick out the towering crags of the Nimrod mountain, and he began to edge further north, over drier, grassy fields, thus ensuring that his team advanced at a right angle to the highway, moving onto the rockface and then climbing the less steep slopes up to the hide under the right-hand side of the approach road.

Once on their final advance they moved into the blessed cover of high woodland, and Ray led them almost straight through, breaking cover within 300 yards of the escarpment. He was obviously hurrying now, because it was almost 0300, three hours before the first pink strands of daylight would begin to illuminate the sky behind them. And they had a climb, and then some meticulous camouflage work to complete. Never had the men from HAMAS experienced anything like the degree of planning, organization, and execution their new Commanding Officer provided.

And now he led them on a zigzag path up the mountain, and they climbed easily, many of them grateful for the brutal three-month training regime he had imposed upon them, ruthlessly weeding out men who could not cope. Of the sixty volunteers who started out, eighteen had been axed from the program. And as they were removed, the standards grew tougher, and men began to feel the pride of the elite warrior.

Two of those who were let go, were overcome with that Arab sense of shame, which is unaccountable, and very dangerous. Both had threatened to cut the new General's throat, but Ahmed Sabah had advised them this was probably a poor idea, if they had ambitions to go on breathing. One very tough young brave, aged nineteen, humiliated beyond his own tolerance at being asked to leave the program, flew at the General with both fists, shouting, '*Who you think you are, you bastard!*'

Ahmed Sabah was furious, and complained bitterly all through the forty-eight-mile journey to the big hospital in Damascus where surgeons would reset the young man's broken arm and collarbone. 'I've killed men for a lot less,' growled Ravi. 'Think yourself lucky.'

Thirty-five men now climbed Mount Nimrod, convinced they were following some kind of a Divine being, sent to them by Allah himself. And when they reached the safety of the hide below the road at 0320 they each, to a man, thanked their God for their mission and their leader.

By 0600 they were invisible, both from the road and anywhere else, protected by layers of brushwood. They were not to know, but this temporary new headquarters was almost a precise replica of another observation post constructed by Ray Kerman, five years previously, 3,500 miles away in West Africa, on the north bank of the Rokel Creek.

Thanks to the stash of water back at the RV Point they all had full canteens, no food, because it was cumbersome, and unnecessary. This was a short mission. They drank sparingly and waited. Some of them grabbed some sleep, between guard duties, and by 1030 hours they were listening for the sound of the decoy vehicle they knew would break down, right above them.

In fact Ray Kerman saw it before they heard it, moving steadily along the highway way down the valley. He and Ahmed waited right below the chalk line they had made on the surface of the road, and when the old, dilapidated Ford Escort finally labored up towards them, they both watched it move into the very center of the road and then stop dead, bang on the line.

They now knew precisely where the supply truck would stop, and they broke cover, positioning themselves for the kill, Ray on the far side of the road, Ahmed, hidden in a clump of bushes on the near side, above the men.

The twenty-eight-wheeler came groaning up the hill, obviously heavily-laden, in a low gear. And with a hiss of giant airbrakes, it rumbled to a halt, its engine ticking over noisily, in the precise spot Ray had planned. The driver hit the horn, but the two Arabs, their heads deep in the car's engine just waved, and did not look up.

The doors to the truck's cab opened simultaneously and the two Israeli soldiers climbed down, and walked slowly to the car, the last steps they would ever take. Each one of them leaned over the engine, one on one side, one the other. Which was where they died, instantly, each with a long combat knife through his back and deep into his heart.

And at that moment the place came vividly to life. The HAMAS warriors swarmed up onto the road from the hide below, and cranked down the steel rear flap. They pulled up the tarpaulin and clipped it high. Within moments they were hauling the big cardboard crates along the floor of the truck to the back end where hands waited to grab them and lift them to the side of the road, then over the edge of the cliff.

General Ravi and Ahmed took two much smaller cardboard boxes out of the trunk of the car, and dumped them both in the cab of the truck. Then four more of the raiders dragged the two bodies off the road, pulled off their jackets and hats, and dumped them over the cliff.

The General shook hands with the two Arabs, who jumped back in the car, made a three-point turn and roared back down the hill to organize their second blockade of the morning, the side-on breakdown which would prevent any other vehicle driving up to the jail.

The men worked fast, sliding, grabbing and hauling the cargo out of the Israeli Army truck. The stuff was heavy and awkward, but there were a lot of hands and a lot of muscle. They worked in pre-arranged teams, four men in the truck, four on the ground dragging the cartons out, then handing over to a relay of twelve carriers, rushing the boxes to the side of the road, where twelve more men had nothing else to do except shove the boxes the last six feet and over the edge. This was the kind of operation which could easily have turned into a Chinese firedrill, but it proceeded like clockwork, smart in its efficiency. SAS smart.

Six minutes later the truck was empty, the cargo gone, resting way below the road in the bracken, along with its dead former driver and guard. And you'd have to get awfully close to the edge, and peer downwards into a specific spot in the low mountain foliage, to see the light brown packing cases, full of eggs, meat, vegetables and bread.

By now Ravi and Ahmed had changed into the Israeli uniforms and were in the cab, with their carbines and two boxes. The rest of the team were piling into the back of the truck, hoods down, MP-5s at the ready. It was a bit tight, but they all made it. Then they pulled down the tarpaulin, but left the rear gate down, for a quick and easy exit.

Ravi released the brake, rammed the truck into first gear, revved the engine, and slowly began to climb the hill. He wound it up to thirty m.p.h., and two minutes later they drove up to the gates of Nimrod Jail. Ravi hit the horn, twice; short, sharp notes, nothing urgent.

Inside the walls, the duty guard casually looked up on the monitoring screen, saw the supply truck and absent-mindedly pushed the button to open the main entrance, returning immediately to his newspaper.

Ravi and Ahmed watched the great wooden doors swing inwardly. Then the truck edged forward, its engine roaring as it pushed into the inner courtyard. Ravi could see a total of six guards, two on one side of the yard, four on the other. Two of them waved cheerfully and Ravi waved back, noting the men were in a civilian prison uniform, not military, unlike the two patrols he had watched so often outside the walls of the building.

He drove the truck in. Almost. And he placed it in such a position that the gates could not be closed until the truck was moved one way or the other. He held his breath and cut the engine, whipping the keys out of the ignition and shoving them in his pocket.

Then he hit the starter, buying time, pretending he had stalled, and knowing the first wave of his attack was under way. Eight of his men were already out of the truck, beyond sight of the guards, racing back through the gate, four swinging left, four right.

The first squad found what they wanted within thirty yards, the two-man Israeli patrol, smoking, one sitting on the old castle wall. One single burst from the MP-5s cut them down. They never knew what hit them. Seconds later, another burst from the other side of the jail signaled another triumph, as Ravi's team gunned down the other patrol, just two soldiers leaning on one of the heavy artillery pieces overlooking the vast flatlands below.

The shots were scarcely heard behind the mighty walls in the courtyard, over the raging of Ravi's disconnected starter motor. But the attack was under way, and a single hooded gunman kicked open the door to the interior gatehouse, blew away both men inside, and obliterated the electronic control panel with a fusilade of machine-gun fire.

All six duty guards began running towards the gatehouse, and three of Ravi's men, lying flat underneath the truck, shot them all dead in their tracks. Not one of the guards even knew where the shots had come from.

This had all taken less then one minute, and now the HAMAS general was leading the way. He hurled one hand grenade clean through the window of the small building on his left, in which four off-duty guards were sleeping. The blast collapsed the entire structure. And the shuddering din, in the enclosed yard, alerted the three-man staff in the prison office, from which a door was flung open.

Framed in the doorway was the governor of the prison. One of the marksmen under the truck shot him dead, while Ravi who could see another officer on the phone through the window, hurled in his second hand grenade, then hit the floor as the prison office was blown apart.

Ahmed, carrying one of the cardboard boxes from the cab of the truck had made immediately for the main gates out of the courtyard into the prison block, and surprisingly found them open. He pushed them both inwards, and his two bodyguards, especially trained by the General himself, rushed in, machine-guns blazing, cutting down the two duty guards who were both gazing out of the window, wondering what to do, and trying to dial numbers on their mobile phones.

Up above, on the second floor cell block landing, another guard rushed to the steel rail and looked over, yelling in English, '*What the hell's going on?*' This was a big mistake because Ahmed's bodyguards looked upwards, and instantly shot him dead. Which left no active guards on duty in the prison. Nimrod, for the moment, belonged to General Ravi Rashood.

And now his men swarmed into their designated positions, using keys, taken from the work-belts of the dead men, to open the gates to the lines of cells, in which were incarcerated the most dangerous terrorists in all of Israel. These were forty-seven ringleaders of bombing attacks conducted on behalf of HAMAS, Hezbollah, and the Jihad over the past several years. Many of them were well-known Palestinian leaders, but this place contained men who would never be released onto the streets of Jerusalem, or Tel Aviv or Hebron ever again.

The Israelis called them political prisoners. And in a sense they were. But only in a sense. All of them had found their way into this specialist high security jail because of diabolical acts of mass murder and killing. And the Israelis were confident the mountain-top site, surrounded by miles of low farmland, would make the place as secure as Alcatraz, the wickedly exposed countryside being as dangerous and unhelpful to a fugitive as the wide, swirling currents of San Francisco Bay.

So far they had been right. And they might still be. General Ravi knew he had time to free the prisoners. But the getaway needed to be as flawless as the attack itself. And now he went to work, issuing the contents of his cardboard box to yet two more men he had personally trained.

He gave them each a high-powered, battery operated electric drill, each one of which would drive two small round holes into the locking bars of the cell gates. The second box was opened on the floor and he began to take out the reels of detcord, handing each one to a separate man. This stuff was precious, absolutely beloved to both the SAS and the US Navy SEALs. Although it is really just a fuse – light it and stand well back – it is unlike any other slow-burning fuse used by Special Forces to detonate high explosive.

Detcord burns at *five miles per second*. Wrap a few turns around a good-sized oak tree and that stuff will blast the trunk in two. Its core is called PETN, a slimline explosive which can be aimed with great accuracy. Detcord explodes so fast you can hook it up to several targets, join the cord together, and knock down the lot, all at one time.

By now one of Ravi's drillers had reached the top of the open staircase. The second drill was already working the lower level, and the scream of the motors was filling the air. Each driller hung a small precision piece of machined steel over the lock, and drilled into two pre-set holes, boring two more holes accurate to one-hundredth of an inch, straight into the unseen steel locking bar behind the outside shield.

And right behind them raced the guys with the detcord, one on the reel, the other shouting in Arabic into the cell . . . *HAMAS! We're getting you out . . . grab the cord and shove it back through the second hole . . . hurry!*

No short instruction was ever carried out faster, and as the length of cord was returned through the hole, an entirely new man moved up to grab it, and drag it through, then wrap it around the bar twice more, and cut it to length with the pruning shears they'd used for the bracken. Another man was ready to tie the end to the next length coming from the next door cell.

Ravi intended to blow the locks four at a time. And in strict relays his men drilled, threaded, dragged, wound, cut and tied the lethal detcord. One task per man. The work proceeding with lightning speed, two of the General's NCOs patrolling the cell blocks, shouting clear instructions . . . *'When your detcord's in place, retreat to the far wall of your cell . . . lie flat facing the ground against the wall . . . if there's a mattress, get it against your back, between you and the explosion on the door lock . . .'*

Six minutes after the first drillings had begun, General Rashood fired, and the explosions ripped into the first four locks, blasting them to pieces. Each of the doors swung open, and two men rushed into each cell to help the inmate to his feet. Thankfully they were not manacled and there were no injuries so far. It had taken approximately ninety seconds to liberate each man, but on the lower level, Ahmed was conducting a concurrent operation, and almost immediately there was another mighty blast and four more doors swung open. Same procedures precisely, sixteen men were now engaged in walking the eight freed men to the muster point behind the truck in the courtyard.

Re-assessing the time, Ravi now calculated he had eight men

out in seven minutes. And he guessed they would get faster. That meant forty-two minutes maximum for all forty-seven. He had under a half-hour's work, but his mind was haunted by the face of the man he had seen on the telephone in the office. *Had he got a message away? And what had he told the military HQ? Was there a direct 'hot line' . . . if there was, it was trouble. If not there was an excellent chance they'd have time to spare.*

He had always known the quandary, the weak spot in the operation. Should he have gone in and knocked out the main electric supply to the jail? Or would this have started off an automatic alarm which would have damn nearly blown the operation before they even made it inside the gates? He had estimated that was a risk too great to take, but now he did not know whether Israeli paratroops were on their way to Nimrod in helicopters.

He had already dispatched two lookouts to the high ramparts of the jail, to scan the skies. They'd been up there five minutes now and could see nothing in the clear blue of the morning. They had principally to look one way. Not east towards the Syrian border, not north to the Lebanon frontier, just south, towards the Israeli military.

The General climbed the gantry to the highest wall of the jail, and dialled a number. The lookouts heard him snap, '*High rollers go!*'

Back on the ground, fifteen minutes had passed and sixteen men were free. His 2 I/C (Explosives), was now detonating on the upper floor and Ahmed was in command of all explosions on the lower area. Two shuddering bangs, in quick succession signaled eight more prisoners free. And still there was no word from the lookouts high above.

Ravi's delight at the absolute precision of the detcord blasts, was tempered only by his chilling awareness that the Israeli paras could arrive any second, in helicopter gunships. He could not have known that possibility had disappeared, because the man in the office on the phone had only had time to shout, 'The jail is under atta . . .'

At the other end, the nineteen-year-old girl soldier who had received the call, was replying, 'I did not quite catch that . . . who is speaking, please? . . . this is Israel Army HQ Northern Command . . .'

The line was now dead, issuing an ominous dial tone and

nothing else. The operator tried again, tapping the phone cradle up and down, saying, 'Hello . . . hello . . . is anyone there?'

But there was no further sound. The girl called her supervisor and reported she had received a 'funny sounding call'.

'I thought they said something about a jail underwater,' she said. 'But the line went instantly dead.'

'What jail?'

'They never said, sir. But I was sure I heard "jail". And I thought I heard "underwater" but it didn't make sense . . . the caller did not say another word.'

'Well, let's give it another few minutes, see if anyone calls back. If not, it sounds like a wrong number. You think jail could have been gale, stale, rail or some other word?'

'Well, I suppose it could have been. But I did think it was jail . . . if it had been gale, and underwater, it could have been a ship's distress call on the wrong frequency. But I still think it was jail.'

'Okay. Let's leave it for fifteen minutes and see if we hear anything else. By the way, did you announce who you were, you know, Northern HQ etc?'

'Yessir. I did. Right at the beginning. And after the line went dead.'

'Okay. Good girl. Lemme know if they come through again.'

Meantime, back on the Nimrod ramparts, one of the lookouts spotted the first helicopter, clattering in from the north, flying low over the Lebanese border, straight towards the jail.

'Helo incoming, sir!' roared the lookout. *'High speed . . . degrees three-sixty . . . low altitude.'*

General Rashood swung around, charged back outside, through the main gates, past the group of truly incredulous political prisoners, who were mostly too stunned by events even to speak, even to express their thanks. They just stared, as the HAMAS CO, trained a pair of Israeli binoculars he had just stolen on the northern skies.

And there it was, one mighty Sikorsky CH-53D Sea Stallion, hammering its way towards them, making 130 knots through clear skies. It looked military, it sure as hell had once been military. But right now it was painted bright white, with blue trim, with a commercial insignia, in Arabic, presented boldly in still-wet paint. . . 'STAY COOL WITH FROSTY'S.' On the fuselage a contented polar bear licked a giant ice-cream cone.

Down on the lower rampart below the level of the jail, two of

Ravi's men were holding orange flags aloft, waving in the big assault chopper, originally designed to carry thirty-eight US Marines, fully-loaded for combat.

But this morning it was empty, and General Rashood bellowed his next order. . . *'Everyone to the lower level . . . straight down the hill to the guys with the flags . . . then board the helo . . . Go! Go! Go!'*

Two distant thumps told him that eight more prisoners were out, and he stood in the courtyard waving them on as they ran into the yard . . . *'Straight on,'* he roared. *'. . . straight on . . . keep running . . . straight down to the helicopter . . . all aboard . . . all aboard . . . we're outta here . . . right now . . . Go! Go! Go!'*

Ravi knew the Sikorsky, right now on loan from the Syrian Army, was built for soldiers carrying huge packs and weapons. These prisoners had nothing, and it would thus carry more, maybe fifty if necessary, with its overload capacity. He had counted on a total of eighty-six and had instructed his loadmasters to board the first thirty-two prisoners, plus sixteen of his own men on the first journey.

By now the Sea Stallion was on the ground and the prisoners were pouring through its open doors. And right then, the lookout called again . . . 'Helicopter incoming, low altitude . . . degrees three-sixty . . . high speed . . . identical . . . repeat identical . . .'

All forty-eight men had clambered aboard the helo and it was already lifting off. Shuddering upwards, almost vertical. Then it tilted, its engine howling, and rocketed east, thundering towards No Man's Land, and then the Syrian frontier.

The second Sea Stallion was now making its approach, and more and more prisoners were racing down the path towards the lower rampart. Two more bangs signaled eight more men were free. Thus far General Ravi's men had been inside the jail for three-quarters of an hour, and there was just one more batch of prisoners to release.

The second helicopter circled, wearing the same commercial livery, and as it did so, the ops room in the Israel Army's Northern Command Headquarters burst into life. A young captain was listening, intently, as a supervisor stared at a computer screen, calling the information. *'Another one, sir. No doubt. Incoming helicopter. Three-sixty degrees. Speed one hundred knots. Altitude under five hundred. American built. But no military radar. Destination Nimrod Jail . . .*

'*First helo taken off, track two-three-eight . . . headed zero-nine-zero, speed one-three-zero knots. Altitude under one hundred feet.*'

'How long was it on the ground?'

'*Four minutes maximum, sir.*'

'Any communication from the jail?'

'*Trying, sir. No response.*'

A new voice . . . '*Did someone say* jail?'

'Right. Nimrod.'

'*Holy shit!*'

'What's up?'

'One of my operators took a call this morning, a garbled sentence . . . she though it said, "the jail is underwater" . . . then the line went dead and no-one called back. No-one mentioned the name of the jail or anything.'

'I wonder if the real sentence was, "the jail is under attack," not water, but he couldn't finish the word.'

'*Air crew go to action stations. Gunships to Nimrod Jail – it may be under attack. Assault Groups One and Three.*'

The station commander bellowed for someone to connect him to the observation post up on the Disengagement Line, due east of Nimrod.

'Yessir. We saw him alright. A big single-screw helicopter, traveling east to Syria. Commercial aircraft, sir. No military radar . . . it was white, looked like an ice-cream van with a rotor . . .'

'A *what!*'

'An ice-cream, van, sir . . . white and blue. It had a big polar bear painted on it.'

'A *what!*'

'A polar bear, sir. It was licking a pink and white cone . . .'

The phone crashed down. '*Fuck me!*' yelled the Captain.

It took twelve minutes to fire up three IDF helicopters, load up the troops and get off the ground, for the twenty-mile flight up to Nimrod. But as the Israelis took off, General Rashood's second big Sikorsky was ready to go. Its rotor was screaming, the big passenger door was wide open, and the General was running for his life, down the path, leaving the massive Israeli truck an inferno behind him, flames from its fuel engulfing the entire front side of the jail.

Ravi hit the fuselage of the Sikorsky running, hauled himself up and rolled into the rear cabin. Someone slammed the door, and they took off instantly, flying east, out towards the Syrian border, hanging on grimly to a ten-minute start, although this was, as yet, unknown.

Sprawled in the rear, the General was talking to his men. 'Well, we never lost anyone, and we got 'em all out. Not a bad morning's work.'

Just then, the Navigator called back, 'Sir, I got three paints on the screen right here, maybe fifteen miles off our starboard quarter, right on our four o'clock, heading for Nimrod. High speed.'

The General nodded, unsmiling. 'As the Iron Duke might have mentioned, this had been a damned close-run thing. Another five minutes in that jail, we would not have made it.'

And as the Sikorsky Sea Stallion thundered into Syrian Air space, the Israelis were on their final approach to Nimrod. They could already see the truck blazing in the gateway, and the obvious bomb damage in the courtyard. And, as they drew nearer, they could see two figures apparently asleep on one of the big artillery pieces.

Soon they would discover a jail entirely devoid of inhabitants. There were no guards, no prisoners, and a total of twenty men dead. All officers of the jail. 'Good God!' breathed the commanding offcer, as it began to dawn on him that every single lock on each cell door had been skillfully and professionally blown out. As indeed had the impregnable reputation of Nimrod Jail itself.

And somewhere out there, beyond the rugged landscape of the Golan, there lurked the most dangerous enemies of the State of Israel; men who had proved they were prepared to die, in the cause of attacking, killing and maiming the Jewish populations of Tel Aviv and Jesusalem. The young commander, whose parents had both been killed in the momentous Israeli drive to the Golan Heights in 1973, was not looking forward to making his report.

And, twenty minutes later when he did so on the helicopter's radio, his message sent a frisson of pure anxiety around the Northern HQ of the Army. *How could this have possibly happened? It was plainly state-sponsored, and brilliantly planned. But by whom?*

The CO of Northern Command requested the satellite be adjusted to photograph Syria's military bases, particularly the ones in which helicopters were parked. And over many days, photographic evidence came in showing lines of the choppers, all painted in grim, functional desert light-brown, with insignia. No-one knew that beneath two coats of this smart Syrian Army livery, two giant polar bears licked their respective cones, uncaring that they would never be seen again.

It took two days for the Israelis to admit what had happened, that they had somehow been the victims of one of the most spectacular jail-breaks in history.

Israel had just lost every one of her forty-seven most lethal political prisoners. They were sworn enemies of the State, who had been incarcerated in a purpose-built prison, designed to render escape impossible. *And where were they all now?* God alone knew that. But they were surely no longer in Israel, and they were probably beyond the reach even of the Mossad, being sheltered in some country which was innately hostile to Israel and would offer no information or co-operation.

The Israelis were careful with their press release, desperately trying not to look incompetent, or even ridiculous. It was released quietly, from a Government Department to the *Jerusalem Post* on the quiet news evening of Saturday, 30 April. It was faxed at around 8.30 in the evening, complete with the name and phone number of the press officer, Abe Stillman, who was no more a press officer than Arnold Morgan. Mr Stillman was a senior field officer from the Mossad. He knew how to block dangerous questions, and he knew how to lie with absolute impunity.

The release read as follows:

Twenty prison officials have died in a Palestinian terrorist attack on a jail in Northern Galilee. The dead men all worked at the Nimrod High Security Prison. They were on duty at the time, some of them working outside the walls of the jail.

The terrorists are believed to have rammed the gates open with a freight truck and then shot down the guards in a cold-blooded, cowardly massacre of civilian personnel.

It is not yet known which group was responsible, but Israeli security forces are assuming that either HAMAS or Hezbollah carried out the raid.

It is also known that certain prisoners escaped by air, in two civilian helicopters. They are believed to have flown into Syria, but the Syrian military has denied all knowledge of the attack.

The names of the deceased will be released when the immediate families have been informed.

Throughout the release, the Israelis played down the

overwhelming importance of the escaped men, placing the onus of the story on the guards who lost their lives.

It was a tactic destined to fool no-one. David Heyman, the young, gifted night editor of the *Post*, read the fax sheet with amazement, lasered in on the fact that no-one was telling anyone which of the most dangerous convicts in the country had escaped, and hit the wire to Abe 'Stonewall' Stillman.

The man from the Mossad lived up to his nickname . . . *I'm sorry we have no further information on that . . . right now we have a team of investigators at the prison trying to ascertain the facts . . . it would be wrong of me to give you inaccurate information . . . Sheik who? . . . I'm sorry, I cannot comment on the status of individual prisoners . . . yes, it was a military-style attack on the prison . . . I cannot comment on the precise nature of the killings . . . I understand some of our people did die of gunshot wounds . . . the telephones? I'm afraid the system is down . . . I don't know how or why . . . when we have further information from the government investigators we will inform you . . .*

David Heyman sensed a gargantuan cover-up. He called the night news editor, and told him to get up to the back bench (the hub of the newspaper where the front page is prepared, designed, and edited).

The ex-Fleet Street reporter, Eddie Laxton, was probably the best hard newsman in the Middle East. He read the fax, listened to the night editor's description of his talk with Stillman, and immediately dispatched a team of six reporters and photographers to the Nimrod area.

He ordered a helicopter to fly them to the small commercial airport north of Galilee, where two cars would be waiting for the twenty-mile drive up to Nimrod. He knew the entire area would be cordoned off, and that there was little chance of being granted access. But his men were trained tough. If they had to, they'd climb the mountain to observe and photograph the state of Nimrod Jail.

Eddie Laxton was something of a crusader, and he did not think governments should be covering up lapses in security. If this story was what he thought it was, he, Eddie, was going to nail it down hard.

And shortly after midnight, one of his boys nailed it. While the photographers were skirting the roadblock in an attempt to reach the jail, lit up now by big military arc-lights, the *Post*'s junior reporter, Ben Lefrak, twenty, decided to place himself in the nearest coffee shop, one which might stay open half the night while emergency teams were toiling into the night.

And at 2.15 a.m. it happened, in the little coffee shop in the Druze village of Majdal e-Shams. Three uniformed members of the IDF, covered in dust, came in and ordered coffee and pastries. And the landlord, sporting the gigantic mustache of his Islamic sect, served them cheerfully.

The place was busy, and when Ben went to the counter to order his fourth coffee, he returned to a different seat, right next to the IDF men, with whom he skillfully struck up a conversation.

'Pretty bad up there, eh?' he ventured.

'Tell me about it,' replied the young soldier. 'Christ, I'm tired.'

'Did they knock the place down?'

'Not really but they blew the hell out of the guardroom, and the office, and exploded a fucking great truck right in the gateway.'

'Wow! Any prisoners injured, you know trapped in their cells and hit by the blast?'

'Couldn't say really. There aren't any prisoners left in there, not so far as we could see. They all got away. The place is empty now, but there may be more bodies . . . that's what we're digging for.'

'Gotta be hard work, right? The place is made of granite.'

'Yeah. None of us are looking forward to going back up there. But the Prime Minister is supposed to be there sometime in the next hour.'

Twenty minmutes later, when Ben Lefrak got outside and dialed the newsroom back in Jerusalem, Eddie Laxton could have kissed him.

And David Heyman's front page was a masterpiece. There was a three-column picture, two inches high, of the Nimrod Jail, then three head shots of the Prison Governor, the Chief of Security, and the Military Commander. Captioned starkly, '*All Dead, Gunned Down in Raid.*' Beneath was the two-deck headline:

HAMAS TERRORISTS BLAST NIMROD JAIL –
EVERY POLITICAL PRISONER FREED

And underneath that was a block of twenty one-inch square photographs, five by four, each one captioned with a name. In a transparent strapline, set diagonally across the pictures was the word 'GONE!'

For the *Jerusalem Post* this was a sensational treatment of any story. And it more than matched the conservative coverage in the *Syrian Times*, the English-language publication, which offered wildly pro-Arab slants on all items of news.

Their headline read:

HEROIC HAMAS FREEDOM FIGHTERS LIBERATE OUR MARTYRS

The stories were remarkably similar in content, each pointing out that every worthwhile political prisoner in the entire country had essentially vamoosed; set free by a brilliantly-led hit squad from across the border.

The details tended to blend together, but within a half-hour of publication in two special Sunday afternoon editions in Jerusalem and Damascus, the news was well and truly out – on all the local Middle East radio networks, plus the BBC World Service, and the Voice of America.

Newspapers in the United States, operating six hours behind Israel, received the newsflash at around midday, which gave them a long time to prepare and research thunderous front pages which revealed that the forty-seven most dangerous terrorists in the entire history of the Arab-Israeli conflict were on the run, free and clear to attack again.

Inside pages were packed with '*Why, Oh Why,*' stories, individual cries from the heart, from 'experts' on jails, security, jail inmates, bank robberies, Middle East politics, Jewish mothers, sons and daughters, culminating in the inevitable . . . *Why This Must Never Happen Again.*

In London, one of the tabloid dailies rounded up a couple of survivors from the Great Train Robbery of 1963, and ran the headline, '*THIS MUST HAVE BEEN DONE BY A PROFESSIONAL'*. It was written with all the irate self-confidence of Fleet Street in full cry, as if they had just delved into the psychological depths of Plato.

Lieutenant Jimmy Ramshawe read the initial briefs from the CIA early on that Sunday afternoon.

Incredulous, like most of his colleagues, that a terrorist group had been responsible for the entire outrage, he sat in his office, consumed with thought. The sheer military precision of the operation was contrary to normal terrorist strikes. Fanatics from the desert were often brave, usually cunning, and quite frequently breathtakingly dumb. This was entirely different. This was meticulous, planned to the last detail, and executed with satanic ruthlessness, its timing perfect. And young Ramshawe thought, 'no bloody errors'.

Shortly before 1800, he stood up and muttered to no-one in particular, 'Nice one, Major Kerman, old mate. You really are a dangerous bastard.'

By 1930 he was in a quickly-convened meeting with Admiral Morris and Captain Wade. All three men had reached the same conclusion at more or less the same time. This could have been conducted only by the SAS or the US Navy SEALs, or at least by someone trained in either Hereford, England, or Coronado, California.

At this stage there was of course no evidence, but Lieutenant Ramshawe, along with his maps of the north Galilee area, and pictures of the jail, had brought in a small file of forensic evidence appertaining to the two robberies at the New York and Beirut banks.

Buried in both reports was an incontrovertible fact: the locks on both gates, the ones situated in front of both vaults, had been blown by the intensely-high explosive PETN. Traces had been found on the gate. Both locking bars had been split in the same place, and the remaining pieces of steel had shown clearly that a drill had been used to bore two holes right through the bar. Both these smashed locking bars had a high degree of PETN embedded in the broken area. The report did not take the matter further, and Jimmy Ramshawe had called Captain Wade to ask what he made of that.

Scotty said instantly, 'Hell, yes. They used detcord. That's a PETN explosive. But it's used almost exclusively by the military, usually by Special Forces. Christ knows where they got it.'

'Raymond Kerman would know how to get it.'

'He would. And he'd know how to use it.'

'James, old buddy, we need to know whether the cell doors in Nimrod were blown by the same method. And the Israelis are not going to be anxious to reveal anything until the fuss has died down.'

And now they had briefed Admiral Morris, and in all three minds, there was no doubt. The jailbreak was masterminded by an ex–Special Forces officer, everywhere you looked there was evidence.

They had plainly driven into the jail in the truck, and then jammed it in the main gateway, having first disposed of the Israeli driver and his colleague.

'Just imagine how carefully this was planned,' said the Admiral slowly. 'First of all they had to get into the country, across a very hot border on the Golan Heights. There must have been at least thirty of them. They must have walked in at night, and then hidden on this mountain. Looks like they carried in the right kit, machine-guns, probably drills, detcord, probably hand grenades. And then they got away in two big helicopters . . . what are the Syrians saying?'

'Not much, sir. Except they applaud the bravery of the freedom fighters, and give thanks to Allah for the safe delivery of the Palestinian martyrs. Of the operation itself, they of course, know nothing.'

'Meanwhile,' said the Admiral, 'We got forty-seven homicidal maniacs on the loose, some of whom might try to come here, even though their crimes have all been committed against Israelis, in Israel.'

'That's corrrect,' replied Captain Wade. 'And there's not a whole lot we can do about it. Except to stay watchful, and step up all surveillance in Damascus, where the prisoners almost certainly are.'

'Okay, guys, keep me posted. I'll debrief the Big Man, and see you both in the morning.'

The phone in Kathy O'Brien's house, in Chevy Chase, on the outskirts of Washington DC, did not often ring on Sunday evenings. She and Arnold Morgan always had dinner at home, and it was well known that this was the one time in the week the National Security Chief tried to leave the cares of his great Office behind him.

Right now he was about to taste a bottle of 1995 Chateau d'Issan, of which he had bought three cases, rather extravagantly on the advice of Harcourt Travis, Secretary of State, and the White House's resident sophisticate.

Arnold Morgan had no intention of revealing to Kathy the source of his advice, unless of course the wine was awful, in which case the ex-Harvard professor currently charged with the entire foreign policy of the United States would most certainly get the blame. Probably loudly.

Arnold rotated his glass, swishing around the red-purple wine from Bordeaux, way up on the left bank of the Gironde River, and smelled its bouquet. Had he known where it was made, in the most beautiful moated, seventeenth-century chateau, from grapes grown in walled vineyards, he would have loved the little ritual even more. To Arnold, bottles of French chateaux-bottled wine were like paintings, to be kept and treasured. But on Sunday nights, he and Kathy always drank one with dinner.

Arnold sipped and savored the d'Issan. Harcourt was spot on as usual. 'Perfect,' he muttered, standing the bottle just to the side of a log fire in the study. 'Little more warmth, another fifteen minutes.'

Just then, the phone rang. 'Fuck,' said the Admiral.

'It's for you, darling,' called Kathy. 'George Washington, National Security Agency, just north of the Beltway, degrees north thirty . . .'

'Alright, alright, goddamnit . . .'

The Admiral, chuckling, stumped down the corridor to the phone.

Kathy caught only snatches of his conversation:

'*How many? Forty seven . . . Jesus Christ! . . . How many they caught . . .? None! . . . Jesus Christ! . . . All dead . . .? Jesus Christ!*'

Kathy basted the roast lamb, giggling to herself, at his obvious amazement. When he replaced the phone and came into the kitchen, she asked sweetly, 'Who was that? George Morris or John the Baptist?'

Arnold laughed. 'I guess we'll see it later on the news, but some terrorist group just released every major political prisoner in Israel, blew up the jail, killed the guards and got 'em all out in a couple of helicopters.'

'Good Lord!' said Kathy.

'That's what I just told John the Baptist,' said Arnold. 'I know it sounds kinda crazy, but there's forty-seven of these fanatics, on the loose. And we don't want 'em here.'

'No, we sure don't.'

'And there's another twist to this. These guys were led and trained by some clever sonofabitch. George and his boys think it was that missing SAS Major we talked about last year. Kerman, from London. They never found him.'

'I remember the stuff in the English papers,' she replied. 'Rich family, but he turned out to be a Muslim.'

'That's him,' said the Admiral. 'And, if I am any judge, he

93

spells real trouble. George thinks his gang not only robbed two banks for a hundred million dollars, he's just liberated the world's most dangerous group of men from an impregnable prison.'

'That's not good,' said Kathy.

'No. It's not . . . and the entire thing smacked of Special Forces. There were no survivors on the jail staff, no witnesses, no-one wounded and left there. Everyone killed absolutely clinically. And, as usual with jails, Nimrod security was totally geared to stop anyone getting out. I'll bet no-one ever gave a thought to preventing anyone getting in.

'First thing tomorrow I want to talk to that new ambassador who just arrived here.'

'Try to be specific, my darling. Ambassador? Ambassador? China? Peru? Mongolia?'

'Iran, stupid,' replied Admiral Morgan, smiling and shaking his head in mock exasperation. 'Iran, state sponsors of international terrorism these past twenty years . . . and birthplace of Major Raymond Kerman.'

CHAPTER FOUR

Eleven months later
Friday, May 5, 2006
Kerman, South-east Iran

General Ravi Rashood and Shakira Sabah sat in deep conversation in the vaulted underground teahouse of the sprawling Bazar-e Vakil in the center of the desert city of Kerman. For Ravi it was a pilgrimage, to the one place he remembered from a far-lost childhood. At least, he remembered the pastries, sweet delicious pastries made with honey and almonds, and he remembered the covered bazaar. The actual teahouse, much more vague in the caverns of his memory, had taken two hours to find, but now they were here, and Ravi held Shakira's hand in their little booth, and told her about his mother.

For Shakira it was a voyage of discovery, rather than re-discovery. She had never been to Iran, and Ravi had never told her much about it, mainly because he could remember so little. But he had told her about the subterranean pastries he and his mother had sampled in a place with great gothic archways, and fine, elegant brickwork, like a church, or a mosque. But he could not remember the tea, nor the house, nor anything else, which was why it had taken so long to find.

Today, they both wore Western clothes, and they had already visited the lofty, yellow stone *Mosque-e Jame*, Kerman's greatest building. Ravi had remembered that, and he knew that he and his family had lived very near. But, try as they did, he and Shakira could not locate the old house, principally because Ravi could only recall its walled courtyard, with a fountain and a tree casting shade on the stone floor throughout the day.

Somehow, though, the teahouse had made the journey worthwhile for one of the world's most wanted men, and the slender, dark-haired Palestinian beauty who was prepared to lay down her life for him, as once she had very nearly done. And that was before she knew him.

'Well,' she said, smiling. 'You kept telling me you would understand everything better if we could just come here. And now we are here . . . did it work?'

Ravi laughed softly. She always wanted answers. Direct, simplified answers. Shades of truth and description, nuance and allusion, went right past her . . . *do you think they should all die? . . . will we be safe? . . . are the Israelis the worst people on earth? Do you love me enough to marry me?*

The words '*maybe*', '*possibly*', '*perhaps*' – phrases like '*let's give it a little time,*' or '*it depends on your point of view,*' or '*sometimes I think so,*' might have been uttered in Mandarin Chinese so far as Shakira Sabah was concerned.

'Yes, but . . .' was her standard parry, before asking the question all over again. Ravi Rashood was enchanted by her, and not just by her beauty and obvious intellect. He had witnessed her courage, her loyalty, and her determination to fight for what she believed was right. And Shakira was devout in the faith of Islam. She read the Koran to the ex-SAS Major; taught him the words of the Prophet as she had been taught; made him understand the path to Allah; the kindness and moral correctness of that vastly-misunderstood religion.

These days, even the amplified call from the minarets, of the mullahs summoning their people to prayer, held a new and soulful meaning for the former Ray Kerman. In the echoing, ancient tones laid down by the Prophet 1,400 years ago, he heard the true voice of his new religion; plaintive and suffering, yet rich in faith and hope.

And now the question stood before him . . . *we are here – did it work?* That ingrained English sense of mannered hedging, honed at Harrow School, urged him to . . . well . . . hedge his reply. But he knew that would be hopeless. Shakira would just ask again, equally bluntly: *we are here – did it work?*

'Yes,' he said. 'Yes it did.'

'How do you know?'

'Because I feel that I belong here. Almost as if I have come home. However long my parents spent turning me into an Englishman, I am not, and cannot be English. I am Iranian, and my forbears were Bedouin. Not my father, nor the British Army could alter that. We are all what we are, even you, my darling.'

Shakira looked serious. 'But if you had never been posted to Israel, never fought in the Jerusalem Road, and never killed two men, just to save me – would you still have one day found your way home?'

'I don't think so. I would have gone on as before, and doubtless ended up in command of a battalion, and then gone into the family business. It was in Hebron that I first felt I belonged, in the market, talking to people. It was strange, but I felt an emotional tie, an excitement, just being there.'

'That was before you even knew me?'

'Yes. It was.'

'So I'm not entirely responsible for your actions?'

'No. No, you're not. I was already feeling this strange sensation, a really powerful pull towards the Palestinians . . . it all reminded me of a story one of my troopers told me in Northern Ireland. He was a nice guy called Pat Byrne, and he had an uncle in Philadelphia, who had left Ireland when he was eleven, and lived for the next fifty-six years in Pennsylvania. And then one day the old uncle – he was a widower – decided to go for a ten-day holiday to Derry, where he still had relatives, but had never once visited in all those years.

'Do you know, he never went back to the USA. He settled into a typical Irish village near the sea with a couple of cousins. Then he called an estate agent back in Philadelphia and told him to sell his two cars, his house and everything in it. He's still in Ireland, some little place in Donegal, happy as a lark.

'And whatever he felt in Ireland was what I feel here in the Middle East. I've hardly any memory of Kerman, but my heart tells me, I'm home.'

'But didn't you feel at home in London?'

'Yes, I did. My family was there. Everyone I knew. But I think I always felt I was different, and that other people thought I was different. When you're a kid you push things like that to the back of your mind. But I knew, when I got here, that I wasn't different anymore. And then I met you . . .'

'Does that mean we're not going to end up in Donegal? We're staying here?'

General Rashood laughed. 'We have a lot of work to do, you and I . . .'

'Yes, but . . . are we staying here?'

'In Iran?'

'Yes.'

'I don't know. But we're going to be here for some time. And even if we leave, it will be to live in Damascus, or Jordan, or even Egypt, or Dubai . . . but it will be in an Islamic country . . . I know that. Anyway I could never return to the West, not to live.'

'They hang you, eh?'

'They might.'

'Well, I won't let them. I'll blow their silly courtroom up, like that Israeli tank.'

'Then they might hang us both.'

'Not us. We're too smart.'

Ravi put his arm around her. 'Smart but careful, that's the trick,' he told her. 'Remember, our business is very dangerous. One serious mistake could end our lives.'

Shakira looked thoughtful. 'Do you sometimes think we have done enough? You know, we should just retire from the battle and go and live somewhere peaceful?'

'I do sometimes think that. But I would like to see a great Islamic State, free of the influences of the West and Israel. Certainly here in the Middle East. And I think I know how to achieve it . . . but not by committing mass murder. Our friend Bin Laden has made that very unfashionable. But there are other ways. Which is why we are here. A lot of people are counting on me, and I'm not ready to let everyone down.'

'I guess you shouldn't be so brilliant, my darling,' she replied. 'At the Nimrod, you showed everyone a standard of professionalism they had never seen before. Now you are some kind of Messiah to half the Arab nations.'

'I can teach them,' said Ravi, quietly. 'But first I must show them.'

They left the teahouse shortly afterwards and took a taxi back to the Kerman Grand Inn, packed and left for the airport for the once-a-week Iran Air flight down to Bandar Abbas, a distance of around 320 miles.

It left on time at 6 p.m. and arrived at the seaport forty-five minutes later. They checked into the now-jaded but once-renowned old Hotel Gamerun on the southside of *Bolvar-e Pasdaran*, overlooking the Gulf. Renamed the Homa Hotel, it still carried an air of opulence, and its restaurant, once famous, was now adequate. Just. But the chef knew how to fry battered prawns, with fresh steamed rice, the staple dish of Iran. They drank mango juice, and then tea, before a walk in the gardens overlooking the ocean.

The night was warm and the moon rose in the east, from out of the desert, casting a light on several strollers along the pathways. The hotel was full, mainly with tourists, as it often was at this time of year. Bookings were impossible, but the Iranian Navy had several permanent rooms under contract, which was how Ravi and Shakira had slipped so smoothly onto the guest list with three-days' notice.

News of the Nimrod jailbreak had had a stunning effect on Arab morale. But it was the Ayatollahs who had insisted on HAMAS revealing who, precisely, had been responsible. And HAMAS had been shy, guarding the identity of their military leader. But as the months went by, the Ayatollahs, who had done so much to finance operations in the Middle East, had their way. The name of General Rashood was given to them, along with the shining fact that he was an Iranian-born Muslim.

This quiet walk in the garden may have seemed like a carefree, romantic interlude, for two people who had been devotedly in love for almost two years. But the atmosphere between them was fraught with tensions. First thing in the morning, General Rashood was to report to the Iranian Naval yard on the western side of the town, where he had been summoned to discuss the future with the top brass of Hezbollah, plus that organization's military sympathizers, and two senior hardline clerics from Tehran, who had for many years provided funds for various acts of destruction against the West.

An Ayatollah paymaster of very senior government rank would chair the meeting, which would take place behind locked doors in the Ops Room Block. Four guards would patrol every entrance. All notes and notebooks would be surrendered for inspection at the conclusion of the discussions. For many months, no-one would ever be informed of the decisions reached, nor indeed what any single person had stated.

As classified military gatherings go, this one was s-e-c-r-e-t. And it would decide the immediate future of General Ravi, and that of his Palestinian bride-to-be. Neither of them knew what tomorrow might bring, even though the main purpose of the meeting in the dockyard was to hear the world view of the revered HAMAS military chief.

Ravi and Shakira slept restlessly, each in turn awakening and

99

wondering where they would go, and what tasks might be allotted them. Shakira would not be permitted to attend the meeting but for the moment she was a guest of the Islamic State of Iran, and would remain at the hotel until the General's business was concluded.

They went down the wide stairs for breakfast at eight o'clock, Shakira eating the traditional *lavash* bread with yoghurt and honey, Ravi insisting on cornflakes and then a couple of fried eggs with toast, despite, by Iranian standards, the monumental cost. The Homa Hotel's accounting department reasoned that anyone who wanted a thoroughly Western breakfast was a thoroughly Western tourist, with thoroughly Western cash, which was, essentially, to be encouraged.

The Navy staff car arrived for the General at 0845. He wore Arab dress, and spoke Arabic to the driver, who steered them westwards, through the seaport, and out towards the headquarters of the Iranian Navy.

Ravi noted the big sign to the left of the main entrance – HEADQUARTERS FIRST NAVAL DISTRICT. Below these large white letters was an uncompromising communication –

Authorized Personnel Only
Intruders Will Be Shot On Sight

Their route to the Ops Center took them past the jetties. Ravi, like all SAS Commanders, was familiar with warships and he recognized a guided missile frigate when he saw one. Right before his eyes was moored Iran's 1,300-ton Alvano Class Vosper Mk 5, *Sabalan*, built over thirty years ago in England, now carrying the very adequate Chinese cruise missile C-802.

Ravi could see the number 73 painted on her stern, and there were seamen boarding her, and others leaving. He couldn't work out whether she was just departing or just arriving. Either way she looked like a force to be considered in a naval confrontation.

They arrived at the Ops Center a little after nine o'clock, and the General was ushered into a downstairs office where he was greeted by the burly, bespectacled figure of Vice-Admiral Mohammed Badr, Head of Tactical Headquarters and the Iranians' most senior submarine expert.

'General Rashood!' he exclaimed, with genuine warmth. 'I am honored to meet you. We have all heard so much.'

'Some of it good?' said Ravi, in Arabic, offering the Muslim greeting, arching his hand down from his forehead.

'All of it superb, General,' said the Admiral, bowing his head and giving deference to the rank of the officer before him. This, despite the fact that Ravi had been commissioned in a dirt cellar, and had never led a force of more than fifty men, while he, Mohammed Badr was the Head of a National Navy comprising 40,000 personnel, and 180 ships, including three Russian-built Kilo Class submarines.

Admiral Badr, a native of the south-coast port of Bushehr, had been in command of the entire Kilo Class program of the Iranian Navy. Indeed he had been in command of the dockyard when an American hit-squad had wrecked all three of the original deliveries, four years previously. The three Kilos now in his possession were brand new, in pristine operational condition, and the Admiral intended they should stay that way.

He loathed America and everything the West stood for. He had actually been known to tremble with fury on the deck of an Iranian frigate when a line of giant US tankers out of the Texan Gulf coast moved arrogantly through the Straits of Hormuz as if they owned it, to reload with crude oil, oil from the Persian Gulf, his country's ocean, his people's oil. Not America's.

On the wall of his office was a photograph of a young naval officer dressed in the dark blue dress uniform of a *Nakhoda Dovom* (Commander), with four gold stripes on his sleeve, the uppermost one containing a gold circle.

'My son,' said the Admiral, glancing across the room. 'Ben Badr, commanding officer of the missile frigate *Sabalan*. He's a good man, thirty-five-years old now. He'll be here in a moment to meet you.'

'I'll be honored,' replied Ravi. 'Did the *Sabalan* just arrive? It looked busy.'

'She docked shortly after midnight,' said the Admiral. 'Been away for about three weeks. North, up the Gulf.'

'Will Ben join us at the meeting?'

'Oh certainly. He is very highly regarded here. A lot of people say I'm just keeping this chair warm for him.'

'Has he worked in submarines, like his father?' asked Ravi, slightly out of context.

But Admiral Badr did not regard it as such, and he replied steadily, 'All of his career. This is his first surface command.'

'Broadening his experience, eh?'

'Precisely so.'

'Can't have a Navy chief who's spent his entire life underwater, right?'

The Admiral chuckled. 'Not these days. But Ben's a quick learner, and he's dedicated to our country and our cause. He'll be promoted to Captain this year, and resume command of one of the Kilos.'

'That's the Russian diesel electric?'

'That's the one. We have three of them. Excellent ships . . . extremely quiet . . .'

'Until they rev up,' said Ravi, smiling.

'Generally speaking,' replied the Admiral. 'We have learned when not to rev up! . . . ah, here's Ben now . . .'

Through the door came Commander Badr, a dark-skinned man with jet-black, close-cut hair, and the build of an athlete, broad in the shoulder but lean, with a light walk, just one step from a full canter, and an easy smile. He was not quite as tall as his father, who was only a fraction under 6 feet 2 inches. But Ben Badr was better looking, classic Persian, with a slim, slightly curved nose, and a high forehead. It was a face of high intelligence.

'Good morning, General,' he said, without being introduced. 'It's my privilege to meet you.'

'Commander,' replied Ravi, smiling and offering his hand in greeting. 'You know little about me, so you should perhaps hold judgement on how big a privilege it is.'

'You already hold a place in my heart,' he replied gravely.

At which point Admiral Badr interrupted. 'One of the martyrs released from Nimrod Jail was Ben's godfather. They were very close. And you have the gratitude of our entire family.'

Ravi was somewhat startled that his exploits were general knowledge here in the headquarters of the Iranian Navy. And Admiral Badr, sensing a flicker of surprise on the ex-SAS man's face, said softly, 'Do not be concerned. The elite high command of Hezbollah expects to know everything from our colleagues in HAMAS. But the secrets of the Nimrod mission remain very secret in our country.'

General Rashood nodded, unsmiling. And the Iranian Admiral continued, 'One thing we do know however is that a very great welcome is in order. We understand this visit is a return to your homeland after more than thirty years in England?'

'Yes. Yes it is.'

'I hope you and Miss Sabah are enjoying it. You are comfortable in the Homa Hotel?'

'Yessir. Very.'

'And your visit to the old teahouse in the Kerman bazaar? Was that nostalgic?'

'It was, sir. Very. I remembered the room – and I *really* remembered the sweet pastries.'

Mohammed Badr chuckled, observing that Ravi Rashood had not as much as flickered his annoyance at obviously having been followed. And he just said, 'General, you understand we all have enemies. We felt it prudent you should have protection during your visit here.'

'I understand,' said Ravi.

'Meanwhile I think we should go upstairs and join the others. The mullahs were here early this morning, immediately after prayers, and we should not keep them waiting.'

They stepped out into the wide stone-floored lobby and made their way to the second floor. The wide wooden doors to the conference room were attended by four armed Navy guards. Admiral Badr wished them good morning, and walked past, opening the door himself.

Inside, set upon a glorious Persian carpet, was a forty-foot long table of polished walnut, around which sat seven men, four of them dressed in combat fatigues, with Arab headdress in black and white patterns. Each of them was introduced to General Rashood, but their names were not offered. It was clear that everyone else in the room knew each other, and Ravi surmised that the four were representatives of the arch-terrorist squadrons of Hezbollah.

At the head of the table was a black-robed Ayatollah, whose name was pronounced obscurely but sounded like Rafsanjani, and may have been a member of the former President's family. He was not referred to as 'His Holiness Grand Ayatollah' but it was obvious he was a Shi'ite Muslim of the highest rank in the government of the Islamic State.

He rose when the General was introduced, and offered both of his hands, saying quietly in Arabic, '*Salam aleikom*, my son. We are grateful to you, for what you have done and for all that you are doing.' Like the Admiral, the Ayatollah had had a close and trusted friend liberated from the Nimrod.

Flanking the great man were two bearded, black-robed *hojjat-el-Islam*, the second highest-ranking clerics, both wearing white turbans. One of them was from the ancient City of Isfahan, the other from Tehran. Each rose in greeting to the visiting HAMAS military commander from Damascus, each in turn thanked him for his achievements.

Ravi and the two naval officers took their seats, and the Ayatollah began by saying, 'I do not, I am sure, need to remind anyone in this room of the great secrecy we must observe. We are discussing matters of great moment, and our plans must not be communicated. The ten people here are representing some of the most important Councils in the Middle East. We are, I know, of one mind. We must also be of one voice. And, when we conclude our deliberations, that voice must be silent.'

Each of them nodded, and the Ayatollah continued: 'We have among us today a most distinguished, and unusual colleague. General Ravi Rashood comes to us not because he has been recruited, but because he has followed his heart, back to its beginnings. And while it is difficult for us to fathom the searching of his soul which led him to abandon family, home, country and career, we are grateful for his decision, that Allah has led him from the Infidel into the embrace of Islam.

'General Rashood in his former life was one of the finest combat commanders in the British Army. But I believe he knew what a cruel, and misguided organization that has proved to be, fighting for government after government against the righteous cause of Islam. Finally, asked to partake in the terrible savagery of the Israelis, backed as ever by the Americans, against the defenseless, peace-loving Palestinians, he turned his back on the conquerors. And he brought his mighty sword arm to the oppressed. Islamic folklore will celebrate his decision for many years to come.'

The Ayatollah paused, and the men around him nodded their approval of his words. General Rashood stared ahead, betraying no emotion one way or the other.

The Ayatollah continued, 'I have learned that in his moment of greatest danger, indeed, in his moment of decision, the General was blessed by Allah with a love which I hope may last them both for their lifetime and beyond. It is not necessary for us to recount his magnificent victories on behalf of HAMAS, only for him to understand our admiration.

'But the time is now upon us, when we must discuss the bigger stage, and the tasks we must move towards. We have hesitated these past two years, because we have not produced the military leader to undertake our onerous requirements.

'But I believe we have one now, in General Rashood, who was I believe, delivered here to us by the hand of Allah himself. And Allah is great, and he has surely sent to us the right commander. And we are grateful to our brothers in HAMAS for recognizing this and for sending the General forward to meet at this summit of Middle Eastern power.'

The Ayatollah nodded towards Admiral Badr, who rose to his feet. 'Gentlemen,' he said. 'Because of the time factor, I do not believe we should concern ourselves with specific objectives, but rather concentrate on much broader strategy. I believe, for instance, there is no further place in this world for the mass killing of civilians.

'Bin Laden tried that with catastrophic results for everyone. He killed innocent people on a scale which brought sorrow to the hearts of every true Muslim. Only the most militant, and stupid, can possibly have approved of the events of 2001. It was not military. It was not justified. And it brought the massive wrath of the Great Satan down upon us. Indeed that heartless action against ordinary Americans came very close to fracturing the great brotherhood of Islam.

'I agree, it was not predictable that the Satan would react as violently as he did. But America is powerful, and greedy, and she is led by vicious vengeful men, who now carry the will of the populace with them. I think everyone in this room understands that any future attack on the USA would result in another pulverizing act of revenge by the Americans, and we do not think we could withstand it.

'We would lose popular support on a scale unimaginable. Not to mention the blood, sorrow and tears. Because for the foreseeable future, the United States of America believes it can, with impunity, smash back at any government or radical group which opposes them. Gentlemen, we do not want to be among the blood, sorrow and tears. No-one will thank us for that.

'The truth is that while the USA remained a sleeping giant, hurt and frustrated by world opinion, then we were applauded throughout Islam for our actions. That is no longer the case. The Americans would not hesitate to slam back at Iraq, Iran, Jordan or Libya, even Egypt or Syria, if they believed those countries had raised a hand against them.

'We have seen their power. There are certainly two men in this room who witnessed the savage bombing of our close, but misguided brethren in al Qaeda. No-one could have withstood the accuracy of the Americans' fifteen thousand-pound bombs. And in that I include our close friends in Beijing.

'No, gentlemen, our path forward must be of a more subtle nature. Which is why we are so fortunate to have a former Western battle commander in our midst, and why we should pay heed to his words.'

The taller of the two *hojjat*s rose, and raised his hand. In deference, Admiral Badr nodded, and sat down. 'Gentlemen,' said the imam. 'Whatever we do, we run the terrible risk of bringing down upon us the full force of the United States military. Remember just a while ago they smashed our submarine force, despite the fact we had done nothing against them.'

Without standing up, Admiral Badr interjected, 'And they just blew away the two biggest dams in Iraq for other reasons.'

Everyone smiled at that. But the *hojjat* continued, 'Should we not consider the present US Administration may be just too tough, too powerful, for any Third World country to grapple with? We hit at them, and they absorb it. Then they come back full of rage and venom against us, using weapons we can never match. Should we not consider a five or ten-year ceasefire in our activities? Perhaps time for a new, soft left-wing government to gain power in Washington. They usually come up with a Clinton or a Carter in the end.'

'Your words are wise,' said the Ayatollah. 'But we must not forget, or ignore, our sacred duty, which is to create a large Islamic State in the Middle East, free of interference or reliance on the West, free of the Great Satan for ever. And in that we have the assistance of the Chinese, who would like to buy all of our oil, and indeed are very easy partners. They ask nothing of us, except trade and co-operation.

'One of the biggest oil pipelines in the world from Kazakhstan to the Gulf of Hormuz was paid for by the Chinese, and it runs right across our country and we are the beneficiaries. No, I am afraid we cannot cease in our struggle. Unborn generations of our people will thank us, and we will receive the Grace of Allah for ridding our lands of the Godless devils from across the oceans.'

'Those also are wise words,' interjected the elderly *hojjat* from Tehran. 'But is there anyone who can explain to me how we can avoid the monstrous anger of the US upon our people? Perhaps I have been here too long. But I have seen much suffering, and much heartbreak. I do not think I could bear to see more death and destruction rained down upon us. Particularly if, in the end, we had brought it upon ourselves.'

The senior Ayatollah placed his left hand on the right forearm of the old cleric. 'You are right to make us aware of the consequences,' he said. 'And I too have many concerns about future attacks on the West. And certainly I have long realized the futility of mass killing, which cannot work, only inflame. I also observe that the United States is beginning a withdrawal of its own from the Gulf. Perhaps not totally, but partially.'

Admiral Badr looked up and saw the nod of recognition from the Ayatollah, and said, 'Your Holiness refers, I believe, to the determination of the White House to cease its reliance on Arab oil, and to tap into its own reserves on the Alaska North Slope.'

'Precisely, Admiral,' replied the Chairman of the meeting. 'You will have noticed a few of the old US contracts with Gulf states have not been renewed, and indeed some of them have been taken up by China. The USA is already intending to become less reliant on oil from our region. His Holiness Grand Ayatollah in Tehran believes the day will come in the next hundred years when the entire American continent, north, central and south, will become one entity, isolationist, and completely self-sufficient in resources.'

'When we have eliminated the State of Israel, that will leave the Middle East, North Africa, and perhaps Muslim Central Asia to us,' said Admiral Badr. 'With, of course, co-operation from the Chinese. Perhaps along the lines of the old Ottoman Empire. Such a dream, a vast Islamic state, free to rule itself, free of the arrogance of the Jews . . . at last.'

He paused and Commander Ben Badr looked up and caught the eye of the Ayatollah, who nodded his assent for the frigate CO to speak.

'I do not think the Americans will find it quite so simple as some people think to become reliant on Alaskan oil,' he said. 'This is a strong and forward-looking Administration, but America is packed with left-wing conservationists. They call them the tree-huggers. And that Alaskan North Slope around

Prudhoe Bay runs into the Arctic National Wildlife Refuge which has a protected status. Has done for twenty years or more. There is a lot of opposition and no guarantee the President will win.'

'Nonetheless,' replied Ben's father. 'They have already laid a major pipeline, running south from an area just beyond Prince William Sound, underwater I think, right into the north-west coast of the US.'

Like all naval officers, both Admiral Badr and his son talked of far-flung places as if everyone in the world spent as much time as they staring at maps and charts. But the drift of the discussion remained on course: *Should we continue to discourage the American fleets from plying their trade in the Middle East, or should we sit back and allow them to drift away in their own good time.*

'The fact is, they are never going to drift away,' said the Admiral. 'The US is a strategic global giant. It sees its own interest in every corner of the world. They deliberately and willfully left Saddam Hussein in place because they knew his removal would probably cause a civil war in Iraq, and we might sweep around the Gulf and conquer them at their weakest point. Which we almost certainly would have done.

'The Americans see advantages for themselves everywhere. They like to keep an eye on Russia, India and China. It suits them to have Carrier Battle Groups in our seas. They will never do what we want, and just leave.'

'And we in turn cannot drive them out,' said the Ayatollah, 'because of their military and naval power . . . and now perhaps would be a good time to hear from the HAMAS commander who has been kind enough to answer our call for help and direction.'

Everyone was in agreement, and General Ravi rose to his feet in the manner of one who had much to impart. 'I have listened carefully to the impressive and thoughtful opinions expressed here this morning,' he said. 'And I do not disagree with any of them. The West is more powerful than we are, and they have the capacity for ruthlessness on a scale we cannot match. However we ought not to dwell upon that.

'If the objective is too difficult, then it is folly to pursue it. As the Americans might say, get yourself a brand-new set of objectives. Crude, perhaps, but perfect logic. They plainly do not like mass killings of civilians, and anyone who does it to them is likely to get obliterated. So don't do it. That's simple. There's not much to gain, except to infuriate your opponent, and the downside is awful by any standards.

'No, gentlemen. This needs a severe rethink. And in my opinion, there are only two things that unfailingly cause an enemy to back down, and the first one of those is sheer exasperation. Not anger, fury and we'll get the bastards for this. But careful studied exasperation. Like Gorbachev displayed when President Reagan archly threatened to wipe his nation out, from outer space if he had to.

'Mikhail was not angry. He was not even frightened. He was just at the end of his tether, exasperated, frustrated and running out of options. In the end he just threw up his hands, said "screw this," gave in. I'm not sure he meant to take down the Berlin Wall and completely dismantle the old Soviet Empire. But that's what happened, so he just advised his nation to get on with living and trading. And he was right.

'And I believe that is what we need to do to the Great Satan. And here we have an even greater advantage than Reagan had over Gorbachev. The Satan has an Achilles heel – it's called dollars. No nation in the history of the world has ever been more conscious of cost, profit, and wealth.

'Which makes our task doubly simple. We have to cause the USA to grow totally exasperated with us, fed up with the inconvenience, tired of endless rebuilding, and above all, fed up with the cost. No killing, no mass murder, just attack after attack on high-tech systems, machinery and institutions. Not people, because that makes them angry and dangerous. Things, gentlemen, things. And everything unattributable.

'That's the only way. Stretch 'em, stretch 'em far and wide. Stretch their resources until they break. Make them think they have to protect this, guard that, send aircraft carriers here, submarines there, troops somewhere else. Make them think the only way they can retain their global empire and trade routes is to guard the whole damn world from attack.

'That way they'll get good and fed up. They'll have those fourth-rate little Democrat congressmen up and whining about the cost, complaining about the effect on the American way of life. They'll bleat themselves to death. But only if no-one gets killed. If that happens they'll smash some nation to pieces again.

'We can get rid of the Americans. We just need to be cleverer than we've been before. Or we'll end up like Afghanistan.'

General Ravi's words had literally slammed around the room, because he was casting aside all of their preconceived ideas. Worse, really. He was standing everything on its head, trying to change the culture of decades of terrorism, making everything that had gone before somehow outdated, old-fashioned, improperly thought out.

Two of the Hezbollah representatives were talking quite animatedly, and it was obvious they agreed with not one sentence of his speech. Indeed one of them climbed to his feet, and said, in Arabic, 'General, we do not think you should come here and decry everything we have done, risked our lives for.'

Ravi did not stand up. He just said quietly, 'I was not asked here to sit in judgement upon the past. I was asked to come here to talk about the future. The past is of no concern to me, save for its lessons. Certainly I had no intention of criticizing your achievements. I do not know what they are. I only know that things which were applicable a few years ago are no longer applicable today. And if you don't change, you will almost certainly perish.'

He paused for a moment and then asked which of the Hezbollah members had seen, first-hand, the American bombing in the mountains around Kabul. Two of them raised their hands.

'How far from the explosion were you?'

'Possibly ten miles.'

'Well, let me say something about that . . . a few years ago I commanded a patrol in Northern Ireland and I know, from very close range, what a fifteen-pound hunk of semtex explosive can do to a street — like knock most of it down. Those American bombs contain *fifteen-thousand pounds* worth of explosive. And I once asked a US Colonel how accurate they were these days. His reply was succinct . . . *which window do you want it through?*'

There was silence in the room. 'They not only have an endless supply of such weapons,' said the General. 'They can deliver them, when and where they want to deliver them. And no-one can withstand that. Trust me. When we strike at them in future, we can afford to make them mad. But not *really* mad.'

'Are you suggesting we can, and should still, strike against them?' asked the Ayatollah.

'Only if we want them the hell out of the Middle East on a

permanent basis. If for instance we were able to damage their Alaskan oil systems, and they guessed it was us, that will cause them to redouble their efforts to become self-reliant, and to get as far away from us as possible. That's what I want – the Satan away from the Middle East.'

'I think this would be an excellent time to break for some tea,' replied the Holy Man. 'Then perhaps, General, you will give us an idea of the military way forward.'

'I believe that is why I am here,' replied Ravi. 'And I will certainly do my best.'

Everyone stood and Commander Badr, the junior ranking officer in the room, walked to a telephone on the wall and ordered tea for ten immediately. Whoever was at the end of the line jumped to it, because four minutes later, three white-coated naval orderlies appeared with two large silver teapots, trays of glass cups set in silver holders, sugar bowls, milk and lemon.

Iranian tea is without question the national drink. They serve it constantly, scalding hot, strong and usually with lemon. It is so bitter practically everyone takes it with sugar. The milk was a concession to Ravi who everyone knew was English. In a way.

They spent fifteen minutes talking among themselves, but the Ayatollah had ears only for General Rashood. He made his way across the room, and inquired, 'Would you be prepared to come to Tehran if His Holiness so wished. I simply have a feeling you are about to propose something rather out of the ordinary.'

Ravi smiled and he looked at the fierce, but highly-intelligent face of the imam. The high forehead beneath the black turban, the calm, penetrating dark eyes, the slightly cynical turn of the mouth. This was not a man to fool with, Ravi thought. Not a man with whom to take any liberties whatsoever, nor indeed to underestimate.

He said, 'I anticipate we are about to become brothers in arms. I would not disrespect our leader. And of course I would attend his wishes in Tehran. Especially if we decide to embark on a great adventure together.'

The Ayatollah smiled. 'General, we may appear to Western eyes to have deep-seated problems among the non-believers and moderates in this country. But in the end, the hardline clerics hold sway here. The disciples of Grand Ayatollah Khomeini still control the country.

'We pay lip service to the West. When it suits us. But we are always guided by the Koran, and our desire for an Islamic State, stretching along the north coast of Africa, right through the Middle East and into Asia. This will one day be achieved. And neither the Great Satan, nor its vicious little puppets in Israel will stop us.'

General Rashood stood motionless. 'I think I can assist you in achieving those objectives and I have confidence that we will succeed.'

'Then we will be seated again, and I will call upon you to outline your grand strategy.' The Ayatollah held out both hands, and said, 'May Allah go with you and with us, General.'

'Peace be upon you,' said Ravi, paradoxically.

Two minutes later he was standing again. And he began with a truly bludgeoning sentence. 'I think we should aim to begin work in two years, by taking out the entire electrical power supply on the west coast of the United States.'

Even the battle-hardened Admiral Badr, who had undergone more scrapes with the US Navy than most Gulf commanding officers, looked up, startled.

'They've already had some quite serious power cuts in California,' continued Ravi. 'And in the next two years there will be millions of barrels of oil traveling down the new pipeline from Alaska, new refineries, new power stations, probably a grid system linking the two biggest cities, Los Angeles and San Francisco to the same electricity source.'

What are you proposing, a suicide bombing raid? Everyone had the same question, so it scarcely mattered who was speaking.

'No, of course not. I am proposing we begin to work on a plan to exact our revenge on them for everything they have done to us. We will start by crippling the new west-coast electricity supply right from the source, at the big refinery in Prince William Sound. Hit the storage tanks, then the actual refinery, then the pipeline itself, then the pipeline underwater along the Washington State coast, maybe three times, then the new refinery they're building in Gray's Harbor, then the main power station which serves the two cities.'

You mean all at once?

'Well, in the course of a few days, we'll be trying to show no connection between a series of accidents.'

Accidents! This sounds like World War Three and Four.

'Absolutely not. We have a fire caused by an unknown source

at the main storage and pumping station. The breaches in the underwater pipe will be a source of total confusion. Another fire in the refinery at Grays Harbor would also be unattributable. Certainly not to us, fifteen thousand miles away.'

You're talking over land and underwater – How?

'Gentlemen. We need a submarine. Actually, we probably need two.'

'General, we already have three,' said the Admiral. 'Excellent diesel-electric powered, silent under five knots. Perfect inshore attack boats. But I simply cannot imagine them creeping undetected down the west coast of the USA, fifteen thousand miles from home. The US Navy would catch us, for certain. And then it would not have been worth it. Because they could repair their stupid crude oil system. But we would not be allowed to replace the Kilos, nor could we replace the men who drove them.'

'Admiral,' said the General. 'Your Kilos would be useless on such a mission. We need a large, fast nuclear submarine, which could neither be detected, nor caught.'

'Nuclear!' The Admiral was genuinely astonished.

'You mean nuclear powered – not an ICBM submarine, carrying nuclear weapons.'

'No. Not nuclear weapons. Nuclear powered.'

'Well before I ask how, let me ask why?'

'Mostly because a nuclear submarine does not need to be refuelled. It has an infinite capacity to run on its reactor, right around the world if necessary, no rendezvous with tankers. A big nuclear submarine can commit an attack in the Pacific, and then head at high speed straight for the Indian Ocean – or the Atlantic, or even the Antarctic. The fact remains, no-one knows where it is. Its range is so vast it just gets lost in literally millions of square miles of water, running quietly, running fast and deep. Invisible to any pursuer.'

'Well, I do see that. We could not get a Kilo to the west coast of the United States and back without refueling five or even six times, and of course she has to snorkel frequently to keep her batteries charged.'

'Absolutely,' replied the General. 'She has to stay at low speeds to remain silent. She's vulnerable in many ways. And in my line of business, vulnerable is bad. In my opinion, the nuclear attack submarine is the finest weapon this world has ever seen. Her speed and mobility are unmatched. Her reactor provides everything, heat, light, power, fresh water, and it gives her the capacity to run deep, almost indefinitely.

'A good one can fire guided missiles from beneath the surface, hitting targets hundreds of miles away with a weapon which appears to have been fired from nowhere. To return to the mundane little objective I just mentioned, a nuclear submarine could fire and hit those American fuel storage tanks in Prince William Sound in total secrecy.

'No-one would know why they had exploded, nor whether it was an act of war. And even if they did, they could never know who had committed it. There would be suspicion, but little else. We would not be among the suspects because we have no obvious access to such a submarine.'

The General glanced around the table, assessing the reaction of his audience. The four men from Hezbollah sat enraptured. The clerics betrayed nothing, but the Ayatollah was leaning forward on his elbows, his head resting on his upraised fingers. He had not been sitting like that before.

Commander Badr, leaning back in his chair right next to Ravi had a thin smile on his face as he listened to the HAMAS commander delve into the future.

The General spoke again. 'I am drawn to the conclusion that we must have a nuclear ship. Without it we are almost powerless. We cannot attack anything from the surface because that will result in instant identification. We cannot use Special Forces beyond the Middle East, because we have no way of delivering them nor retrieving them after a mission.

'And we certainly cannot attack anything or anyone from the air, because again that represents instant detection. We could, I suppose, copy the methods of Bin Laden and infiltrate Western countries, but that is very clumsy, and if our operatives get caught, the US will not hesitate to lambast the country they think is the country of origin. And they wouldn't even care if they were right! They'd still do it.

'The acquisition of a nuclear submarine, gentlemen, changes everything. We can strike in deadly silence, unseen and unknown. And if we can be quick and decisive, the chances of anyone catching us are close to zero. No modern nation, with an agenda such as ours, has ever had a nuclear submarine. And it is my opinion that we should make all efforts either to buy or lease one, under whatever deceptive means we can.'

'May we presume you would not wish our acquisition of a nuclear submarine to become public knowledge?'

'You may, Admiral. I would not even want it to enter an Iranian port or any other Islamic port.'

'And I must also assume you are recommending we have an accomplice in this operation – another country, whose facilities we can utilize.'

'Of course. And the nation to whom we should turn for help, is obviously China.'

'Are you also suggesting we purchase a nuclear boat from them?'

'No. They do not have one good enough for our purposes.'

'Have you made any kind of study of the possibilities?'

'Yes. Of course. And our options are very limited. We plainly can't buy from the West, because they wouldn't sell. China does not yet have sufficient technology. Which leaves India, Pakistan and Russia. India and Pakistan are too afraid of each other to sell anything as critical as a nuclear boat. Which leaves, all alone, Russia, which happily will sell just about anything to anyone.'

'That may be so,' replied Admiral Badr. 'But Russia is a very strong signatory to all aspects of the Nuclear Non-Proliferation Treaty. They were among the first to sign it back in 1968. They don't approve of nuclear tests, underground or underwater, they have always voted to limit the spread of nuclear weapons of any kind, and they have never gone back on that. They even made certain that Belarus, Kazakhstan and the Ukraine signed up for the NPT.

'Certainly they've never sold a nuclear submarine to anyone. Nor have any of the big powers, the USA, Great Britain, or France. It would be an earth-shaking move if they suddenly sold a nuclear attack submarine to Iran.'

'That would depend largely on how it was done,' replied the General. 'I think an element of subtlety might be in order. We would not be involved in any way.'

'That might be difficult,' replied the Admiral.

'That would depend on how hard we seek out the Achilles heel of each party,' said General Rashood. 'Russia is easy. They need money desperately, and will sell just about anything to get it. Their biggest customer by far is China. You may assume what China wants, with its big checkbook and smiling face, China will get.

'Their Navy already has nuclear submarines, which will assuage Russian conscience. If we want to buy a submarine, China will have to do it for us.'

'And why should they?'

'Well, I think we are China's Achilles heel. It is very hard for her to refuse us for several reasons: Firstly, China understands the advantages of a full-scale Sino-Iranian partnership, which is already in place because of the pipeline from Kazakhstan to the Strait of Hormuz. Secondly, China does not want to disturb that friendship with Iran, since we guard the gateway to the Gulf, and without our co-operation it would be difficult for them to operate their new Hormuz refinery efficiently. Thirdly, their partnership with Iran provides an excuse for their warships to roam at will in the northern Arabian Sea and in the Gulf itself. Fourthly, there are many oil and gas contracts coming up in the next two years all around the Gulf, and China knows that with our support and influence they have a very good chance of landing them. And finally, under American pressure, the Chinese reneged on their contract over the C-802 missile which was supposed to be supplied to Iran. They are fervently hoping it has been forgotten. I think this might be an occasion for a timely reminder that Iran has *not* forgotten. And China most certainly owes the Islamic State a very big favor.'

The Ayatollah looked very thoughtful, reminded as he had been, of the still vexed and still simmering bad feeling between the two nations over the C-802.

This sleek, jet-black, near supersonic cruise missile was built by the China National Precision Machinery Import and Export Corporation. But for its range of a little over eighty miles, it relied on an excellent French-built engine, manufactured at Micro-turbo in Toulouse.

The entire saga took place over several months, but Iran was counting on this Exocet lookalike, ultimately to threaten ships moving through Hormuz to the Gulf. The C-802 had the capacity to carry the most sinister types of warhead, and the Americans were pressurizing China not to fulfill the orders from Tehran.

But Iran had a contract, with heavy front money, and ended up raging at the Chinese ambassador and anyone else who might have been able to unclog the deal. Communications between Tehran, Beijing, Hong Kong, Toulouse and Washington were almost blocking the airwaves at the height of the dispute.

And the National Security Agency in Fort Meade was eavesdropping on everyone. Admiral George Morris's men were the only people who knew precisely what was happening.

Nonetheless China saw the danger in alienating the Americans and over several months, despite a great deal of very nifty footwork, claiming things were beyond their control, they elected not to fulfill Iran's order for the missile.

Iran hit back by stripping down one of the C-802s they did own, and going in for a spot of 'reverse engineering' – rebuilding it from scratch with parts they made themselves. Thereafter, Tehran clammed up, and it was assumed by all parties they had found a way to manufacture their own cruise, without further recourse to China National Precision Machinery.

But there had been a lot of bad blood and mistrust. And it was China who wished to repair the damage, and General Rashood had pinpointed an area where the Dragon of the East might wish to ingratiate itself with the Ayatollahs, perhaps even make amends by acquiring a nuclear submarine for them.

Admiral Badr, however, still thought the Non-Proliferation Treaty would prove to be a major stumbling block. 'I realize that the Treaty only covers the matter of nuclear weapons, not nuclear power,' he said. 'But the nations which do have nuclear weapons are very sensitive about letting anyone else get their hands on them.

'And a ship's nuclear reactor contains a substantial mass of uranium, the residue of which is weapons-grade U-235 from which nuclear bombs can be made. That's one reason no country with a nuclear submarine has ever even considered selling a ship, with its reactor room full of live uranium, to any other country. No-one has ever purchased a nuclear submarine. Anyone who has one, built it.'

General Rashood nodded his understanding of the subject. Then he said firmly, 'If we can persuade China to make an offer for two Russian nuclear boats, I would not expect them ever to enter a Chinese port, and most definitely not an Iranian port. I would expect them to make their journey either from the Baltic or from the Northern Fleet and find their way to one of the Russian bases on the Siberian coast, probably Petropavlovsk.

'There would be no need for anyone to know they had even been sold. I don't think a regular submarine movement along the Arctic waters north of Russia, heading east would even attract anyone's attention. They'd just think it was a straightforward Fleet transfer. The Russians do it all the time.'

'You mean our mission would leave from a Russian port?'

'Correct. And not even *they* would know where we were going.'

'Well,' said the Ayatollah. 'This all sounds very intriguing. And so far I am not opposed to any of these advanced ideas. My only question is, do we have a crew who could handle such a submarine?'

'We do have three commanding officers who have undergone several months' training in Russia – and I believe that a part of the course did involve working in a nuclear boat . . . Ben?'

'Yes it did. We found there were a lot of similarities anyway in a diesel-electric. It's mainly the power plant which is different. We were shown the rudiments of how it works, and we were at various times shown in some detail the differences in driving these much bigger ships. But of course we were there to perfect our commands of the Kilos.'

'How long would it take a diesel-electric commanding officer to learn to take a nuclear ship around the world?' asked the Ayatollah.

'Probably nine months of intensive training. Maybe six months for a top man.'

'Like yourself, Ben?' asked the Ayatollah, smiling.

'Thank you, sir,' said Commander Badr, seriously. 'Probably six months . . . actually, I think a group of submarine officers could quickly become quite proficient at moving the ship around the oceans. Diving procedures, torpedoes, even missiles, navigation, gunnery, hydrology, air cleansing . . . they all operate on much the same principles. It's the nuclear reactor. sir. The toughest job on that boat is the Nuclear Engineer's. And he needs to have a half-dozen men around him who know what they're doing. On a project like this, we might need a couple of Russian engineers on loan for a while.'

'Or even Chinese,' said the Ayatollah. 'They have trained men for nuclear boats. And they might be more sympathetic to our cause.'

'Sir,' interrupted General Rashood. 'I do not plan to tell anyone what our cause is. Certainly not a nation like China, which has already betrayed Iran once, entirely in its own interests, and may well find it agreeable to do so again.'

'Of course, General. Forgive me. It is taking me a little while to grow accustomed to a complete professional, on an international level. I might say I am enjoying the experience.'

Admiral Badr smiled in obvious agreement, and added to the conversation by pointing out that his son, Commander Badr, would be working towards a full command on such a mission. 'I do not think I am being biased by assuring the meeting that he is without question the most advanced of our submarine officers. And he has worked with the Russians.'

One of the *hojjat*s nodded a very obvious assent to that remark, and addressed the Admiral by his first name. 'Mohammed,' he said. 'You have brought your son up, throughout his life to be an underwater warrior on behalf of this nation. And we are all very aware of that. My question is, does the General himself intend to accompany our team in person on such a highly dangerous mission. Or is he merely planning it? Down to the last detail, of course.'

'I intend to take overall command of the entire operation,' replied the General. 'I understand, of course, the submarine must have a CO and that he will be responsible for the safety of the ship and the crew. However I will be in the Number One position. As a point of clarification, I should like to record I would be privileged to have Commander Ben Badr as my number two. But on missions such as we anticipate, there can be only one overall commander. And if that commander is not me, then I will not be going.'

All eyes turned upon Ben Badr.

'I should be honored,' he said, 'to serve as Number Two to the great Ravi Rashood, conqueror of the Nimrod. It would be a learning partnership for both of us.'

'As a point of procedure,' said the Ayatollah, 'I must return to Tehran and present the case to His Holiness. It promises to be expensive and fraught with danger. And yet I accept the wisdom of the General – either we change our methods of operation, and move up to a nuclear boat, or we retire from the fray until the United States comes up with a soft left-wing government.

'Off the record, I can promise the Grand Ayatollah will not be in favor of the latter option. For he will be always mindful of the great Islamic ethos, which goes all the way back to the Prophet's journey from Mecca to Medina in 622, the ethos of *Hegira*.'

The Ayatollah looked up and saw a somewhat quizzical look

on the face of General Rashood, and he spoke as if to him alone. '*Hegira* may be just a little advanced while you are studying, my son. But its concept is the clear command of the Koran that our people must not live in oppression from those of other faiths.

'They must remake their lives elsewhere, where Islam is dominant – *Dar-Ul-Islam*. If required, they may have to fight, to convert a non-Muslim territory . . . *Dar-Ul-Harb* . . . into *Dar-Ul-Islam*. But there can be no compromise. The Grand Ayatollah will not agree to sit back and abandon the conflict, because the Koran forbids it.'

It was almost midday now, and the Admiral suggested they break for prayer, and then lunch which would be served downstairs. He suggested that General Rashood and Ben might like to stroll down to the jetties and back for a breath of hot, but fresh air . . . and a chance to become better acquainted.

The two officers, both of similar age, jumped at the chance, as Ben put it, 'to get out of a roomful of mullahs and outlaws.' At which point Ravi considered he was probably the right type.

They walked down the grand staircase of the Iranian Navy and into the heat of the day, both wearing white shirts, and shorts, with long socks and lace-up shoes. Ravi wore no insignia.

And the first thing Commander Badr said was, 'You know, Ravi, you really remind me of someone.'

'I do? I thought I was unique.'

'You nearly are. But we had a submarine officer here, helping us plan an operation, during the last couple of years, and he was exactly like you. A sailor, rather than a soldier . . . tough, strange, brilliant man . . . name of Ben Adnam. Commander Ben Adnam.'

'Was he an Iranian?'

'No. He was an Iraqi, but he had somehow served undercover in the Israeli Navy for many years. His rank was Israeli. But he was a Muslim, very much on our side.'

'Yes. I see the similarities.'

'Oh, I was not referring just to background, Ravi. I was referring to methods of operation. The way you both absolutely know what you are saying before you speak. The way you understand the weak points of other nations. And you both have the same assurance, a kind of certainty that your views are correct, that to take a different course of action would be folly. But above all, you both have a code of caution, which is more prevalent than your obvious daring.'

'That's probably why we're both still breathing,' said Ravi.

'I am not sure that Ben is still breathing,' said Commander Badr. 'His mission was very dangerous. And we had no further use for him after it was complete. He accomplished all that we had hoped, but then he disappeared, as we assumed he would.'

'Did you work with him yourself?'

'Very much. I was a kind of disciple. He was here in Bandar Abbas for several months, and my father put me very close to him, to see his methods, and to observe his knowledge. He knew more about submarines than anyone I ever met. Taught me a great amount.'

'Are you now as good as he is?'

'Close. We spent a lot of time together. And he was a natural teacher. He trained in Great Britain for a while – that's the toughest CO course in the world. He told me he'd finished first in the class, and I believe him.'

'Had he been on projects against the West, or was he strictly an Israeli submarine officer?'

'He would never discusss specifics with anyone. But my father believed he was responsible for destroying the US carrier, the *Thomas Jefferson.*'

'Jesus!'

'Yes. He was quite a man. And you know, there's something he told me I've always remembered . . . he said, "On any classified mission, in any submarine, you will assume that every man's hand is turned against you – if you spot an enemy, on the sea, or in the air, you will assume immediately that he has also spotted you, and will come after you. Always take instant evasive action, no matter what you are doing." '

'Sounds good to me. I like him already.'

They walked on towards the ships, but they were moving slowly in the heat, and after ten minutes they turned back, towards the air-conditioning in the Admiral's headquarters.

'Do you really think we might get ahold of a nuclear boat?' asked Commander Badr.

'I think so. The Russians are always ready to sell to the Chinese. And the Chinese will want to co-operate with Iran. I think there's every chance, so long as we come up with a master plan which will hold China virtually blameless.'

'And do you think we could mount an attack against the oil/power infrastructure of the west coast of the USA?'

'Oh, yes. I'm sure we could. And I think we'd get away with it, so long as we don't kill *people*. That's what agitates them. Civilian death. Steer clear of that, and we can continue to drive them mad. But not so mad they again decide to eliminate an entire country.'

'But mad enough, Ravi, for them to increase their defenses against such acts.'

'Keep stretching them. That's the way. Until they decide it's just not worth retaining their global role.'

'Or until they do decide to make someone pay.'

'That's when we do not want to be present, Commander. When the Great Satan gets *really* mad, rush for cover, that's my only advice.'

They walked back in silence, two men with much on their minds. Lunch was served, more fried prawns with delicious spiced rice, and the conversation was animated, while the most hawkish members of the Islam Fundamentalist movement considered the views of the former SAS Commander.

Back in the meeting, the Ayatollah began by saying, 'I believe we are all in sympathy with the perceptions of General Rashood and I intend to relay them to His Holiness. If we receive an agreement in principle, I will appoint a delegation to make the journey to Beijing to discuss the matter with our Chinese colleagues.

'Meanwhile, I wonder if the General would explain whether he has a particular Russian submarine in mind for us. Or whether Admiral Badr should make a study and provide us with recommendations before anyone goes to Beijing.'

Ravi reached for his notes and replied immediately. 'Sir, in the broadest terms we need a good-sized ship, because the crew are going to be on it for a long time. I'm thinking an eight thousand tonner, probably three hundred and fifty feet long. We want speed of around thirty-five knots dived. A single shafter will do fine.

'Obviously she must have a guided missile capability, and the ship I have in mind will fire those excellent Russian RADUGA SS-N-21s, special 'Granat' type, land-attack, ship-launched from below the surface. With those you're looking at a good range of around one thousand miles, with a big warhead. They fly at Mach point seven, at a height of one hundred and forty feet. The ship I like most, also carries forty torpedoes.'

'Is she old?'

'Average, launched around twenty years ago. She was very expensive because of a new titanium hull. And she's very quiet, well–maintained.'

'Did you not say we wanted two?'

'Yessir. And this submarine has a sister ship which was laid up, for no real reason, a few years back. Both of them were built to excellent standards in the Gorky yards. I think the Russians just found them too expensive, both to build and to run. And I think they might gladly sell them.'

'Where are they?'

'The operational one is in Araguba, the Northern Fleet submarine dockyard. The other one may be there as well.'

Admiral Badr interrupted. 'An SSN, right? What class of ship is this?'

'They were modeled on the old Sierra I, as a modern replacement for the Akulas. But these two were a special class.'

'Name?'

'Barracuda, sir. Barracuda Type 945.'

CHAPTER FIVE

0930 Wednesday, May 16, 2006
Iranian Naval HQ, Bandar Abbas

General Rashood and Commander Ben Badr sat awaiting the arrival of the Vice-Admiral. For almost two weeks now, they had been on stand-by while the most senior clerics in Tehran discussed the possibility of purchasing a nuclear submarine from the Russians, under the auspices of the Chinese.

Ravi and Shakira had spent a thoroughly relaxing time at the hotel, where the ex-SAS man had spent hours trying to teach her to play tennis, concluding at the end of the first week that Shakira was a lot more dextrous with a hand grenade than a backhand. Ben Badr had been busy with crew changes and adjustments to the guided missile systems on board *Sabalan*.

This morning, they had both been told, a communiqué had arrived from the Ayatollah, 'clarifying the situation with regard to China'. And because the entire project would involve the acquisition of the heaviest naval hardware, it had fallen distinctly into the realm of Admiral Badr, and the two younger officers sipped tea, nervously, wondering which way the Ayatollahs had decided.

Admiral Badr arrived with a flourish, in his air-conditioned staff car. He carried with him a black leather briefcase, and he wore no jacket, just white shorts, long cotton socks and shoes, with a white short-sleeved shirt, with epaulettes and insignia, one thick gold stripe, with two thin ones, set on navy blue, depicting the rank of Vice Admiral.

He came briskly into the office and wished his son and his new military ally a very good morning. He ordered fresh tea and came quickly to the point of the meeting.

'I believe you both know we have heard from Tehran this morning,' he said. 'And the news is encouraging, though not quite decisive. The Ayatollahs have decided they will request our friends in Beijing to purchase on our behalf the two Russian Barracuda nuclear submarines.

'Since we last met together, I have ascertained their whereabouts – both are based in the Northern Fleet at the Russian submarine base in Araguba, way up on the Barents Sea, near the Finnish-Norwegian borders. One of them has been laid up for almost ten years, the other, hull K239, the *Tula,* formerly the *Karp,* was operational until a year ago but has been in the dockyard ever since.

'One way and another, gentlemen, I believe either one would serve our purposes very well. The question is, will the Russians sell them?'

'I suppose it's too early to make an assessment?' said Ben.

'Partly,' replied his father. 'But we have made a few discreet initial inquiries from our own office in the Ukraine, and the Russians seem unconcerned about the ramifications of selling a nuclear boat to a foreign power.

'Most of them have not been paid for several months, and they would all be most supportive of any scheme to pull millions and millions of dollars into the Navy's economy. They all reminded our man, the Russian Navy owns those ships, so the cash will be theirs.'

'Did anyone mention price?'

'No. Not specifically. But a Barracuda would probably cost around six hundred and fifty million dollars to build new. These are twenty years old, but lightly-used, and well maintained. Which means they'd still cost around three hundred million dollars each to purchase second-hand. However, there's a distinct lack of customers, which might give Chinese buyers an edge. The Russians are very reliant on Beijing for cash these days. I'd say a flat offer of five hundred million dollars for the pair, might just do it.'

'How about work on the ships? Where would you want that done?' Commander Badr looked sceptical.

'I think we'd insist it was all done in Russia,' said the Admiral. 'Because the work has to be done anyway, and it would sweeten the deal for the Russians if we were paying to keep one of their shipyards open and helping to pay the men.'

'Did you get the feeling the Ayatollahs were worried about the costs?' asked General Rashood.

'No,' replied the Admiral. 'I did not. However they made it

clear that although they consider the purchase of two nuclear submarines extremely desirable for our Navy, they did not wish to confirm any operational plans at this stage.'

'And where, Admiral, would you guess that puts me for the moment?' said Ravi.

'I think back in a comfortable house in Damascus,' he replied. 'In fact I am instructed to fly you and Miss Sabah home this evening by military jet. Meanwhile I am personally ordered to join a delegation to Beijing later this month. We intend to ask the Chinese formally to act on our behalf in the purchase of the submarines. In strictest confidence of course.'

'Do you have any further instructions for me?'

'Most certainly,' smiled the Admiral. 'His Holiness wishes you to refine your plans down to the finest detail for an attack on the Great Satan some time in the next two years.'

'Will this all be at my personal expense, sir?'

'It will not. You will be rewarded at the same salary as an Admiral in the Iranian Navy. And there will be two hundred and fifty thousand dollars in addition, deposited in your bank in Damascus for your out-of-pocket expenses.'

Ravi nodded, unsmiling. But it was Commander Ben Badr who spoke. 'Sir,' he said, addressing his father formally. 'Was there any objection, or stumbling block, to the broad outline of our plans?'

'Not in specific terms,' he replied. 'But I was most interested in the general objection voiced by one of the *hojjat*s.'

'The older man, who was here with us?'

'Yes. He told us very carefully that he was afraid of one man in the White House. Not the President, nor any of his right-wing colleagues in Government. The man our *hojjat* fears is called Admiral Arnold Morgan, the President's National Security Advisor. He believes this Admiral is more powerful than the outgoing President, and that he is quite capable of acting alone.'

'Well, what makes him more terrible than the rest of the Republican gang who run the affairs of the Great Satan?'

'Just about everything. He has the mentality of an Israeli. Strike at him, and he'll strike back. He is vicious, short-tempered and very clever. The *hojjat* thinks every blow we have taken in the past half-dozen years has been on the direct orders, or influence, of that Admiral Morgan. He also thinks that if we make any move against the west coast of the United States, Admiral Morgan will order a savage retaliation against us and probably Iraq as well. Maybe even China.'

'Even if he has no idea who has done what to whom?'

'Especially if he has no idea who has done what to whom. He's done it before. And Bin Laden's escapades apparently put his temper on a hair-trigger.'

'Hmmmm,' mused Ravi. 'Maybe we should think about getting rid of him – without of course blowing up Washington, or even the White House.'

'I think that might prove beyond our capability,' said Admiral Badr. 'Arnold Morgan is under heavy guard night and day. It would be just about impossible to get anywhere near him, without having your head blown off. And what kind of assassin would want to try? Hell, if we missed, he'd probably have Bandar Abbas wiped out.'

Ravi Rashood was thoughtful. 'I suppose it would be *slightly* more possible to eliminate him while he was in a foreign country, wouldn't you say?'

'Maybe,' replied the Admiral. 'The Soviets used to specialize in that. All I can say is that Arnold Morgan represents a very grave danger to any kind of action we may take. Because he's apt to behave as judge, jury and executioner. He is without doubt our biggest enemy. And according to the *hojjat*, he's ruthless, and operates with a religious zeal on behalf of the United States.'

'A one-man intifada,' muttered Ravi.

'When riled, that sounds accurate,' said Admiral Badr. 'At least that's the view of the *hojjat*, who, we know, is a man who would not exaggerate.'

'Is he saying we ought not to act at all, while this Morgan character is in power?' asked Ravi.

'No. No. He has not gone that far. He has just warned that our chances of unruffled success are greatly diminished while Morgan reigns over the US Armed Forces.'

'What about the President, and the Vice-President and the Defense Secretary, and the Chairman of the Joint Chiefs?' said Ben Badr. 'Don't their opinions count for anything?'

'Not, apparently, when the Lion of the West Wing roars. He's an ex-nuclear submarine commander, former Director of the National Security Agency. The President won't hear a word against him. Won't move without him. Everyone else is scared of him.'

'I'm not scared of him,' said Ravi, quietly. 'I think we should make some effort to get rid of him.'

'General Rashood, you are going home tonight, to begin work on our detailed plans for the future. I will make you this promise. If Arnold Morgan is going abroad any time in the near future, and we manage to find out, I will keep you informed. Perhaps then we may put a scheme into place. Meanwhile let's not worry about him.'

'Very well, Admiral,' said Ravi. 'But let's not forget about him either.'

Two weeks later
Damascus
General Rashood and Shakira were in Arab dress, strolling along the Sharia Maysaloun towards the Chan Palace Hotel. They'd taken an after-lunch stroll from the excellent Elissar Restaurant near the Touma Gate through the city's ancient Roman Wall; all the way west across Damascus, three-quarters of a mile, past the massive eighth-century Umayyad Mosque, around the Citadel, and on through Martyrs' Square.

They were in the right area now, headed for the most famous bookshop in the city, the Librairie Avicenne, a block from the Chan, and Ravi looked forward to buying a few English newspapers. There was nowhere else in Damascus where anyone could be certain of locating these days-old publications, and he came here two or three times a week.

They were only just in time. Ravi bought the last copy of Monday morning's London *Daily Telegraph*, and they spent a contented half-hour looking through the shelves in search of books which might contain details of the principal cities on America's west coast, Seattle, San Francisco, Los Angeles and San Diego. There was little available, but Shakira found an April edition of French *Vogue*, and two Hollyood show business and film magazines. Shakira was devoted to American movies.

It was almost 4 p.m. and they walked back through the warm afternoon breeze, back to Martyrs' Square for a drink at the Karnak Bar above the Siyaha Hotel. This is a cheerful place, full of Westerners and Arabs alike drinking cold beer, or a *raki* – Damascus not being an observer of the strict Muslim code of no-alcohol.

They found a small table overlooking the square and ordered

a couple of glasses of beer. They sat reading for a while, until Ravi tired of the newspaper, skipping over the last few pages, and then stopping dead at an unlikely headline:

PERSIAN LADY FOR ROYAL ASCOT
Kerman Mare's New Target

He folded the paper back and read the story with interest: *The brilliant victory by Persian Lady in Sandown's Henry II Stakes last Monday is now widely regarded as the best performance by any stayer seen out this season. On fast, firm ground, the daughter of the Irish-based stallion Saddlers' Hall, covered the extended two miles in only two ticks off the track record, quickening away up the final hill to win by eight lengths from the Newmarket-trained favorite, Homeward Bound.*

Persian Lady's new trainer, Charlie McCalmont, was delighted with her, and reported she had come out of the race without a mark. Last night he said she would certainly now go directly to the Ascot Gold Cup at the Royal Meeting, on Thursday, June 22.

Her owner, the London shipping tycoon Richard Kerman, said last night it had always been his ambition just to have a runner at the Royal Meeting, never mind the second favorite for the Gold Cup.

"We were never quite certain Persian Lady would stay beyond 12-furlongs," he said, "But the way she finished up the Sandown hill was electrifying. Charlie is very confident she'll go the extra half-mile of the Gold Cup. For my wife and I, this is the thrill of a lifetime."

Last night Ladbrokes were offering 6-1 against the compact, bay Persian Lady. Prince Abdullah Salman's rangy grey five-year-old High Five remained 3-1 favorite in all offices.

The newspaper made no connection to the mystery of Richard Kerman's son Raymond, the missing SAS officer who had occupied front pages all over the country a couple of years ago. Right here they were dealing with the Ascot Gold Cup, the Holy Grail for the stamina racehorse. Hebron? Where the hell's that? Sports departments are inclined to be insular places.

Meanwhile, 3,000 miles from London, Ravi stared at the story. He was overjoyed at his father's success, and handed the newspaper to Shakira, pointing out the headline.

'That's my father's horse,' he said. 'I remember her when she was a two-year-old. Dad bred her out of an elderly mare by High Line. He's always wanted a staying horse . . . but he never thought he'd get one this good.'

Shakira read the few paragraphs, understanding little of the jargon which racing people take for granted. Then she said, quite suddenly, 'Do you miss your parents?'

Ravi replied, 'Sometimes.'

'You've never contacted them, have you?'

'No. I couldn't, really. It would have put the most awful pressure on them. They would have felt obliged to inform the authorities I was alive, and then there would have been a desperate investigation. Phone-tapping, mail-searching and God knows what else. I didn't want to put them through it.'

Shakira sipped her beer. 'I suppose the only way you could ever see them would be to meet them somewhere.'

'But that would mean contacting them, prior to the meeting, and I'd never quite trust someone not to find out. In the end, I probably wouldn't turn up.'

Shakira persisted. 'But what if you were to meet them without contacting them?'

'Well then they wouldn't know how to find me. Nor I them.'

'I know how you could find them, without a single word to anyone.'

'Lay it on me.'

'Royal Ascot, or whatever it is. Thursday, June 22. They'll be there. And easy to find. Especially if Persian Lady wins.'

'If she wins, they'll probably have tea with the Queen or something. That'd be harder than getting next to Admiral Morgan.'

'Then you better meet them before she wins. I expect they'll be watching the horses before the race.'

'Shakira,' he said, smiling. 'Have you ever been to Royal Ascot?'

'Of course not.'

'Then I will tell you about it. First of all, there's about ten zillion people in attendance. Everyone in the Royal Enclosure wears a little colored badge with their name on it. Each man is required to wear morning dress . . .'

'I thought it was in the afternoon?'

Ravi knew the girl he loved was just joshing him, and he carried on regardless. 'Morning dress is just an English expression. It means top hat and tails . . .'

'Like Frederick Astaire?'

'Precisely. He'd fit in a treat, especially since he married a jockey.'

'A *jockey*!'

'Lady jockey, dingbats. Super rider, and a very beautiful one. American.'

'Anyway Mr Astaire is dead.'

'And his morning suit wouldn't fit me. So I'd have to get my own. But what *I am trying to tell you* . . . in this ocean of irrelevance . . . is that Ascot is literally crawling with security guards, officious men in top hats and green uniforms as I remember, checking people's badges, making sure the person wearing it is the person who's name is written on it.'

'How do they know?'

'They don't. But they can make some very shrewd guesses. They're always catching someone wearing a badge issued to someone else. And they take it damn seriously. Those Royal Enclosure badges are precious and non-transferable. Are you really suggesting I could get ahold of a false badge, and then pull off a meeting with the owners of one of the main horses in the Ascot Gold Cup? I'd get caught, and probably end up in the Tower of London, before standing trial for murder.'

'Is the place where the horses go before the race in the Royal Enclosure?'

'No. It's outside down the lawn, where everyone can see them parade. Before that there's a kind of saddling paddock with boxes where trainers fix the girths and stuff.'

'And is that in the enclosure?'

'Well, no. No it's not.'

'So you wouldn't even need one of those badges?'

'I suppose not. But I am on the Ascot list . . . I've been on it since I was at Harrow . . . I'd have to have a badge . . . and that badge would probably finish me.'

'Ravi, my darling, you're going to talk to your parents . . . to give them reassurance . . . just for a little while . . . just to put their minds at rest . . . to let them know you're not dead. Nothing else is important. Anyway I would like to come too . . .'

'Shakira. I'm not going. You're not going. I love you, and I'm not taking you into England. It's too dangerous.'

'So it might be. But I still think a big crowd is a very good way for you to disappear, then make contact and spend a half-hour with your mother and father, before you vanish from their lives again . . . perhaps for ever.'

'Maybe,' said Ravi. 'But it's a risk I cannot take. Putting my mother's mind at rest is not worth the sacrifice of my own life. And that's what it would mean. They'd almost certainly make me stand trial for treason, killing two serving SAS NCOs in cold blood. To save a Palestinian girl . . . I don't think so.'

Shakira put her arm around his shoulder. 'It's nice to know we are safe here, though,' she said. 'Safe from the horrible English. I do love you.'

At which point they changed the subject to more relevant matters like future HAMAS attacks on the Israelis, and a long-term strategy for stretching the forces of the United States wider and wider, until one day the Americans just grew tired of a long and pointless conflict.

The days in Syria were long, and growing hotter. Ravi and Shakira had been given a large, rambling, eighteenth-century house around the corner from the Elissar Restaurant in the eastern part of the old city. They had air-conditioning installed and settled into a relaxed and pleasant life in their new country.

Most weeks they hosted at least two HAMAS meetings, and most days they wandered around the covered bazaar. Sometimes Shakira cooked for just Ravi, other times for friends. They kept a near permanent private table at the Elissar, which served the best food in the city, and they used her brother as a paid general helper, delivering messages, chauffeuring their medium-range Ford car, occasionally collecting visitors from the airport.

Ravi had no money problems. He had been awarded 'prize money' of $2 million after the two sensational bank hoists in Israel, the quarter of a million dollars 'expenses' had been wired into his account by the Iranians, and his annual 'Admiral's' salary of one hundred thousand dollars was wired into an account he kept in Switzerland, approximately two thousand dollars a week. There was no question of tax.

The house, on Sharia Bab Touma, was rapidly filling with travel books which contained information on all United States embassies, consulates, and military garrisons, in Europe, South America and Asia, and in far-flung outposts in the South Pacific, New Zealand and Africa.

With no active operations, they moved through the month of June calmly, even discussing their forthcoming marriage. But on Tuesday morning, June 13, he picked up an encrypted e-mail on his portable computer direct from Iranian Naval HQ, which jacked Ravi's pulse up by several notches.

'*To General Rashood. FYI. Admiral Arnold Morgan believed to fly to London, Thursday, June 22nd, 1800 hours. Andrews Air Force Base-Northolt. Air Force One, ETA 0500 Friday, June 23rd. Staying privately, US Ambassador, Regents Park. Funds, if necessary, through Iranian Embassy, 27 Prince's Gate. Prefer you employ third party. Adm. B.*'

Shakira was asleep when he read it, at 5 a.m., and thoughts tumbled through his mind. *Parents. Ascot. Same Day. Gold Cup. Assassination. England. Danger. Terrible danger. Was it worth it? Why? Time. Eight days from now. Planning. Assistance. No time. And yet . . . perhaps his finest hours lay just ahead . . . a dagger to the very heart of the Great Satan?*

At this precise moment, Ravi was stopped dead in his tracks. He recalled his final farewell to his mother, and the pain was as sharp as if it had happened yesterday. He doubted a day went by without her thinking of him. His father's hurt was probably worse. They, who had never wished anything but the best for him. He doubted God would lightly forgive him for this flagrant violation of their trust and hopes.

Ravi committed the e-mail to memory, erased it from the computer, and retired to the kitchen, to brew some tea. As if tuned in to the raging neurons in his brain, Shakira joined him, alert to his mood, dressed in a long white robe. She was sensational upon the eye, beneath her tousled jet–black locks.

'What's happened?' she said.

'Oh, nothing. Just making some tea.'

'Yes but . . . what's happened?'

'Nothing really. I had an e-mail from Bandar Abbas, and it made me wonder again whether I should try to find my parents at Ascot on the day of the horse race.'

'What did the e-mail say which made you wonder?'

'Oh, it just mentioned a certain US diplomat who might be in London in late June.'

'Surely no-one you might want to meet.'

'No. Not really. Someone I might want to assassinate.'

'Wow! You mean personally. Or on behalf of a government?'

'On behalf of the Nation of Islam.'

'Will you take him out before the horse race, or after?' Shakira spoke with complete seriousness, and Ravi laughed.

'Oh, I shan't be involved myself. But I think they might like me to try to hire someone.'

'Good. Can I come?'

'No. But I may take you some of the way.'

'Meaning?'

'We might both go to Paris. Where I will leave you for two or three days.'

'And you go to London to the horse race and the assassination without me?'

'More or less.'

'What's that? Yes or no?'

'Yes. I would have to leave you, because my mission may be dangerous, and I don't want you to end up in a British jail. Even if I do.'

'Oh.'

'And we don't have much time to make our arrangements. Later today, I must call Admiral Badr, and the Syrian Embassy in London. It's in Belgrave Square. I need to fix a badge for the horse races. The Syrian diplomats are more acceptable to the British than the Iranians.'

'But I thought we said you did not need one to see the horses before they race?'

'No. You said that. But I know I must have a proper badge. Royal Ascot is like a club for some people, the English upper classes. Without that little colored badge I'd feel half-dressed. And if I did need to talk to anyone, the badge will give me status, make me look *bona fide* – as if I am there legally, still a part of the regiment. But this is not a military place. And you see very few serving officers. It's too expensive.'

'What about Frederick Astaire's morning clothes?'

'I need my morning coat, top hat and tails. That way I can relax, properly dressed, with proper credentials. Nothing suspicious. I'll just be a smart public school-educated Army officer enjoying a day at the races.'

'What will it say on your badge?'

'The least possible. Just *R. Kerman Esq*. Unobtrusive. And I'm not going into the Royal Enclosure so I won't have to run the gauntlet with those bloody gatemen.'

Six days later,
Monday, June 19
The Air France Boeing 737 from Damascus touched down at Roissy-Charles de Gaulle Airport, nineteen miles north-east of

Paris, two-and-a-half-hours late at four o'clock in the afternoon. Ravi and Shakira hurried through Terminal Two and picked up a cab, directing it to the long narrow Rue du Bac in the Saint Germain area of the city, on the Left Bank.

In moderate traffic, they pulled up outside the Hotel Bac St-Germain forty minutes later. To Shakira it seemed she was visiting the City of Light with the most sophisticated man in the entire world. But Ravi's hotel selection was made from horizons more narrow than she knew.

He had only ever been to one hotel in Paris in his life. And this was it, his parents' favorite, a charming, moderately priced, twenty-one-room establishment which served breakfast in the summer months high on a rooftop terrace with a grand fountain in the center.

Richard Kerman always stayed here, mainly because he liked the terrace and the discreet, semi-luxurious nature of the place. Young Ravi had never forgotten the sweeping views over the city he saw as he tackled his first ever croissant and poured himself hot chocolate from a special pot with sideways handles.

Behind him to the west, jutting into the sky above the grand buildings of the French Government Ministries, was the Eiffel Tower. Out in front, a few hundred yards away was the Cathedral of Notre Dame set on its ancient island in the middle of the River Seine. Nothing had ever tasted so good as the *chocolat chaud* to the twelve-year-old Ravi. 'This,' he had muttered, 'is plainly the life for me.'

And now, twenty-four years later, he was back, under very different circumstances, some of which were markedly better, such as the beautiful Palestinian girl with whom he would sleep and have breakfast. Some were sharply worse, like the need for secrecy, the false name, the forged passport, the wariness, the need to remain separate from other guests.

But, in general terms, Ravi was pleased to be here, however briefly. And she, in turn, was breathtaken by the size and beauty of the French capital.

They checked into the Bac, as the French call the hotel, without incident or questions, Ravi taking the greatest care not to reveal he was the son of one of the hotel's best and most long-standing clients. He thought he recognized the proprietor from all those years ago, but he betrayed nothing, and wondered cheerfully whether the same lady still mixed the *chocolat chaud*. He certainly hoped so.

Shakira was thrilled by the mass of foreign satellite channels on the television in the room, and had to be coaxed away to dine on that Monday night. It was raining lightly outside, and they were both tired, gladly accepting the recommendation of the hotel doorman to try, just a few doors away, the Gaya Rive Gauche, the Left Bank outpost of the famous Paris seafood restaurant on the Rue Duphot.

They ate tiny clams prepared with thyme as a first course, and then a superbly grilled fresh sole for Ravi, and turbot with Hollandaise sauce for Shakira. The maitre d' recommended a bottle of 1998 *Chablis* from the impeccable Tonnerre estate of Monsieur Jean-Marie Raveneau. At the conclusion of their dinner, the vivacious freedom fighter and bank robber from the backstreets of the Palestine Road in Hebron, found herself echoing the distant sentiments of General Rashood. 'This is, quite probably, the life for me.'

And so it was. But not for long. The next morning, Tuesday, time was short. The rain had stopped and the weather was bright. They had a hurried breakfast on the roof, croissants and fresh fruit, and Ravi was nearly certain the same lady had made the *chocolat chaud*.

But he had to leave. Back in their room, he packed quickly, gave Shakira 1,000 Euros to sustain her in Paris until Friday evening, when he would, hopefully, return with the love of his parents rekindled, and the elimination of Arnold Morgan among his list of achievements.

He settled the hotel bill in Euros, cash, and handed Shakira a piece of paper containing the name of a contact in the Syrian Embassy to whom she should report in any crisis, or indeed, in the event of his death or capture.

He kissed her lovingly goodbye, and took a cab straight along the river and up the wide Boulevard Sebastopol to the Gare du Nord train station, a ten-minute ride. His booking on the 11 a.m. Eurostar express to London's Waterloo Station was confirmed, and he slept most of the three hours it took to cross northern France, traverse the tunnel under the English Channel, and then charge through the county of Kent at high speed into central London.

By 3 p.m. he was inside the Syrian Embassy in Belgrave

Square, his headquarters until Friday morning, and a living tribute to the iron bonds that held the unspoken world of Islamic Fundamentalism together. Syria and Iran, Palestine and Iraq, blood brothers in Jihad, in the fight against Israel and the West.

That night Ravi dined with two military attachés, and a member of the Syrian 'security' forces. None of them had much to add about the arrival of Arnold Morgan, except to confirm the times, and to re-confirm they knew nothing about his schedule.

No-one seemed hopeful, but first thing on Wednesday morning they drove a car with diplomatic plates around Regent's Park, checking out vantage points which might give a view of the US Ambassador's private residence. It was not promising. The top advisor to the American President would arrive in a military staff car, surrounded by agents. It would take a huge slice of luck for security to be so lax a marksman could hit Admiral Morgan with a silenced rifle and then make an escape.

It might be possible from somewhere near the boating lake, or from a 'hide' in Queen Mary's Gardens, but there would almost certainly be too many people. Nonetheless they decided that this early morning rendezvous at dawn was an opportunity to be explored.

A hit man would be loitering outside the Central Mosque, west of the boating lake from 5 a.m. onwards. He would take instruction from General Rashood only, and no instruction would be given if there was the slightest risk either of them would be apprehended. This would depend on the size of the police escort and the US Security staff.

Ravi was not optimistic, but luck is an unexpected ally at times. Maybe the Admiral would arrive with just a couple of agents, and no extra police on duty because of the early hour. In any event, there would be three getaway cars positioned on the Outer Circle near Hanover Terrace, Clarence Gate and opposite the Royal Academy of Music.

If the Syrian sniper could make a couple of shots, it was the best possible time to hit and run. Clear roads, light traffic, and minimum law enforcement. Ravi would make his decision at first light on Friday morning when the US Admiral arrived.

If the operation suceeded Ravi would lie low in the embassy through the weekend and then leave for Paris by train from Ashford Station, in Kent, on a British passport under the name of John Farmer, a local landowner from nearby Bethersden.

Meanwhile he had another task to attend; a visit to number 86, The Bishop's Avenue, which would, he was certain, be completely empty. His parents always rented a house in Winkfield Row for the Ascot meeting and they took with them their permanent in-house staff of Joe and Edna Wallace, butler/chauffeur, cook/housekeeper. Mrs Kerman did have an extra daily cleaner in London, and there was a three-days-a-week gardener, but none of them would be at the main house during Royal Ascot.

The Kermans entertained quite lavishly on the Tuesday, Wednesday and Thursday of the Ascot meeting, but dined out on Friday, usually at the home of the former Conservative cabinet minister Sir Henry Tattendon-Sykes.

Ravi elected to go home by taxi, confident he could have it pull into the drive, behind the high walls and out of sight of the neighbors. He was right. It went off without a hitch, and he walked quietly around to the back of the house to a line of large terracotta tubs full of flowering geraniums. Under the third one from the left, he knew, was the spare key.

He stood at the rear door and prayed the numbers had not been changed, which, amazingly, they had not. And he immediately disarmed the burglar alarm by punching in the numbers of his own birth date 180570. That stopped the buzzer, and he bounded through the house, up the main stairs, hard right along the corridor to his old bedroom.

Inside, nothing had changed since the day he had left. He opened the door to his wardrobe and everything was exactly as he expected, his morning coat hanging neatly on the left-hand side, next to three dark gray suits. He grabbed the coat and striped pants on the same hanger, took the gray waistcoat from the upper shelf, a plain midnight blue silk tie from the rack, then dived into the drawer for the correct shirt. He had black socks and shoes with him.

He ran down the stairs, clutching everything under his arm, banged in the numbers to the burglar alarm, watched the digital sign '*Leave Now*' light up on the little screen, and slipped out of the door, double-locking it behind him.

He replaced the key and walked back to the taxi, which was now turned around ready to drive him back to the embassy. Risky, sentimental mission accomplished.

Ravi ordered the cabbie to drive down to Regent's Park and

to take a turn around the Inner Circle, then make a slow circuit of the Outer Circle, before heading west along the Marylebone Road and then south to Marble Arch, Park Lane and Belgrave Square.

The driver did as he was instructed, charged forty pounds for the trip and was glad to be handed fifty pounds for his trouble.

Ravi spent the early evening with his Syrian colleagues, working on a detailed map of the Regent's Park area, and inspecting the beautifully-made SSG 69 Austrian sniper rifle the marksman would use on Friday morning, Allah willing, in Regent's Park.

This is one of the most deadly long-range rifles in the world. Superbly engineered, in the right hands it can achieve a six-round grouping of less than 15½ inches at a range of a half-mile. Bolt-actioned, with a 6 × 24 ZFM telescopic sight, it fires a lethal, single 7.62mm shell which leaves the cold-forged barrel at a speed of 860 metres per second.

The specimen currently in the hands of General Rashood was engineered into three pieces, to fit into a seventeen-inch long, hard leather briefcase. Its black, mat-finished cycolac stock unscrewed at the thin neck right behind the trigger-guard. The barrel unscrewed at a point four inches in front of the iron rear-sight. This delicate conversion work had been carried out by an Austrian jeweller, with the help of a precision gunsmith, and it fitted snugly into deep velvet grooves, in the black innocent-looking briefcase.

Ready-to-fire, with a five-round drum magazine in place, it would take no more than twelve seconds to assemble, and even less to dismantle. The marksman would be dressed in City clothes, his hands spotless having made the professional sniper's routine check, wiping off *any* excess oil inside the rifle, thus eliminating any tell-tale puff of smoke on firing.

General Ravi liked it. General Ravi actually loved it, and he hoped to hell the man he would meet on Friday morning knew how to use it. Knew how to blow away Arnold Morgan's head from the cover of a carefully selected forsythia bush, long beyond flower, but large and leafy, and strategically perfect to hide a lone assassin, east of the boating lake.

There would be no sound, save the whine of the 7.62mm shell, and the smack of steel, crushing bone. The sniper would then walk softly, a full quarter-mile distant from the ensuing uproar, through the grounds of London Regent's College and out through Clarence Gate, holding his briefcase, a picture of preoccupied innocence, joining other early morning workers.

'Maybe,' muttered Ravi. 'But maybe not.' *A heavy guard outside the ambassador's residence will kill this mission stone dead. The police will cordon off the area in a split second. I don't take chances, and I don't like surprises. I'll try. But no more.*

They all dined with the ambassador and the head of security at the embassy that night. They served a fish and rice dish in the Arab style, and it did not compare with the sole at Gaya Rive Gauche. However the dinner did reveal one illuminating fact. The head of security, a lean, swarthy Damascus-born, ex-tank commander, was in fact Friday's marksman. He spoke little, but the ambassador confirmed he was a distinguished soldier, and probably the best sniper in the Middle East.

Ravi slept fitfully, thinking of his parents, wondering if he would find them easily, wondering how they would greet him. He could hardly have blamed them if they were furious with him, and of course he ran the risk that his mother might faint at seeing him back from the dead in full Ascot rig. *Christ, that'd be attractive, a prostrate mother, right out there in the paddock, in front of the Monarch, and God knows who else . . . worse yet, he would probably be found guilty of committing the cardinal sin of the English upper classes — frightening the bloody horses.*

As dawn broke over Belgrave Square, General Ravi slipped out of the embassy, into a chauffeured staff car and headed for Hyde Park Corner. They drove quickly through near deserted streets and turned up Portland Place towards Regent's Park. It would be Ravi's last recce.

He noted there were no police on duty, at least none that he could see, and traffic conditions were certainly in his favor. If the Syrian sniper could get an accurate shot in tomorrow, the getaway would not be difficult. They drove slowly along the Outer Circle, all around, past the zoo, and then back to Belgrave Square.

Before midday, General Ravi was on his way to the Gold Cup, dressed immaculately, with the little cardboard pink badge, acquired easily by the ambassador, pinned to his lapel. The inscribed words, *R. Kerman Esq.* were written beneath the date, June 22, and the day, Thursday. Tomorrow's badge would be green.

He made the journey to Ascot in a taxi. After the last race, he would walk down the road to the forecourt of the train station and pick up a different one. Today he was anonymous, dressed identically to about 5,000 other men. But he deliberately did not speak to the driver on the way to the racecourse, burying himself in a corner of the backseat, studying the *Racing Post,* attempting to spot the dangers to his father's second favorite for the big race. He read with some satisfaction that the early favorite High Five was withdrawn, injured. And that Homeward Bound, beaten by Persian Lady at Sandown, was now favorite, regarded as more likely to last out the marathon than the stamina-suspect Kerman mare.

They hit heavy traffic as soon as they left the M4 motorway, crawling in a long queue towards Windsor Castle, but Ravi had left plenty of time, and they drove slowly along the straight road bordering the western edge of the racecourse, arriving at the main intersection just after 1.25.

Ravi jumped out, and headed across Number One car park, entering the racecourse at the less busy end, God's little acre where English families had for generations occupied the same picnic spots. The place was awash with champagne. There were small trestle tables, set behind large Mercedes and Rolls Royces, groaning under the weight of mighty plates of poached salmon, hauled out of the Scottish rivers, drenched in mayonnaise, and now consumed boldly with cold new potatoes . . . the standard rations of the British establishment at play.

Ravi strode through the morning suits, looking neither left nor right. He reached the ticket checkpoint and walked past the gateman, his badge plain to see. Inside, he purchased a racecard, and stood under a towering oak tree, finding his bearings.

He sensed a determined movement of the swarming crowd around him, heading for the Royal Enclosure. He checked his watch which showed 1.40, and as he did so, he heard the distant announcement that the horse-drawn Royal carriages were now inside the gates, and were proceeding up the racecourse towards the Enclosure.

The nineteen-year-old Queen Victoria made that same procession in the first year of her reign back in 1838, and it looked much the same now, the reigning monarch in the lead carriage, drawn by four Windsor grays, followed by an assortment of royal princes, princesses, dukes and duchesses. The Gold Cup itself has a similar pedigree dating back to 1807. Ravi Rashood, terrorist, killer and danger to society, sensed again his omnipotent lack of empathy towards the pageantry of England.

He checked out the saddling enclosure, then strolled down to the main parade ring, where he knew Persian Lady would make her entrance at around 3.10, walking from the upper paddock, down the broad, grassy, white-fenced walkway, in the hoofprints of the mighty.

He considered he would need to be in place by then, perhaps walking down behind the mare with his parents. He resolved then to see them at the saddling boxes, where Charlie McCalmont would be tightening the girths, and his parents would be waiting outside, hopefully alone. Luckily he had never met Charlie.

His plan laid out, Ravi sat quietly on one of the little round stools leaning on the fence, watching the first arrivals for the Ribblesdale Stakes, a high-class twelve-furlong contest for fillies. As the space around the ring filled up with throngs of racegoers, he stood up and walked back through the crowd. But then fate struck a near-mortal blow.

He felt a tap on his shoulder, and a very cultured, very English voice said cheerfully, 'Ray . . . Ray Kerman . . . Christ, old boy, I thought you were dead!'

Ravi half-turned and found himself staring into the pink, round, smiling face of Rupert Studley-Bryce, resplendent in a black silk top-hat, and grey morning coat, a scarlet carnation half-concealing his little pink badge. He and Rupert had shared a study for two years at Harrow.

Ravi smiled carefully, overwhelmingly pleased that his badge was engraved with his correct name. 'Hello, Rupe,' he said. 'What a surprise. Didn't know you were a racing man.'

'Well, I'm not really. But I usually have a day at Ascot . . . but gosh! It must be twenty years . . . not since we left Harrow . . . last time I heard about you there was a worldwide hunt going on . . . what was it . . . missing in action somewhere in Jerusalem? People thought you were dead.'

'Not quite. But it was a bit close. Actually I've been on a highly classified mission for the Regiment in the Middle East – been back for about six months . . .'

'Look, forget this bloody fillies race . . . come and have a drink in the White's tent, just over there.' Rupert was a big man, and he steered Ravi so determinedly forward, the ex-SAS officer found himself en route to the private Ascot oasis of the world's most eminent, and oldest, men's club, as if dissent was out of the question.

White's main building stands in unannounced glory at the top of St. James's Street, around the corner from the Ritz. It was founded in 1693, a haven for the English aristocracy, cabinet ministers, and great business leaders; men who prefer the company of their own kind. Its doors are, broadly, closed to show business, bookmakers, professional sportsmen, flash Harrys, and other persons of low rank and breeding.

The Club's Committee has erected its private marquee just above the parade ring at Ascot for the better part of a century. The caterers serve a very good lunch, and copious amounts of alcohol. Television sets line the inside for those disinclined to watch the races live. White's stands as an unashamed bastion of privilege and elitism, members only, and even they have to give prior notice of intent to attend.

There are wealthy men who would kill to be invited for membership. General Ravi Rashood was probably the first person in White's history to be absolutely appalled at being invited inside the sacred tent flaps.

But inside he was. 'Couple of glasses of champers,' Rupert called to the barman. 'Krug. Large.'

And then to Ravi, who had removed his hat, 'This is really nice, old chap. I remember distinctly being very upset at the reports of you going missing. You sure you're okay?'

'Never better, Rupe,' replied Ravi, slipping easily into that old-public-schoolboy mode of speech, perfected at Harrow, and nurtured by some for all the days of their lives.

'Well, you know about me; dull army officer, scratching around the desert looking for terrorists. How about you?'

'Well, you must know I'm a Member of Parliament? If you've been back in England for a few months. Last election. Nice safe seat in Buckinghamshire.'

'Yes. Of course,' said Ravi, hastily. 'Absolutely. I just meant lately, any great excitement? We get pretty insular down at Hereford ... dealing with military matters we think are important, when no-one else gives a damn.'

'You *sure* you've been here six months? I like to think my maiden speech in the Commons caused a national uproar,' said Rupert, quaffing deeply the magic bubbles from Rheims.

'Well, I've been here on and off. I'm involved in heavily classified work, and I can never talk about it.'

'Turned you into a bloody spy, eh? Anyway, I expect you remember the bit where I said the Labour Government was the least able, the worst group of would-be executives ever to attempt to run anything? You must remember . . . I said they had never made one single correct executive decision in nine years, and that I would hesistate to ask any one of them to take charge of a country pub, never mind a country. It was all over the front pages and the television.'

'Oh, of course, Rupe. I'd just forgotten it was you. I remember the bit about the country pub.'

'I hope you haven't forgotten that three national newspapers came out and said that here at last was a fighting Conservative who might one day lead the Tory Party. Your old room-mate, eh? Future PM.'

'Can't say I recall that part,' said Ravi, with care, but smiling.

'Well, never mind that, old boy. It's damn nice to see you . . . just having a drink together, after all these years. Takes you back. Remember that little room in the old Dog and Fox, eh? Remember when we used to sneak out to that pub?'

'God, do I. Those were the days, right? Away from the cares of the world . . . tell you what, how about some dinner next week. I'll be at the MOD for another couple of weeks . . .'

'Perfect . . . I'd really enjoy that. I'm mostly on my own during the week, in the London flat – you know, wife and kids at the old family home in Bedfordshire. I usually get down there on Friday nights. How about Tuesday?'

'I'm sure that'll be fine. Let me have your office number, will you? I'll confirm it with your secretary tomorrow.'

'Great. Call oh-two-oh-seven, six-nine-one, four-double-three-seven. Ask for Lizzie. She'll probably answer the phone. Why not come over for a drink in Annie's Bar in the Commons? We can dine at the club if you like.'

'Rupe, that all sounds great. But I have to go right now. Meeting the parents just before the second race. This has been real fun. I'll call in the morning.'

'God, I'm just so glad you're alive . . . there's an Old Harrovian golf meeting at Sunningdale in three weeks. There's a lot of the chaps will be delighted you're still with us . . . g'bye, Ray.'

Ravi replaced his hat, and walked up to the now empty rail around the early saddling enclosure. He pulled out his mobile phone and dialled 0207-691-4337.

'Hello, Lizzie . . . yes, this is John Farmer, an old friend of Mr Studley-Bryce . . . we were at Harrow together . . . matter of fact I just left him in the White's tent at Ascot . . .'

'Yes, Mr Farmer, how can I help?'

'Lizzie, he wrote down his home address for me to send him an invitation to a lunch in Oxford, and I must have thrown away the piece of paper with a couple of betting slips. Losers, of course! He said to send the invite to his flat, and there's so many people here, I just can't find him. Luckily I took down his office number. You're my lifeline!'

Lizzie laughed. 'You could just send it to me . . . I'll see that he gets it.'

'I don't care where I send it,' chuckled Ravi. 'But he did say specifically, send it to the flat.'

'Okay. It's Flat nine-b, Priors Court, seventy-two, Marsham Street, London SW-oneV two-SA.'

'Thanks very much. I'll pop it in the post.'

By now he could hear the commentary on the second race, the Norfolk Stakes, five furlongs for two-year-olds. It would take only around sixty seconds, less if one of them was really classy. And already he could see stable staff leading up the runners for the Gold Cup, the next race.

He waited discreetly at the far end of the preliminary enclosure, knowing the trainer would appear any moment, carrying the saddle, and the number cloth for Persian Lady, who was already walking briskly around the perimeter, so close he could touch her as she went by, her name carried on the stable girl's right armband.

He guessed his parents would accompany Charlie McCalmont on the long walk from the weighing room, down the lawn, through the middle of the empty parade ring, and on up the hill to the paddock. And sure enough, there they were, and his heart missed several beats as he saw his mother, and his father marching resolutely towards possible victory.

They both looked immaculate, his father in a black, tailored morning coat, a navy blue shirt with a white collar, the perfectly knotted, maroon silk tie, tucked into a gray waistcoat with a gold watch chain. Charcoal-gray striped pants.

His mother wore an elegant dark green suit, which showed off her slim figure. And her lustrous dark hair was almost hidden beneath a very chic, wide, black hat, obviously from Paris. But she looked older, and walked in a self-conscious way, as if aware that the eyes of the crowd were upon her, as the fabulously lucky owner of one of the leading runners in the Gold Cup. She was walking just behind Richard and the trainer, and she was smiling a smile of immense pleasure, imperfectly masked by modesty. Ravi guessed her heart would be pounding, but perhaps not so hard as it might be a few minutes from now, when he made his opening appearance.

Persian Lady's connections came within twenty-five yards of Ravi, heading straight to the first saddling box on the left. For a few moments, they stood watching the mare coming towards them, and then Charlie gestured to the girl to bring her in.

Persian Lady dipped her head, and turned, walking into the box, turning again, easily, facing out of the door, the girl at her head, Charlie gently placing the saddle on her back.

Ravi ducked under the rail and set off across the grass, walking swiftly approaching his mother, bang on her six o'clock. Silently he stood behind her, before leaning forward and saying softly into her ear, 'Steady, mum. Don't scream or faint. I'm right here and I'm just fine.'

Naz Kerman almost died of shock. She heard the familiar voice and spun around, her hand flying to her mouth. Helplessly, she just said 'Oh, my God,' twice, with tears cascading down her face. Then she dropped her racecard, and her binoculars, and her handbag to the ground, and flung her arms around him, sobbing uncontrollably, careless of who saw her, disinterested in what anyone might think.

They were both off to the side of the saddling box, and could not be seen by Charlie or the groom, but Richard Kerman turned around and his heart literally stopped for a few seconds, as he saw the commanding figure of his only son, perfectly dressed, in the arms of his wife.

It took only a half-minute but it seemed to the owner-breeder of Persian Lady that the whole world had gone into slow motion. He watched Naz try to pull herself together, and he saw Ray step towards him, and he felt the steel arms of the SAS Major enfold him, and was conscious of just one sentence . . . 'Listen, Dad. I'm fine. And you two are busy. Say *nothing*, but meet me in one hour under that big tree over there. I have much to tell you. *And don't worry.*'

With that, Raymond Kerman was gone, striding back across the grass, disappearing into the big crowd now gathering around the paddock, and making his way down to the packed parade ring, where thousands of racegoers were anticipating the arrival of the big gray Homeward Bound and the hugely popular Persian Lady.

Mr and Mrs Kerman were in a daze, but Naz was laughing at the world, months of grim acceptance now being replaced by a euphoria which bubbled up inside her.

'Darling, he's alive,' she whispered, unnecessarily. Richard just shook his head, and there was a wry expression on his face, as the afternoon sun warmed the old red brick of the saddling box, and Charlie McCalmont pushed a dripping cold-water sponge into the mouth of Persian Lady, washing out the saliva, preparing her for battle.

He softly pulled her right ear, and ran his hand down the white blaze below her headband, which bore a neat diamond pattern in the black and scarlet colors of her owner. Then he said, quietly, 'Okay, Julie. Let's go.' And the girl led the mare out, setting off across the grass, almost in the footprints of Major Kerman, five minutes before.

Meanwhile General Rashood was doing his best to steer clear of any possible human contact, which was not easy in a crowd of close to 75,000. He went into the Royal Enclosure, keeping his head well down, and then made his exit through the tunnel and into the infield where he hoped he would be least likely to see anyone he once knew.

He positioned himself on the rail, and stared at the grass for a full fifteen minutes until the pounding of hooves, thumping past him, signified the horses were going to post. Thus far he had betrayed nothing, no information about his parents' runner to Rupert Studley-Bryce, no bets on Persian Lady, in case a bookmaker should recognize or even remember him. No contact. No lunch. No tea. Just a heartrending reunion with Naz and Richard.

He watched the horses go by, all fifteen of them in a big competitive field. And he waited for six more minutes until the announcement came over the racecourse system . . . *Under starter's orders . . . and they're off.*

Ravi knew the status of this race, and he understood the quality of the blue-blooded thoroughbreds who would contest it . . . most national racing authorities consider a mile-and-a-half about as far as a racehorse wants to run. There are a few high-class two-mile races but not many, the Goodwood Cup, and, in Australia, the Melbourne Cup.

The Ascot event is over two-and-a-half miles, $200,000 to the winner. This is an arena for gladiators only, for the Titans of the track, racing into the thunder of the Ascot crowd, bringing lumps into the throats of every true horseman, just because of their power, their speed and their unending bravery.

There was a big television screen behind him, but Ravi could not take his eyes off the emptiness of the dark green carpet before him. He stared ahead, watched the runners come by for the first time, five furlongs already behind them. He spotted the scarlet cap of Persian Lady in the middle of the pack, on the fence, going easily. And then they were gone, away from the stands, thundering out into the country, swinging right, up the slight rise in the ground and then on down towards Swinley Bottom.

Five furlongs out Ravi could hear the announcer calling the race . . . *and Persian Lady strikes the front . . . opening up a six-length lead as they race down to the turn.*

And twenty-four seconds later, Ravi heard the traditional Ascot bell toll, as the leaders entered the home straight with two-and-a-half furlongs to run. By now most of the field was half-dead with exhaustion, and Persian Lady had the leaders off the bridle. Right behind her, three lengths adrift, came Homeward Bound, answering the desperate calls of his jockey, trying to shake off the outsider, Madrigal, running the race of his life.

Inside the final quarter of a mile, the favorite collared Richard Kerman's mare. Racing fiercely on the outside the big gray gelding matched strides and then took a half-length lead. Madrigal was not out of it either, and as they raced into the bedlam of the massive crowd, there were three in a line, driving for the eighth pole, 200 yards from where Ravi was standing.

Right there, Madrigal had had enough. And that left Persian Lady, with a half-length to find, as they hurtled towards the wire. Jockey Jack Carson, aged nineteen, went to the whip, slashing Persian Lady three times on her left quarter. But she was already digging deep, racing to within an inch of her life.

Again Carson hit her, and now she shied from the whip, slashing her tail, but she still kept running gallantly, struggling to level with Homeward Bound. And the giant grandstand literally shook from the deafening roar of the crowd, as the mare went after the favorite, fighting her way home, coming again in the dying strides.

There was pandemonium in the announcer's voice as they charged past the winning post. And like him, Ravi could not separate them when they crossed the wire. He just heard '. . . *They've gone past together . . . photograph . . .'*

And so they waited, Richard and Naz Kerman up in the owners' and trainers' stand, Ravi in the infield and the connections of Homeward Bound standing near the Winners' Enclosure.

It took six minutes . . . *Result of the photograph . . . first number two, Homeward Bound. Second number eight Persian Lady. The third horse was number 14, Madrigal. Distances, a short head, and nine lengths.*

The mare lost nothing in defeat, save for around $150,000. And when her owners finally walked to the meeting place they found their son still breathtaken at the formal drama of the contest. He shook his head, and said, 'I definitely picked the right day to come and find you.'

And then he stood by to cope with a blizzard of questions, all on the same theme . . . *Where have you been? What have you done wrong? How long will you stay? Does the army realize you are here? Have you given yourself up?*

Most of them he could not answer. But he explained they must never admit he had been to England, and that he doubted he would ever return. He plainly could never contact them. He was settled in a Middle Eastern country, though not in the land of his birth. He hoped soon to marry, and he had a prosperous career in front of him.

His father of course wished to know what had really happened in Hebron, but that was something they could never discuss. Ravi had much explaining to do, but his parents understood the high stakes – to discuss their son with anyone might cost him his life. And after one hour they parted, with immense sadness, Ravi assuring them he would find them again, probably in an equally unguarded moment, as this had been. Possibly in Paris.

Confident their secrets were safe, he ordered them to return to the Royal Enclosure, and he stood under the tree, watching them walk away. He could see them making for the enclosure gate, and as they entered, his mother turned around, just fleetingly, and waved in a half-hearted way up towards the paddock where he stood. He tried to raise his own hand, but it didn't work, and his eyes were suffused in tears, as indeed were the eyes of Naz Kerman.

General Rashood stood alone for a while, but the last race was starting and he decided to leave before the crowds. He left the way he had come, through the top gate, and then he turned left, down towards the train station where he found a taxi. They pulled up outside the Syrian Embassy at 6.45.

He had dinner at around eight with the security chief with whom he would work in Regent's Park the following morning. But at 10 p.m. he left through the main door and hailed a cab in the square, instructing the driver to take him to Marsham Street, SW1.

It took just a very few minutes and it was growing dark by the time they arrived. Ravi paid off the driver and walked slowly down one side of the street, the side with the even numbers. Prior's Court was about halfway along the rather gloomy road. He pushed open the swing doors, presenting himself to the doorman.

'Good evening,' he said. 'I'm meeting Mr Studley-Bryce — if he's not in, he'll be back shortly — he's given me a key.'

The doorman gazed at the immaculately dressed man who stood before him. 'Sir, I'm sure he's not in yet,' he said. 'But if you have a key, please go up. You know the number . . .?'

'Nine B,' said Ravi.

'The lift is just across there, sir. Ninth floor.'

Ravi, thanking God for the curious authority his formal morning clothes gave him, boarded the lift and stepped out on the correct floor. He walked to 9B, and used his credit card, sliding it in and pushing back the lock. If Rupert had double-locked it with the other key, flicking the safety steel bolt into place, he was out of luck. But Rupert had not bothered. And the door swung open, and Ravi Rashood entered the flat, sitting down in a large comfortable chair to await his old friend.

He did not turn on the light, but he did turn on the television, watching the 10 o'clock BBC News and almost cheering out loud as Persian Lady once more set about cutting down the lead of Homeward Bound.

There was another half-hour to wait before he heard the obvious sound of a key in the lock, and a slightly drunk Rupert came into the room, swaying lightly and demanding to know if anyone was in here, or has the bloody doorman gone mad?

Ravi came at him from behind the sofa, and the MP just had time to cry out '*Ray, what the hell . . .?*' They were the last words he ever would utter. Ravi slammed a small onyx ashtray right between his eyes, splintering the bone in the center of his forehead.

Then he rammed the butt of his right hand with all of his force into the nostril-end of Rupert's nose, driving that bone deep into his brain.

'Sorry about that, old chap,' he muttered, lowering the body to the floor. Then he slipped into the kitchen, selected a ten-inch long steel carving knife from a rack above the wooden work-surface, picked it up with a dish cloth and left the apartment holding the weapon inside his jacket.

The ground floor was deserted as he crossed the floor towards the entrance, but he could see the doorman watching a small television behind a glass door. He stopped and beckoned him to come out, which he did, sharply, as if obeying a command from a superior officer.

Ravi killed him on the spot, instantly plunging the knife deep into the man's heart, all the way in, right between the ribs. He pushed the still-standing body back into the little ante room beyond the desk, turned out the light and the television, shut the door and left, wiping his hands on the dish cloth and taking it with him. The knife remained embedded in the heart of the security chief of Prior's Court, though no-one could see the body, now crumpled on the floor behind the door.

He waited on the embankment for a cab, and went straight back to the embassy, which was quiet now. All of the ambassador's staff were sound asleep, and Ravi let himself in the little side door with a key presented to him by the sniper.

It was almost midnight, and he placed his cell phone on the charger before grabbing four hours' sleep. They called him at 4 a.m., and he packed his suitcase, before writing careful instructions to a staff officer to deliver it personally to Waterloo Station, outside Coach Five, Eurostar Express, 8 a.m. to Paris.

And once more General Rashood stepped outside the Syrian Embassy, into Belgrave Square, an hour before dawn. Safe now from the possibility of a phone call being traced, he called Northolt Airport, and in an American accent informed them he was the United States Military Attache in Grosvenor Square, and could someone give him the ETA of *Air Force One*?

'This morning sometime, sir. Not allowed to give details to anyone.'

'Thanks, pal,' said Ravi, briskly. And to himself, *Well, he's not here yet. But 'this morning'? What the hell does that mean . . . 0500 or 1130?*

Twenty minutes later he was at the edge of Regent's Park looking along the line of houses where the United States ambassador lived. It was just about 0500 and the sky was growing lighter to the east, but the street lights were still on. He could see a detail of four US Marine guards in tight formation outside the building. Four London policemen, visibly armed with sub-machine guns waited on each corner of the block. Another four were outside the Residence talking with the Marines. Every light was on in the front of the building.

'Holy shit!' breathed Ravi. 'This does not look promising.' He tuned his little short-wave radio into that of the sniper, who was currently hiding somewhere across the lawns near the boating lake, lining up his sights. He signaled two blips – *hold everything*. Then he walked back westwards, not especially noticeable because of his regular dark gray suit and light briefcase.

He reached Clarence Gate, and there at the entrance were six more armed policemen. Worse yet, he could hear the rotors howling on a landed helicopter somewhere behind the houses. He stared up to the rooftops and in the distance he could see what looked like an entire SWAT team fanned out in surveillance mode, high above the park.

It was 0540 and suddenly, advancing down Marylebone Road was an unmistakable convoy, two police escort cruisers, four motorbike outriders, and then two long black US Navy staff cars, the American flag fluttering from both of their front wings.

The motorcade swept left, into the wide entrance to the park, policemen waving them in. The first cruiser turned across the road, blocking it northwards, the second skewed across the entrance immediately the US Navy cars were past. Ravi, standing some fifty yards south of the Residence, saw the rear door of the cars open and six obvious agents emerged.

Then two more people disembarked, and in the gathering

light, Ravi could see a smallish, broad-shouldered tough-looking character accompanied by a stunning looking redhead. The agents closed around them, and the US Marines moved up tight, all four of the original guards by the cars, two accompanying the tall figure of the US Ambassador as he came out of the house.

Ravi sent four blips to the Syrian assassin – *weapons tight!* Then he sent five blips – *abort mission instantly*! Because one thing was for certain, any shot fired could not possibly hit the Admiral, not in this mob-scene of security.

And if anyone did get a shot off, he stood a near 100 percent chance of being shot down like a prairie dog before he'd travelled ten yards. These guys were not joking. They were ready for anything, and Ravi knew how to weigh up danger.

'Fuck it,' said General Rashood, graphically to himself. 'I'm outta here.' And he called a cab, snapping somewhat irritably to the driver, 'Waterloo Station, in a hurry.'

But his mood lightened as he pondered lunch in Paris with his Palestinian goddess. Followed by a relaxed afternoon in bed, and then a wonderful dinner.

His trip had been, he decided, a bit of a disaster. His parents were in tears, Persian Lady was defeated, two completely innocent men were dead, and Arnold Morgan was cast-iron safe.

And now he had a long journey ahead of him. But not as long as Rupert Studley-Bryce's. And in the back of the cab, there was a thin smile on the face of the HAMAS terrorist.

CHAPTER SIX

Thursday, June 29, 2006
Damascus

The splash headline on the front page of last Saturday's London *Daily Mail*, was, well . . . arresting. And General Rashood stared at it intently:

RUPERT STUDLEY-BRYCE MURDERED
Tory MP's body discovered
in London flat

Ravi had just brought the newspapers home from the Librairie Avicenne, and though he had expected to see some coverage of his old room-mate's death, he had not imagined it would be quite on this scale.

Before him was a large photograph of Rupert in his Ascot clothes, taken by the photographers who permanently loiter around the main gates to the racecourse. Beneath it, the caption read: '*A day at the races for the Tory firebrand – he died in his top hat and tails.*'

The story described how the body had been found mid-afternoon on Friday, the final day of the Royal Ascot meeting. His House of Commons secretary, unable to locate him, had phoned his wife Susan in Bedfordshire, who had also heard nothing. Receiving no reply from the flat, the secretary had arrived at Prior's Court with two policemen at 3 o'clock in the afternoon.

And there she found the place was already swarming with detectives trying to find out who had stabbed the sixty-three-year-old doorman, Alf Rowan, to death, on the previous evening.

The story continued: *Police believe the same killer murdered both men, probably because the doorman refused him entry, on this quiet Thursday night when very few people were around. Residents were being interviewed last night, but no-one admitted seeing anything, or anyone, suspicious in the building.*

A spokesman at New Scotland Yard said the causes of death were very different. Mr Studley-Bryce, who was thirty-six, had not been stabbed, but had died as a result of head injuries inflicted by persons unknown.

Little was known about the MP's movements during the day, save that he did attend the Royal Ascot race meeting and had spent some of the afternoon with friends in the private tent of White's Club. It is believed that he dined out in the West End, but no-one at the Club would confirm that he had been there.

Police are continuing with their inquiries.

There followed a two-page biography of the Member for South Bedford, detailing his schooldays at Harrow, his three years at Oxford University, and his rambunctious entry into politics. Of Mr Alf Rowan, who was equally dead, but considerably less important, there was a small, single-column story, and a short interview with his heartbroken wife.

Ravi Rashood put down the newspaper and poured himself some afternoon tea. Then he scanned the sports pages of the London *Sunday Telegraph*, noting that the six-year-old Homeward Bound had been sold for nearly $300,000 to go jumping. The purchasers were John Magnier, boss of Coolmore, the world's greatest thoroughbred stud farm in County Tipperary, and his friend JP McManus, the hugely wealthy Irish sportsman and gambler. Homeward Bound would be trained in Tipperary by Aidan O'Brien.

Meanwhile Shakira had settled down with the *Daily Mail* and very quickly asked, 'Did you know that MP who was murdered in London? He went to your school and he's the same age.'

'Yes. Yes I did. Knew him quite well . . . he was not a friend. Guess someone had it in for him. Those MPs get mixed up in a lot of shady stuff these days.'

'I suppose so. His wife was only twenty-nine. And they had three very young children. It's got the English guessing by the look of it.'

The problem with buying newspapers which are nearly a week old is you can get behind the times very swiftly. And 6,000-miles away, in the National Security Agency in Maryland, Lt. Jimmy Ramshawe was doing some very advanced guessing on precisely the same subject.

He had spotted a paragraph in Tuesday's London *Telegraph*

which had seriously intrigued him. '*Police investigating the murder of Rupert Studley-Bryce admitted last night that a small part of the inquiry was being conducted by the anti-terrorist squad based at New Scotland Yard. However they had no further information.*'

Lt. Ramshawe knew what that meant – some reporter had discovered the anti-terrorists were on the case and had tried to find out what was going on. The police, not willing to tell an outright lie, had confirmed, and then fobbed him off.

'So what,' murmured Jimmy Ramshawe, 'are the bloody anti-terrorists doing in there? That's pretty unusual for a straight-forward civilian murder. I don't think this Studley-Bryce had even served in the military.'

This was precisely the kind of puzzle which appealed to the Lieutenant, but he was busy today and had no time for luxuries like a foreign murder inquiry. It was a story in Wednesday's London *Daily Mail* which really switched him on.

'*Police admitted to being completely baffled by the news that the knife which was used to stab doorman Alf Rowan to death in Westminster last Thursday night almost certainly came from the kitchen of the murdered MP Rupert Studley-Bryce.*

'*Unlike Mr Rowan, the MP was not stabbed, but died from head injuries. They now believe Mr Studley-Bryce may have been killed BEFORE the doorman. And that the killer may have murdered the doorman on his way out of the building.*'

Jimmy Ramshawe thought long and hard. *He came for the MP, didn't he? And then he killed the only man who could possibly recognize him, or even identify him. Hmmm.*

But what Jimmy wondered was why the doorman had let him in in the first place? *But he did, because the guy went upstairs and entered the flat without busting down the door, killed Studley-Bryce, then nicked the bloody carving knife and hopped back downstairs and murdered the bloke behind the desk. Bloodthirsty little bastard. But effficient. Damned efficient. And I still wonder what the anti-terrorists are doing in there.*

Jimmy spent another fifteen minutes pondering this mystery. Then he decided to call an old Navy buddy at the CIA in Langley, Virginia, just to see if they knew what was going on over there in London.

He did not, however, hear anything back for twenty-four hours, but it was worth the wait.

'Jimmy, hi. Sorry to take so long. But our guys have been very interested in that murder case for one reason. Studley-Bryce was killed by a professional man, probably one who had served in Special Forces – it was a classic blow to the face, drove his nose bone right into the brain, killing him instantly. The Brits don't have a clue who might have done it or why. But not many civilians know how to kill like that. And it's got a lot of people wondering.'

'Have they announced anything about this.'

'No. And they're not going to. Our guys know, because any murder which may have been committed by any person who could have been a terrorist is shared between Scotland Yard and the CIA. But don't for Christ's sake shout it around. This is supposed to be classified.'

'You can count on my discretion,' said Jimmy. 'Hey, thanks for that. It's damned interesting.'

Lt. Ramshawe had trouble remaining seated, there were so many antennae leaping out of his head. Only twice in his short career had he been told of men being killed by plain and obvious Special Forces unarmed combat techniques – once early last year, that SAS NCO whose body was found in the rubble in Hebron, and now again today. New body, same technique.

There was something else which was also itching his brain . . . *where the hell's that biography of Studley-Bryce? Here we are . . . right here . . . he went to Harrow School and he's thirty-six years old . . . now where's my file on Major Raymond Kerman . . . here we are . . . right here . . .*

'*Holy shit!* Or, as that Greek bastard might have said, *Eureka*! . . . they went to the same bloody school and they're the same age! They fucking knew each other. WOWEEE! I think this bastard killed him. Same as he killed the SAS Serjeant, same as he did everything else. But I'm buggered if I know why. I'd better tell Scotty and George.'

Jimmy Ramshawe had taken a very short time to establish a significant reputation in the National Security Agency. He was obviously thorough to an extreme degree, and he was smart as hell, one of those most unusual young men, born to operate at the highest level of Military Intelligence. He was suspicious and cynical, with a memory like a bull elephant. He could match facts, recalling seemingly unconnected incidents. If three-dimensional jigsaw puzzles had been an Olympic sport, J. Ramshawe, representing either Australia or the USA, would have won a Gold Medal.

'My bloody oath,' he told Admiral George Morris. 'Did you ever see such a set of facts? We're damn nearly certain he murdered his SAS colleagues, one of 'em with a blow no civilian could deliver. And suddenly we've got another body, killed in *precisely* the same one-in-a-million way – and it turns out to be a bloke he actually went to school with, same age, must have known him well.'

Admiral Morris grinned. 'Jimmy,' he said, 'I have the greatest respect for your powers of deduction. But I have a couple of questions: Why do you think this wanted terrorist was in London? And, if he was, what the hell's he doing wandering around murdering Members of Parliament? You wouldn't be in possession of anything so unusual as a motive, would you?'

'Gimme a break, Chief? I'm just getting bloody started.' In times of stress young Ramshawe was apt to become more Australian than Banjo Patterson. And he kept going: 'This is a very big guy in the terrorist world,' he said. 'And big guys tend to make big waves. You told me that yourself. And every instinct I have tells me to watch out for this character.'

'I don't disagree with any of that. And I think you could very usefully spend the rest of the day trying to shed a little more light on what we already know . . . Scotty?'

The US Army Captain Scott Wade, sitting in on behalf of the Military Intelligence Division, nodded carefully to the Director. 'Admiral,' he said. 'We have taken this vanishing SAS Major very seriously since he first went missing. And we got a lot of alarm bells going off right now. If he really was in London, he was there for a darned good reason, running a big risk of capture. I don't know what that reason was, nor why he suddenly killed a Member of Parliament, but I am completely in favor of Lieutenant Ramshawe going after some more facts . . . I mean, we know how dangerous he is . . . this guy could turn out to be a new Abu Nidal.'

No-one smiled. And Admiral Morris murmured, 'We don't even know his goddamned name anymore.'

'Dollars to doughnuts he's gone back to his original name from Iran,' interjected Lt. Ramshawe. 'What was it . . . Ravi? Ravi Rashood?'

'Very likely, among his Middle East guys,' replied Admiral Morris. 'But there's no way he went to London using that.'

'Oh, no. He went into the UK as a Pom, in dress, voice, and attitudes. No doubt of that,' said Jimmy. 'Even the dead doorman wouldn't have let a robed Arab, a total stranger into the apartment block, not without specific instructions from a tenant.'

'What's a Pom?' asked Scotty.

'That's Aussie for Brit,' said Jimmy. 'Usually whingeing Pom. But in this case, just Pom. Major Kerman's no whinger.'

'Jimmy,' said Admiral Morris, good-naturedly interrupting this discourse on the finer points of Outback elocution. 'You better get right back on the case. I don't know where you'll start. But I expect you have a few ideas.'

'Yessir,' said the Navy Lieutenant. 'I'm on my way.' And with that he stood up and left, carrying a large file, heading right back to his post in Security Ops, his computer and his phones.

A thought was already formulating in his mind, and it concerned Mr and Mrs Richard Kerman. Everyone accepted their son had made no contact since his disappearance. After all, phones had been tapped, constant surveillance had been in place, and all mail to the Kermans' home had been monitored. And there had been no contact from the fugitive. But was that still true? Ramshawe ruminated.

Would have been just as bloody difficult to contact them from a London hotel, as from a Jordanian hotel. The phone checks would have picked it up. Don't know about e-mail, but the Brits would be capable of intercepting. And a personal visit to the house would have been spotted by the surveillance guys.

Nonetheless Jimmy believed that Major Kerman *must* have contacted his parents if he had been in London on some kind of a murder mission. Jimmy did not of course know whether the Brits had even connected the two killings in Westminster with the lethal unarmed combat blow perfected by the SAS.

But he, Jimmy, had connected it. And he Jimmy wanted to know what Richard Kerman and his wife had been doing during the week of June 19. And whether it looked like a rendezvous had taken place.

He switched on his computer, and immediately went on line, initiating a search for Richard Kerman. He was surprised at the list of headings which faced him – a catalogue of newspaper articles about the father of the missing Army officer; another catalogue of magazine articles and broadcast transmissions about the London shipping tycoon; more data involving the City, shares and oil prices; and finally a list of newspaper stories about his involvement with thoroughbred racehorses.

Jimmy elected to leave that one 'til last. But they would be only a few minutes away. He had read much of the other stuff, and took little time to ensure nothing much had happened in the last four weeks.

The racehorse section was much more current, and it immediately revealed the second favorite for the Ascot Gold Cup, Persian Lady, was owned by Mr Richard Kerman, the London shipping tycoon, and his wife Naz.

Ramshawe's eyes opened wide. He jumped out of the Kerman file and keyed straight into Royal Ascot Results 2006. He searched for the Gold Cup, and found the two-and-half-mile marathon had been run on Thursday afternoon, June 22.

Jimmy prayed Persian Lady was 'in the bloody shake-up' – and there she was, placed second to a gray gelding called Homeward Bound . . . beaten a short head . . . ridden by Jack Carson . . . trained by C. McCalmont . . . owned by Mr and Mrs R. Kerman.

The Lieutenant scrolled down for a report on the race, looking for an interview, cast-iron confirmation that there had been no mix-up. The Gold Cup runner-up was indeed owned by the parents of the missing SAS man.

No doubt. '*London shipping tycoon Richard Kerman was magnanimous in defeat . . . "We're very proud of Persian Lady. She gave it everything," he said. "And it took the best staying colt in Europe to defeat her, by the width of your hand, after twenty furlongs."*'

Jimmy Ramshawe rifled among his papers '*. . . body discovered Friday afternoon June 23 . . . murder committed the night before, Thursday, just a few hours after the Gold Cup was run . . . and the bloody MP was right there at the racecourse. Now there's another coincidence for you . . . there's gotta be a connection.*'

He swiveled his chair around and picked up the phone, called his buddy at the CIA.

'Can you do me one quick favor – find out whether the Brits have talked to Mr and Mrs Richard Kerman about their missing son, the SAS Major, any time in the last ten days?'

'Shit, you're a nuisance, Ramshawe . . . gimme 'til the morning, will you?'

Jimmy leaned back and tried to put himself in the Major's shoes. *He's buggered off from home and family, everything, every connection he's ever had, and parked himself in the middle of the bloody desert . . . he knew the score . . . knew he could not possibly contact home . . . not even to reassure his parents he was alive . . . this guy's a Special Forces forward commander . . . he would not have taken that risk . . . mostly to protect his own mum and dad.*

He stood up and paced his small office. 'Poor bastard couldn't even risk a message, could he? Somehow to make a rendezvous,' he muttered. 'No. He was buggered all ways by the bloody Secret Service, and he, of all people knew how thorough they would be.'

It took another few minutes for the light of truth to dawn upon him. '*Gottit!*' he exclaimed. 'Major Kerman went to make his own rendezvous without even telling Richard and Naz. He didn't have to tell 'em. Because he knew, beyond doubt, exactly where they would be standing at around three o'clock on that Thursday afternoon . . . with their trainer, getting ready to saddle the horse.

'And what happens? He runs straight into this bloody joker from his old school. Who stops him . . . has a chat to him . . . it must have been like a horror story . . . and the guy's a Member of fucking Parliament . . . and he's longing to tell the entire world he has discovered the missing Major, an old friend. Ray had just one possible course of action. And he took it.

'He found out where Rupert lived, and to his dread discovered it was not a house, but an apartment, in a block, with a doorman. He conned his way in, and waited upstairs. Killed poor old Rupe to shut him up. And got rid of the doorman with a knife on his way out. That way his visit to London was still a secret, and his parents had the endless comfort of knowing he was alive and well. More importantly, they would not risk arrest for deliberately witholding information on a wanted traitor to his country.'

Jimmy hit the line to his Director, and was summoned to the office immediately. And there he convinced Admiral Morris and Captain Wade of the unique set of circumstances. The Gold Cup, which his parents almost won, the murder that night of the MP who had been at school with the Major, and was *known* to have attended the race meeting.

'If the old Brits can just get up to The Bishop's Avenue, and seriously put the arm on Mrs Kerman, she'll end up admitting her son turned up at the races for a don't-worry-mum chat. She will of course know nothing about the murder of Rupert Studley-Bryce, or the doorman, for that matter. And they may never prove he did it. But I'd say we'll know a lot more about the Major by the time MI5 have finished talking to the Kermans.'

'We might even get a handle on where he lives,' offered Major Wade.

'I doubt it,' said the Admiral. 'But Lieutenant, that's an outstanding bit of detective work. And I can't fault the logic. It all fits. And don't you all get the feeling we're closing in on our man?'

'Well, sir, we are on the verge of proving beyond any doubt that he's alive. And that has a value of its own.'

'And in a way,' said George Morris, 'that may make everyone's task just a little more onerous . . . this character is a big thinker . . . we have good reason to think he pulled off one of the biggest bank robberies in history . . . and when he decided to strike a blow against Israel, he didn't just loose off a couple of political prisoners . . . he released the whole fucking lot!

'I'm afraid he might be planning some massive strike against the West – something so huge it'll take our darn breath away. I get the feeling this guy could do damn near anything he wanted. He's got class. Not as much as the late Commander Ben Adnam, but still class, and we have to believe he's damned dangerous.

'Let's put a rocket up the Brits' asses. See if we can't catch him, before the galloping major strikes again. Because when he does, I've a feeling it might be memorable, in quite the wrong way.'

0900, July 10, 2006
Headquarters, Chinese Northern Fleet
Qingdao, Shandong Province
It was a large but unprepossessing conference room, high in the oceanside office block which overlooked the cool, south-flowing tides of the Yellow Sea. Nonetheless the long, plain, milk-white walls of the room made a stark backdrop to the jet-black robes of the two Iranian Ayatollahs.

Both clerics now sat impassively beneath the glowering portrait of Jiang Zemin, the party politician whose rise to supreme authority in Beijing had included the chairmanship of the all-powerful Military Affairs Committee of the People's Liberation Army/Navy.

Again and again, while China's defense budget climbed into

the billions, irrevocably to an all-time high every single year, Jiang had masterminded its distribution. Now his successors were in place, and they were listening to the most extraordinary request.

These two Holy Men, from the hot dusty lands which surround the Gulf of Iran, were here to discuss the possibility of the Chinese Navy purchasing *two* nuclear submarines from the Russians; in strictest confidence, never revealing to anyone the identity of the real buyer, which would be of course, Iran. The two Ayatollahs were accompanied by the Commander-in-Chief of their Navy, Admiral Mohammed Badr, plus his 'senior military advisor,' General Ravi Rashood, who flanked them at the large conference table.

Their staff of fourteen Iranian Naval orderlies awaited them, occupying the entire twenty-third floor at the 500-room complex of the *Huiquan Dynasty Hotel*, overlooking Qingdao's beach No. 1, a ten-minute ride from the Northern Fleet Headquarters.

Arms dealers are no strangers to the inner counsels of modern military states. But the sight of the two Muslim mullahs, all dressed up trying to get their hands on the world's most lethal weapon, the underwater strike submarine, possessed a certain unreal quality of its own.

And the bushy eyebrows of the Chinese Navy's Commander-in-Chief, Admiral Zhang Yushu, were raised high as he listened, through his interpreters, to the totally outlandish request of the imams from Tehran.

'But gentlemen,' he began. 'Surely you must be aware of the restrictions of the Non-Nuclear Proliferation Treaty . . . surely you anticipate Russia will have the gravest reservations about becoming the first nuclear nation ever to sell a ship of this quality to a foreign power?'

'We believe,' replied the less senior Ayatollah, 'their desperation for cash may override their . . . well . . . conscience . . . about selling such a weapon of war. Let's be honest, they've never hesitated before about selling any hardware to anyone, particularly to yourselves. And in that I include big guided missile destroyers, Kilo Class submarines, and even, I believe, an aircraft carrier.'

'Well,' interrupted Zhang, 'you yourselves purchased at least three diesel-electric submarines from them . . .'

'Yes, but not nuclear. Nuclear is different.'

'Gentlemen,' said Admiral Zhang. 'You seem disinclined to let the mere existence of a ship's nuclear reactor stand between yourselves and progress.'

'With your assistance, Admiral, I am rather hoping not.'

'Yes,' said Zhang, slowly. 'But I sense you are asking us to take a very large risk on your behalf . . . one which is guaranteed to infuriate Washington . . .'

'Quite frankly, we do not see a need for Washington ever to discover that you have acted on our behalf . . .'

'Washington has a way of finding out any damn thing in the world which it considers in any way significant,' said Zhang, roughly.

'But perhaps not this,' replied the Ayatollah, gently enough. 'You see, we are asking you to purchase the submarines, which is not in itself so shocking. Then we are looking for a delivery route along the northern coast of Siberia, into the Barents Sea and a docking in the Russian Navy base of Petropavlovsk on the Kamchatka Peninsula. We intend to take delivery there, and set off on our mission from there.

'We do not intend to involve you in any way except financial. We pay, you buy, the Russians deliver, we take over, in the utmost secrecy. It is likely that Washington will not even know the submarine has been sold out of the Russian Navy when it clears Petropavlovsk.'

'Hmmmm,' said Admiral Zhang. 'You see us as a kind of agent, handling the sale, eh? But yet, right in the firing line, should the Americans discover the formal owners of the ship?'

'Well, the documents could scarcely disclose the true purchaser . . .'

'Of course not,' said Zhang, interrupting. 'The Russians may very well agree to sell us a couple of nuclear boats, but I do not believe they would fly in the face of world opinion and sell the ships to an Islamic State in the Middle East. That would be a step too far, even for them.'

'Which is after all why we are sitting around this table . . .'

Admiral Zhang stood up. He was a big man, burly and tough-looking, son of a Southern sea captain, former Navy commanding officer.

'Gentlemen,' he said. 'I accept that the rudiments of your plan are sound. Yes, we could probably buy the ships you want. Yes, it would be of little consequence to us, so long as you were paying. And yes, there would be little enough risk to us so long as it was delivered to a Russian naval base and stayed away from China.

'But what, I ask, would happen, if you go off in your nice new submarine and make some astounding attack on your Great Satan, and the Russians, under extreme pressure from the West, admit the ship was sold to us? That it sails under the flag of the Chinese Navy. Then what?'

'I have thought of that,' said the Ayatollah, referring to notes written out for him by General Rashood. 'You admit the truth, the ship was purchased by the Chinese Navy, but you have never taken delivery, and that it has never set foot in Chinese waters, nor indeed in any Chinese port.'

'Which would of course be perfectly true,' mused Zhang.

'You simply deny all knowledge.'

'But where will the *second* submarine be at this time?'

'That, Admiral, must remain a matter for negotiation. But I was rather hoping we could smuggle it into a Chinese base and hide it. Maybe take a different route to China altogether.'

'I suppose that would be possible,' said Zhang, 'but I am at a loss to see what possible advantage any of this could have for either my Navy or our country?'

'It would come under the heading of *continued agreeable relations* between China and Iran,' said the Ayatollah. 'You remember, the great Sino-Iranian Pact we have so often mentioned. The one which was very nearly broken when you reneged on our contract over the C-802 missile, leaving us defenseless in the face of American aggression. This is such a perfect opportunity for you to make amends . . .'

Admiral Zhang's Political Commissar, Vice Admiral Feng Lu Dong, visibly winced. China's massive interests in Middle East oil, and overwhelming reliance on the goodwill of the Ayatollahs stood before him. And the former Deputy Commander-in-Chief of the PLAN spoke for the first time, addressing the vexed and simmering dispute over the Exocet lookalike C-802 missile which had caused such friction between them.

Feng nodded to the chairman of the meeting, and noted the short bow of Zhang Yushu's head. 'Your Holiness,' he said. 'I know of course your deep and understandable hurt at the failure of that contract, as you in turn must understand the dreadful position in which we found ourselves. And I trust you understand we always acted in your best interests, as well as our own.

'You surely know the Americans would have stepped up and taken military action probably in Bandar Abbas had you taken delivery of the C-802. And the possible destruction of your Naval Headquarters would have been very bad for both of us . . . not only that, the French were in the middle of it, threatening to refuse us delivery of the missile's turbojet engine . . . there were so many circumstances completely beyond the control of us both . . .'

'And yet,' said the Ayatollah, smiling, 'we seemed to rate less of your consideration than all of the others . . .'

'Most certainly not,' protested Admiral Feng. 'But we could treat the others as businessmen – you we had to treat as brothers.'

'And you decided to become your brother's keeper?' asked the Ayatollah, still smiling.

'What more could you expect from your greatest friends?' replied the Chinese Admiral.

Both Zhang Yushu and Ravi Rashood smiled wryly at the dazzling skill and brevity of the exchange.

'Which brings us back to a poignant question,' countered the Ayatollah. 'Are you still our greatest friends?' And this time, his face was passive, devoid of even the thinnest of smiles.

'Of course,' replied the Admiral. 'Nothing less. We honor you and trust you . . .'

'Then you will surely wish to convey those thoughts to us in a way which would earn our own gratitude and thanks . . .'

'Most certainly . . . but . . .'

'I am afraid, but nothing . . . when we leave this room, at the conclusion of these discussions, we expect to be bidding a temporary farewell to our blood-brothers, friends and sales agents. In so doing you will have bought the continued devotion of the most powerful nation in the Middle East. And I would most respectfully remind you, your partners in so many great future ventures.'

'Yes, of course we do see that,' said the Chinese government's Political Commissar, turning once again to Admiral Zhang, looking for help.

And Zhang obliged. 'I am afraid,' he said, 'the bonds that hold us together are much stronger than the issues which occasionally separate us. I accept in principal your request to have us purchase two Russian submarines on your behalf, because that in itself is not unreasonable among friends.

'However, I must also speak to you as a former CO of a Luda-Class guided missile destroyer, by that I mean a professional Naval officer. And I have several questions which I shall ask in no particular order.' And now Zhang read from the pages of a small notebook:

'*One: Who's going to drive this submarine?*

'*Two: What experience does your Navy have with nuclear ships?*

'*Three: Can you raise any kind of a Command competent to handle a sizeable SSN on a long distance mission?*

'*Four: Do you have at least six officers capable of running the nuclear propulsion systems, and I include in that a top-class reactor room Lieutenant Commander, plus at least two Chiefs who have experience in that environment?*

'*Five: In short, can you raise a proper crew, complete with nuclear engineers, to operate an 8,000-ton SSN, both at high speeds and, if I guess correctly, for slower, silent running?*

'*And, finally, we require an answer to this sixth question — what precisely do you want the submarine for?*'

The Ayatollah gave way to Admiral Mohammed Badr, who stood formally, and spoke without notes.

'Admiral,' he said, 'as I explained earlier the two ships we wish to acquire are the two Barracudas, the Type 945s. And the first operational one will come under the command of my son, Commander Ben Badr, who I trust you will remember.

'He studied right here in Qingdao at your Submarine Academy four years ago, and like the rest of his class, took his final diploma in Nuclear Propulsion. His six-month work-experience program took place in Shanghai the following year, and I hope you remember it was almost entirely in your Han-Class Type 091 nuclear boats – Ben worked in hull 405, right after her refit.'

'He'll find that Barracuda a sight more difficult than Han 405,' replied Zhang. 'She's a lot faster, a lot bigger and a lot more complicated.'

'The principles, however, remain the same,' replied Admiral Badr. 'And there were four other young Iranian officers taking the same courses in Qingdao as Ben. Two of them are commanding officers in our Kilo-Class program and the other two command surface ships. Indeed, in the past month we have sent eight Lieutenant Commanders to study advanced nuclear physics at the University of Tehran. We are not complete novices in nuclear ships.'

'No, I understand that. You do have the basis of an SSN crew, and of course the majority of the ship's company can operate an SSN on much the same lines as they operate a diesel electric. The systems are, after all, Russian.'

'Precisely so,' replied the Iranian. 'Nonetheless we shall require training, and I am hoping the Russians will agree to undertake this under the usual terms. Perhaps you could send a group of Chinese personnel, acccompnied by a dozen of our own people, and they could join the crew making the delivery along the northern route.'

'You are assuming much, Admiral,' said Zhang.

'I am really assuming only one thing,' said Admiral Badr. 'That when you threaten to open that vast check-book of yours, the greedy, half-starved Russian Bear will very nearly bite your hand off.'

Everyone laughed. And Mohammed Badr continued, 'It will take perhaps six or eight months. But I am confident we can put together a competent crew to run a Barracuda submarine.'

'Perhaps,' said Zhang. 'But question six remains. And for us, it's a deal-breaker. We have to know, in the strictest confidence of course, precisely what you intend.'

'That is simple. We intend to take out the new American oil pipeline which runs from Alaska down the west coast, and which will in the coming months provide all of America's electric power from Washington State south all the way to the Mexican border.'

'You do?' said Admiral Zhang, smiling but plainly incredulous. 'And do you expect to be blamed for this?'

'Certainly not, if we can mount our attacks in silence, from deep water, using both missiles and torpedoes.'

'And your basic objective?'

'In the short term to drive the United States back into the world oil markets, and to cut off her supply from Alaska . . .'

'And in the long term?'

'To continue with a steady stream of attacks on US institutions and businesses, always stretching them, making them defend themselves, until they decide their global position is untenable, and retreat into a new policy of isolationism, probably in partnership with Canada, Central and South America. But gone from the Middle East.'

'You are moving into waters which we would deem very dangerous,' interjected Admiral Feng Lu Dong. 'Very slowly we are picking up large contracts for Middle East oil, and we are already seeing the United States in retreat from the Gulf. Why attack their oil interests in Alaska?'

'Because America will always be America,' replied Admiral Badr. 'She will be stung by any attack on her pipelines. And she will raise heaven and hell to repair, and protect. This White House wants the US to be self-sufficient in oil. And when she finally recovers from the blows we inflict against her, she will consolidate her interests around Alaska, moving in a very heavy Navy presence to defend her interests.

'It's just one more step in our strategy to stretch her forces out – until the USA becomes just a passive oil-trading customer of both yours and ours. Not some sort of Goliath trying to rule the Middle East as well as everywhere else.'

'You intend to cause the USA to abandon its global role because she will no longer consider it worthwhile?'

'We intend to remove the USA from the Middle and Far East with a policy of exasperating our enemy to death. And that way lies the construction of a great world-dominating Sino-Iranian trading partnership, and, very possibly, a giant Islamic State stretching the length of North Africa, in the image of the Prophet's own magnificent vision.'

Admiral Zhang looked pensive. He nodded, sagely, and suggested a ninety-minute break, since it was almost midday, in order that both sides may consider the ramifications of the discussions so far. The Ayatollahs agreed and the Iranian contingent prepared to leave the sprawling Northern Fleet base and return to the hotel, driving through the pleasant streets of the oceanfront resort which had once been a colonial outpost of the German Reich, back at the turn of the nineteenth century.

The town of Qingdao still bore the remnants of its colonial past. Indeed parts of it looked like a small Gothic town in Bavaria, dotted with houses set beneath steep sloping roofs made of bright red tiles with half-timbered facades. Tall towers of Protestant and Catholic churches led up to the former Governor's mansion, which looked precisely like a Prussian hunting lodge, set at the top of the old Bismarck Hill.

The Iranian negotiating party drove along the former Kaiser Wilhelm Ufer, and once back at the Huiquan Dynasty, Admiral Badr and General Rashood sat in the hot sun, out on the terrace while the Ayatollahs prayed. They drank large cool glasses of beer, still made locally in the Germania Brewery under the city's old name of Tsingtao, and exported all over the world.

'What do you think, Mohammed? Have we got 'em?' Ravi's words betrayed no anxiety, but he was very focused.

'Absolutely,' replied the Admiral. 'There's no doubt Zhang will act as our agent in the purchase of the Barracudas. But I'm sure he's going to ask for a five percent commission. Like thirty million dollars if they cost six hundred million dollars. I think the rest falls into place for them very well. Any disruption in the US fuel economy will please them, especially as they will suddenly, for the first time, find themselves important, supply-side traders with the US. They will love that. Equality with the Great Power, and all that. Their oil contracts in the Gulf will suddenly look very good indeed.'

'Yes. I agree,' said Ravi. 'The operation plainly has a lot of appeal to them. I suppose their worry is that the Barracuda will somehow get caught, perhaps even before she has made her silent attack. And the Chinese will not want the ship to be apprehended with crew from the People's Liberation Army on board . . .'

'No. They certainly will not. But our ace is the fact that we will ensure the Barracuda never sails into a Chinese port . . .' The Admiral had another deep draft of beer, and then added, 'If there is a stumbling block here it will rest on the reply of the Chinese to the Russians, if the Americans start to blame Moscow.'

'I'll brief them on that,' said Ravi. 'And it's very simple. They will admit nothing. They will operate under the guise of mass confusion, hold Naval inquiries, find out why the submarine never came to Shanghai, swear to God the Russians have done nothing wrong, express total bewilderment at the problems on America's west coast. Deny all knowledge. Offer help. Smile like hell. And look concerned at the misfortune which has befallen their great friends across the Pacific.'

Mohammed Badr chuckled. 'The Chinese will also hope the Barracuda is never caught, eh?'

'It won't be. That SSN can turn away from the eastern Pacific, and run non-stop without fueling through deep water all the way to the Indian Ocean, the Antarctic, the South Atlantic. Anywhere it wishes. There is, as we both know, nothing quite so elusive as a smooth-running nuclear submarine.'

They ate a light lunch overlooking the giant cul-de-sac of the Yellow Sea – just slippery sea cucumber, prawns and scallops, all local specialities from one of China's oldest fishing ports, situated for centuries on this remote coastline, more than 300-miles due north of Shanghai, yet 340 miles south-east of Bejing.

They reconvened shortly before 1400. And now Admiral Zhang brought with him his oldest friend, Admiral Zu Jicai, the wise and wily Commander of the Southern Fleet, plus a Deputy C-in-C (Northern) Vice Admiral Zhi-Heng Tan, and the Northern Fleet Commander Vice-Admiral Zhu Kashing.

They sat in a tight group at the head of the table, and Zhang opened the proceedings on an extremely optimistic note.

'I think, gentlemen, you may assume that the Navy of China will make every attempt to purchase your two Barracuda submarines for you. However I am sure you will understand this will entail a certain amount of time and almost certainly several journeys to northern Russia. It is essential that we act as if the submarines were to be for ourselves, and I thus conclude that a small remuneration in the form of a commission would be in order . . . say ten percent of the cost . . .'

Admiral Badr interjected immediately, saying, 'We had factored that in, Admiral, but we would not like to lose sight of the fact that this little venture is a very small favor returned to us . . . in the light of the . . . er . . . misunderstandings over the C-802 missile. I conclude therefore that five percent would be a more agreeable commission.'

Admiral Zhang turned and whispered to Admiral Zu, who was sitting, as always, at the right hand of the great man. They both smiled, having known full well from the start the commission would be five percent. And Zhang beamed at the meeting, secure in having just earned $30 million for the Navy of China, and said, 'Well, we would not of course undertake this for anything less than ten percent – at least, not for anyone else. But you . . . ah, that is very different. You are our brothers, and five percent is the correct number between us.'

And he rose to shake hands on the deal with the Ayatollahs, and with Admiral Badr, and the somewhat mysterious General

Rashood. There was much bowing from the Chinese, and much hugging, shoulder to shoulder from the Muslims. The deal was cemented with declarations of love and affection. And trust.

The discussions were not however completed. And the conversation swerved towards the departure of the first Barracuda on its mission to Alaska.

'Of course,' said Zhang, 'we will make every effort to capture a berth for the first delivery in the Russian Naval base at Petropavlovsk. But their dockyards are so crowded these days, with ships laid up, it may not be so simple. They've just about reached the point where they are cannibalizing one ship in three for spares, and even then they can't really afford to go to sea. I read somewhere last week that two of the dockyards in the Northern Fleet were threatening to seize ships from the Navy and sell them for scrap, unless their bills were paid.'

'Sounds like an ideal atmosphere in which to purchase a couple of laid-up submarines,' said General Rashood. 'Perfect in fact, for us.'

'It would seem so,' said Zhang. 'And with your agreement, we will inform the Russians we intend to bring in crew of – perhaps twenty-four to thirty personnel on the journey from the submarine base at Araguba to Petropavlovsk. Thereafter we will take control and leave there for home, under our own crew.'

'Correct,' said Admiral Badr. 'And you'll attend to the question of training our men. The nuclear engineers. But we've always found the Russians especially co-operative in that regard. Especially if they know they are about to get paid.'

'Do you have any thoughts about the terms of payment?' asked Admiral Zu.

'Yes,' replied Admiral Badr. 'We intend to try for five hundred million dollars for the two. But that may not work. If we have to go to six hundred million, we will pay a two hundred million down-payment with the order; then one hundred million when the first ship is ready to accept our crew. Then two hundred million more when the first Barracuda docks in Petropavlovsk. That's our terms, on that first ship, delivered-freight Petropavlovsk.'

'And the final hundred million?'

'That's payable when the second Barracuda clears Araguba.'

'Sounds acceptable, particularly when the seller is close to bankrupt,' said Zhang.

'Meanwhile,' said the senior Iranian Ayatollah, 'you might like to tighten up your new oil futures, especially the contracts with the Royal family of Saudi Arabia.'

'Yes, that would be sensible,' replied Zhang. 'But we never look forward to it. They are hard to deal with, probably because they are about as royal as I am. Just a group of nomads who found a sugar daddy in Washington . . . someone to find their oil, drill for it, lay the pipelines, store it, refine it, and then buy it.'

General Rashood chuckled. The process had not been a lot different when the Pahlavi dynasty took over Persia with successive Shahs declaring themselves royal. And Ravi noticed the Ayatollahs, avowed enemies of the Peacock Throne, subtly joined in the Chinese merriment about the Saudis.

'Do you really think the United States will have to buy from us?' asked Zu Jicai

'If the Alaskan pipeline suddenly dries up, they'll have to get oil from somewhere, in a very major hurry,' said the Ayatollah. 'And China's big contracts in the Middle East will make them the logical seller. Direct from our joint refinery. There may also be a little price rise, to our mutual advantage.'

'You are thoughtful people,' said Admiral Zhang. 'And I think we are about to embark upon a great adventure together.'

Two months later. September, 2006
Bandar Abbas Naval Headquarters
The coded message from Qingdao to the Commander-in-Chief of the Iranian Navy was succinct – *Old Razormouth 600 Affirmative*. The agreed satellite signal if the Russians accepted a deal to sell the two submarines at an agreeable price.

Mohammed Badr, who had always enjoyed a spot of deep-sea fishing, had thought up the code name for the Barracudas himself, remembering a trip he had once made in the western Pacific near Miyake Island south of Tokyo. The young Lt. Commander Badr had actually landed one of these lightning-fast, dulled-silver predators after a one-hour battle, and he recalled his captain's shouted warning, 'You watch out for old razormouth – he bite your dick off!'

He now stared with immense satisfaction at the satellite communication, confirming Iran's purchase of the two nuclear ships. He also experienced an even greater satisfaction; that he had heeded his captain's warning so assiduously.

He hit the telephone wire to a number in Damascus, and instructed the answering voice to meet him in Bandar Abbas, immediately. An Iranian Navy jet would pick him up at 0700 (local) from Damascus International. The Admiral informed General Rashood they would both then fly to Qingdao, in company with a lawyer, to read and sign the contracts on behalf of the Islamic Republic of Iran.

0800 December 20, 2006
National Security Agency
Fort Meade, Maryland
Lieutenant Ramshawe scrolled down the list of coded messages the CIA had deciphered off the satellite of the People's Liberation Army/Navy. In fact the signals were originally overheard by the eavesdroppers at the NSA itself, but the CIA then sorted them out, reading the routine Navy messages and forwarding them on, with anything that looked mysterious, sinister or unusual. *Old Razormouth 600* was right up there with the unusual.

It landed amidst twelve other pages of naval and military signals, and it stopped Lieutenant Ramshawe dead in his tracks. *Old Razormouth 600! What in the name of Christ is that all about?*

Jimmy ran the word through his mind with the alacrity which came naturally to him, and the Aussie's total disdain for the confusing, which came even more naturally to him – *razorblade, razor wire, razor's edge, razorback – Arkansas – beats the shit out of me. Might even be a misprint . . . who the bloody hell's Old Razormouth?*

'Funny word, that,' he muttered to himself. 'Never even heard it before – suppose it means sharp-tongued, kind of waspish. Bloke with a quick turn of phrase. Probably some Chinese captain taking the piss out of his boss. Hope for his sake Old Razormouth never reads the comms . . . the guy'd probably get fucking shot.'

At which point Jimmy Ramshawe consigned the signal to his private filing system, on computer, just a little list he always kept, of all things baffling, yet interesting. 'Get in there, Razormouth,' he said, hitting the *SAVE* button.

January 20, 2007
European North Russia
The gray-painted Tupolev Tu-22, the multi-mission ASW

Russian 'Bear,' was making 500 knots as it thundered through the freezing skies, 55,000 feet above a stark white frozen landscape, towards the equally stark white frozen White Sea. The time was 0140, which was essentially irrelevant, since the sun never made it above the horizon up here, not during the 'polar nights' between November and January.

On the ground the temperature was minus six degrees, and there was still an hour's flying left of their 950-mile journey from Moscow, all of it due north, before landing at Severomorsk, headquarters of Russia's Northern Fleet, 125 miles inside the Arctic Circle.

It was almost impossible to distinguish land from ocean, so thoroughly ice-bound was this petrified corner of north-west Russia. The 'Bear' was actually headed straight on over Murmansk, the most northerly city on this planet, to an airfield right on the shores of the Barents Sea, which does not freeze thanks to the Gulf Stream flowing around the North Cape. When the wheels of the Tupolev reached out for the last rock-hard runway on the Kola Pensinsula they would be positioned at 69 degrees north, way closer to the Pole than Iceland, on a latitude identical to the shores of the Eastern Siberian Sea.

'Looks a bit cold out there,' said General Rashood, staring through the window into clear sunlit skies, above the White Sea. 'You ever been this far north before?'

'I've never even been cold, never mind this far north,' said the Iranian Admiral, chuckling. 'Are you sure this was absolutely necessary?'

'Well, I need to meet the guys who will be driving the ship, and you better check up on that two hundred million dollars you just handed over.'

'I'm just joking,' replied Mohammed Badr. 'I'm looking forward to seeing Ben. He's been up here for almost two months now.'

They arrived at Severomorsk a little before 1400, stepping out of the plane into almost total darkness. All the runway lights were on, and the airport was lit up everywhere. A Russian Navy staff car awaited them on the runway and the driver set off immediately across a light snow covering towards a wide road which plainly led down to the dockyards.

It took only twenty minutes and they were escorted immediately to a waiting high-speed fast-attack Mirazh patrol boat, which made a little over forty knots up the flat-calm Kola River estuary, thirty minutes to the port of Polyarny. And from there they were driven up the small 'Navy' road, running behind the granite cliffs which sweep down into the Barents Sea. It was about thirty miles to the top-secret Russian submarine base of Araguba, which lies in sinister seclusion at the head of a long steep-sided fjord.

Admiral Badr thought it was touch and go whether he would be able to breathe the frigid air without his lungs caving in completely. And he stood gasping, astounded at the temperature, as Commander Ben Badr came hurrying over to greet his father.

He hugged the Admiral and shook hands with the General, though Ben was hardly recognizable in his coarse, heavy Russian Navy greatcoat, dark blue scarf, and thick fur hat that looked to contain the hides of an entire pack of grizzlies.

Behind Ben, moored alongside, was the unmistakable shape of a 350-foot long Russian-built nuclear attack submarine. To Admiral Badr it bore the hallmarks of the Sierra I, with a relatively short sail, tapered for'ard. But it looked somehow more expensive, more serious. It bore the white painted hull number K-239. This was it, the jet-black Russian nuclear hunter-killer, Barracuda Type 945.

Right now she flew the Russian Navy ensign, pure white with a blue diagonal cross. It would be many months before she flew any other flag, if ever. Admiral Badr could see her commanding officer, *Kapitan* Gregor Vanislav standing at the head of the gangway to greet them. A native of Murmansk, he wore no overcoat, just his uniform, the thick gold bar with one star on the sleeve denoting his seniority.

He saluted in deference to the rank of the shivering Admiral Badr, and then said carefully, in English, 'I am pleased to meet you, sir. You have fine son Commander Ben, very, very fast learner.'

He welcomed, too, General Rashood and led the way into the submarine, Ben Badr's place of work since November. On board, awaiting them were four Iranian Naval engineers, trained in nuclear physics, but currently acclimatizing themselves in the Barracuda's reactor room – they were Commander Ali Akbar Mohtaj, Lieutenant Commander Abbas Shafii, Chief Petty Officers Ali Zahedi, and Ardeshir Tikku.

They were all currently registered as personnel in the People's Liberation Army/Navy, and they were all wearing Chinese Naval uniform, surrounded by ten officers, plainly Chinese, and crew executives. If the Russians had any suspicions they never voiced them. Not a word or inquiry about either the trainees, or indeed the recently-arrived guests, whom they obviously knew represented their valued clients the Iranian Navy.

They knew precisely who Admiral Badr was, and they had always known the identity of Commander Ben Badr. As for the rest, the Russians had obviously decided they were from central Asian Muslim states halfway between Russia and China – Turkmenistan, Kyrgystan, Uzbekistan or Godknowswhereistan. Either way it was no-one's business.

Anyway, the Iranians had an office in the main dockyard in the Ukraine, right there in Sevastopol on the northern shores of the Black Sea. And the Ayatollahs are very important customers for all manner of Russian Naval hardware. Also the Russians knew very well of the slightly unnerving and robust partnership between China and Iran in oil and arms deals. And $600 million had plainly helped to instill a keen sense of discretion among the former owners of the nuclear submarine. For Three Wise Monkeys, read Three Hundred Wise Russian Admirals.

Two further local crewmen, both Petty Officers, joined the party and they moved through the Barracuda, informing the visitors of her excellence . . . *she very fast, thirty-four knots dived, no trouble, very comfortable at that speed . . . good wide submarine . . . considerable stand-off distance between hulls . . . makes big advantage for radiated noise reduction . . . also for damage resistance . . . all titanium hull . . . excellent . . . very, very quiet . . . made her expensive . . . maybe too expensive . . . they don't build no more . . . probably big mistake . . . she was our best . . . dives to almost 2,500 feet . . . we all sorry Barracuda going . . . good ship . . . very, very good ship . . . keep you safe, eh?*

Admiral Badr nodded. He was getting the message. This had been an excellent buy. The Barracuda was almost twenty years old, but she was built in the outstanding shipyard at Nizhny Novgorod, the former Gorky, in the opinion of many experts the home of Russia's finest marine craftsmen. They had floated her proudly up the Volga and all the way through the Belamorsk Canal all those years ago, on one of the great 600-foot-long Tolkach freight barges. Her weapons and reactor room were fitted out in the high-tech nuclear workshops in Severodvinsk on the White Sea, west of Archangel. Again, the home of some of Russia's best scientists and engineers.

And her service record was impeccable. The first Barracuda, commissioned with such ceremony back in 1987, was built as pure front-line muscle for the Soviet Navy, and they had treated her like an empress, refitting and replacing every part which showed stress or wear. She was probably as good today as she had ever been. Worth every cent of the $300 million the Chinese had paid.

The Barracuda had lived in these cold northern waters all her life, through the end of the Cold War, and beyond. Now she was just too expensive to run for a navy which sometimes found it difficult to raise the cash for the dockyard lighting systems. General Rashood's original estimate of the Russian position had been accurate to a degree. The Russian Bear had indeed nearly taken Admiral Zhang's hand off when he made the offer for the massive cash sale.

They broke for dinner at 1900, the visiting Admiral and General from Iran being guests in the officers' mess. They were joined by Ben Badr, and dined with several high-ranking Russian officers, though none as high-ranking as Mohammed Badr. It was as if this was strictly a lower level operation, just 'working up' a recently-sold submarine. Nothing like a flagrant breach of the Nuclear Non-Proliferation Treaty, with a big attack nuclear boat possibly being sold to an Islamic Republic, with major terrorist connections, and many, many uses for the lethal U-235 uranium in an active nuclear reactor.

They ate superb blinis, the delicious little Russian buckwheat pancakes served with caviar and sour cream. And the former Major Kerman delighted his Russian hosts by telling them the allegedly true story of the visiting Texan and his family who dined at the Dorchester Hotel in London and had not really tasted Russian caviar before.

Just what is this stuff, worth a hundred bucks a shot? How could it cost that much?

'Well, sir, it's something of a ritual,' said the head waiter. 'We serve it with finely chopped egg, and onion, and small pancakes, plus a generous glass of the finest Smirnoff vodka, chilled, the favorite of the last Czar of Russia.'

Yeah, but what is caviar? What's it look like?

'Sir, it's the eggs of the sturgeon.'

'That right? Beautiful. Lemme have two. Sunnyside up.'

This was greeted by roars of laughter, and glasses of vodka, since no-one was likely to be going to sea for a couple of days.

But then the conversation returned to the deadly serious nature of the visit. And two ex-Soviet nuclear *Kapitans* were detailed to supply notes on the differences and similarities in the ship, beyond the reactor room.

You got a SAM missile system you're all going to recognize, the old SA-N 5/8, plus a Strela portable launcher . . . the SSM Novator Alfa SS-N-27 on the new Kilos is not much different from the A/S Novator 15 Starfish Tsakra on the Barracuda . . . 53 cm tubes, nuclear warhead or regular Type 40. Whatever. Anyway the big missile on this ship is the long-range RADUGA . . . . . . the SS-N-21 Sampson Granat . . . that's a cruise . . . flies at O.7 Mach, around 200 meters above the surface . . . 1600-miles. It's just been in overhaul. Top of the range.

Torpedoes. Hardly any difference. Mostly 21-inch tubes, 53 cm weapons.

Countermeasures . . . some similarities. ESM, Rim Hat/Bald Head intercept with radar warning on this ship. You're probably more used to the Squid Head on the Kilos. But they're much the same.

Radars: same . . . surface search Snoop Pair . . . back-to-back ESM aerials.

Sonars: the Barracuda has regular Shark Gill hull-mounted passive/active search and attack, low to medium frequency . . . you're used to the more modern Shark Tooth and Shark Fin, the MGK-400 system. But there's not much difference . . . and we have the same Mouse Roar system . . . hull-mounted active attack, normal high frequency.

You'll notice a V-shaped casing on the port side of the sail – that's to cover the releasable escape chambers . . . that bulbous casing on the after end of the sail is for a towed communications buoy . . . very useful.

They retired to bed at 2200, and reconvened at 0500 for a further tour of the ship. To the east, out into the Barents Sea, they could see a glow along the horizon, but there was no daylight and nor would there be daylight for another two weeks.

Admiral Badr and General Rashood took time to inspect the second Barracuda they had purchased, hull number K-240. But it was in a floating, covered dry dock, with several large plates currently being fitted into the underside of the hull. It would plainly be a few weeks before she was seaworthy, but the other one, hull K-239, had already been in sea-trials, and would resume in late May when the new RADUGA missile system was complete.

They left at noon, the same way they had arrived, car to Polyarny, patrol boat to Severomorsk, military aircraft south to Moscow. Commercial jet to Ankara, then change for Tehran, navy jet to Bandar Abbas. General Rashood would not complete his 2,800-mile journey back to Damascus for four more days.

But the news was excellent. The first Barracuda would clear Araguba by July 20th, in time to make the summertime easterly route along the north coast of Siberia, south of the ice-pack. She would be accompanied by an Udaloy Type-1 frigate and the gigantic 23,500-ton ex-Soviet Arktika-Class ice-breaker *Ural*. This was a triple-shafted nuclear-powered monster with a reinforced steel bow, enabling her to ride up, and then bear down on ice, eight feet thick, and smash it assunder.

The waters ought not to be frozen at all in July, but there would be ice floes, and the Russians proposed to take no chances whatsoever with the safe delivery of the first Barracuda. Not with $200 million awaiting them in the port of Petropavlovsk. You can pay a lot of electricity bills with that.

On the journey home, Admiral Badr could hardly contain his excitement about the new purchase. And he talked ceaselessly about her speed, her lethal missiles, and, above all, her ability to run endlessly, in near silence, through all of the world's oceans, without ever needing to surface, either for oxygen, water or fuel.

He was also aware that any missions mounted by the Barracuda would enjoy the clandestine protection of both the Russians and Chinese, both in the release of misinformation regarding their whereabouts, and in the case of China, a hiding place not yet revealed, but one, apparently, so secret, so unexpected, it was entirely possible they would never be located. Not in a thousand years.

Even the somewhat taciturn, close-mouthed Ravi thought that last part was pretty nifty. Though he was unsure whether the men from the Pentagon would accept defeat that lightly. He doubted it, but China was still one hell of an ally.

And he looked forward to hot, peaceful spring and summer months with Shakira, interspersed by short planning visits to Bandar Abbas, before he returned to northern Russia to join the

Barracuda on the long, working journey all along the icy waters of the northern coastline, and into the Bering Straits.

Right there they would begin their deep run down the Pacific, south along the barren wasteland of the Kamchatka Peninsula to Petropavlovsk where they would put the finishing touches to the plan for a sophisticated attack on the USA which would never be forgotten.

'Are you looking forward to our adventure?' asked Admiral Badr.

'Yes, Mohammed. I am. And may Allah go with us.'

CHAPTER SEVEN

General Ravi headed back to the cold north of Russia in the last week of July, 2007, with no further price upon his head. The twin murders of Alf Rowan, and Rupert Studley-Bryce were never solved in London, indeed the Brits never even admitted to the faintest suspicion that the Member of Parliament had been taken out by a professional. At least, they never admitted anything publicly. Neither, however, did they remove their constant surveillance and permanent phone-tapping at 86, The Bishop's Avenue.

As Admiral Arnold Morgan was often at pains to point out . . . *the Brits talk funny, and because of their weird upbringing, they find it damn near impossible to speak plainly . . . but stupid they ain't. So don't underestimate 'em. Ever.*

In fact MI5 had interviewed Richard and Naz Kerman on eight different occasions in the past twelve months, but the Iranian-born couple had revealed nothing, and flatly denied they had ever laid eyes on their only son, not since he was posted to Israel and then vanished in the Jerusalem Road, Hebron, more than three years ago. MI5 even tried telling the Kermans they *knew,* beyond any doubt, that Ray Kerman had attended Royal Ascot. Richard and Naz said if he did, they never saw him. For the record, MI5 did not believe them.

And there it remained, at a strange and frustrating standstill. Two SAS men murdered in Hebron, two gigantic bank robberies in Jerusalem and Tel Aviv, the incredible liberation of *every* important political prisoner in Israel, and a brutal double murder in London: the same man suspected of committing each and every one of those crimes; the same man everyone knew, but no-one knew.

Lieutenant Jimmy Ramshawe had essentially blown the whistle six times, every time. And everyone believed him, at least everyone who mattered at the National Security Agency in Fort

Meade believed him. And they had relayed their deductions to MI5, and they believed him as well. MI5 were even on close speaking terms with his mom and dad.

But no-one even knew his name. Not now. And no-one ever found him. No-one ever even saw him, except for Alf Rowan. And no-one really knew whether he was dead or alive – which country he was in, which hemisphere he was in. Nor indeed what he might do next. The Mossad offered nothing. Jordan offered nothing. Neither did Iran, Libya nor Saudi Arabia. But they wouldn't, would they? MI5 had even had the Queen's Ascot Representative search the offices in St James's Palace for any badge application for a Major R. Kerman, and of course they drew a blank.

They did find an application for an R. Kerman Esq. from the Syrian Embassy. But the highest possible government authority in Damascus told them it was for a professor of poetry named Dr. Rani Kerman who was writing an ode to Hafez al-Assad. They even enclosed a photograph of the man, and his address and office phone at the university in Damascus. MI5 never even followed up on this exercise in futility. Neither did they wholly believe the Syrians.

Jimmy Ramshawe, on receipt of the information in Fort Meade, summed it up with Australian terseness . . . 'Lying towelhead bastards.' And the fact remained clear in his mind: 'The NSA and MI5 are trying to find a Bloody Phantom. And they know it.'

Which made it all the more astounding, that the Bloody Phantom was right now striding, large as life, across the jetty in the top-secret Russian naval base in Araguba, which stands behind several miles of razor-wire, out on the frozen edge of the universe. He was accompanied by two Admirals, ex-Soviet *Kapitans*, and three commanding officers, one of them the son of the Commander-in-Chief of the Iranian Navy. The Bloody Phantom had just popped in to inspect a $300 million cruise-missile nuclear submarine someone had just bought for him.

Ben Badr, after almost eight months in Araguba, was delighted to see Ravi, and keen to regale him with his expertise on the workings of a nuclear-powered warship. For the journey to Petropavlovsk, along the Siberian coast, Captain Gregor Vanislav would be in command, and Ben would be his number two, the Executive Officer of the Barracuda. Ravi himself would be given no rank during this 4,000-mile voyage of learning. But the next time she sailed, he would be her operations director.

When they boarded the submarine, the entire party headed straight for the torpedo-proof reactor room, constructed on all sides with walls of lead, eight inches thick. This area contains the power-plant of the ship, the impenetrable stainless steel, domed nuclear reactor, its core of U–235 uranium, the business end of a nuclear bomb.

The reactor is the steel heart of the pressurized water system which creates the steam to drive the turbines of the submarine almost endlessly, requiring only water to keep moving along on full power. The pressure inside that system heats the water to a searing 200 degrees centigrade, under a phenomenal 2,500 pounds pressure per square inch. As a point of comparison, we live in fifteen pounds pressure per square inch.

Ben Badr led them immediately to the reactor control room where *Kapitan* Gregor Vanislav awaited them. He was standing quietly behind three watchkeepers, all Petty Officers, who were operating separate panels of keyboard control, each one containing six computer screens. The three areas under such close observation were the propulsion system, the reactor itself, and the auxiliary panel.

One of the screens in this latter group records the tests which reveal the efficiency of the condenser. This is the machinery which turns seawater into fresh water of the purest type, hopefully devoid of every molecule of the dreaded, ultra-corrosive NaCl, sodium chloride. Two parts NaCl per million in the pure water system of a nuclear reactor is two parts too many. Way too many.

And it was this screen to which Gregor Vanislav was turned when Ben Badr led his team into the control room. 'Hello, Gregor,' he said, cheerfully. 'Always checking on our purity, eh? Pristine water to make us run good, the first concern of a nuclear engineer.'

Kapitan Vanislav turned to Ravi and smiled. 'You see, I teach him priorities, months ago. And he never forget. You got a good man here, General. Young Ben Badr. I like him. Make no mistakes, hah? That's the trick, you wanna stay alive.'

'Yes. I've often found that myself,' said Ravi, smiling back. 'But I'm afraid you'll have to be more patient with me. I know very little, and I have to learn fast.'

'Right here's a very good place to start,' replied the Russian Captain. 'These screens show you the quality and temperature of the water flowing into the reactor . . . but I think Ben should be your professor. That way I can listen to him, make sure he's learned everything good.'

Commander Badr nodded, and stepped up to his task. 'Okay Ravi,' he said in English. 'I start by telling you the danger of sodium chloride. It's just salt, of course. Seawater is full of it, and we have to get rid of it because it's probably tbe most corrosive stuff on the planet. You get that stuff in our water system, it seeks out little crevasses, maybe in the joints, or the welding, and it builds up, weakening the steel, until one day, under the terrific pressure, it blows. Blows a damned big hole, and a blast of pressurized scalding water rips out of the fracture into the room, flashes off into wet steam of terrific heat.'

'Christ,' said Ravi.

'You know what happens then?'

'Not really.'

'Well, remember the whole system works on stability . . . inside the nuclear reactor, the core consists of these cleverly shaped and machined slugs of highly active uranium, and in general terms, the neutrons split away, millions of them, and if they were allowed to just get on with it, they'd collide with U235 atoms, hitting and splitting, causing a too–rapid chain reaction, generating colossal heat, until you had, in a very few minutes, a core meltdown . . .

'However, we don't allow this . . .'

'Oh, good,' said Ravi.

'No. We have a system of rods inside the reactor . . . they're made of some stuff called hafnium which absorbs the neutrons, stops the reaction running out of control. So when all these rods are down, deep in the uranium, the activity is negligible. Just a quiet, scarcely active, hunk of machinery.

'Then we want to get going, right? So we begin to "pull the rods" – lifting first one group and then another out of the uranium core. And as we do so the neutrons have more and more freedom to split and cause further fissions. And as this happens, the system gets warmer. But we have total control of the process, and we create the heat precisely as we wish – a self–sustaining critical mass . . .'

'Okay,' said Ravi. 'I'm with you.'

'But remember,' said Ben Badr. 'This is a circuit. The pressurized water is pumped out of the reactor, into a simple steam generator, and this surges off down the pipeline to drive the turbines. The whole thing is just a steam engine. But we control how much steam goes to the turbines, and we control how much turns back into water and surges around the circuit, back into the reactor to begin the process all over again . . . it's called the Carnot Cycle, the difference between water temperature coming *out* of the reactor and going back *into* the reactor . . . this is the power factor driving the ship.'

'When the water flows into the reactor, does it actually touch the uranium?'

'Oh, yes,' replied Ben. 'It flows right over the solid U–235, and the temperature of the water is absolutely critical. If it's a little too cold, the neutrons react, speed up and get hotter. And in my view the really scary thing about a nuclear reactor is that the hotter it gets, the hotter it wants to get.'

'So we get a corrosion leak, like you just said,' asked Ravi. 'And the pressure drops and the water cools, and comes in at too low a temperature, we have big trouble?'

'With a leak like that in the prime circuit, the core loses its water flow, and rapidly starts to overheat.'

'I imagine you have some kind of "fail safe" in there, right?'

'Absolutely. The rods crash straight back in, all of them, immediately reducing the activity of the core. But in a submarine, you have a problem right there. The rods actually stop the reactor. It's called a reactor SCRAM. But at that moment the submarine's power plant is dead. That means we soon have no propulsion, no fresh water plant, no fresh air system, and no heat. Should we be 1,000-feet below the surface this is relatively bad news.'

'There's an emergency system, I suppose?' said Ravi.

'Yes. One to keep the now inactive reactor cool, and a diesel engine, which we immediately fire up, once we get back to periscope-depth or on the surface.'

At this point Captain Vanislav interrupted. 'Remember, General,' he said. 'Ben is speaking to you as a submarine officer, not a scientist. And you don't need to be a scientist to command an SSN. But you do need to *understand* the system, and you need to know what those screens are telling you. But most of all you need the ability to recognize a problem, and to know what action to take. You will have very knowledgeable nuclear engineers down here in this part of the ship. They will keep you well informed. But you must be aware of the potential snags, and how to react to them.'

'Have you taught Ben everything during sea trials?' asked Ravi.

'Oh no. We have a superb simulator on shore, and all of our future submarine officers learn the profession in there. Ben has spent literally weeks in that simulator, just like an airline pilot studying big passenger jets. He's been right through the entire course, from the smallest emergency to core meltdown.'

'I'm not sure I like the sound of that last part,' replied Ravi.

'No,' interjected Captain Vanislav. 'That last part is bad.'

'When does it happen?'

'Tell him, Ben.'

'It is most likely caused by either a leak in the prime circuit, as we mentioned. Or by the sudden arrival in the reactor of very cold water. For whatever reason. If, for instance, there is no returning water, because of a chronic system failure, an emergency valve will open, and seawater will gush in from outside the hull. This is not good, but it's not as bad as no water at all, because no water increases the fission of the neutrons to a very severe degree in about seven seconds. Right then you have the potential for a core meltdown.

'Not a bomb, just uranium getting so hot, it will eventually melt through the stainless steel floor of the reactor, maybe through the deck and then both hulls. But this is rare. Almost unheard of.

'The most common crisis is a slug of cold water surging in through the emergency valve which will trigger increased fission. But it's all a bit slower, in time for the rods to drop, get things back under control. Back to what we call the Negative Temperature Co-Efficient, which means the reactor is self-governing, heating the water right where we want it, self-regulating.'

General Rashood was all business right now, concentrating all of his considerable intellect on the words of Ben Badr. 'Okay,' he said. 'You say self-regulating? What changes? What's getting regulated?'

'Every time we open the throttles on the submarine, we are drawing off power, drawing off the steam, cooling off the returning water, effecting a change in the temperature of the water being received by the reactor.

'Always remember one thing, Ravi . . . the neutron population increases immediately to that cooling water, more fissions occur, more energy is released in the core. That gets transferred to the primary coolant, then to the secondary system. That's the water that boils to steam to drive the turbines. Thus when you draw off more power, the reactor automatically increases its fission rate to provide it.

'Vice versa, it's a similar chain. Reduce power draw-off, increase temperature of water back into the core. Reduce neutron population, reduce fission rate.

'But that doesn't mean we all have a nervous breakdown whenever we speed up. The whole system is very largely self-regulating. Strictly hands-off. We don't do anything; we watch. We watch like fucking arctic eagles for anything that can go wrong . . . that's the engineering officer's task.'

'Ben's a very good student, right?' said Captain Vanislav, chuckling, and adding with a mock serious expression, 'Of course, I had to get him into shape at first. He's a little impatient, sometimes little bit arrogant . . . you know, his daddy's a very big man. But he's very good. He was Russian, I give him command of nuclear ship any time.'

And he placed his arm around the shoulders of Commander Ben Badr, and stated quietly, 'Right now, I can say that in thirty years in the Russian Navy, I never met a better young submarine officer.'

'I'm feeling better about this by the minute,' said Ravi. 'But I have one question . . . what's the range of our power accelerating . . . do we have two pumps, one for each turbine, with, pre-sumably, slow and high speeds?'

'No,' said Ben, quickly. 'We have six pumps. Very powerful. At low speeds we use two of them, working slowly. But we can have six of them, working fast, if we really want to get moving. That's a big power range. This *Barracuda* can make over thirty-five knots under the water. Very hard to catch.'

General Rashood nodded, gazing back to where the watch-keeper was checking the purity of the water. 'That's a key man, right there,' he said distractedly. 'Two particles of sodium chloride per million, and he's searching for them . . .'

'And remember the testing process,' said Ben. 'We take a

sample from the circuits frequently. And even the beaker we use must be surgically clean – in chemical terms, as clean as a hospital operating theatre.'

Ravi Rashood had stood among the supreme professionals of his trade before. But rarely had he experienced such a degree of confidence and efficiency as he sensed in this Barracuda Type 945.

Captain Vanisalav seemed to sense his thoughts. 'We're not supermen, General,' he said. 'But we make fewer mistakes than most people. It goes with the territory. Mistakes down here can mean a very quick, and somewhat unpleasant death. So, we tend not to make them.'

Five days, and more than forty hours intensive study in the simulator, had transformed General Ravi Rashood into a passable, theoretical submarine engineer. And now they were almost ready to go. In wide Kola Sound, downstream from Severomorsk, a small Navy escort out of Murmansk awaited the Barracuda on her final voyage under the command of Russia's Northern Fleet.

One of the latest nuclear submarines, the *Gepard*, a 9,000-ton Akula II, built in Severodvinsk and commissioned in 2004, was on the surface six miles east of the Cypnavolok headland. Two hundred yards off her port bow stood the frigate *Neustrashimy*, a four-year-old guided missile ship with an exceptional 4,500 mile range.

She was a Jastreb–Class Type 1154, larger than the old Krivaks with the same turbine propulsion system as the Udaloys, but, like the Barracuda, she was very expensive. The Russians built only two of them, and then sold the third hull for scrap to pay outstanding debts.

The *Neustrashimy* was commissioned in the Baltic, but moved north a year later. Now she was bound for the Pacific Fleet and almost certainly would not return from Petropavlovsk.

One mile to the east, stark against the bright, low sun, which had only briefly dipped below the horizon all night, was the giant ice-breaker *Ural*. This broad-shouldered, steel-hulled ruffian of the Arctic would lead the way as they moved across the gleaming, but freezing, blue waters of the northern ocean, avoiding or smashing the lingering ice floes, hugging the immense, bleak coastline of Siberia.

Back on the jetties of Araguba, a small crowd had gathered to watch the departure of their former Barracuda–Class submarine, *Tula*. General Ravi and Captain Vanislav stood with a Russian navigation officer on the bridge. Commander Badr, the Executive Officer, was below with the helmsman, another Russian veteran.

Deep in the reactor room, Lt. Commander Ali Akbar Mohtaj had observed the Russian Chief Petty Officer 'pulling the rods', bringing the reactor up to self-sustaining at the correct temperature and pressure. Chief Petty Officers Ali Zahedi and Ardeshir Tikku were positioned at two of the three panels in the reactor control room – Zahedi in propulsion, Tikku in auxiliary. Both men were now experienced in their areas of operation, and in overall command of the control area was the most senior of the Iranian submariners, Lt. Commander Abbas Shafii, who had been in Araguba for more than nine months.

Eight other Iranian Naval staff, four young officers and four seasoned chiefs, were also in the crew, occupying positions of serious responsibility in the turbine room and the air cleansing plant. Two others had understudied the planesman, another worked in the electronics area. He was a Lt. Commander from Tehran, with two excellent degrees in electrical engineering, and three tours of duty in one of the Iranian Kilos.

All of the Iranians were dressed in the uniform of the Peoples' Liberation Army/Navy. And in addition there were fifteen Chinese members of the crew, five officers including a Lt. Commander who had been missile director in a large, absurdly noisy, ICBM submarine out of Shanghai. Four Chiefs and six regular POs made up the number, and they were spread evenly through the ship mingling with the thirty Russians, and two interpreters who would often be working longer days than anyone.

Captain Vanislav called down through the communications system, '*Attend bells!*' And the Chief of Boat ordered the last dock line cast off.

The turbines came to life, and the huge propeller churned the water, as the jet-black hull moved off the jetty, assisted by a tug; first in reverse, then sliding forward, on Vanislav's command, '*Half-ahead.*'

The helmsman settled on to his ordered course north, straight at the Pole, 1,250 miles away. Ravi Rashood, standing on the bridge felt on his face the winds off the Kola Peninsula, which now gusted out of the north-west, from across the vast ice cap which covers the top of the world, 1,800-miles in diameter.

They held course for only one mile as they stood down the outward channel from the sound, running fair through the short sea, to make their rendezvous with the *Gepard* and the *Neustrashiny*, and then falling in behind the mighty *Ural*.

Captain Vanislav called a course change to the north-east . . . *zero-four-two, half-ahead . . . make your speed twelve knots . . .*

Up ahead they could see the colossal outline of the *Ural*, moving forward now, towards the outer edges of the Skolpen Bank, one of the shallow inshore shoals of the Barents Sea, where there's only 200 feet of water.

By 0600, Barracuda 945 was tucked in, 300 yards astern of the ice-breaker, with the frigate steaming on her starboard quarter, 400 yards south of the *Gepard*, which was also on the surface.

Ahead of them stretched 800 miles of deep ocean, all the way to the northern headland of rugged Novaya Zemlya, a 460-miles-long, crescent-shaped island, only fifty-miles wide. It looks like a forgotten extension of the Ural Mountains, which peter out just to the south, on the jagged hills of Vajgac Island. Almost certainly, when the mammoth roamed the tundra, a million years ago, Novaya Zemlya was actually joined to the mainland.

But right now it was not joined to anything, though in winter the pack ice shelf sweeps right down to its seaward shores, but the North Cape Stream just manages to keep the tides flowing to the south.

Captain Vanislav's 200-mile-a-day journey passed without incident until they came towards a ten-mile-long ice-field still floating, months after it had broken off the Arctic cap. The *Ural's* ops room judged it still to be three to four feet thick, 100 miles east of Novaya island.

Ravi and Ben both watched from the bridge as the ice-breaker headed straight for the outer edge of the ice floe, and then drove right up onto the floating skating rink. Her reinforced bow rode up, almost 100 feet beyond the water, and suddenly there was an almighty, echoing crack in the clear silent air, and then another, then six more, as the ice split asunder, forward and sideways, crushed beneath 23,500 tons of solid steel.

And into this newly-created bay, the *Ural* drove forward, until she reached the end, and once more forced her way up onto the ice, her twin propellers ramming the stern forward another 100 feet. And again there was the thunderous crack as a zillion tons of four-foot thick ice split in half, causing a rift almost a quarter of a mile long.

'Christ,' said Ravi Rashood, staring in amazement at the sheer brute power of the *Ural*. 'One more of those and we're through.' He picked up his binoculars and stared ahead. The ice-breaker seemed to be steaming through a bay now, with the floes splitting off on all sides.

He watched fascinated, as the *Ural* repeated her crushing assault on the remainder of the ice field, pulverizing the last couple of hundred yards seemingly without breaking stride, ramming the baby icebergs aside with that iron-fisted bow; cleaving the way for the Barracuda and her consorts to reach the East Siberian Sea and on to the Bering Strait.

Clear of the ice pack, they rounded the seaward headland of Novaya Zemlya. Right here they were due north of the estuary of Russia's longest river, the 3,362 miles River Ob, which rises in the hilly borders of Mongolia, and then flows north right across the Siberian Plateau, east of the Urals, under the Trans-Siberian railroad bridge, and on into the icy depths of its fifty-mile-long hook-shaped estuary, twenty miles wide, all the way.

The end of Novaya Zemlya signals the end of the Barents Sea, and now they entered the Kara Sea which stretches another 500 miles into the Severnaya Island group, two days away. There were no more ice floes, but well-charted shoals along the Central Kara Rise kept them well south, inshore, leaving the Nordenshel'da Archipelago to starboard as they made their easterly swerve through the narrow Strait of Vil'kitskogo, south of the Severnayas.

Which was where US Surveillance first saw them clearly on photographs taken by 'Big Bird,' as it passed silently overhead.

0700 Thursday, August 9, 2007
National Security Agency
Fort Meade, Maryland
Lieutenant Ramshawe liked satellite photographs. However samey, however grainy, however routine they were, he looked forward to keying in through his computer to Intelink, the National Reconnaisance Office's private internet system of secure and encrypted cable networks. Jimmy could pick up surveillance

photographs taken from anywhere in the world on the NRO-built constellation of satellites which endlessly circled the globe.

He always scrolled down to find anything of interest in the China Seas, and habitually had a look in the Bering Strait and along the Kamchatka Peninsula where the big Russian Pacific Fleet operates. He rarely, if ever found anything worth researching, but that never stopped him looking. Ramshawe was one of the most natural-born Intelligence Officers ever.

In summertime he always checked out any Naval activity in the seas to the east of the Severnayas. Up to that point the ocean was essentially Russian. They patrolled it, ran navy exercises, and tested ships all along that coastline from way back in Murmansk for more than 1,000 miles to the east of the Kola Peninsula.

Sometimes there were halfway interesting pictures, perhaps showing a new Russian warship, but mostly Jimmy found himself looking at the routine functions of a near moribund Navy. East of the Severnayas, however, was the place to spot fleet transfers, and it was important that the USA knew precisely where big Russian warships were stationed. Essential in fact.

And today Jimmy was taking serious note of a four-ship convoy pushing along the north coast of Siberia. He zeroed in close, and then pulled right back. 'Shit,' he muttered. 'That Siberia's a bloody big place. Gotta be the biggest place in the world.'

He was right, too. Siberia represents one-twelfth of the entire land mass of the planet earth. It might be cold, and it might be lonely, and it might have a somewhat chilling history. But small it's not.

And Jimmy stared hard at the three ships, pulling up a square overlay which would tell him the identities of the four Russian ships moving east from the Barents to the Bering.

'Here we go,' he said to himself, as the insert caption box flashed up onto his screeen ... *One good-sized frigate, the* Neustrashimy. *9,000 tonner, guided missiles . . . one bloody great ice-breaker . . . this big bastard out in front, right? One Akula II nuclear submarine. One Sierra Type nuclear submarine, believed to be one of two Barracuda-Class ships. Hunter-killers. Type 945 . . . All on the surface . . . nothing secret . . .routine summertime fleet transfer, Northern Fleet to PacFleet. No problem.*

The Lieutenant knew about Russian Akulas. and he knew about Sierras. Barracudas were a mystery. With only one operational, there was really only one Type 945 ever seen in open water. And for the past five years, the entire term of Jimmy Ramshawe's service in Fort Meade, the ship had only been out a half-dozen times, so expensive was she to run.

He keyed in one of his most highly-classified CD-Rom pages, and pulled up the details, noting the high speed and deep diving depth of the Russian's most pricey attack submarine, first-in-class, named the *Tula*. He also noted they were planning, in a half-hearted way, to fit her with cruise missiles with a 1,600-mile range. But apparently not for another year.

He pulled up the picture and looked at the shot of her, running through cold, calm seas, a clear white bow wave breaking up over her deck and splitting at the sail, to form two swirling vortices on both sides of the hull.

'Looks like a bloody dangerous piece of work to me,' he muttered. 'Wonder where they keep the other bugger.'

He scrolled back the page to the operational section, and noted there was some doubt whether the second hull was ever completed. If it wasn't, he read, it's probably in the Northern Base at Araguba, possibly in a covered dock. *If it did get as far as sea trials, we never saw it.*

'Funny name, Barracuda, for a bloody Russian,' he said to his empty office. 'That's a big, vicious warm water fish, never found far beyond the tropics. I've seen a picture of my dad catching one in the Caribbean. Barracuda? Up there in the arse end of nowhere, north of the bloody Tundra, inside the Arctic Circle. Doesn't make bloody sense. It's like the Jamaican Navy calling their bloody ships 'walrus' or 'polar bear'. Like Nelson Mandela being elected President of Iceland.

'Where's the national identity? Silly bastards. There's never been a bloody barracuda within a thousand miles of Russia. Ought to be Sturgeon-Class, or Killer Whale. Or Sea Lion. Fancy having your best attack submarine, in ice-bound Arctic waters, named after an overgrown tropical goldfish.'

He wandered out to find a cup of coffee, and then wandered back, still wondering about the Barracuda. 'I think I'm right,' he said. 'Don't wanna clobber the old Ruskies for nothing, though. I'd better check it out . . .'

He hit the keys, pulling up barracuda, the fish not the warship. He slipped the 'mouse' onto game fish. Then he found *Gamefish of North America* written by the greatest writer about fishing there's ever been, A.J. McClane, author of the *Encyclopedia of World's Fishing.*

'Here we go,' he said. 'Page 240. There's a whole section on 'em, right before the bloody sharks.'

He scanned the pages and swiftly found out he was right. Barracudas do not venture into cold water, and the illustrations were beautiful. He decided to read a little from the opening paragraph, and found out that this fish has a diabolical set of teeth, two lines of razor sharp nashers, and, wrote A.J., the *disposition of a cornered wolf . . . its bite can be poison . . . the mere sight of it . . . can nearly induce cardiac arrest.*

And so, indeed, could the subtle prose of Mr McClane. Almost. Because the next paragraph, right there on page 240, halfway down the text, contained the sentence . . . *yet in shallow water, old razormouth has the speed of a rocket.* And that very nearly did send the young Intelligence Officer directly into cardiac arrest.

Old Razormouth! When did he last hear that? Jimmy's mind raced, but his heart stopped. It always did when he thought he was on to something. He took a deep slug of coffee, and exited the barracuda section of *Game Fish.* He hit the keys for his secret file, logged into the index.

Christ! It was nearly a year ago. September 2006.

Here we are . . . OLD RAZORMOUTH 600 AFFIRMATIVE. Signal sucked off the Chinese Navy satellite – original source: US SIGINT listening station in the underground bunker at Kunia, Hawaii. Rock solid.

Lieutenant Ramshawe considered the unlikely possibility that some Chinese admiral had landed 600 barracudas, as forecast. *Six hundred. Affirmative.* That last word implied a clear suggestion that the subject had been mentioned before. Otherwise, thought Jimmy, old Admiral Tai Mai Hook would have sent a signal that read: 'Holy shit! I've just caught half the world's population of barracudas.'

No. *Affirmative* meant something which had been expected. Or half expected. And it was not a netful of fish. Old Razormouth, the barracuda, on a Navy satellite had to be code for Russia's most dangerous attack submarine. But what about *600*? The Russians only have one operational. *I suppose the number could refer to anything – depth beneath the surface . . . hours running time . . . a radio band . . . stockpiles of torpedoes . . . miles from home* base . . . missile range . . . or even dollars . . . maybe the Chinese have bought the bloody thing.

Lt. Ramshawe decided he had better things to do than try to connect a year-old, four-word Chinese satellite signal with a perfectly innocent-looking Russian Naval Fleet Transfer along the Siberian coast.

'Nonetheless,' he muttered. 'I'll be keeping a weather eye on those four little bastards creeping through the frosties. 'Specially Old Razormouth.'

August 14. 73N 138E.
South of the New Siberian Islands
They were at the eastern end of the Laptev Sea now, still hugging the coast, having already passed the 5,600-square-mile delta of the River Lena, which, like the Ob, flows clean across Siberia from the center of Asia. Ahead of them was the fifty-mile-wide strait between the northern headland and the southernmost island, the gateway to the East Siberian Sea.

Out in the lead, the *Ural* was still making on average 200 miles a day. Both submarines remained on the surface holding a regular speed of nine knots, a constant watch kept from the bridge for smaller ice floes which could damage a submarine, if hit hard enough, head on. The fact that it was only dark for an hour each day made this task somewhat easier.

Ravi Rashood had spent much of his time with the commanding officer and Ben Badr. But he had served regular four-hour watches in the navigation area, the sonar room, and the radar room. He joined the two other Iranian officers, plus an interpreter, talking with the planesmen. And he spent two entire days with Chief Petty Officer Ali Zahedi in the propulsion area. This coupled with a day in the reactor room with Lt Commander Mohtaj gave General Rashood a hard grounding in the way a nuclear submarine moves through the oceans.

He knew the screens to watch, the dials to check, the location of the electronic circuits and their breakers. He was now well-versed in all emergency procedures, and he used all of his spare time talking with Ben Badr. In this particular nuclear submarine, dealing with any kind of problem, any possible kind of hitch or failure, there was an excellent chance that these two disparate military characters, from opposite cultures, religions and upbringing, would arrive at the correct solution.

All that remained for both of them to study was a crash–course in firing procedures for the big RADUGA cruise. Commander Badr was probably 50 percent proficient. Another Lt Commander from Bandar Abbas had been working almost exclusively for nine months right through the system's overhaul in Araguba. And an outstanding CPO from Ravi's home province of Kerman had completed a degree course, with an interpreter, in cruise missile technology and guidance systems.

Ravi had some catching up to do. And he would spend much of the Fall in Petropavlovsk attaining the level of mastery in the subject any submarine commander must have.

Meanwhile they pushed on through the southern strait of the New Siberian Islands, and the wind began to back around to the south, bringing a soft warmth to the air. There were few discernible signs left of the terrible Siberian winter, but snow still marked the dark and distant summer shores of Russia's vast, sleeping land.

It was a 1,000–mile five–day run down to the Chukchi Sea and then into the Bering Strait where the little convoy would steam within a half–mile of United States waters. All the way down to the Strait, they would hug the inshore waters, and Captain Vanislav ordered the required course change to east–south–east as they entered the East Siberian Sea, right in the wake of the *Ural*. He called the swing to starboard – *Conn-Captain . . . steer one-one-two . . . advise Ural immediately.*

Still running through smooth water, they pushed ever more southwards, away from the deep thrust of the permanent ice field which lurked back over the port side horizon, flat lethal solid all the way from the North Pole and at this point within 100 miles of the Siberian coast.

However it had been a mild summer in this northeasterly corner of Russia and their passage was relatively simple. They saw no ice floes, and they kept the speed down to nine knots, night and day, cleaving through the dark blue waters watching the surface up ahead.

And all this time, the Iranians became more and more efficient. General Rashood himself was not, of course, ready to take command of the ship in the high-tech manner of a seasoned nuclear captain. But Commander Badr most certainly was, and he was building an extremely capable afterguard to sail with him. General Rashood had already shown himself to be the ideal

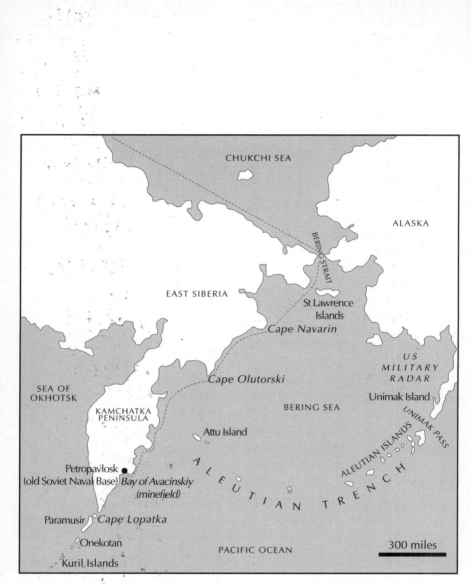

CHUKCHI SEA

ALASKA

BERING STRAIT

EAST SIBERIA

St Lawrence
Islands

Cape Navarin

Cape Olutorski

US
MILITARY
RADAR

SEA OF
OKHOTSK

KAMCHATKA
PENINSULA

BERING SEA

Unimak Island

UNIMAK PASS

Attu Island

ALEUTIAN ISLANDS

A L E U T I A N   T R E N C H

Petropavlosk
(old Soviet Naval Base) *Bay of Avacinskiy*
(minefield)

Paramusir *Cape Lopatka*

Onekotan

Kuril Islands

PACIFIC OCEAN

300 miles

THE BARRACUDA'S LONG VOYAGE AROUND SIBERIA - TO THE EAST LIES ALASKA

Special Ops Commander, and the long days of study in the submarine meant he was well able to conduct any mission he wished, with this ship's company, and, particularly, in this ship.

If Commander Badr had dropped dead, General Rashood, with his Iranian officers and crew could have successfully avoided capture, and brought the ship home. There was no doubt in anyone's mind, that this SAS-trained officer, was a man they could follow to gain any objective. Even without Ben Badr, Ravi could probably manage. With Ben Badr they would form a competent combination.

The five-day run down to the headland of Cape Uelen which guards the Russian side of the Strait was completed in solitude. They passed the high cliffs and the little trading post on the Dezhneva Peninsula sighted about twenty-five miles inshore, and in the distance they did see some local activity, small fishing boats and a barge. But they never saw an ocean-going ship from anyone's navy, and the only eyes watching them belonged to faraway Jimmy Ramshawe, who was checking out the satellite shots every couple of days from 7,000 miles away, still wondering why the hell Old Razormouth was any concern of the Chinese.

They steamed out of the Chukchi Sea and into the Bering Strait in a cold gusting wind, right on the Arctic Circle. The seas were getting up now, the temperature had returned to zero, and long Pacific swells caused the Barracuda to ride up slowly and then pitch into the trough. Captain Vanislav ordered them to periscope depth, which made the journey a little more comfortable, but not much. He would have preferred to take her down 100 feet out of the weather, but the waters of the Strait are notoriously shallow and, all submarine captains believe, badly charted.

And so they just pushed on, with snow dusting the surface, and the swells still making the big underwater ship rise and fall. Captain Vanislav ordered a course change to the south-west right off Lavrentiya Point, straight along the dividing line in the ocean which separates Russia from the USA, west of St. Lawrence Island, forty miles off the most easterly stretch of Siberian coast. Where the Barracuda ran, it was around 0200 on Tuesday, August 21. Three miles to port, across the international dateline, it was still Monday, same time. Ramshawe was looking at photographs before they were taken. In a way.

Ravi continued his studies, spending time in the reactor

control room, and especially with the sonar officer, an English-speaking Chinese officer, who had worked on the PLAN's Kilo program. Ravi had a natural affinity for the precise yet creative thinking required in the sonar room, and this was also true of Ben Badr. As always they had much to discuss.

They pushed on across the 300-mile-wide entrance to the Anadyrskiy Sea, with its steep gray cliffs and circular summer currents. The tides were still flowing here in late August, but in a few short months these northern parts of the Bering Sea would freeze over completely.

Two days later, they began the long voyage down the Koryakskoye Nagorye, a wild, desolate Eastern Siberian landscape, containing a vast mountain range stretching for 500 miles, north to south: great snow-capped peaks visible from the ocean, sheer rockfaces reaching right down to the sea. With the weather still rough, the ship's company in the Barracuda could of course see nothing, and for three more days, they never saw daylight, as they ran south at periscope depth, along one of the most remote coastlines in the world.

Eventually the land begins to narrow and at the Gulf of Karaginskij it develops into a thin isthmus, which joins to the Siberian mainland the 500-mile-long, shillelagh-shaped Kamchatka Peninsula. The mountains go straight through the isthmus and cleave through the center of the peninsula, Russia's Rocky Mountains. Their most spectacular peak is the volcano Kljucevskaya Sopka, at 15,500 feet, the highest mountain in Siberia, fifty miles inland, and 120 miles north of Petropavlovsk.

The Barracuda, miraculously in the mind of the ex-Kilo officer Ben Badr, did not have to refuel. But they made two very slow stops, once while the frigate escort took on more diesel from a Russian Naval oiler in a sheltered bay behind the jutting headland of Cape Kamchatka, and once while the CO of the escorting submarine checked a leaky seal in another bay near the mountain. Both ships could have made it to Petropavlovsk, but warship COs dislike running on empty, and submarine COs are generally allergic to shipping water unless it is unavoidable during a fast getaway from an ops area.

On the first day of September, they left the two-mile-wide south-running shipping lane and made a rendezvous with the Russian Navy pilot sent out to meet them. Because an extensive minefield lies right across the entrance to the wide bay of

Avacinskiy, extending ten miles seaward, fishing and anchoring here are banned. No ship is permitted to enter the bay, because beyond its entrance lies one of the most secretive naval seaways in the world, Russia's forbidden dockyard, classified, ringed with steel, the port of Pretropavlovsk, still harboring the mentality of the Cold War, the glowering, eastern outpost of the old, Soviet Pacific Fleet.

They made their right-hand turn around steep Majacny Head, and turned into the narrows, heading north up the bay, directly to a covered dock, where a shore crew awaited them, maneuvering the Barracuda into position away from the seeing-eye of the US satellites. Lieutenant Ramshawe would see the submarine head into the Base, from the open ocean. But he would not be able to observe it further, at least not until it broke cover and headed back out into deep water.

Ahead of the Sino-Iranian crew lay a program of intensive missile testing, mainly concerning the computerized direction-finder in the head of the weapon. The RADUGA was essentially a 'fire-and-forget' type; launched while the ship was submerged, and then left to find its own way to its target, relying totally on the pre-programmed route, punched into its electronic 'brain'. This enables it to fly at Mach 0.7, almost 500 m.p.h., or around eight miles per minute, one mile every seven and a half seconds.

Even if you saw it, ripping through the skies, 200 feet above your head, there would not be a whole lot you could do about it. Even if you had some kind of an anti-missile device. This Russian-built heavy steel road-runner of the skies can outthink you, and then outrun anything you throw at it. Unless of course you catch it head-on, long before it reaches you. And that's very nearly impossible with a submarine launch from below the surface. The surprise is too radical.

General Rashood disembarked a much wiser, better-educated submarine officer. He was to spend two more days here, and then fly out direct from the military airfield east of Petropavlovsk, in company with Ben Badr – first stop Shanghai, then commercial jet direct to Tehran where Shakira would meet him.

In the coming months Ravi would work on his plan in solitude in Damascus, with occasional visits from Commander Badr. They would study the most detailed charts of Alaska and the safest routes to get there. They would study the new US oil pipeline which runs mostly underwater from the brand new

Alaskan refinery, all the way down the American west coast. And they would study the grid of electrical power stations which are spread throughout California, especially the ones which faced the Pacific Ocean.

And during these months there would be much wry laughter. In the old days, when the USA relied totally on Arab oil, such a strike would have been impossible because it would have hurt too many of their own people. But the US was beginning to use its own supplies, for the first time, and since China had entered the picture as a new player, and become, in many ways, a savior of the Arab economy, there were undoubtedly more adventurous possibilities.

Ravi and Ben had no intention of ever being wanted in the way Osama Bin Laden had been. They had no intention of killing or injuring the US population. Their aim was simple – havoc, pandemonium, the great superpower humiliated, like a Third World country, right in front of the entire world. Commander Badr and his father loved it. Shakira, too, thought it was going to be superb. So indeed did Ravi. There was one terrible unspoken fear in his mind. And it stemmed from that Friday morning in London, over a year ago, June, 2006 – when the Syrian assassin had been unable to put a bullet through the head of Arnold Morgan.

Aside from that, his considered opinion was that the Barracuda could not, would not, be stopped from its appointed task. And no-one would ever know who had perpetrated a crime on this scale. He smiled often at the thought of a bewildered White House, and a baffled Pentagon. But it was always tempered by a slight fear of the terrible Admiral who sat at the President's right hand.

By September 8, Captain Vanislav, plus the nucleus of the Barracuda's crew, including all of the Iranian officers and men, and all of the Chinese crew had flown back to Severomorsk. And there they settled into a truly clandestine operation, the sea trials of the second Barracuda, hull K-240, conducted in the submarine roads beyond the Gulf of Kolskiy.

The schedule required them to exit the submarine docks before the US satellite pass at 1100 each morning. By that time it would need to be submerged, working out beyond the Skolpen Bank, in 600 feet of water. This particular ship, while identical in every way to the hull now under cover in Petropavlovsk, had not been completed until late June, and was still having a few wrinkles ironed out, especially in her sonar systems. But her reactor, fitted out in the excellent nuclear engineering plant at Severodvinsk, ran sweetly. The most difficult part was to make absolutely certain no-one ever knew she existed.

Every day she was pulled from her covered dock in Araguba by two tugs, then sent on her way out to sea, at least one hour before America's silent 'Big Bird' came drifting past, 22,000 miles overhead in space, probing, photographing, checking, making absolutely certain that nothing on the planet earth moved or changed direction without the express, incontrovertible knowledge of the National Security Agency in Fort Meade, Maryland.

Once clear of the shallows, Barracuda II dived out of sight at the earliest possible moment. Captain Vanislav was still in overall command, and he had essentially the same team with him as that which took Barracuda I through the Arctic seas to the Kamchatka Peninsula. But only Iran's torpedo and missile crews remained in Petropavlovsk. The men from the desert who now made the ship run, and listened to the echoing caverns of the deep, were all busy in Russia's cold north.

Returning the Barracuda to the dockyard after two or three days at sea was a rather simpler process. The United States surveillance program required one look every day at submarine movements in the Barents Sea. In truth these movements were irregular these days, owing to the monstrous shortage of money. But it was safe for Barracuda II to go home in the evening, lethal for them not to be clear of the land and underwater by 1030 hours.

Ravi and Ben had drawn up a schedule for more and more Iranians to be indoctrinated into the nuclear submarine program. Twelve at a time, they flew to Petropavlovsk from Bandar Abbas, for their initial instruction. Then, after four weeks, they flew on to Severodvinsk to join the sea trials of the second Barracuda. In that way, Iran was able to send twelve men back to Petropavlovsk, and they slowly built two crews which with some assistance could operate either of their new Barracudas.

It was a masterpiece of organization, conducted with speed and thoroughness. Inside a very few months, Iran had become a dangerous nuclear submarine power; prepared to make *two* major journeys, which would absolutely bedevil the West, in underwater warships *no-one* even knew they owned.

By late January 2008, Barracuda II was ready to make the first of these journeys, its maiden voyage, from Araguba, west into the Atlantic. Three weeks later, Barracuda I would leave from Petropavlovsk, past the minefield and into the Pacific.

US surveillance would see only one of them leave, because General Rashood wanted one of them to be seen. One would move slowly and secretly, under the command of newly-promoted Captain Ali Akbar Mohtaj. The other, under the command of the senior military leader of HAMAS, would make rather better time.

The most confusing aspect of all, from faraway Jimmy Ramshawe's point of view, was that he only knew of the existence of one of the two ships. And anyway, both were in Russian ports where they belonged. The only, tiny glitch in the armor of the Sino-Iranians was Ramshawe's slender grasp of a connection between China and Old Razormouth. And if he added up his total knowledge on that subject, on a scale of 1 to 100 it would have trouble making it onto the chart.

And on Thursday morning, January 31, 2008, in the Arctic darkness, around 0500, Barracuda II slipped her moorings and ran swiftly down the bay towards the open wastes of the Barents Sea. She turned due north, and dived in 135 fathoms of water. Her crew would not see daylight again for six weeks, as she crept around the globe, striving twenty-four hours a day to remain unseen, undetected and ultimately without naval identity.

The first part of the journey was unquestionably the most difficult. Four hundred feet beneath the surface Captain Mohtaj ran slowly towards one of the most sensitive submarine hunting grounds in all of the earth's oceans – the GRIUK Gap, the narrowest part of the North Atlantic. A straight line on a chart with a ruler will demonstrate the precise dimension – start at a point 69.00N 35.20W on the craggy ice-shores of Greenland, ninety miles south of Scoresby Sound. Come south–south-east for 250 miles, crossing the Arctic Circle, across the half-frozen Denmark Strait to the northern shore of Iceland at Husavik. Cross the island, and then continue your line SSE to the northern coast of Scotland, a distance of 450 miles.

The last section is the business end of the Greenland–Iceland–UK Gap, in navy parlance, the GRIUK, the seaway through which every Russian submarine, for the duration of the entire Cold War, had to pass. Still is. Ships tend to avoid the Denmark

Strait because of its weather, its ice floes and its terrible reputation. Anytime you're looking for submarines, Russian, British, or American, steer into the eastern section of the GRIUK, between Iceland and Scotland, take care over the Iceland-Faeroe Islands Rise, where the ocean is a little shallow, and routinely respected by all submarines.

All around this Rise is the domain of the sinister, black, underwater killers; prowling, slowly, silently on their softly-humming nuclear reactors. And it was to these waters that the rookie Iranian nuclear Commanding Officer Captain Mohtaj was headed in his brand new Barracuda II, running the gauntlet through the submarine patrols of the Royal Navy and the US Navy, and above all trying not to set off the hair-trigger alarms of America's ultra-secret Sound Surveillance System.

SOSUS is the US Navy's fixed undersea acoustic network of passive hydrophone arrays, sensitive listening equipment connected to operational shore-sites which collect, analyze, display and report acoustic data, relayed back from the strings of hydrophones laid in the deep sound channels.

They are installed in all of the key areas of the Pacific and North Atlantic, criss-crossed over the sea-bed. And boy! Are they hot and heavy in the GRIUK Gap . . . you know what they say . . . *if a whale farts in the GRIUK, seventeen shore-based American technicians die happily of sheer excitement.*

You can imagine what happens when SOSUS picks up the steady engine lines of a possibly hostile submarine.

Captain Mohtaj was treading on eggshells.

And he cut the speed of the Barracuda as they came deep, through the icy waters of coastal Norway, a country which claims the entire northern swathe of the continent of Europe – right around Finland, Sweden and Lapland, up to the Russian border. Those Norsemen of old were the masters of these Arctic waters. They owned and controlled the Atlantic coastline from the city of Stavanger in the south to Russia's Kola Peninsula, more than 1,100 miles away, 500 miles up to the Arctic Circle, 600 beyond.

In summer the steep fjords and bays of western Norway and the Islands represent some of the most spectacular cruising waters in the world. Bright, lonely, devastatingly beautiful seascapes, where the summer sun never sets, and the waters are blue, and the people friendly.

Even in late January, the great tidal ocean still flows freely because of the Gulf Stream, and the Barracuda moved slowly past, following the contours of the legendary Lofoten Isles. This windswept 100-mile-long group of islands juts out from the mainland, forcing passing submarines into the 4,000-feet deep waters of the Voring Plateau.

From here it took Captain Mohtaj another ten hours to reach the Arctic Circle, running south–west. The Barracuda's sonar room thought they heard another submarine here, but the acoustics were too distant, too faint.

And it was as well they were, the 8,000-ton Los Angeles Class patrol submarine *USS Cheyenne* would doubtless have been fascinated at an unscheduled Russian nuclear boat, from right off the charts, creeping down the North Atlantic. The Americans might have sunk it, and in any event they would have blown a very loud whistle, summoning ships of the Royal Navy, maybe even an air search, to find out precisely what was going on.

But neither submarine was close enough to make a firm classification. It was judged by both ships to be just another noise in the ocean, probably a passing trawler.

The *Cheyenne* continued its patrol, running north. Captain Mohtaj slowed down some more, to seven knots, and continued south–west. It took him two and a half days to make the next 400 miles, creeping along, still 400 feet beneath truly violent, gale-tossed seas. At 1630 on the afternoon of February 6th they crossed the unseen line in the ocean which told them they were in the GRIUK Gap, moving over the Iceland-Faeroe Rise in a little over 850 feet of water; speed: five knots. Ten degrees west, 61.20N.

They stayed well west of the notorious Bill Bailey Banks, two underwater mountains which rise up to only 250 feet below the surface, and they barely increased speed for another 150 miles until they reached the great abyss of the Iceland Basin, where the Atlantic suddenly shelves down to a depth of nearly two miles.

Captain Mohtaj knew this was time he must go slower, because SOSUS is always watching in deep water. He felt vulnerable in these cavernous depths, but he risked a little more speed, asking the Barracuda's turbines for nine knots, and making a course change . . . *come left* . . . *steer one-eight-zero*.

The Barracuda maintained speed for the next four hours, then made a swing towards the Rockall Trough, 100 miles west of the Irish coast, bang over the tremblingly-sensitive American hydrophones. SOSUS picked them up, no ifs, ands, or buts.

Cocooned inside the brutishly classified US listening station on the windswept granite shores of Pembrokeshire in South Wales, staring out across the gray and choppy Irish Sea, two US operators had picked up the Barracuda simultaneously and had been listening for twenty minutes.

'*Submarine, sir. It's Russian. I'm checking, but right here I've got initial classification, a Russian nuclear. Probability area large.*'

'*Degree of certainty on that classification?*'

'*Thirty percent, sir. Still checking . . .*'

Back in the Russian ship, there had been a problem. And right now the Chief Engineer was in the process of having a heart attack, having just found a toolbox carelessly leaned against the side of one of the turbo alternators and left there for the biggest part of three hours. It was rattling quite sufficiently to cause a serious 'noise-shout', and the Chief was raging around the engine room deck trying to find the culprit.

'Jesus Christ!' he ranted, siezing the tool box. 'This is fucking unbelievable.' He stopped the rattle instantly, and he was very quick, but not quite quick enough. The Americans had not only picked up the 'shout' of the toolbox, but SOSUS had already given the heads-up.

Back in Pembrokeshire, the operator knew his quarry had gone suddenly quiet, but he did not know why. '*Contact disappeared, sir. Still checking. It looks like a Russian turbo alternator at fifty-hertz, not sixty like ours.*'

'*How big's the probability area?*'

'*We're looking at a square, ten-miles-by-ten-miles.*'

'*Nearest US submarine?*'

'*The* Cheyenne's *last-known eighty-miles east of Iceland, about six-fifty-miles north of the datum. Almost twenty-four hours away.*'

'*Contact regained?*'

'*Nossir. Nothing. I guess she must have shut it down.*'

Both men knew that was much, much worse than simply hearing her again. Because it meant the Russian was being deliberately clandestine, evasive. And there was no reason for that. The Cold War was long over. Russia was not normally perceived as a threat. She had every right to be running a patrol down the middle of the North Atlantic, as did the Americans.

She could have been training crew, testing systems on a long-distance run. She could even have turned around and headed home. Maybe SOSUS had just picked up acceleration noise as she made her turn. But, if she had been going home, why was she not making proper speed north? And how come *Cheyenne* had not heard anything as she came south?

Submarines traditionally pose a lot of questions. But the US Navy Lieutenant Commander in Pembrokeshire did not like his information so far, and he drafted an immediate signal to Fort Meade:

Pembroke Facility picked up a twenty-minute contact on very quiet vessel 071935FEB08. Insufficient data for certain classification – fifty-hertz line, indicating Soviet turbo-alternator. Abrupt stop. Possibly submarine. Nothing on Russian networks correlates . . . 100 square-mile probability area, checking longitude 15.00W, south end of Rockall Trough, off Irish coast.

The Navy's Atlantic desk in the National Surveillance Office drafted a request to Moscow to clarify the situation. But two days later, there had been no reply, neither had anyone heard a squeak from the Barracuda, which was creeping south at low speeds, tiptoeing over the SOSUS undersea wires. Not quite undetected, but almost.

It was February 8, a Friday afternoon, when Lieutenant Ramshawe took an hour off and scrolled through the pages on the NSA internet system. He'd been looking and reading absent-mindedly for more than forty-five minutes when he caught the word submarine in a transmitted message.

˘˘˘˘his brief acquaintance with Admirals Morgan and Morris had taught him one thing, if nothing else – *you see the word submarine, you drop everything and find out what the hell's going on . . .* to quote Admiral Arnie, as Jimmy was prone to call him in unguarded moments . . . *these are sneaky, dangerous little sonsobitches. Anytime, anywhere you discover one of 'em skulking around, without an excuse the size of the Grand Canyon, you will check, check and then check some more.*

Right now Jimmy was checking some more. He understood the signal. A couple of days ago, Wednesday evening, one of the guys in a SOSUS listening station on the other side of the ocean had picked up a Russian nuclear submarine running quietly down the Atlantic west of Ireland.

He downloaded the signal immediately, then logged into his Classified Intelligence CD-Rom and turned to the section on Russia. He pressed 'search' and scanned for the fifty-hertz line, which in turn revealed the Sierra I list. It seemed these old Soviet warhorses had at last been phased out with the old 'Alfa' class. But the American did find a couple of Sierra II's, Kondor Class Type 945A's based in the North Fleet at Araguba. There were no Sierra I's.

So he hit 'search' again, looking for any and all Sierras still floating. And he came up with just one, a ship called the *Tula*, stationed in Araguba, Hull 239, a Sierra I, Barracuda Class, Type 945.

'*It's fucking Razormouth! H-o-o-o-o-l-y shit!*' he yelled to his empty office.

And then, 'No. Wait a minute. It can't be. Razormouth's in Petropavlovsk. I checked it in myself, straight into a covered dock, beginning of last September . . . lemme see . . . hold hard . . . yeah . . . here we go . . . sighted it eight times since then, making short patrols. Probably sea trials. It's always back in the evening, because we always catch it at the same time. Last sighting . . . February 3rd.'

Lieutenant Ramshawe knew beyond any doubt that whatever the guys in Pembrokeshire heard, it was *not*, repeat *not*, the Barracuda, Hull number 239. Because there was no way that ship could have got within 10,000 miles of the west coast of Ireland in three days.

'Mind you,' he told himself. 'They never said it did. They just said they picked up some lines. I suppose they could have hauled a second Barracuda out of mothballs, if they've got one. But Jesus . . . the west coast of Ireland is a bloody long way from home, for an old ship that's been out of service for several years. Beats the shit out of me.'

Nonetheless. Jimmy Ramshawe was left with a puzzle. And if Admiral Arnie found out there was a rogue Russian submarine running loose in the Atlantic and no-one knew anything about it, there'd be hell to pay. He requested a copy of the last signal asking the Russians for an explanation, found it, noted Moscow still had not replied.

Then he sent a message to Admiral George Morris suggesting they send another, this time personally to the Commander-in-Chief, the Admiral of the Fleet Vitaly Rankov.

George Morris knew this ex-Soviet battle cruiser commander was a former Intelligence Officer and a friend of Arnold Morgan. He also knew that if Rankov did not reply to a communique from Washington, Admiral Morgan would be on the telephone to him. He expected that Admiral Rankov would not view that possibility with much enthusiasm, and would probably reply soonest. He told Ramshawe to re-send the signal to Moscow.

It took two more days for the giant ex-Soviet Olympic oarsman to send an answer, personal to Admiral Morris, who sensed it was carefully worded, in the extreme:

111200FEB08. The Russian Navy currently has no patrols in that part of the Atlantic. We have only the two Kondors moored alongside in the Northern Fleet. And one Barracuda Class conducting trials out of Petropavlovsk. Your operators could be mistaken. I am told there is sometimes a similarity between our boats and the new French nuclear SSN which is replacing their old Rubis Class. It's not yet named, but it is working in the Atlantic out of Toulon. The French refer to that program as Project Barracuda. Sorry can be no more help. Rankov (C-in-C).

Admiral Morris called Lieutenant Ramshawe into his office to examine the reply. And they both came to the same conclusion. It did not state flatly there was no Russian-built submarine there. Only that they were not patrolling that part of the Atlantic. Which was slightly different. But the reply had been sufficiently friendly, and sufficiently helpful to make another communique seem rude, unnecessary and undiplomatic. Admiral Morris would have to let the matter rest. As Vitaly Rankov knew he would. He was of course keenly aware of the 600 million reasons he had for remaining very discreet about Chinese activities.

Jimmy Ramshawe left the Director's office muttering, 'From what I can see, there's bloody Barracudas all over the place – but at least the French have warm water.' He returned to his own office, concerned that there was no further information they could present to the President's National Security Advisor, no hard-copy whatsoever on the identity of the disappearing submarine. Jimmy was frowning when he entered Admiral Rankov's message into his mystery file. Right next to Old Razormouth.

And the following evening, February 12, 2,500 miles away, right off the Portuguese Azores, clear now of the North Atlantic SOSUS traps, Captain Mohtaj ordered an increase in speed. He was headed for lonely waters now, down the coast of Africa, which the US Navy regards as largely irrelevant.

The water was at least two miles deep all the way to the Cape of Good Hope, 4,700 miles away. For the first time the Barracuda was in near-deserted waters, but Captain Mohtaj's propulsion team only marginally opened the throttles of the 47,000-horsepower GT3A turbine.

The nuclear reactor responded with a little increased steam. *'Make your speed eight,'* called the CO. *'Depth five hundred. Keep steering one-eight-zero.'*

Old Razormouth II was on her way, at nearly 200 miles a day. And no-one in the Western world had the slightest idea where she was, even *whether* she was. And certainly not where she was going.

CHAPTER EIGHT

Shakira Sabah, at the age of twenty-seven, married the former Major Raymond Kerman in a Muslim ceremony in their Damascus home on Sharia Bab Touma in early November, 2007. The marriage was conducted by a local law officer, and because of the groom's lack of family, indeed any relatives, they were obliged to dispense with most of the traditional Muslim five-day festivities, and the giving of many gifts. They did, however, receive a private blessing from the imam, at the nearby beautiful Mosque of Sheik Farrag.

For the wedding ceremony, attended by only six people, Shakira wore a simple, long, white dress, with a traditional hat and veil, which made her look even more like a goddess than usual. The groom wore a dark gray Western suit and promised to care for Shakira for all the days of her life, having already deposited $100,000, the muslim *mehmet*, into her private bank account.

This lifelong pledge appeared to reflect the ancient Islamic creed that women, beyond the home, must play a somewhat subservient role to that of men. And General Rashood thought that was not too bad an idea, given his new wife's inclination to assert herself, not to mention her flair for blowing up the armed battle tanks of those who displeased her.

However, as the cool, wet month of January wore on, the newlyweds were hovering around the edges of their first major row. Not to beat about the bush, Shakira Rashood wanted to take part in the Barracuda's mission to the eastern side of the Pacific Ocean. Not in a shore-based, non-operational, executive role, which Ravi assumed she meant. Shakira actually wanted an executive position on the submarine itself.

And on this rainy Friday evening, as it grew dark outside, they returned to the subject for the third time in twenty-four hours.

'Locked up under the water with sixty men, the only woman

in the crew – you can't do that,' said Ravi, smiling but dismissive.

'Yes I can,' said Shakira, not smiling, not submissive.

'Might I remind you that no woman has ever served on board a submarine, not in any navy, anywhere in the world? It's too confining, too claustrophobic, and it's surely no place for a woman.'

'Yes it is,' said Shakira. 'When I work, I'm no different from you. Oh yes, I understand the Arab world believes you to be some kind of a God of War . . . and I know I'm not in that league – but I'm as good as most of your soldiers, you'd have to admit that.'

Shakira's gaze was steady. Ravi knew that look only too well. His wife had no intention of backing down. And he was obliged to resort to reason.

'Look,' he said. 'There have been great strides to include women in the navies of both the UK and the USA. They have recruited them, allowed them to serve on warships. But they've often proved to be a complete bloody nuisance . . . people falling in love with them, trying to get their clothes off in parked helicopters and God knows what. And that's just in big surface ships. No-one has ever dared to recruit them to serve in submarines.'

'I expect the instances of women getting into sexual situations with the other members of the ship's company are less than one in ten thousand. It's just that newspapers are not interested in the other nine thousand, nine hundred and ninety-nine. I bet there are more examples of theft on board warships. Anyway it won't apply to me, will it? No-one's going to try to undress the Commanding Officer's wife, are they?'

'I should bloody well hope not,' said Ravi, in mock effrontery. 'But I'm sure you see, it's such a close confinement in an operational nuclear submarine, working underwater. It's just not a suitable environment. No-one's ever allowed a woman aboard, and I could not possibly break with that rule. Especially as I'm a rookie submariner myself . . . can we go out now? I'm starving, and we're meeting Ahmed in five minutes at the *Elissar*.'

'We can go out when you tell me I can come on the Barracuda to the west coast of the USA,' said Shakira, flatly. 'I've already coped with the destruction of one family, and I have no intention of losing you, thousands of miles away, when I do not even know what's happening. I'm coming with you, and that's that.'

'Christ, Shakira. People could die on a mission like this.'

'I'm not afraid to die,' she replied. 'And I know you aren't either. But if we're going to die, we'll die together. I won't remain here, waiting for someone to tell me you aren't coming home. Either we go together, or no-one's going.'

Ravi was not accustomed to defiance on this scale. But of course he'd never been married before. 'You are asking the impossible,' he said, carefully.

'No I'm not. It most certainly is possible. Because you are able to do anything you like. No-one is going to argue with the great General Rashood, Liberator of the Palestinian Martyrs.'

'I am not following rules set by someone else,' he said. 'I am following my own rules. And I would not dream of allowing a woman, any woman, to serve for several weeks in a submarine.'

'Well, then you can tell me why not,' she said. 'Proper reasons, not just too crowded, or too fraught. Proper reasons. In simple sentences. Why can't I work in the Barracuda, like anyone else?'

'First of all you are not a submariner. You know nothing of nuclear reactors, turbines, propulsion, hydrology, electronics, engineering, mechanics, missiles, navigation, sonar or torpedoes.'

That slowed down Mrs Rashood.

'Hmmm,' she replied, not terribly eloquently.

'And to put you in that ship would be to take up precious space. You'd be a *passenger*, who could make no contribution to the running of a Special Operation, underwater.'

'Hmmm,' she added.

In Ravi's view, Shakira's head of steam was gone. He thought he could see her will for this argument disappearing before his eyes. He should have known better.

'You've forgotten something,' she said.

'Oh. What?'

'The maps.'

'What maps?'

'Exactly,' she said. 'Forgotten. You don't think I'd have a discussion like this without thinking out a proper job for myself, do you?'

'Well, no. I am acquainted with your tenacity.'

'Well, what about the maps?'

'What maps?'

'The navigation charts you asked me to order from England,

via the Syrian Embassy, and then have them sent to that freight company here in Damascus.'

'Oh, you mean the American charts?'

'Yes. You had me order them, and collect them. And I studied them very carefully before I gave them to you. Remember? I even took copies, and marked them up in blue pencil, according to your notes. Back in September, before we were married.'

'Well, yes. I do, of course, remember them.'

'And you probably also remember I plotted certain courses for certain weapons from your notes. Marked up the check-points and made a record of the terrain.'

'Well, yes. And I'm grateful, of course. You did it damn well, I remember.'

'And perhaps I might remind you of something else?'

'Yes, but not now. Ahmed's waiting.'

'Ahmed can go on waiting until I'm finished . . .'

'But I'm starving . . . we have to go . . .'

'We're not going anywhere right now . . . but I want to remind you of how our organization is funded.'

'I know how it's funded. From the banks we hit in Jerusalem and Tel Aviv.'

'And who made the floor plans of those banks, got friendly with the senior teller, drew the maps from scratch, drew up a diagram of the entire alarm systems? Then penetrated Schwartz Locksmiths and drew up the diagrams of the most secure locks in the country, the ones at both banks, not to mention the ones in the Nimrod Jail? Who did all that?'

'Well, you did . . . I'm not saying you didn't. But what's any of that got to do with the submarine?'

'It has everything to do with it. Because the whole lot of you would probably have got lost, shot or arrested, without my work in the planning department.'

'I accept that,' said Ravi, warily.

'And another thing,' she added. 'In my spare time this past few weeks, I've been looking at American coastal radar defenses, mostly civilian, at sensitive container and tanker ports, but in some cases, ports of the US Navy.

'As it happens, I have a few rather critical changes to make in certain trajectories. And I'll be making them in a small office-space, in the ops room of the Barracuda, right next to the missile director . . .'

'But . . .'

'No buts. Are you ready to take your new Precision Target Officer out to dinner? Lieutentant Commander Shakira, reporting for duty . . .'

Ravi wanted to laugh. But this was no laughing matter . . . 'I can't appoint Lieutenant Commanders to the Iranian Navy,' he said.

'I assure you, this is not the Iranian Navy. They'll want to stay well distanced from this. That Barracuda will sail under the Command of the HAMAS Fundamentalists. And you are the military C-in-C of that organization. You can appoint anyone you like, to any position you like. No-one will even question it. I'll just go aboard like anyone else.'

'My God!' said Ravi, in a voice altogether stronger than he felt. 'And where do you think you will live? In a torpedo tube?'

'I shall be sharing your private cabin, as your wife and principal assistant in the area of weapons control and plotting. I know you have a private room, and I know it's got a small shower, basin and head, because I've read it.'

'It's tiny, just about enough room for one, a bed and a chair and desk.'

'Then we'll have to work alternative watches. Sometimes,' she said. 'Anyway, we'll manage. I'll bring a double sleeping bag and spend the night on the floor, if you'd prefer.'

'It's not a floor. It's a deck,' said Ravi. 'And anyway I wouldn't prefer. We'll put the big sleeping bag on the bed, nice and cosy, stop us falling out . . .'

Shakira walked over and put her arms around him. She kissed him long and lanquidly. Then she pressed her cheek to his and whispered, 'You're not dying without me. And that's final.'

'I know it is,' he said. 'And I'm going to give it serious thought. But I'd be awfully grateful if you'd hurry up. Otherwise I'll be *eating* without you.'

Ravi stared out into the drizzle which had made the streets shiny, and tried to come to terms with the rather pleasurable prospect of taking his wife with him on the submarine. Her general arguments had been considered, and well-thought out. But she'd managed to get some kind of a jump on him, taking the time and trouble to elucidate her plan, and her reasons, into a disciplined argument.

In the normal run of events, that was his strength; the strength of all SAS officers. Well thought-out plans. No surprises. Well it was more than three and a half years since he and Shakira had fled the devastation of the street in Hebron, and she had never stopped surprising him.

He had not caved in to her demand for a place in the crew because he loved her, and could deny her nothing. He had caved in because she had pointed out her talent, and her contribution to the operations of HAMAS. And she was correct. Her role in three massive operations had been critical. He had given in to the logic, not his love for her.

And he thought again what a huge help she always was, how that pliant, direct mind of hers could really get at a problem. He remembered her words when he had first mentioned the possibilities of the bank robberies.

You'll need maps, floor plans, diagrams of the alarm systems . . . do you want me to start work on that?

And now she came through the door into the drawing room. And her hair was brushed, she wore a bright scarlet lipstick, and she was as slender and beautiful as she had been that first day he met her.

'Ready?' she asked.

'Lieutenant Commander Shakira,' he said. 'You are really something.'

Ravi pulled out a big umbrella, and they stepped out into the rain, and they both knew Mrs Rashood was about to join the Barracuda crew, and that she would be sailing from Petropavlovsk within the next fourteen days.

0900 Thursday, February 7, 2008
Beijing Airport
Shakira knew as well as anyone how important her husband was, but she had no idea he was *this* important. The Iran Air flight from Tehran, which had taken eight hours, had no sooner landed than three Chinese officials came aboard to collect their bags which had unaccountably been stowed in the cupboard of the forward cabin.

Throughout the 3,500-mile journey they had four rows to themselves, no-one sitting in front, no-one behind and no-one opposite. They had been served excellent caviar, a privilege Iran Air passengers normally enjoy only on flights to Japan.

Here in freezing, snowy Beijing they were led off the aircraft

217

before the other passengers, downstairs onto the refueling area and directly into a Mercedes Benz which took them 500-yards to one of the Russian Navy's new long-range reconnaissance Tupolev Tu-204Ps.

Its engines were already running, had been since the Iran Air Boeing came into the Beijing Air Traffic Control area. Ravi and Shakira were led up the stairs into the seating area behind the cockpit. Their baggage was brought in and placed behind the rear seats. Doors slammed, and the fast Russian naval aircraft moved up to the head of the take-off runway, and then hammered its way noisily into the cold, cloudy skies north-west of the Yellow Sea.

It was 1,200 miles up to Petropavlovsk, right across the northern Chinese Provinces of Liaoning, and Jilin, before entering Russian airspace and heading out across the iron-gray wilderness of the Sea of Okhotsk to the Kamchatka Peninsula.

There are times in summer when the gigantic mountain range which runs down the backbone of this cold and rugged land can rival the Alps or the Rockies for pure grandeur. But in winter, which this most certainly was, the entire place looked like a travel commercial for Eastern Siberia, into which it most certainly fitted.

The new supersonic Tupolev was cruising through sunlit skies at 60,000 feet, like Concorde, and going very nearly as fast at 1.8 Mach. But the weather was ferocious down below on those snow-swept high peaks. Lashing winds off the tundra were gusting ninty knots. With a blizzard raging, human life was impossible. Even polar bear life was marginal.

It was not that much better on the runway, east of the mountains above the Bay of Avacinskiy, but the blizzard had eased, and in a freezing, still-gusting wind, the Navy pilot put the Tupolev down, hard. It was a difficult landing, and not pretty, but the veteran *Kapitan* had faced worse – mainly landing the old SU-25 fighter-bomber *Frogfoots* on the gale-torn decks of elderly Kiev-Class Soviet carriers in the Barents back in the 1980s.

He taxied to the terminal where a Navy staff car awaited them, and drove them immediately to the Petropavlovsk base. Ben Badr was outside the main offices to greet them, and he expressed no surprise at the sudden appearance of Shakira, but shook hands with her warmly, and then hugged Ravi.

'I did not know you were coming up to see us off,' he told Mrs

Rashood. 'But I am delighted to see you, and wish very much you were coming with us.'

'Well,' said Ravi. 'That is a wish I am able to grant very easily. Lieutenant Commander Shakira is coming with us.'

He spoke in a very matter-of-fact voice, not smiling, and very much the commander of the mission.

Ben Badr, who himself had now been promoted to Captain in the Iranian Navy, never missed a beat. 'Of course, sir. I assume under your command, rather than mine!'

All three of them laughed. As they turned into the warm building, out of the biting Arctic wind, Captain Badr used the moment of levity to reiterate the delicate balance of power which would be observed in the Barracuda submarine.

'Sir,' he said. 'This ship will sail under my command, as if it had a Fleet Admiral on board. That's you. My responsibilities are solely involved with making sure we get safely from one place to another, without endangering the lives of the crew. However, all decisions appertaining to the actual mission, where we go, what we hit, when, and how, are made by you. You can overrule me. I cannot overrule you.'

'As we have always agreed,' replied Ravi.

'Correct. And as my father has agreed,' added Ben. 'We should both be very clear. This is not a mission of the Navy of Iran. It is not a mission of the Navy of China. And it is most certainly not a mission of the Navy of Russia. This is an operation of the Islamic Resistance Movement, HAMAS, which is committed to the total liberation of historical Palestine, and the creation of an Islamic State. Ravi, you are the highest ranking military leader HAMAS ever had. This is your mission.'

Ravi smiled. 'Just so long as you do not think I am taking advantage of my exalted rank to bring along my wife, like some Roman emperor.'

'The thought never crossed my mind,' replied Captain Badr. 'Many people know of Shakira's important contribution to HAMAS operations. I am sure you have thought it through very well.'

'I made my decision based on her long weeks of work in the area of precision targeting,' said Ravi. 'She has made a detailed study of our objectives, and put forward a plan which, if I am honest, is more hers than mine. I know I should miss her in a strictly operational sense, if she were not on board.'

'Sounds like *we* should miss her,' said Ben Badr. And he stepped forward, and in the Muslim manner, lightly kissed her on both cheeks. 'Welcome aboard, Lt. Commander,' he said.

'There is, of course, the question of where Shakira will work,' said Ravi. 'And since it involves charts, and maps, and computer screens, I think it will need to be near the navigation officer . . .'

'Not a problem. We've room there. She will of course outrank him. He's only a Lieutenant . . . still, we might as well get used to that . . . as the wife of General Rashood she will outrank almost everybody!'

They retired to a private room for lunch, during which they discussed the most awkward part of the entire mission – where to go when the operations were complete. They had the world's ultimate getaway vehicle – a fast, silent nuclear submarine which would never need refueling and, properly handled, would be impossible to detect.

Ravi had always been unhappy about the lack of planning which had gone into this final aspect of the mission. But he now took some assurance in the report of Captain Badr.

'I have talked to the Chinese Political Commissar and he has pointed out that China, above all others, cannot be associated with the activities of the Barracuda. As a nation they have too much to lose. They must not be caught with an involvement in this.'

'They could of course eliminate us, and then claim to have helped the Americans by doing so,' said Ravi. 'In my native land, it's known as playing both ends against the middle.'

'Like the Americans, China too, would be quite unable to find us.'

'Yes. That's true,' said Ravi. 'Which leaves us out in the cold rather. Can't return to Bandar, can't go anywhere near China, can't even think about Russia. That's a lot of coastline to be banished from. Half the world. A lot of people to embarrass.'

Ben Badr was thoughtful. 'Ravi, I must tell you what the Chinese have told me. They have a plan they say is foolproof. They have a place for us to go, to get rid of the submarine, and to make a simple escape, all of us, back to Iran and Syria. They are saying by air. They are also saying the submarine will never be found.'

'That sounds very like them,' said Ravi. 'Devious Orientals. But do we have any guarantees?'

'Not many. They just say they have helped us from the start. That it is equally in their interest, as much as ours, that no-one should be caught. They will continue to help until everyone of us is safe. They honor us and trust us, as we should honor and trust them.'

'If anyone should find even a trace of the submarine,' said Ravi, 'China is in big trouble. That's true. It will come out they bought it from the Russians. Whatever crimes were perpetrated against the West, China would have to accept the blame. Even worse for them if they should be forced to admit they bought a nuclear submarine for a known stronghold of terrorism. No, I agree with one thing. Discovery of this mission is worse for the Chinese than anyone.'

'The tricky part is they are paranoid about security. And they are not prepared to divulge their getaway plan. They have stored it in an impenetrable safe on board the submarine. It will open on a timed device ten days into the mission. That way no-one will ever have the chance to reveal to anyone where we are utimately going.'

'I thought we were honored and trusted?'

'Up to a point,' said Ben. 'Until Chinese self-preservation kicks in.'

'Do we trust 'em?'

'No choice really. And anyway what's the point of worrying. We are undertaking this mission on behalf of Islam. If Allah requires us to be martyrs, then martyrs we shall be. I'm not afraid to die.'

'Neither are we,' interjected Shakira Rashood. 'But if there is a chance of postponing it, I think we should do our best.'

'I think Allah would always agree with that,' said Ben. 'We are here to complete his work. Certainly not to squander the great opportunities he has given us. Allah is great.'

'Okay, Ben, that's all very clear then. Do we have an ETD yet?'

'Saturday morning. February ninth. First light. Meanwhile we're moving into the submarine. I had the Russians construct an extra private office, larger than the regular CO's. As the overall commander, that one's yours. It has a bed which folds into the wall, a fairly large table and chair. I'll have a second one delivered. The bed's only a single but there's room for a small sofa or an armchair in that room. I'll get one.'

'Thanks, Captain,' said Ravi. 'Shall we go now?'

A Russian naval driver took them down to the submarine jetties, where Iranian seamen awaited them, to help with the bags and move the Mission Commander into his quarters. Ben Badr introduced Lt. Commander Shakira, and told them she had accepted a position as the Precision Targeting Officer and would be working in a special office close to the navigation area.

He revealed the news in an understated way, communicating an unspoken gratitude that one as accomplished as Shakira had condescended to join their humble operation along the west coast of America. He realized the news that a female naval officer was joining the ship's company would travel around the crew in a matter of seconds.

The fact that it was Shakira Rashood, wife of the God–like HAMAS warrior General Ravi, would probably render them speechless on the subject. And Captain Badr hoped they would stay that way.

Shakira herself, far from seeming overawed, was apparently oblivious to the fact that she was storming one of the last all–male garrisons in the entire world. She strode confidently up the gangway, huddled in her unlabeled dark blue Iranian Navy greatcoat and scarf, black fur hat, lined fur sea boots and gloves, and stepped on board Barracuda Type-945. She was the first woman ever to do so, anywhere, in anyone's navy, as a member of a submarine crew.

The ship was running on electric power from shore cables right now, and Ravi hoped there would not be a cut in supply owing to unpaid dockyard bills. But the Russians had done everything in their power to make this mission run flawlessly. The Chinese had been prompt with their payments, and although no Russian personnel would accompany the voyage across the Pacific, there were several seamen from Murmansk still in attendance, particularly in the area of torpedoes (for self-defense only), cruise missiles, and sonar.

Lieutenant Commander Abbas Shafii had been back working in the reactor control room for more than a week, and the CPOs, Ali Zahedi and Ardeshir Tikku, who would assist him as chiefs of the propulsion and auxiliary control panels, were also in residence. All three men had spent nine months in Araguba, and then made the long journey along the Siberian coast in the Barracuda.

There were eight other Iranian officers in the ship's company, all of whom had made the Arctic voyage from Araguba. They would however now set sail without their Russian and Chinese tutors, relying entirely on their intensive study-courses in nuclear submarine management. Some forty Iranian seaman, new to the ship, had all served in the Kilos.

Only six men would sail from Petropavlovsk devoid of any experience in submarines – they were all members of the 20,000-strong Islamic Revolutionary Guards Corps (IRGC), Iranian Special Forces, modeled on US Navy Seals and the British SAS. All six were veteran 'hard men' trained and bloodied as hitmen in the long war against Iraq. All six were expert frogmen, who believed they were fighting for Allah and that He would protect them, and, if necessary guide them home, into His arms forever.

Their leader, Lieutenant Arash Azhari, a superb soldier, could have been offered a position as a SEAL instructor anytime, had his politics been somewhat different, not to mention his nationality and his religious beliefs.

Aside from Arash and his boys, every other man who would occupy a critical position, particularly in the Barracuda's reactor area, was trained and experienced. Captain Badr was the most experienced of all of them, and his father Admiral Mohammed had been closely associated with the fine detail of the mission. He had, for instance, eliminated all uniforms, thus preserving anonymity in the event of capture. The two commanding officers, and now Shakira, would all wear navy blue sweaters. Lieutenant Commanders and Lieutenants would wear royal blue, Chiefs and regular petty officers, maroon, and the remainder, seamen, cooks, laundry men gray. Everyone would wear jeans (made in USA), with white socks and trainers (also made in the USA).

General Rashood asked to inspect the torpedo room and the missile director's section of the ops room. He authorized only twelve torpedoes, since they were only for self defense and he did not imagine any need for the full complement of forty. He noted there were twenty-four land-attack cruise missiles as he had specified. The programming area for the electronic computer brain carried by each missile in its nose cone was adjacent to the navigation area, where Shakira would work.

Ravi already knew the ship well, and he toured all three decks, meeting again the men who would sail with him, and carefully introducing Shakira, as the 'Precision Target Officer', who had masterminded the original plan, and who would be responsible for further adjustments and variations.

Mrs Rashood was a model of politeness. She made certain of everyone's name, rank, and area of responsibility, jotting down the details in a small leather notebook. She told everyone she met, how greatly she looked forward to working in co-operation with all members of the crew. She mostly did not sound very maritime, but she sounded sincere, and intelligent. And everyone was captured by her beauty, which was more or less why women had been banned from every submarine service in the world for almost a century.

However no other female had ever joined a ship's company as the wife of a high-ranking officer. Which ruled out the possibility of any wayward behavior. At least, it would on this ship, because the Barracuda was not under the formal command of any navy. It was under the overall command of a known Special Forces killer, on behalf of a terrorist organization, backed up by a known commanding officer, whose father held in his hands the careers of every last man on board. Disrespect to Shakira, on even the most innocent scale, was out of the question.

General Rashood and his wife moved into the principal officer's room, which was extremely spartan. They shared the wardrobe, loading it with a succession of shirts, sweaters, jeans, socks, shoes and underclothes. No uniforms. They tested the bed and decided it was wide enough for them mostly to sleep in it together, with the aid of the big camping bag. If the incoming Russian Navy sofa was around the same height, it would be an even simpler task.

As it happened the incoming sofa was one of the worst pieces of furniture ever made. It was the right height, made of plastic and only marginally softer than the floor. However, pushed against the bed, it made a passable extra area for the double sleeping bag, allowing an arm or a leg some extra space, and preventing either Ravi or Shakira falling overboard onto the deck. The danger of this latter occurrence was, however, remote. General Rashood and his wife tended to sleep very closely together.

They spent Friday working their way through the day, Shakira with her charts, Ravi touring the ship with Ben. At 1830, with snow again falling on the jetties, they began to pull the rods in the core of the nuclear reactor. As the sun endeavored to struggle out of the Pacific, the Barracuda would be on its way.

There were no goodbyes. The Russians had removed the last of their seamen in the small hours of the morning, and were now keeping their distance. All Chinese personnel had returned to Shanghai the previous evening. Ravi and Ben Badr were about to go it alone, in an all-Iranian warship. At 0548 on Saturday morning, they cast off the docklines, and with the Pilot already on board, his boat chugging along off their starboard beam, they headed out of the Bay of Avacinskiy, through the minefield, and east into the wide Pacific Ocean.

The pilot disembarked at the end of the minefield, and Captain Badr stayed on the bridge, watching the surface of the choppy sea for another half-hour. Then he swung south, in order to catch the lenses of the American satellite at the earliest possible time. But just before 0730, out beyond the 500-metre mark, he ordered the Barracuda beneath the waves. Then he ordered her to turn north-east again.

'*Conn-Captain . . . bow down ten . . . make your depth four hundred . . . speed fifteen . . . make your course zero-four-five . . .*'

The Barracuda made its turn 300 feet below the surface, and headed across the wide Gulf of Kronockiy, where the inland shores of the Pacific begin to shelve down to depths of more than 6,000 feet.

Above them the weather worsened, and somewhat to the surprise of the Barracuda's sonar room they picked up engine lines, five, maybe ten miles off their port bow. But it was raining now and the surface picture was confused. Nonetheless the sound of the oncoming engines grew closer, and while it was definitely not a submarine, neither Russian nor American, Ben Badr ordered the ship to periscope depth to get a fix with the sailor's best friend, Eyeball Mark One.

And way up ahead, they could just make out the outline of a clear and obvious fishing boat, big warps stetching down on yellow davits from both beams. It did not carry an inordinate amount of antennae, nor was it making any recognizable naval transmissions, but it was a good size, maybe 1,500 tons.

Captain Badr held the Barracuda at PD and identified the trawler as Japanese. Through the powerful periscope lenses they could just make out her name, *Mayajima*. And the navigator had made her course 225 degrees, heading, doubtless into the rich fishing grounds of the Gulf of Kronockiy.

Since the submarine was headed north-east and the trawler was headed west south-west, their path of approach was digressing by the minute. Right now they were two miles apart and going very clearly away from each other. Ben Badr ordered his helmsman to hold course and take her deep again . . . *four hundred feet . . . make your speed fifteen.*

What the Barracuda's CO could not have known was that Captain Kousei Kuno, master of the trawler *Mayajima*, had just been given a very strong heads-up from his own sonar operator, pinpointing a huge shoal of fish, far north for this time of the year, and very deep, possibly 2,000 feet.

He ordered the trawl net lower in the water, releasing the warps, to 1,500 feet, and even on a fishing boat of this size, they felt the big otter-boards at the head of the net dig into the water, forcing the giant entrance-gap open wide at the top end.

The sonar man called out depth and range of the shoal again. And Captain Kuno pushed his speed up as far as he could, and turned his wheel hard to port, changing his course to due east, in hot pursuit of the precious fish. Right across the path of the oncoming Russian-built nuclear submarine.

After four minutes, he cut his engines, wallowing at only three knots, and turning back west, right above the shoal. Literally tons of fish floundered into the net, trapped by the baffles, forced into the narrow cod-end in the time-honored tradition of deep-sea commercial fishing.

Except that at that precise moment, Captain Ben Badr's nuclear submarine thundered into the net, coming north-east under the port quarter of the *Mayajima* and ramming its bow straight into the heaving trawl, powered by engines generating 47,000 h.p.

The warps stretched and held. Then one snapped in two sending its ten-foot wide otter board clattering into the casing of the submarine, making an enormous din inside the hull.

'What the hell's that?' said Ravi, who was standing next to the CO.

'God knows,' said Ben Badr. 'Sounds like something just fell off.'

He could not of course have known that one of the warps was holding, while the other was hooked around the sail, and the mighty Barracuda was dragging the *Mayajima* down by the stern, with a single otter-board still clattering away against the sail.

'*Are we shipping water?*' called the CO.

'Negative, sir.'

'*Reduction in speed?*'

'Maybe four knots, sir.'

Back on the *Mayajima*, there was pandemonium as Captain Kumo realized they were being dragged down. Water was cascading over the stern flooding into the hold and sloshing into the navigation area. Despite their propeller being almost at rest they were making fourteen knots, backwards. The strains were enormous, and he hit the emergency levers which would release the steel-enforced warps which held the trawl net.

Immediately the *Mayajima* righted itself, returning to an even keel, with no serious damage. They were stationary in the choppy water, having lost their massive fishing equipment and their valuable catch, and sustained damage to the lower deck interior. The pumps were working overtime to haul the water out of the hold, and there was no point remaining at sea one moment longer.

These ships carry no spare trawl net, mainly because of the expense. The loss of the net ends their voyage, and confines them to harbor, until the insurance company, or someone else, stumps up. Captain Kumo turned south, back to the Pacific seaport of Ishinomaki, on the east coast of Honshu. He had suffered losses he would later claim added up to $200,000.

In the submarine, the clattering on the hull ended as abruptly as it had begun. With the release of the second warp, both lines holding the otter-boards were slack. There was one final bang as the board whacked the casing for the last time, but it did no harm, and the net, full of cod, slipped easily off the Barracuda's bow, down into the depths. Free and clear of the impediments, the submarine accelerated north-east as if nothing had happened.

'*Are we shipping water?*' Ben Badr called again.

'Negative, sir.'

The CO turned to Ravi and said, 'We just got entangled in something that was not metal, and therefore not a ship. It must have been a very large fishing net. Those bangs on the casing were the otter-boards. I've never done it before, but I've met submariners who have. It's not dangerous for us, because ultimately we're not in the net, we're just dragging it. But it is very dangerous for the fishermen, who must release it, before we drag them down . . .'

'Do we go to the surface to check up on possible damage?'

'We never go to the surface, Ravi. Not until the day we exit the ship for good . . .'

'But they might be sinking,' replied Ravi.

'If they are, we shall do nothing to help them.'

One month later Captain Kumo would claim he saw their periscope, jutting out of the water.

Meanwhile the Barracuda pushed on. Three hundred and fifty miles of open ocean lay before them to the western point of the Aleutian Islands, which stream out in a narrow 1,000 mile crescent from the seaward tip of the Alaska Peninsula, the great south-western panhandle of America's largest state.

The Islands, which stretch more than halfway across the Pacific Ocean at that latitude, divide the Bering Sea to the north from the Pacific in the south.

Populated for some 9,000 years, they stand in some of the cruelest winter weather on earth, valued principally as a storm-lashed natural outpost for the US Navy, which guards the western approaches to Alaska and the coasts of both Canada and the United States.

In recent years, the level of military surveillance from the Aleutians has been increased tenfold with the rise to global importance of Alaskan oil. The great terminal of Valdez in Prince William Sound, with its huge storage capacity, its convoys of south-running VLCCs (Very Large Crude Carriers), and the new west coast undersea pipeline, have turned it into a main cogwheel in the American economy. And it requires heavy protection.

With the President's insistence on less reliance on Arab oil, the estimated sixteen billion barrels of reserves on Alaska's North Slope represents the very heart of White House policy. The USA owns enough oil on the freezing land south of the Beaufort Sea to replace all Middle East supplies for the next thirty years.

A minor problem has been the oil beneath the protected acres of the sensitive Arctic National Wildlife Refuge. And there has been a certain amount of protest from a tribe of native Indians, who fear new drilling may drive away migrating deer – never mind the irony that they hunt the deer from the back of gas-guzzling snowmobiles, with high-powered rifles.

No matter. The Republican Administration of the early twenty-first century, ignoring the tree-huggers, greens, wets and other romantics of the environment, believed that most Americans think inexpensive and plentiful energy comes with liberty, and will put up with some damage to the near-deserted wilderness of Alaska, in order to get it. Yessir.

If the Administration harbored any doubts, the events of 11 September 2001 dismissed them all, in a major hurry. The prospect of the United States economy operating almost entirely on oil owned by Abdul, Ahmed and Mustapha was plainly out of the question.

The President, backed by trusted advisors, some of them dyed-in-the-wool oil men, called immediately for increased energy production. The Democrats did not like it, neither did the Eskimos, nor presumably the migrating deer, but a frenzy of new drilling was unleashed, most of it on government land, which included eighty-six percent of all oil exploration in Alaska.

By the end of the year 2006, a brand new pipeline was close to completion, right across Alaska, following, for much of its 800-mile journey, the route of the old Trans-Alaska Pipeline System (TAPS). For decades, this has carried crude oil from the vast, 150,000 acre Prudhoe Bay Field in the north to the giant Valdez Terminal in the south, on the shores of Prince William Sound, 120 miles east of Anchorage, as the crow flies.

The new pipeline, the Alaska Bi-Coastal Energy Transfer (ABET) has been built on the same lines, a zigzag formation which allows it to withstand enormous stresses, because the above-ground pipeline contracts and expands, as the tundra melts and then freezes. Both lines cross the mountain ranges of the Brooks, the Alaska and Chugach, plus thirty-four rivers and streams, including the Yukon, Tanana and Chena Rivers.

The pipes are highly visible, crossing tremendous areas of wasteland, each section holding 840,000 gallons of oil, held at bay by the massive strength of the jet-black, four-foot wide, galvanized steel transport system. The two pipelines diverge shortly before reaching Valdez, the new one cutting left, through the south foothills of the Chugach Range, to the new transfer terminal in Yakutat Bay.

There the crude is pumped into the brand new undersea pipeline system which, from the winter of 2007, ran from the south shore of Alaska, down to the Queen Charlotte Islands, 600 nautical miles south just off the coast of British Columbia in relatively shallow water.

And that was only half of its underwater journey. The rest took it down the coast, past Vancouver Island, and into American waters off the shores of Washington State, and the only deep-water port in that State, that of the ten-mile-long Grays Harbor.

These increasingly busy sea-lanes, 100-miles south of the Canadian border, are now known as the Coastal Super Corridor, the west coast's newest hub for business and international trade. Grays Harbor represents an outstanding confluence of road, rail and marine transport routes, north-east to Seattle, south to Portland and California.

Its new status had prompted the Republican White House to force through a Bill which allowed the construction, deep in the harbor, of a new refinery to handle the incoming piped crude from Yakutat. It was built, using every possible modern technique, on the south shore, two miles from the sprawling port of Aberdeen, a town of 17,000 citizens, now joined in an urban sprawl to its neighbors, Cosmopolis and Hoquiam.

The oil refinery was making a lot of people very rich. And the VLCCs were coming in line astern to Grays Harbor, loading up with refined crude oil, and then turning south again, down the coast to the Panama Canal and America's giant oil distribution system on the north coast of the Gulf of Mexico.

Perhaps even more importantly to the new boom towns at the head of Grays Harbor was the Canadian Pacific Railroad, which brought colossal tanker rolling stock right into the refinery, before running south for 900 miles, to yet another massive, new US Government initiative, the biggest electricity generating power station in the country, Lompoc, California.

This towering construction was christened Superpower West. It is the mighty plant built on the express orders of the President, to end forever the constant power-cuts, which had been erratically blacking out parts of California for several years. Superpower West, solely reliant on Alaskan oil, was born to take the pressure off the other fifty main California generating stations. It was born to light up, exclusively, the cities of San Francisco and Los Angeles.

It was into this multi-billion dollar power grid, stretching from the first snowy American soil halfway across the Pacific, to the very last hot, dusty US acres on the Mexican border, that Ravi Rashood and Ben Badr were now headed.

The Barracuda was out in open water now, running deep, west-south-west from the incident with the fishing boat. Captain Badr held her speed at fifteen knots, 500 feet below the surface, heading towards the Kamchatka Basin where the ocean shelves down to depths of almost two miles.

The Commanding Officer was trying to run the ship as if it were a part of someone's navy, but they still had an unresolved, life-and-death navigation issue – whether to take the shorter route along the south side of the Aleutians, or to take the route north of the islands and try to duck back south through the Unimak Pass at the far eastern end of the chain.

No modern navy would dream of allowing the matter to be a subject for discussion during the voyage. All routes and objectives would have been signed, sealed and delivered in orders long before departure. Even in Special Ops. But this was, in the end, not a navy. The Barracuda was staffed with professionals and experts on all decks, but the mission was unorthodox and would need refining, like the Alaskan oil, during its long journey.

It was Lieutenant Commander Shakira Rashood who was waving a red flag, casting grim and academic doubts on the wisdom of taking the short route south of the islands.

She was not being dogmatic, nor even insistent. But she was saying to the CO, and the Navigation Officer, and indeed to her husband, 'If I were an American, I would have a patrol submarine right there, moving along the northern edge of the Aleutian Trench over that very deep water . . . right here . . . look . . . where it's over three miles to the seabed.'

Ben Badr plainly found this an extremely difficult exchange, since he was unused to being questioned in his own ship, particularly by a woman, whose species he had never even seen in a submarine. But Shakira had spent months studying charts of the area, and gleaning information off the internet from defence papers and Pentagon data.

Ben knew she would be unlikely to speak out unless she knew a great deal about the subject. And he bit the bullet, smiled and told Ravi he had a very learned wife, which defused the situation and allowed Ben to avoid a direct confrontation with a lady, 500 feet below the surface.

Ravi too had studied the charts with Shakira, and in fairness was in two minds about the best route past the Aleutians. However the chart he and the navigator now studied with the Commanding Officer was not so full of information as Shakira's, whose main concern had been with American surveillance.

'For what it's worth,' she said. 'I have seen a pattern of more and more precautions being taken by the US Navy. For instance, immediately after September 11th, they stepped up security around the Valdez Terminal, and they are still running naval patrols a mile out of Prince William Sound. I don't know if those patols include submarines, but it is my opinion, the US Navy would *sink* any interloper detected in those waters . . . just imagine a foreign submarine creeping around in the waters near the very heartbeat of their west-coast economy. Trust me, they would not hesitate to open fire.'

General Rashood looked carefully at the chart, and then said simply, 'OK, Lieutenant Commander, why the north route?'

'Well, take Attu Island, the first place we come to. The chart marks an air reconnaissance post just to the east. Remember, this is the very tip of the islands. I would be amazed if there was not a Loran Station, a proper US naval facility somewhere on that coastline. It may be a straightforward radar station, or even a SOSUS processing unit. Either way, it will look like a cowshed, or reindeer shed, and either way, they could hear us come by. The water's shallow to the south, and noisy, but we don't want to go that way.'

Ben Badr nodded in agreement. 'Well,' he said, 'it's certainly a lot deeper to the north. The seabed falls away right offshore to two miles deep, and it stays that way for a couple of hundred miles.' He and Ravi stared at the chart, looking at the distinctive soundings which lay to the south, where the ocean floor shelves steeply down into the Aleutian Trench, which in places is four miles deep.

'I doubt there's SOSUS, not right down in the trench,' said Ben. 'And I agree with Shakira. All the signs are there for a US Navy listening station right here – 173E 53N.

'And I agree there is a very good chance of a US submarine patrol to the south . . . come here, Ravi . . . and Shakira. Let me show you a slightly bigger scale chart . . .'

He produced a large white, blue and yellow chart, which showed the ocean well south of the Aleutians, the sprawling undersea area known as the Great Pacific Basin.

'This large plateau,' he said, 'is loaded with US SOSUS surveillance, which means we cannot go anywhere near it. But since we have to move from one end of the Aleutians to the other, we have to go somewhere. Now look at these depths here

. . . all through the Basin, for miles and miles, north, south, east and west, we're looking at 5,000 metres. The whole place is lethal. Because during the Cold War, the Americans were paranoid about Russian submarines crossing that stretch of the Pacific into American waters.

'And you both know the Americans. When they want something, they make sure they get it. What they got here was an impenetrable area, in which no-one could move without US surveillance picking them up instantly. What they could not do, was operate the same system to the north, close in to the islands.

'Here . . . look at these depths. Heading north from the Basin, we move into a sudden decline, where the seabed reaches a kind of cliff edge and then plunges rapidly down to depths of over seven thousand feet, and stays there for several miles.

'Then,' he continued, 'right here, still heading north, over the deepest part, the ocean floor starts to rise steeply . . . here . . . six thousand . . . five . . . four . . . three . . . two . . . then one thousand . . . then way under, five hundred feet . . . three hundred off Attu Island. We just crossed a very large ditch, the Aleutian Trench. It's the one place the US Navy cannot operate SOSUS. It's too deep, too steep. The US equipment on the great plateau of the Basin cannot see across the ditch . . .'

'I know it can't see across, but why can't it?' asked Shakira.

'The undersea cliffs are too steep. SOSUS does not like looking up walls,' replied Ben. 'And that's why they almost certainly have a submarine patrol in there. If you've got billions of dollars worth of equipment guarding your western approaches, you wouldn't begrudge yourself a nuclear submarine to try and make it foolproof, would you?'

'I guess not,' said Shakira.

'And where does that put us, in your estimation?' asked Ravi.

'It puts me right with Shakira's original argument, that it would be folly to try to run south of the Islands, because we'd almost certainly get detected by any US submarine which happened to be in the area. They may not catch us, but they'd sound an alarm that would be heard all the way to the Pentagon. And I don't think we'd like that very much.'

'There could even be two submarines in there,' said Ravi, thoughtfully.

'I would not disagree with that either,' said Ben. 'Because even if they have SOSUS arrays on the ocean floor inshore, from eighty miles all the way to the beach, it's awfully difficult to listen "uphill", 'specially out here . . .'

'How do you mean?' asked Ravi.

'Well, in this area, coming from the Basin up to the Trench, there are some huge swells, which have been building for a thousand miles. The weather is bad, force eight or nine gales, pretty big seas. There's a ton of noise from the sea hitting the underwater cliffs – a lot of turbulence, water bouncing around, strong currents sluicing in and out of deep underwater holes.

'This is bloody awful anti-submarine country. There's cold water running past the islands from the north, warm from the south, forming marked thermoclines. It's appalling for SOSUS, and a whole lot easier to simply put a patrol in there, right in the middle. If I were in charge of US surveillance I'd have a patrol right here, at fifty-one degrees ten minutes north, one-seven-nine degrees east, off the island of Amchitka. I'd probably have an air patrol lurking around as well, just in case we found something and wanted to force it to the surface.'

'You mean it could be just one submarine, or maybe even two?' said Shakira.

'Correct. But everything is telling me we want to stay out of the south.'

'That's what it was telling me,' said Shakira. 'And I only have about one-hundredth of your knowledge.'

'Agreed?' said Ben.

'Absolutely,' said Ravi. 'We'll take the north route.'

'Meanwhile, can someone give me the latest on the US Loran stations, so I can fill my chart in?' said Ben.

'Well, I don't have that much,' Shakira replied. 'But I've entered everything I found. There's something definite for Attu Island, and I also had a mark on Amchitka. That's about two hundred and forty miles east of Attu, next to the wide seaway here . . . right through the islands.'

'Gottit,' said the CO. 'We'll be way north of there, in water a mile deep . . . here, just north of this sandbank . . . the Petrel Bank it's called . . . there's only one hundred feet in the middle . . . another forty miles east.'

'Okay,' said Shakira, 'I have a definite US naval facility on Atka Island, fifty-two degrees thirty minutes north, one-seven-four degrees east. And a possible, another couple of hundred miles on, Chuginadak Island. Not definite, just possible . . . then

I have two definite US Naval facilities – one on Umnak Island, right here . . . the other on Unalaska . . .'

'I can see four flashing beacons in this group,' said Ben. 'If we can see them through the periscope, we're probably too close.'

'I realize this sounds a little naive,' said Shakira. 'But somewhere, somehow we have to cut through the islands, from the the northern route back into the southern, right? Has anyone thought of where we might do that?'

'I have,' said Ravi. 'I'm not enough of a naval officer to select the correct side of the Aleutians to take a submarine, but I am enough of a military officer to realize that if we go north, we must eventually come south again. The main route for cargo ships is through the fairly busy Unimak Pass. I took the trouble to get hold of a very detailed chart on the area, better than anything we've seen so far . . .'

'I'm glad you did that, Ravi. I have good charts, but not excellent ones,' said Ben. 'And when we cut through the Aleutians, we must be very careful. If we're going to be detected anywhere, it'll be in there, surrounded by US radar and sonar, and unknown SOSUS cables.'

'Better that than a big armed Los Angeles Class nuclear ship,' replied Ravi. 'Because that American bastard will probably open fire on sight.'

February 11
They checked the Global Positioning System in the early afternoon and found themselves in precisely the right place, 53.45N 170.30E, ninety miles west north-west of the northern shoals of Attu Island. Captain Badr ordered an immediate reduction in speed because they now had no idea which SOSUS arrays were in place, and which weren't.

Ben erred on the side of caution. He was steaming in more than 9,000 feet of water, and he ordered the Barracuda to 800 feet . . . *speed five* . . . *course one-one zero*. The possibility of them being heard at that depth running so slowly was close to zero.

At this rate it would take them almost a day to cover 100 miles, and Ben Badr wanted to go no faster. It would thus be eight days before they were in the approaches to the Unimak Pass, eight days of stealth, cunning and restraint. Ravi was especially good at all those things. General Rashood was confident.

They crept slowly forward, easing their way along the northern route, about five miles offshore. They stayed in minimum depth all the way, and eight times the sun tried to struggle out of the Bering Sea in front of them, and eight times it failed. The weather on the surface remained stormy and rough, but no-one saw it. The Barracuda never came to the surface, only to periscope depth for a fast GPS update. They just kept going along, the big reactor running sweetly, providing all the heat, fresh water, fresh air, light and power they needed. The HAMAS terrorists were breaching the outer defences of the United States in the utmost comfort, given the circumstamces.

They never knew it, but only once in the entire run did they come close to being heard. That was about thirty-miles north of the eastern headland of Unalaska Island. A big fishing boat out of nearby Dutch Harbor somewhat unnerved the sonar room when it suddenly hauled full nets noisily, and close, perhaps hurrying to make home port before the weather.

The Officer of the Deck already had the Barracuda cutting the coastline somewhat fine, and he had no wish to get tangled in *another* fishing net. He desperately wanted to turn away, but this was a bigger problem than it might seem – hard rudder turns are noisy, well capable of giving a four- or five-second transient on US Detection equipment. The US operators would not know this was a submarine. In fact they'd probably blame the trawler suddenly speeding up, and classify it as such.

But the OOD knew that any detection was bad, and somewhat rashly elected to come to PD to confirm he was well out of the way of the fishermen. Big mistake. The Barracuda's periscope came thrusting out of the icy water, just for a few seconds, and was instantly picked up by shore-based American radar on Akutan Island. Just a fleeting contact, three sweeps on the screen.

As it happened they put it down to debris from the trawler's catch. But five minutes later Ben Badr himself wanted to take a look at the surface picture – and this time the contact was spotted on radar, and logged, by the Americans . . . *transient* . . . *insufficient data for positive identification*. But it was sufficient to be recorded formally as a possible intruder.

And they waited with new vigor for it to appear again. But it never did, and the Barracuda continued towards the Unimak Pass. The mighty Los Angeles Class hunter-killer submarine, *USS*

Toledo, cruising through the Aleutian Trench, was too far away to detect then.

The Barracuda was just a few miles short of the seaway through the islands early on the morning of Wednesday, 20 February. They took up a position ten miles off the flashing beacon on the northern headland of Akutan Island. They were not able to see it, but the GPS had them accurately placed. Up ahead was the beginning of a 'safety fairway,' drawn up by the Admiralty in London, for all shipping using the Pass.

In those lanes, the chart informed them, there was no impediment to safe navigation. Not even man-made . . . *no artificial island or structure, fixed or permanent.* It added that it was not mandatory to use the 'fairway', but recommended.

'Thanks, old chap,' said Ravi, in a sudden spasm of homesickness. 'I'm with you all the way.'

But Ravi's chart showed there was a shallow area, two miles long, in the middle of the fairway, under eighty feet at its worst, and fine for surface ships. But it was not fine for submarines which wished to stay undetected. It was possible, because most of the sandbank was ninety feet deep, but it was not advisable. Without putting a mast up, the Barracuda was fifty-five feet high from the top of its sail to the keel. Ben Badr would want twenty-foot clearance from the seabed, because to hit the bottom would be a crisis of diabolical proportions.

It was simply begging for trouble to make a slowish run at periscope depth, with the mast jutting out of the water, probably in the slavering teeth of powerful US radar. Ben Badr did not like it, and was actually considering making a fast run for it, on the surface, in the dead of night, and then heading for deep water.

General Rashood, however, considered this had an edge of hysteria to it, and was quite certain it would have given any ultra-cautious SAS Commanding Officer a heart attack. He said quietly, 'Ben, I have been taught to back off, any time I find myself weighing up a risk which will threaten my "mission critical".'

'So have I,' said Ben. 'But in this godforsaken place, we must have a ninety percent chance of getting away with a fast surface run, for maybe five minutes. They'd probably think we were a fishing boat, or a freighter.'

'Don't like the odds,' said Ravi. 'Forget it. Anyway I think I have a better plan.'

'I should hope so,' replied Captain Badr, grinning. 'You're in charge.'

'When I was in Araguba, a Russian officer, who I think had drunk a little too much, told me . . . and he probably shouldn't have . . . about a Russian submarine . . . he thought it was a Kilo-Class boat . . . which went right through the Bosporus submerged . . . and was never detected by heavy Turkish radar.'

'He did? That's incredible,' said the CO. 'Every submariner knows the Bosporus is impossible, with all that fast freight traffic, and terrible currents, sandbanks, wrecks, and God knows what.'

'I know. But this Russian told me it was done. And you know what? He told me how it was done . . .'

'He did?' said Ben, eyes wide open.

'Yes. Dead simple, really. He went through in the wake of a big freighter, right up his backside. The stern wake confused the radar so badly, they never saw the periscope.'

'Is that right?' said Ben Badr, even more incredulously. 'But I wonder what would have happened if the surface ship had stopped?'

'Funny. That's what I asked. But the old Russian just smiled and told me a good submarine captain would be on high alert for that. No problem.'

'Are you saying that's what we should do, Ravi?'

'Why not? We'll hang around waiting for a big freighter, and follow him through. Much less dangerous here, the channel's wide, and just about deserted. If that Russian could follow a ship through the confined area of the Bosporus, we ought to be able to chase one through a safety fairway, in the middle of a seaway nearly ten miles wide.'

'Yes. I suppose we could. I'm not sure how long we'll have to wait . . . we'll come to PD every half-hour and see what's going on . . . keep our speed right down . . . and then get in close.'

The trouble was, throughout the day, there were several small ships moving through the Pass, but no big ones. It was quite late in the afternoon, almost dark up here in these latitudes, when the veteran Kilo CPO, Ali Amiri, Chief of the Boat, called from the periscope:

'Captain, sir . . . I have a possible . . . three-three-zero . . . twelve thousand yards . . . I'm about thirty on his starboard bow . . . he's got a commercial nav radar . . .'

'*I'm turning towards for a better look . . . before the light gives out on us . . .*' Captain Badr was all business now.

'*Up periscope. All-round look.*'

Seconds later – '*Down!*'

'*Bearing?*'

'Three-three-five . . . bearing that. Range that . . . on twenty-four metres . . . seven and a half thousand yards, sir . . . put me twenty-five on his starboard bow . . . target course . . . one-two-zero . . . distance off track three and a half thousand yards . . .

'*Come right to zero-six-zero . . . down periscope . . . make your speed five knots.*'

The Barracuda moved forward in the water, running slowly towards the track of the oncoming freighter. They took another look closer in, and assessed her as a 6,000-tonner, Japan registered, heading straight into the Pass, nicely on a steady relative bearing as it approached.

For the next ten minutes they hectically worked the periscope up and then down, until finally Captain Badr ordered a gentle starboard turn, falling in hard behind the freighter.

With her bow right behind the merchantman's prop, range locked on the stern light, the Barracuda matched speed precisely with the leader.

Eighty five revolutions . . . speed over the ground eight-point-eight by GPS . . . eight-point-three through the water, sir.

Only 100 yards of choppy, foaming water separated the two ships as they made their way down the narrow safety fairway. No-one, obviously, in the Japanese ship had the slightest idea they were being closely tracked by a nuclear submarine. A rogue submarine at that.

And the team in the Barracuda kept station to the nearest few yards, watching the angle between the horizon and the freighter's stern light; knowing if it increased they were too close. If it decreased they were falling behind, out of the broiling wake which was protecting them from US radar.

The Japanese ship held a far steadier course than the last one they had encountered, the *Mayajima*. It set its speed and held course for mile after mile. It probably drew only around twenty feet, so it was not in any way neurotic about ocean-depth, just kept rolling through the Pass, on course to a distant land. 'Probably full of computers,' said Ravi. 'Though I can't imagine where they were coming from up there in the Arctic.

Unless it was Prudhoe Bay . . . they've got a lot of electronic kit up there.'

It was twenty-five miles to the shallowest point of the Pass, and it took two and a half hours. And all the way across the shoal, Ben Badr's men kept calling out the depth of water beneath the keel. It only once went under twenty feet – all the way to fourteen feet, which made the CO somewhat nervous. But within fifteen minutes they were hearing the ocean bottom was shelving down again.

Ninety-feet, sir . . . now one hundred . . .

They were positioned at 54.15N 165.30W – and no longer required their Japanese escort. Sixty miles south-east of Sanak Island they made a course change to due east, running deep now, straight along the 54th parallel, away from the great volcanic arc of the Aleutian Islands, into the Gulf of Alaska.

CHAPTER NINE

For five days and five nights the Barracuda ran deep beneath the windswept waters of the Gulf of Alaska. Captain Badr never let her speed rise above six knots, nor her depth above 500-feet. She tiptoed past the menace of the US Navy's SOSUS arrays and stuck to the shallowest water she could find at that depth.

A lot of very large oil tankers rumbled overhead on the high-octane highway to and from Prince William Sound and the terminal at Valdez. But no-one heard the near silent thrum of the Russian turbines, carrying the marauders from the Middle East towards the spectacular archipelago of Alaska's south-eastern islands and fjords.

On Thursday afternoon, February 28, the submarine arrived in 500 feet of water, west of minuscule Forester Island. Ben Badr's log book read 54.47N 133.45W. The Barracuda was thirty miles off the coast of Prince of Wales Island, the third largest in all the Americas, and that includes Hawaii.

The Commanding Officer put his ship into a slow racetrack pattern, moving at only three knots through the water, now 300 feet below the surface. As it grew dark, there was heightened activity in the missile compartment, as eight big RADUGAs were moved into firing position.

Two decks above, in the navigation area, Shakira Rashood was locked into her charts, preferring the sprawling Admiralty layouts to the smaller neater versions which appeared on the computer screens. She used dividers, a three-foot-long clear plastic ruler, a protractor, and calculator. Ravi stood next to her, mildly amused at his wife's capacity to turn his own broad outlines and objectives into careful details. She was, he thought, at heart, a natural-born civil servant, which was unusual for a terrorist.

From the moment he had explained to her his objectives, she had set about turning ideas into concrete plans. She had studied the success/failure rate of the RADUGAs. The defenses, both probable and certain, of the targets in the USA. She plotted routes, changed them, suggested positions for the launch platform – the Barracuda – and finally presented her work in carefully drawn diagrams, in thin blue lines on her charts.

As far as Ravi could see, her strategy, and geographic understanding were without flaw. For weeks he had put up with . . . *how far is this? . . . what about this? . . . what about that? . . . too far . . . too direct . . . no possibility of working . . . absolutely not . . . there's a US listening station right here . . . you can't take a submarine in there . . . they'd hear you . . . it's too shallow . . . too busy . . . too close to the shore . . . too far out . . . too near the main tanker lanes . . . too near this coastguard patrol area . . .*

Shakira was tireless. Thorough, intelligent and cautious. But still tireless. Grand strategy was not her game. It was the minutiae that absorbed her. And long ago, Ravi had considered that minutiae might keep them safe from discovery and attack.

She had no personal ambition to be seen as brilliant. Indeed she checked with her beloved Ravi every step of the way. Shakira's ambition was to help produce a perfectly executed operation, eliminating mistakes, catching miscalculations, listing snags, drawbacks and dangers.

Ravi had never met a better executive, working in a confined area like maps and missiles. And during that long Thursday evening he watched her working with the missile director, the two of them checking the distances, the flight trajectories and courses. And he thanked God for the long weeks his missile team had spent in Petropavlovsk, mastering the big cruises which would now strike a blow for Allah deep in the heart of the Great Satan's power base.

Even if all failed, and they should be caught and eliminated by the US Navy, nothing could now prevent the strike. The power grid of the west coast of the United States was at their mercy.

At 2200 hours, Ravi ordered the Barracuda to alter course to ninety degrees, to face east, towards Mecca, across the great frozen prairies of Canada to the Atlantic. And then he took the ship's broadcast system and asked every man to spend a few moments in prayer. Those who could, knelt in the Muslim fashion.

He reminded them their immediate actions might bring about the coming turmoil, and that they would hear the angels sound the trumpet three times. And that when God read the angel's reports, the righteous would cross the bridge, into Paradise. And that surely all of His children now dwelling in this great weapon, built to carry out Allah's will, would be among the righteous.

'I have turned my face,' said Ravi, 'only towards the Supreme Being who has created the skies and the earth, and I am not one of those who ascribes a partner to God. To you be glory, and with this praise I begin this prayer. Yours is the most auspicious name. You are exalted and none other than you is worthy of worship . . .'

He prayed for guidance in their great adventure and he ended with these lines from the Koran . . .

> . . . *from thee alone do we ask help.*
> *Guide us on the straight path,*
> *The path of those upon whom is thy favor.*
> . . . *Light upon light,*
> *God guides whom He will, to His light . . .*

At which point he ordered the ship back around to the west, and he summoned the Missile Director to the control room, checking one last time the pre-firing routines and settings. The program was immaculate. Only missile malfunction, or unexpected enemy action, could stop them now. The big RADUGAs, the guidance programs pre-set, were ready to go, straight along the route Shakira Rashood had masterminded.

At 2300, Ravi gave the order. *Stand by tubes one to eight.*

Then, seconds later . . . *Tube one launch!*

And the first of the opening salvo of four nine-foot-long steel guided missiles blew out of the launcher, arrowed up to the surface and ripped out of the water, as its engine ignited

It roared upwards into the black night sky, with a fiery trail crackling out behind it. At 200 metres above the surface, its cruise altitude, the missile adjusted course to 290 degrees and hit flying speed of 600 knots. The gas turbines cut in, eliminating the telltale trail in the sky. And the RADUGA was on its way.

Right behind it, the second one was in the launch process, out of the tube and on its way to the surface. The third was only seconds from ignition, and the fourth was already under the control of the launch sequencer.

There would be variations in each of the four designated indirect routes to Valdez, but they would arrive on target twenty seconds apart no matter what. And now they fanned out, streaking above the night waves of the Gulf of Alaska, growling surprisingly softly as they sliced through the wind and scattered low cloud.

The initial 860 miles took the salvo ninety minutes, and it took them more than 200 miles *past* the natural right turn up into Prince William Sound on longitude 146.20W. It also took them far south of the US Navy radar which sweeps the Sound night and day.

It took them to a point high above St Augustine's Island at the gateway to the Cook Inlet, which leads up to Anchorage. At the island the missiles made a sharp adjustment, swerving right on to a northerly course of 35 degrees, straight up the wide Inlet, and then over the Alaskan mainland for 375 miles.

Shakira had programmed a complete about-face at this point. And the missiles now made a 150-degree turn to the south, hurtling still at Mach 0.7 towards Valdez from a direction no-one could reasonably predict.

0115 Friday, February 29
On the Glenn Highway, Central Alaska
Harry Roberts, and his hunting buddy Cal Foster, ought not to have been driving. It was pitch black, the lights on their old truck had seen brighter days, and they had drunk about nine pints of Alaska Ambler apiece.

Both of them were twenty-one, the legal drinking age in the state with the highest level of alcoholism in the USA. Fortunately, the highway was just about deserted at this time of night, which left Harry to execute a few free swerves and steering corrections without actually killing anyone.

They were around four miles from the town of Glennallen when Cal announced from the passenger seat that he had a desperate need to unload a half-gallon of Alaskan Ambler, and the truck had to pull over right away.

Harry understood the feeling, and drove onto the hard shoulder, narrowly avoiding driving headlong into the ditch. They both stumbled out of the cab and positioned themselves for one of the great pees of their young lives.

Cal held his head back and belched luxuriously into the night, unleashing a shattering bark which could have petrified a bull moose. He reopened his eyes and it was then that he saw it, coming towards him, high above in the clear skies. At first he

244

thought it was a shooting star, then he realized it was an aircraft of some type. Then it went by, directly overhead, with that soft growl, and a s-w-i-i-i-s-s-s-h-h of disturbed air.

'Harry!' he said. 'Did you see that? A fucking UFO just flew straight over mah pecker . . .'

'What are you talking about?' repled Harry, swaying but still aiming steadily into the wilderness.

'I just saw a UFO. Straight up there. Flew over us. I saw it, heard it. Honest. Like something from that movie . . . what was it . . . Close Encounters of the Most Fucking Awful Kind.'

'Never heard of that movie,' said Harry, distractedly.

'Harry. I'm telling you. I just saw a fucking spaceship fly straight over us.'

'You're hallucinatating.'

'*I'm not*! Hey, look, Christ! There's another one. Look over there. To the right,' he added, pointing left.

Harry stared up the wrong way. But Cal was still yelling, '*Look! Look! Look! . . . Up there . . . that light in the sky . . . shit! Is that baby moving . . .!*'

Harry turned and looked left. And he saw it too. 'Christ! What is it?'

'It's a UFO, whaddya think it is?'

'What's a UOF?' said Harry, slurring his words.

'Unidentifiable fucking object in the sky, asshole,' said Cal.

'You can't spell,' grunted Harry. 'It was just a regular plane, maybe a little late for something.'

'You ever see a regular plane go that fast, that low? Jesus Christ, I could hear it swishing through the air. Ain't never heard nothin' like that before. Nossir.'

The oil terminus of Valdez lies at the end of a twenty-four-mile long deepwater fjord in the north-eastern corner of Prince William Sound. It is beautifully sheltered, standing in the seaward foothills of the 5,000-foot-high Mount Hogan, located north-west of the giant clusters of storage tanks.

These great steel structures, thirty of them, glinting in the starlight of this bitterly cold February night, stood in groups of four and six, all over the terminus, each one thirty feet high, and sixty feet across. They are essentially connected at one end to the inflowing crude pipeline from the Prudhoe Bay, and at the other to a further galaxy of pipelines stretching only a few hundred feet,

245

but leading out to the shipping berths where the world's largest tankers wait in line, to fill up and then head south. Valdez is the most northerly ice-free port in the Western Hemisphere.

The Valdez terminal never sleeps, and neither do the waters of Prince William Sound freeze. The crude keeps right on flowing, summer and winter, seven days a week, night and day. The natural protective geography of the place is the result of modern thinking, because the entire City of Valdez was constructed after 1964 when the Good Friday earthquake practically wiped the place out, including many citizens.

The oil terminus itself was completed in 1977 at a cost of $9 billion and the project made Valdez a rich city, its economy glittering behind the huge taxes paid out by the oil companies. Half the town worked in the local oil industry, and everyone knew the value of the Valdez Goose, which laid eggs of the purest black gold.

Within hours of the September 11 catastrophe in faraway New York, the Valdez city fathers were calling for additional radar, and indeed sonar, for their priceless port. They got them too, double quick, all aimed across, above and through the water. But all aimed essentially south, to the area of potential danger. Nothing was aimed at the desolate, freezing, snowbound mountain range to the north, where human life is just about impossible during the winter months.

But it was from out of the north that Ravi and Shakira's missiles were coming, ripping through the night, frightening the life out of one extremely drunk Alaskan, who nonetheless made a mental note that some kind of a spaceship had just flown directly over his pecker.

The first missile came flashing over Mount Hogan's western heights at around 0130. It leveled off over the descending ground, and came scything through the icy air, pointing downwards at an angle of almost forty-five degrees.

It hit Tank 18 head-on, with a colossal explosion, which detonated the adjacent Tank 17, which in turn blew Tank 15 and 16 to smithereens. Almost a million gallons of crude oil, blasted by the incinerating heat, hit flashpoint in under two seconds, and a scarlet-black mushroom of fire rumbled into the air, 200 feet high.

Just then the second missile came in, slamming home slightly to the right of the blaze, and blew to high heaven the small gas refining plant and the entire control section of the terminus.

Missile Three shrieked through the smoke and devastation and knocked Tank 14 flat, setting fire to Tanks 9, 10, 11, 12 and 13. For whatever reason, the fire was less volatile, but was somehow even hotter and it blew the big main pipeline out to Berth 4 where the *Exxon Prince* was taking on thousands of gallons of crude being pumped right now into its two for'ard holding tanks.

The incinerating flame ripped across the jetties like a massive length of detcord, slower but bigger. And before the astonished eyes of the ship's master a thunderous explosion, caused by the vast amount of inflammable gas in the tanks, blew the entire bow of the 400,000-ton tanker clean off the front of his ship.

Nineteen seconds later Missile Four came spearing through the smoke and devastation of the terminus and crashed into the middle of Tanks 1 to 6, four of which were only half full of crude, but were loaded with volatile gasses – they went up like an atomic bomb. The searing explosion was visible in the night sky for fifteen miles to the south. And the fire lit up the sleeping city of Valdez.

By some miracle no-one on the burning tanker was injured, mainly because of its size. Every one of the crew was in quarters way back in the stern of the ship, close to the bridge, the oil control room, and the engine room. The explosion up for'ard had taken place almost 400 yards from anyone. The crew would have to abandon ship, fast, but even when the tanker finally settled on the bottom, there would still be the equivalent of a six-story building jutting out of the water.

Meanwhile, General Rashood's second salvo of four RADUGAs was well on its way, fanned out two miles apart, whipping through the night skies over central Alaska, again traveling the precise same final track, north to south. Eight minutes after the *Exxon Prince* had blown up, the final four Russian cruises slammed into the gigantic fuel farm above the city – lines of vast storage tanks which, when full, held up to nine million barrels of crude oil piped from the North Slope.

Right now, they were full, and the tanks split asunder, unleashing a burning river of oil onto the hillside. Crude needs ferocious heat to ignite, and those four missiles provided that heat in spades. People in the town, awakened by the gigantic explosions at the main terminus, would later describe a succession of 'kinda soft' explosions up the hill. Not the *Ker-bam!* of a bomb.

More a series of *W-h-o-o-o-o-s-h!* sounds, like that from a petrol-sprinkled bonfire when the first light is thrown in.

The fuel-farm fire above the city was terrifying, because people thought it would rage downhill and set fire to the entire town. But the crude was burning at such a rate, and at such heat, it scarcely moved, settling quickly into a contained twenty acre inferno, roaring and crackling, destroying every last gallon of Alaskan crude on the shores of Prince William Sound.

And no-one had even the first idea what had happened. Nor how it happened. Certainly not why it happened. The 4,000 citizens of Valdez knew only that the great terminus, and all the oil in it, owned and operated by Amoco, BP and Phillips Petroleum, was gone. The entire place was on fire, and there had been, plainly, a disaster on a monumental scale.

There had been just a skeleton night staff of three in the oil control area – two of whom were luckily having coffee in a mess-room 300 yards away – and all communications from the terminus were down. But the scale of this blaze was so great you didn't need a telephone. A passing husky could have told you the oil port was on fire.

Dick Saunders, the local stringer for the *Anchorage Daily News,* was the first reporter on the case, fifteen minutes after the last missile ploughed into the fuel-farm. He had missed the last edition of the newspaper by a long way, but he nevertheless called the night desk in Anchorage and told a tired, bored-sounding editor that the entire port of Valdez was on fire and right now they were facing the total destruction of the Alaskan economy.

This definitely stopped the night editor being bored, and he, in turn, hit the wire to his brother who worked the night shift at KBBI (AM 890), the public radio station over in the little port of Homer on the Cook Inlet. Eight minutes later the story was out, and every late-night radio station in Alaska was on the phone to Valdez, verifying the scale of the disaster. The broadcasters were in full cry by 2.30 a.m. and CNN were out nationally with the drama onscreen by 3 a.m.(Pacific Coast Time).

By 4 a.m.(Pacific), 7 a.m. on the east coast, the National Security Agency was calling key operatives into the Fort Meade headquarters, the FBI was dispatching west coast staff in a private military jet from San Diego to Anchorage, the White House was informed, the President was headed for the Oval Office, and

Admiral Arnold Morgan's driver was hurtling along the Beltway direct to Fort Meade. Admiral George Morris was doing his level best to get there before the Big Man.

The staff of the Chief of Naval Operations was already in the Pentagon dispatching two frigates directly out of San Diego immediately to Prince William Sound. The LA-Class nuclear boat *Toledo* was out of the Aleutian Trench and headed at flank speed south of the islands, direct to the deepwater channel inside the Sound itself.

Meanwhile Captain Ben Badr had turned away from the datum, and was quietly leaving Forester Island astern to the north-west while he aimed the Barracuda east into the Dixon Entrance, a wide seaway which marks the end of America's Alaska Territory and the beginning of Canada's western coastal waters. The Dixon runs north of Canada's Graham Island and then swings south through the broad Hecate Strait to Queen Charlotte's Sound, and on to the northerly waters off Vancouver Island.

This is a well-traveled, sheltered route for tankers heading out of the Gulf of Alaska and on down the west coasts of Canada and the United States. It is also the route of the brand new coast-hugging underwater pipeline joining the Yakutat Bay transfer terminal, east of Valdez, to the gigantic refinery in faraway Grays Harbor, Washington State.

General Ravi and Shakira stood next to Ben Badr as he conned the submarine, 500 feet deep, in 200 fathoms of water, quietly south of the great shoal of the Learmonth Bank. The journey of 130 miles to their next area of operations would take them more than a day at their restricted speed of only five knots through these Canadian coastal waters. They did not even have much to talk about, since no-one on board the submarine had the slightest idea what had taken place after their two salvos of 'fire-and-forget' RADUGA missiles had blasted off on their journey to the Alaskan coast.

Shakira was confident. She had read the reports of every test-firing there had ever been on the RADUGA. In her mind there was no doubt they had reached their final destination. The missile's refined guidance system, stolen from the Americans by the Chinese in the late 1990s and shared with their friends in Moscow, was as reliable as anything being manufactured in the West. And so far as Shakira could tell there was no modern precedent for the missile failing to explode on impact.

249

'I believe there is a very large fire burning in the port of Valdez,' she said, clutching the arm of her husband in the Barracuda's ops room. 'Almost as big as the one in my heart.' As a terrorist, Shakira Rashood had all of the passions required for the task, and she never lost sight of her avowed hatred for the Americans, whom she believed had armed, financed and encouraged the Israelis in the most monstrous atrocities against her own people.

The GPS position which awaited them was 54.15N 131.39W, a mile north of the 100-fathom line, less than two miles from the notoriously shallow Overfall Shoal, which stretches six miles out from Rose Point, the north-easterly tip of Graham Island. The new pipeline runs straight across the edge of this very large sandbank, at one point only thirty feet from the surface at low tide.

The hazard is well marked, away from the main shipping lanes to the east, towards the Canadian coast. More significantly, the water is 600 feet deep less than two miles to the north of the Shoal. Four hundred yards from the Shoal, it is still 200 feet deep. The insertion of Lt. Arash Azhari and his frogmen from the Islamic Revolutionary Guards Corps should not be a problem.

While Ravi, Shakira and Ben crept through the dark waters south of Alaska, Admiral Arnold Morgan's driver Charlie gunned the big staff car, engine roaring, headlights blazing, straight at the main entrance of OPS-2B, the huge one-way glass building which houses the eighth floor lair of the NSA Director.

The car following them, containing three armed agents, had had trouble keeping up with them all the way from Chevy Chase, and the Big Man was well inside the main doors before his 'minders' arrived.

Armed security guards were awaiting him, and he moved straight up to Admiral Morris's office in the private elevator, a full four minutes before the Director himself made his entry.

When he did so, he pushed open the door to his office and was greeted by a voice from behind his own desk, from his own office chair.

'Where the fucking hell have you been, sailor? Vacation?'

George Morris understood that when Arnold came visiting he lost his chair, desk, and seniority in more or less that order.

He ignored the greeting, and chuckled at his old friend sitting once more behind the big desk. 'Hello, sir,' he said as he always did, before slipping back to 'Arnie' as befits close friends of over thirty years' standing. 'Has anyone told us what the devil's going on in Alaska?'

'Not really,' replied the President's right-hand man. 'I've seen only the pictures off the internet which CNN are showing. But I'll tell you what. That looks like some kind of fire. You hear if anything's suspected?'

'Not a thing. The media don't have a clue, but I did notice there seem to be two very definite areas of destruction – the second one quite a way from the main terminal. I don't really know about connections between storage areas, not in a plant as big as Valdez. Maybe there *are* adjoining pipelines . . . but if there are no connections, it's hard to see two massive, simultaneous fires breaking out in the same place, but nearly a half-mile apart, within ten minutes of each other, without there being something pretty damn fishy about it.'

'Hmmmmm,' said Admiral Morgan. 'We got a surveillance report in yet? You know, details of local shipping, surface contacts, aircraft movement . . . anything?'

'If we have, the newly-promoted Lt. Commander Ramshawe's consolidating it along the corridor in his own office. Couldn't have him do it in here. That boy makes more mess than any other five people I've ever met. Paper! Christ he can fill a room, every day of his life.'

Arnold Morgan grinned. 'Shall we get him in here, since he is now your personal assistant?'

'Sir, I wanted to check something with my chief of Military Intelligence, Captain Wade. But he's very busy, I've been on the phone to him twice before I got here. I'm going down to his office for ten minutes.'

'Okay, George. I'll go pay a surprise visit to James Ramshawe, check he's on the case . . .'

Both Admirals made for the door, George Morris headed for the elevator, Arnold Morgan for a big office twenty yards down the corridor.

The sign on the door read, '*Lt. Cdr. J. Ramshawe, assistant to the Director.*' Arnold did not knock. Arnold did not knock when he entered the Oval Office. He probably would not knock on the Pearly Gates.

He pushed the door open to find J. Ramshawe in his shirt-sleeves, hunched over a table on the left of his room, putting sheets of paper in various stacks, and working his computer with his right hand only. 'Wait a minute, whoever the hell you are,' he grunted. 'Someone's made a blue here. I've gotta fix it before I stand up.'

'What's a blue?' asked Admiral Morgan.

'Australian for balls-up,' replied Ramshawe, still not turning around. 'How some people reach the conclusions they do reach beats the absolute shit outta me.'

'And me,' said the Admiral. At which point the young Lieutenant Commander sensed something familiar about the rasping tone of the voice, and just found time to mutter, 'Oh Christ,' before leaping to his feet and apologizing profusely for his rudeness.

Admiral Morgan chuckled and offered a handshake. They had not seen each other for several months, not since a very difficult operation in the Gulf of Hormuz, which had led to the National Security Advisor literally telling George Morris to elevate Ramshawe to his present exalted position.

'Well, the Alakaska catastrophe's almost four hours old . . . I'm counting on you to have a theory, cause and effect, guilt or innocence, fact or fiction?'

Lt. Commander Ramshawe loved Admiral Morgan, and he was one of the few people not completely fazed by his disconcertingly tough manner.

'Sir, right now I have not seen much more than anyone else. But I've noticed the definite evidence pointing to two separate areas of explosion and fire, damn nearly half a mile apart. I have not been able to connect them, mainly because all the phone lines to the oil terminal are down.

'I have been through to the Police Department, and I've got a computer hooked up to a local radio station which is interviewing a lot of Amoco people. The fuel-farm and the actual terminus went up in flames separately, about ten minutes apart. No doubt about that.

'Almost all of the key operatives from the plant were in the town asleep, thank Christ, or they'd all be dead. Several of them have been on the radio, and they are all expressing total bewilderment at the fact that two quite separate, totally devastating fires broke out. I've heard three different oil execs say that a flash fire was impossible. Every last barrel in Valdez was crude, and it quite often doesn't burn at all. Not unless something makes it very,

very hot, some kind of an explosion, a bloody bomb or something . . .'

'You've seen the coastguard surveillance reports?'

'Only the prelim. There's no record of any ship movement anywhere in Prince William Sound any time after twenty-three hundred the previous night . . . and that takes care of a lot of ocean . . . the bloody place is a hundred miles long . . . out to the hundred-metre line . . .'

'Air traffic?'

'Not even a private aircraft after twenty-one hundred.'

'Nonetheless the oil guys must be thinking someone blew the holding tanks up?'

'They're not saying that, sir. At least not yet. But they must be thinking it. Let's face it, crude oil doesn't suddenly go off bang by itself, does it? And that bloody fuel-farm has nothing anywhere near that would cause even a spark, never mind a twenty-acre inferno . . .'

'Hmmmm,' said the Admiral. 'No ships, no aircraft, no suspects, no apparent motive, no clues. Not much of a start to an investigation, eh Jimmy?'

'Nossir. Not much at all.'

'Who was it said, *When you have eliminated the impossible, only the truth remains?*'

'Sherlock Holmes, sir. Front and center.'

Admiral Morgan laughed. 'What do you have to do around here to get a cup of coffee?'

'Oh, Christ. Sorry, sir. I'll fix it. The usual . . . black with buckshot?'

No-one ever forgot Arnold Morgan's coffee requirements, honed during his years in nuclear submarines. No cream, just two or three little white sweetener pills. Buckshot, he called them.

'Right. Better get some coffee for the boss too. He'll be back in a moment. But before that I want to talk to you . . . so hurry up.'

Lt. Commander Ramshawe picked up the phone and ordered coffee for three, with hot English muffins, since it was now after eight in the morning and the two Admirals had been up half the night.

He replaced the receiver, and turned back to the President's National Security Advisor. 'Lay it on me, sir. What do you need?'

'Jimmy, in the absence of any further evidence to the contrary, we'd better face up to the fact that some bastard just blew up the biggest oil terminus in the United States.'

'Yessir.'

'The total impossibility of an attack by sea or air, means that whoever did it must have escaped by land. That means the range of mountains right behind Valdez, correct.'

'Yessir. The coastguard will be combing the area with three helicopters by first light in about one hour. I've already spoken to them.'

'Do you think it likely that a bunch of crazed terrorists crept through the snow and ice, down Mount Hogan, and put a few bombs in the oil storage area.'

'Nossir. And even if they did, they'd get caught pretty sharpish this morning. The place is gonna be alive with helicopters and anyone making a getaway will be leaving footprints in the snow all over the bloody wilderness, right, sir?'

'Precisely. The chances are nothing will be found. So what does that leave?'

'Sabotage,' said Jimmy. 'By a local person, or persons. Or an enemy attack with at least two missiles, which no-one saw.'

'Fired from where, Jimmy?'

'Well, not from the land. Not from the air. And not from a surface ship.'

'Why not from the land?'

'Have you seen the size of those storage tanks, sir? And the area that's burning? You couldn't cause that much catastrophe with a hand-held missile like a Stinger. If the fires were caused by a missile strike, it was a big, highly-explosive, unbelievably accurate guided weapon. Sophisticated military. Nothing less. You don't keep that kind of stuff in a bloody cave.'

'And you can't fire that kind of stuff from a bloody cave,' said the Admiral. 'There is only one place from which you can fire that kind of stuff. It's known as a warship.'

'And there wasn't one of them within hundreds of miles, sir.'

'Not one which we could see, James. Not one we could see.'

Ramshawe smiled his lopsided Aussie grin. 'I was just thinking you might get around to that, sir,' he said.

'Likewise,' replied Arnold Morgan. 'And this is my real question . . . when I arrived in this office you were too pre-occupied to care whether it was me, the President of the United

254

States, or Jesus Christ. Whatever you were working on was extremely important to you. What was it?'

'Sir, I don't want to be accused of irrelevance. Not on a day like this.'

'Jimmy,' said Admiral Morgan, walking across to the window and staring out over the gigantic parking lot, 'what was it?'

'Well, sir. I arrived at the conclusion that if the culprit was a salvo of big guided missiles, they must have been unleashed from a warship, one that we somehow couldn't see.

'I've actually been here all night, sir, because I've been working on a minor problem since yesterday evening . . . it keeps running through my mind. I've pulled a file up in hard copy, and I've been reading it carefully. When the fires broke out, and the guys on the radio kept saying it could not have happened, I found myself putting two and two together and making about three-hundred-and-ninety-five . . .'

'I know the feeling,' said Arnold. 'Tell me the minor problem.'

'Okay . . . lemme get these papers in order . . . right . . . on February twenty-first, our Naval attache in the Tokyo Embassy receives an inquiry from the Japanese Government about US submarine patrols off the Kamchatka Peninsula. In particular about patrols off the Bay of Avacinskiy, you know, sir, that godforsaken place in front of Petropavlovsk . . . ?'

'Gottit. Go on.'

'Well our man in Tokyo makes a few inquiries and discovers no American submarine has been on patrol in the Western Pacific for at least three months. Nothing nearer than the southern waters of the Aleutians. But being a careful and cunning diplomat, he doesn't tell this to the old Japanese. He decides to withhold all information until he finds out why the hell they want to know.'

'Good man,' said Arnold. 'Rear Admiral Whitehouse, I believe?'

'That's him, sir,' said Jimmy, long accustomed to Arnold Morgan's encyclopedic memory. 'He tells the Japanese Government they can count on full US co-operation, but first they have to explain why they want classified naval information. We don't just bandy this stuff around, right?

'Anyway, he gets what he asks for. The Japanese Ministry tells him they have received a very large claim for compensation from the master of a fifteen-hundred-ton trawler out of Ishinomaki, that's Honshu. The Japs not only tell him, they enclose full, signed affidavits from Captain Kouisei Kuno and his senior crew members, who all claim they were damned nearly dragged to the bottom of the Pacific Ocean by a submarine which charged straight into their trawl-net.'

'What made them think we were the prime suspects?'

'That's the thing, sir. They didn't. They went straight to the Russians, and got a surprisingly fast and comprehensive reply. The Pacific Fleet Commander immediately cited a Sierra Class Barracuda nuclear boat which they said left Petropalovsk early that very morning, February ninth, bound for the South China Sea.

'Their memorandum said the ship had turned south, immediately beyond their restricted area, outside the bay, and could not possibly have collided with any fishing boat some fifteen or twenty miles north of the Petropavlovsk area . . . and it just so happens I've been watching that particular ship for several months . . . followed it on the satellite all the way from Murmansk . . . and right here, sir, I have a dated photograph . . .'

He handed the Admiral a black and white 10 × 8-inch print. 'See that sir . . . it *did* leave Petropavlovsk on that day, very early because we take satellite photographs at around oh-seven-thirty. And it *did* turn south . . . there it is . . . right there, sir . . . check the GPS . . . it really was exactly where and when they said it was . . .'

'Then what did the Japanese do?'

'They checked with the Chinese, who told them they have not had a submarine in that area for more than six months. Nothing beyond the Yellow Sea.'

'So what's vexing you, Jimmy? As if I don't know.'

'That's right, sir. I've checked the boards. I've had Naval Intelligence check every goddamned submarine in the world. And they've found them all. Either the Japanese fishermen are lying, just because they lost their net, or something bloody weird is going on.'

'And then you sat here twisting and turning over what hit the oil tanks, and you couldn't get that phantom submarine out of your mind, correct?'

'Yessir.'

Just then a waiter tapped on the door, and entered bearing the coffee and muffins. These were immediately followed by the entry of the Director himself, George Morris, clutching a sheaf of papers, every last one of them containing statements by Alaskan oil execs who were unable to come up with a reason between them as to how the oil fires could possibly have started.

Arnold Morgan himself filled in the details of the discussion for Admiral Morris, who nodded thoughtfully. 'If it was one fire in one place,' he said, 'we'd be pursuing the accident theory. Two fires, in two places, same time, same area, doesn't make any sense. If it wasn't sabotage, someone just hit us. Simple as that.'

'I don't think sabotage is entirely out of the question . . . possibly someone in the pay of a terrorist organisation . . .' Arnold Morgan was pensive.

'Sir, when the bloody fires cool off,' said Jimmy, 'there's gonna be some evidence of some kind of incendiary device. If it's a couple of bombs there should be something for the forensic guys to identify. Missiles are more difficult because they tend to blow themselves into much smaller pieces . . . plus the heat from those fires will melt everything – but they'll probably find clues.'

'As far as I am concerned,' said Admiral Morgan, 'we should already, between ourselves, as the senior military Intelligence academics in this country, be considering the possibility of a military strike against us as an absolute priority. We should also accept that if we were hit, we were hit by missiles fired from an enemy submarine. And that possibility will magnify over the next few days when we discover exactly how far away the nearest foreign warship was.'

'Which makes the word of the captain of the *Mayajimo* another priority,' added Jimmy. 'I've read a translation of his evidence, and it's pretty convincing. He has produced the broken end of the warp which held the trawl net – snapped about fifty feet from the boat . . . way underwater . . . plastic reinforced by steel, almost two inches thick. You couldn't break that stuff with a buzz-saw . . . never mind pull it clean in half.'

'What else does he say?' asked Admiral Morgan.

'Plenty,' replied Jimmy. 'He wants two hundred thousand dollars' compensation. Says he lost his trawl net, and his entire catch, because he had to let go the remaining warp. He says the submarine was dragging them backwards at more than twelve knots, pulling the stern of his ship down. He says water was piling in over the stern, flooding some interior areas. He enclosed polaroid photographs which he took immediately after the ship righted itself.'

'I suppose the other crew members confirm his story?' said George Morris.

'Of course they do, sir. And on the face of it, you'd have to believe them. The question is, what submarine was it? Because a submarine it most certainly was. There's no doubt in my mind.'

'Nor mine,' said Admiral Morgan. 'That was a submarine alright. It's got all the classic signs of what happens when a big underwater ship hits someone's net. Doesn't happen often, but when it does, it's pretty well obvious.'

'But according to the Russians, the only submarine within hundreds of miles was their own Barracuda. And that was almost twenty miles from the datum, and definitely headed the wrong way.'

'Just remember one thing, young James . . . the words of my old friend, Admiral Sandy Woodward, the Royal Navy Commander who won the Falklands War for the Brits in 1982. He was giving evidence about the sinking of the *General Belgrano*, and he faced questions from some half-assed know-nothing politician who was telling him the *Belgrano* was one hundred and eighty miles away, and going slowly in the wrong direction anyway, away from the Royal Navy fleet.

'Admiral Sandy just said, *The speed and direction of any enemy ship is irrelevant . . . because both can change in a matter of seconds.*'

'Jesus. That's right too,' said Jimmy. 'Are you suggesting, sir, the Barracuda could have dived, turned around and headed north-east.'

'Yes I am. Because it easily could have. And there was no other submarine which could possibly have hit the trawl net. *There is no other explanation. And nor can there ever be.* If missiles hit Valdez, they must have been fired from that Barracuda. One sneaky little bastard, I think we'll discover.'

0100 Sunday morning, March 2
53.15N 131.39W. The Dixon Entrance
North of Graham Island
Lt. Arash Azhari and his highly-trained frogmen were making their exit from the submarine which was positioned thirty feet below the pitch-black surface of the water. One by one they went into the exit chamber which flooded down, and then opened, allowing them to float out onto the casing of the motionless Barracuda.

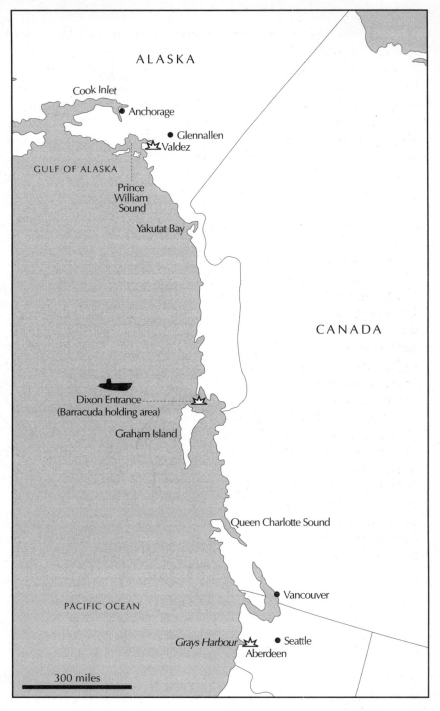

ALASKA AND THE NORTH-WEST - THE BARRACUDA'S
PRINCIPLE TARGET AREA

Each man carried black, French-made scuba gear, and a frogman's suit distingushed by extra-large flippers and a working flashlight set onto the tight-fitting rubber helmet. They were unarmed save for fighting knives, but four of them carried, strapped to their backs below the breathing equipment, a powerful 'sticky' bomb, magnetized, with a twenty-four-hour timing device.

By 0115 all six members of the Islamic Revolutionary Guards Corps were grouped in the icy water, around twelve feet below the surface, right on the escarpment of the underwater cliff which forms the Overfall Shoal. They were just 300 yards from the south-running pipeline out of Yakutan. And if they swam due east, they must run over it sooner or later. This was the choke-point, the narrow waters over the shoal, across which the pipe *must* run, according to the minute calculations of Shakira Rashood.

Lieutenant Azhari led the way, checking his wristwatch compass every three minutes. They kicked long, hard, slow strokes with the big flippers, conserving their air, heading for the shallowest part of the shoal. And shortly before 0130 the beam of Azhari's flashlight picked out a wide dark shape on the seabed, more or less where Shakira's map said it would be, snaking out of the Dixon Entrance and down the Hecate Strait.

All six men could see down through the clear, unpolluted water, and they could see the pipeline still rising towards the surface. Right now it was around eighteen feet below them, and Arazhi gave the signal for two men to join him almost directly below. Two men with bombs, and, like the other four, experts in underwater demolition.

Swiftly they kicked down eighteen more feet, and then they unclipped the two 'stickies' and set both timers for twenty-two hours. The four-foot wide pipeline was encased in steel and carried no barnacles in these very cold waters. The first bomb clamped on magnetically with a dull 'clump' sound.

The second was placed exactly opposite on the other side of the pipe, the timer reversed three minutes and twenty-one seconds, the precise time Lieutenant Azhari's stopwatch measured between the fixes. The bombs would detonate simultaneously, shortly before midnight tomorrow.

They joined their three colleagues and showed the leader the time on the stopwatch which showed the start of the twenty-two-hour cycle. Then the second three men broke away and began swimming downhill, following the pipeline back north, into deeper water, down the escarpment of the shoal.

They kept going for 1,000 yards, and unclipped the last two bombs, placing the first one on the steel pipe and taking a total of seventeen minutes off the twenty-two-hour setting. Then they clamped the fourth and final 'sticky' on the precise opposite side of the pipe, set the timer for twenty-one hours thirty-nine minutes and fourteen seconds, and turned back west.

They were almost 100 feet deep here, and as they swam back westwards, they kicked towards the surface, settling twelve feet below the waves for the final 200 yards, back to the submarine, which was now emitting a slow *b-e-e-e-p* every twenty seconds to guide them back.

When they arrived, Lieutenant Azhari was waiting, the other two frogmen having already boarded through the wet-hatch. Ten minutes later they were all inboard, and the giant US oil pipeline from Yakutat was doomed in this part of the ocean, barring a zillion-to-one fluke.

Captain Ben Badr turned his ship slowly west, and they headed back out through the Dixon Entrance, into the 12,000-foot-deep waters of the Gulf of Alaska, where they could run 1,000 feet below the surface, and where they would be virtually impossible to find. They were headed due south.

Noon, Sunday, March 2
Ops Room Valdez Police Department
Officer Kip Callaghan's telephone never stopped ringing. Local people were literally in line to give information, ask for information, or just to talk about the savage, roaring blaze which still thundered into the smoky skies on two sides of their town.

It had taken almost twenty hours to stop the flow of crude oil flooding out of the inflow pipe from the north, directly into the terminus, and igniting with the rest of the stored fuel. The electronic control center was still completely out of action, but they had managed to turn off a huge valve on the pipeline, by hand, some two miles north of the city.

Wearily, Officer Callaghan picked up the ringing phone again . . . 'Valdez police – situation room . . .'

'Sir, I'm calling from Glennallen . . . with a little information you may want . . .'

'Okay, sir. Just give me your full name and address, and age. Plus the number you are calling from . . .'

'Cal Foster, P.O. Box fifty-eight, Glennallen. I'm twenty-one, and I'm calling from Glennallen nine-oh-seven, eight-two-two, three-six-double seven . . .'

'Thank you, sir. Please tell me your information . . .'

'Well, I'm really calling about a UFO I saw in the sky on Friday morning around one-thirty.'

'A UFO! You mean a kinda flying saucer, sir?'

'Well, kind of.'

'Sir, this is the situation room for the fire catastrophe. You'd probably be better to let the main police department know about a flying saucer. Right here I'm strictly in the combustion area . . .'

'Officer, I'm in the right department. I may have a connection to the fire . . .'

'Okay, sir. Tell me . . .'

'Well, me and my buddy, Harry Roberts, had just stopped on the Glenn Highway on our way home, and we were like taking a leak, facing north, when I saw this missile flying through the sky. Real quick, right above us. I could see a flame coming from the back, and it made a kinda growling noise . . . it was heading directly south to the mountains and Valdez . . .

'Then, just about a half-minute later, I saw another one, maybe a mile to the east, but going the same way. Just as quick. Identical. I was thinking they could have been missiles – you know, aimed at the oil terminal . . . and maybe they started the fire . . .'

'Sir, did your buddy also see the objects?'

'He wasn't in time to see the first one. But I yelled when I saw the second one, and he saw that alright. Mind you, he didn't really believe it was a missile. He thought it was a low-flying aircraft, and he might have been right. But I don't think so . . . I ain't never seen anything go so fast through the air, not that low to the ground . . . that was no aircraft. Nossir . . .'

'You took a while to let us know . . . how come?'

'Well, I never knew about the fire until the middle of the day Friday . . . and I'd kinda forgotten about the rockets I'd seen. Then I got to thinking about 'em, and last night I suddenly thought there might be a connection . . .'

'Sir, I'd like to speak to your buddy Harry . . .'

'Well, right now he's up at the Caribou Cafe.'

'They got a phone?'

'Sure. It's eight-two-two, three-six-five-six . . . don't listen if he tells you it was a seven forty-seven or something . . . it wasn't.'

'Okay, Cal. I'm gonna try to get this corroborated. I'll call you back . . .'

Officer Callaghan called the Caribou and asked to speak to a customer named Harry Roberts. Half a minute later the reluctant spotter of the UFO was on the line.

'I saw it, yessir. I definitely saw it. And Cal was right. It was traveling real quick. And I saw it much later than he did, only seconds, but it was going away from us time I turned around . . .'

'You didn't see the first one at all?'

'Nossir. Cal just caught it as it went over us. I wasn't in time. But I saw the second one. Flying straight for the mountains . . .'

'Well, your buddy Cal thinks those rockets might have been headed for the oil terminal, and were the cause of the fires . . .'

'Coulda been . . . coulda been . . .'

'Do you think they were kinda mysterious? Like not an aircraft . . . more like a missile . . .?'

'Well, I haven't given the one I saw much thought. But it was kinda creepy. The thing you'd notice was how fast the bastard was going . . . and Cal's right. It was a lot too fast for a regular aircraft . . .'

'One more thing, sir . . . what time was it when you and Cal saw 'em?'

'Well, I got home at exactly one-thirty a.m. So Cal musta spotted the first one at around one-twenty . . . took us about ten minutes to get home from there.'

'Okay, sir. That's all. Thanks for your time.'

Kip Callaghan knew the first explosions in the oil terminal were now put at 1.30 a.m. It was ninety miles up to the Glenn Highway where Cal and Harry saw the possible missile. If the damn thing was making ten miles a minute, that was around nine minutes' flying time.

The coincidence was too hot for Officer Callaghan. He phoned his boss and gave him the information. Superintendent Ratzberg immediately reported the phone calls to the newly arrived FBI Chief, who passed it on to the coastguard, who alerted the appropriate US Navy Department, Pacific Fleet San Diego.

Ten minutes later, news of a possible sighting of guided missiles was in the Pentagon, and four minutes after that there was a message on the secure Fort Meade internet, direct to Lieutenant Commander Jimmy Ramshawe, Personal Assistant to the Director.

Jimmy, who was on duty that Sunday afternoon, buzzed Admiral Morris, who instantly called Admiral Morgan, encrypted, at home in Chevy Chase. It was late afternoon now, bitterly cold and already growing dark. Arnold was sitting by the fire glowering at the *New York Times*, the liberal left-wing views of which unfailingly made his tight-cropped steel-gray hair stand on end. At least it would have done, had it been sufficiently long.

Meanwhile he just glowered, and waited for Kathy to bring him some China tea, which he counted as one of his Sunday afternoon luxuries. The interruption of the phone call from Admiral Morris caught him entirely unaware, and he greeted his old friend tersely. 'What's up, George?' he said, 'I suppose you're on a special mission to ruin what's left of the weekend?'

'Don't be ridiculous, sir,' replied George, 'I bring you critical information . . . the police in Valdez have interviewed two local men who apparently saw two very fast missiles ripping through the sky, due south towards the Valdez Terminus, at one-twenty on Friday morning, ten minutes before the storage tanks blew up, ninety miles away.'

'Who are the guys . . . sane . . . sound mind . . . etcetera . . .?'

'Yes. Apparently. Both twenty-one years old, clear sighted and identical in their observations. One of them saw two missiles or rockets, the other saw only one . . . said it was traveling too fast to be a commercial aircraft. Both confirmed a short fiery tail in the stern of the object, and both were struck by its very high speed.'

'Did they want anything out of it?'

'No. Nothing. The first one meant to report it as a UFO. It was only when he saw about the fires he decided they might be connected.'

'Uh-huh . . . may we presume that at after one o'clock in the morning these two kids were several sheets to the wind?'

'I expect so, Arnie. Nonetheless, according to the police, they are both kinda unassuming guys. They agree on the basics, and their time-fix is probably accurate within seconds. And they had no way of knowing that, not before one of 'em made the call.'

'I'd say they're correct by the sound of it,' said Admiral Morgan. 'I now accept that we were probably hit by at least two missiles, fired from an enemy unknown, almost certainly from a submarine, probably Russian. We got a lot of sleuthing to do, George.

'Meanwhile we better keep a tight lid on this. We can't tell the populace someone is trying to wipe us out. Make certain no-one releases anything, and I'll have the President make a short national broadcast later tonight . . . just expressing his regrets at the terrible accident in Alaska. That way we'll take the sting out of it. The Press won't catch on till someone tells 'em . . . and no-one better do that. Yet.

'George, be at my office tomorrow morning 0600. Bring Ramshawe. Does he know about the missile sightings . . . ?'

'Sure does. He told me.'

'Fluky little bastard. Tell him not to be late.'

The remainder of the evening went cosily and gastronomically perfectly for the President's National Security Advisor. He carefully drafted the text of the President's broadcast, then called the White House to tell the Press Officer how to handle it and what to tell the man in the Oval Office.

Submitted by anyone else, this would have taken several drafts and a committee of God knows how many people to write and rewrite, suggest and re-suggest, criticize and re-criticize. The fact that not one of these literary minnows could come within a bull's roar of writing anything one-tenth as good as the original was not considered relevant.

Even the great Ronald Reagan had a White House plagued by these fourth-raters, trying to look thoughtful, and mostly failing. The wondrous political writer Peggy Noonan, a talent of genuine stature, revealed in her book, *When Character Was King,* they were known as the Three Blind Mice. She once observed, in hysterical detail, precisely how they would have rewritten Lincoln's Gettysburg Address.

It was as well they were not in residence during the reign of Admiral Arnold Morgan, who had all of the flinty, idealistic, conservative character of President Reagan, the same selfless regard for what was right for the country, and much more capacity to be flagrantly rude to people whenever he felt so inclined.

The Three Blind Mice would have lasted about ten minutes with Admiral Morgan on the prowl. On one occasion when the duty Press Officer did venture to tamper with a draft speech the

Admiral had penned for the President, Arnold sent for him, tossed the offending sheets of paper into the bin, and growled: 'When I write something, with all the implications of National Security involved, don't ever again dare to change one word of it. What I write is what I mean. You don't like it, get another job. Join a fucking poetry society. Just remember, there's a thousand goddamned writers around, but not one of them, *not one*, hear me? *not one* understands what to do, like I understand what to do. That's all.'

That particular Press Officer, not the head of the department, was in shock when he left. And his mauling in the lair of the National Security Advisor became legend among the writers. No-one had ever wanted to tangle with Admiral Morgan again.

And on this Sunday evening, when he told the Press Officer his requirements, the only words he heard were, 'Yessir. White House Press Room, twenty-one hundred. No questions afterwards.'

'Correct,' said Admiral Morgan, banging down the phone, without saying goodbye.

Thereafter his mood mellowed. He and Kathy always had dinner together at home on Sunday nights. They started with a couple of glasses of champagne. Then, with their main course, drank the best bottle of wine Admiral Morgan could lay hands on.

Tonight Kathy had prepared roast lamb, and Arnold had opened, warming by the fire, a bottle of superb burgundy, 1997 Corton Rouge, a Grand Cru from one of France's historic Domaines, the Bonneau du Martray. Eleven years old, from a great vintage, the wine was another recommended by Harcourt Travis, the Secretary of State, connoisseur of the French grape, wine advisor to the National Security Advisor.

The Admiral poured two glasses and tasted his before he carved the lamb. Then he handed one to Kathy and kissed her, asking her, as he did every Sunday evening, if they were to be married this week.

Her reply varied no more than the question. 'Only,' said Kathy, 'if you resign from the White House and allow us to spend carefree years together without you trying to run the world.'

'Guess we'll have to hold off for another week, then,' he said. 'Otherwise there's not going be a light left on in the country . . .

no oil whatsoever coming out of Alaska . . . and the goddamned Chinese running off with all the crude in the Middle East.'

Kathy O'Brien for a moment looked pensive. 'Do you really think,' she said, 'that someone actually hit that oil terminus in Valdez?'

'Honey, I know full well someone hit it,' he replied. 'Hit it good and hard, blew up and incinerated Christ knows how many acres of stored fuel, in two places, with guided missiles, which two witnesses saw going in. They were fired from a submarine that somehow crossed one of the narrowest parts of the Pacific Ocean, into either the Gulf of Alaska or the Bering Sea.'

'How come you don't even know which ocean the missiles were fired from?'

'Because that's the nature of SLCMs,' he said unhelpfully.

'What's an SLCM?' she asked.

'Submerged launch cruise missile. Flies itself. Steers itself. Finds its own target. All pre-programmed. It's just about the trickiest weapon in the world because it launches suddenly, from out of an ocean. From a launch pad which seemingly does not exist.'

'Well, if it's caught on radar you'd surely know where it's come from, roughly?' said Kathy.

'And therein lies the problem,' said Admiral Morgan, archly. 'Among the many secrets our last Democratic Government somehow allowed the Chinese to get their hands on, was a brilliant pre-programmed flight direction system which allows these missiles to make whatever course you want 'em to make.

'Let's say you gotta target a thousand miles away to the north-east . . . you can make one of these missiles go right round it, swinging north a hundred miles early, then heading east, then homing in on its quarry . . . flying due south – right out of the north. At that point, no-one knows where the hell it's come from.

'The final flight path is irrelevant. It just came from nowhere. So in this case, you can only stick the point of your compasses into Valdez and describe a circle to about twelve hundred miles and anywhere there's ocean more than three hundred feet deep, inside your circle, is a place a submarine could have launched from. Right here, on this enchanted Sunday evening, we're looking at around a zillion square miles.'

Arnold sipped his burgundy.

'Well, my darling,' said Kathy. 'You don't seem over-anxious to send out a posse to find him?'

'No point. You can't search that big an area. All you can do is get your defenses and surveillance systems on high alert, and wait for the sonofabitch to make a mistake. As he will.'

'What about refueling. Won't someone have to come and deliver him some gas.'

'That, Mrs O'Brien, is what really worries me. He may not have to.'

'Oh, does the submarine run on fresh air?'

'No. Water.'

At which time Arnold spent ten minutes explaining to his fiancée the principles of a nuclear submarine, how its reactor just goes on working, how it can stay underwater for years, if necessary. How it's *the goddamned sneakiest little sonofabitch ever invented, and every time we run into a major problem, I look for an enemy submarine.*

'Wow,' said Kathy. 'You mean it's possible there actually could be an enemy submarine, lurking off our coast?'

'I'm afraid it is. But the little bastard might already be chugging its way back over the Pacific Ocean,' he replied.

'To which country, though,' she persisted.

'If I knew that, life would be a great deal easier,' rasped the Admiral.

In fact it did not get any easier at all. Arnold and Kathy retired to bed at around 10 p.m. since he had to be up and on his way by 0530. And while they slept, an appalling catastrophe happened on the eastern shores of the Gulf of Alaska.

At precisely 11.35 p.m. (2.35 a.m., Eastern), two simultaneous, muffled underwater explosions breached the biggest oil pipeline in the United States. Right inside the entrance to the Hecate Strait. In the pitch dark, crude oil began to pump out into the ocean, millions of gallons, and no-one could see it. And it pumped for seven hours, until someone did see it, a Canadian fishing boat at first light.

A breach in any oil pipeline is bad. Back in 2001, a disenchanted and very drunk Alaskan fired a .338 calibre hunting rifle into the overland pipeline at point blank range, punctured it with one bullet and caused a spillage of 300,000 gallons of crude over a two-acre area.

Several fathoms below the surface of the ocean, out near the

Overfall Shoal, the situation was 100 times worse. The fires in Valdez had caused thousands of barrels to be diverted down the new pipeline causing a marked increase in the pressure.

All through the night the massive pumping station in Yakutat Bay was driving tons and tons of oil into the pipe and it was all thundering out into the ocean, over 500 miles away, causing an ecological disaster of satanic proportions. It was also the beginning of a stark and terrifying shortage at the new refinery in Grays Harbor.

By dawn, the coastguard had alerted everyone, and the slick was ten miles long, already washing on the rocky shores of Graham Island. The Canadian Government, always sceptical and knee-jerk jumpy towards any environmental problem, was beside itself with indignation.

CNN was on the air in Washington by 10 a.m. but the radio news bulletins were earlier. Meantime there were tugs, frogmen, oil pipeline emergency crews, support vessels, cranes, and divers, hurtling towards the shallows north of the Overfall Shoal from where the pumping oil seemed to emanate.

From the Gulf coast of Texas, crews of disaster specialists were preparing to fly north. Many of them were veterans from the 1991 Gulf War, men who had worked on the massive grid of oil fires in the Kuwaiti desert, ignited by Saddam Hussein once he realized all was lost. These repair crews would bring with them the cutting edge of modern disaster technology. Anything to stop the flow.

Obviously, valves would be turned off, but in an undersea pipeline, these are far apart, and several miles of oil could just go right on leaking into the ocean.

By the time Admirals Morgan and Morris, plus Lt. Commander Ramshawe were briefed on the scale of the disaster, the media already had experts on the airwaves explaining what had happened.

It was Professor Jethro Flint, a mining and energy expert from the University of Colorado who was the most lucid. Answering questions from a CNN news reporter he stated: 'The fires in the Valdez terminus have plainly shut down the entire Trans-Alaska Pipeline System. Nothing is currently flowing south through the line from Prudhoe Bay to Valdez. But, back in the north, the oil is still flowing into the pumping station from the deep wells which are active in a very wide area up there.'

The Professor paused. 'What to do with the extra capacity?' he said. 'Since the crude can't go where it always goes, down the TAPS route, and it's gotta go somewhere.'

Where, sir? Where will it go?

'That oil,' replied Professor Flint, 'will be diverted down the new south-running oil freeway, the Alaska Bi-Coastal Energy Transfer, direct to Yakutan. And there they will increase the traffic flow, pumping much more crude into the underwater system.'

Will that matter, sir?

'It will matter to the extent they will never have tested that pipeline with those kind of real-life pressures. And when you subject something to stresses it's never undergone before, it can rupture. And in my view, that's what this has done. They've overloaded the pipeline, somewhat thoughtlessly, and it's come unraveled.'

That was sufficient to send afternoon newspaper editors, and media newsmen into a collective dance of death, preparing headlines such as . . . *OIL EXECS BLAMED FOR ALASKA PIPELINE DISASTER . . . ALASKAN PIPELINE – ACCIDENT WAITING TO HAPPEN . . . PIPELINE TESTING SNAFU – ACCIDENT PREDICTABLE . . . PIPELINE ACCIDENT CAUSED BY OVERLOAD.*

Admirals Morgan and Morris watched the drama unfold with Lt. Commander Ramshawe. The three of them had lunch together in the White House, poring over the charts, studying the distances, trying to work out from where a rogue submarine might have unleashed a salvo of missiles at Valdez, and then blown up the pipeline.

'I'll say one thing,' said Arnold Morgan. 'The media, for once in their miserable fucking lives are being helpful. They keep saying "accident" and that's what we want . . . not just to calm the populace . . . but so no word gets out we're suspicious.

'Once someone realizes we're on the case, our chances of finding out what the hell's going on get diminished by fifty percent.'

'You're not yet ready to start ordering a search?' asked George Morris.

'No. Not without some evidence there is a definite submarine out there. Right now we're chasing our tails, but I hope not for long.'

'Do you think there's any possibility this is all just a huge accident?' said George.

'Not a chance,' snapped Arnie. 'How about you, Jimmy?'

'Not a chance,' replied Lieutenant Commander Ramshawe.

CHAPTER TEN

Admiral George Morris left the White House right after lunch, without his personal assistant. Lt. Commander Ramshawe was required by the National Security Advisor for a brainstorming session, to think, and essentially to play war games.

On a large computer screen on the left-hand side of the office, was a close-up chart of the entire area of southern Alaska, the coastline west to east, from the Aleutians all the way around to the Queen Charlotte Islands, passing the Cook Inlet, Prince William Sound, and Yakutat Bay. The route of the Alaskan Bi-Coastal Energy Transfer pipeline was marked in thick black against the light blue tone of the inshore ocean.

Admiral Morgan, however, was not quite ready to delve into the main thrust of his investigation. Right now he was grilling Jimmy Ramshawe for every last contact he may have had with any foreign submarine in the past two years.

And Jimmy was telling him about Old Razormouth, and how he took that to be a code name for a Russian Barracuda. He told Arnold about that message, *Old Razormouth 600 confirmed*. And he told him how the US SOSUS men in South Wales had briefly picked up the transient engine lines of a similar Sierra I in the Atlantic, off the west coast of Ireland, on February 7.

And he mentioned how Admiral Morris had asked Moscow for an explanation. And how they had both judged the reply to be polite and helpful, but evasive.

'Rankov?' growled the Admiral.

'Yessir.'

'Lying Russian bastard,' added Arnold.

'Anyway, sir, I did check on the Barracuda program and we have no record of a second hull *ever* being operational. Hull 239, the *Tula* was always with the Northern Fleet, and we then tracked it, last summer, along the north coast of Siberia – an obvious transfer to the Pacific Fleet. Admiral Rankov confirmed that himself. Then we saw it leave Petropavlovsk and turn south . . .'

'Do we *know* they completed the second hull?'

'No, sir. Not really. There is a slightly shaky report that it was launched. But we have no record of it ever going to sea. It was reported laid-up, in a covered dry dock, out of commission, in the Northern Fleet at Araguba back in the early 1990s. That's the last we heard.'

'Guess they couldn't afford to run 'em. They were expensive ships . . .'

'There was never much doubt about that, sir. The Russians canceled the class, and laid one hull up. They never made a secret about that. It was obvious.'

'But we still don't know what submarine the guys heard off the coast of Ireland?'

'Nossir. We never got a handle on that.'

'And neither do we know what submarine hit the trawl nets on the goddamned *sushi* ship off Pretropavlovsk?'

'Must have been the Barracuda. But no, sir. Nothing confirmed.'

'Well, well,' said Admiral Morgan. 'Who plays games with us, Jimmy? Very big, very destructive games, eh?'

'I'm not sure, sir. But I got a creepy feeling Old Razormouth is somehow right in the bloody thick of it.'

'I would not disagree with that, Jimmy. Not at all.' And with that the Admiral stood up, and walked over to the chart, and with the touch of a couple of keys, he described a big seaward arc 1,000 miles out from the port of Valdez. It was a long arc, extending south-west to south-east, starting way down, off the Alaskan Peninsula, and slicing across the Gulf to the southern half of Graham Island.

'If he exists, Jimmy, he's somewhere in there,' said Arnold. 'At least he was in the very early hours of yesterday morning. Christ knows where he is now.'

'Why yesterday, sir? The pipeline ruptured early today?'

'Jimmy, if you and I were going to blow a big hole in an oil pipeline, or a ship, or any underwater target, and we were using modern high explosive, we certainly would not wish to be anywhere near when the charge detonated. In fact we'd want to be as far away as possible. If we happened to be operating out of a submarine, I guess we'd give ourselves the maximum clearance time. And most of those limpet mines can be set for twenty-four hours.

'So I guess we'd place our charges, and allow almost a day to get the hell outta there – so we'd be, what? At ten knots, two hundred and forty miles away? At five knots we'd be one-twenty miles away. And since no-one knows our direction, that's an awful lot of ocean to search, like maybe fifty thousand plus square miles . . .'

'So you think he's now been on his way home, for perhaps a day and a half?'

'Without question. Except I'm not sure he's going home, Jimmy. I'm not sure he's finished his work . . . but come and look here at this chart . . .'

The young Lt. Commander with the Aussie accent stood and walked slowly across the room, deep in thought. 'Bloody oath, this character has a set of balls, hasn't he? Sometimes, during these conversations I start thinking it's all a fantasy . . . I mean we're talking about a guy who's taking on the US Navy, and is marauding along our coast like some fucking pirate, raping and pillaging, and we have no idea who he is, where he's come from, or where he's bloody going.

'In the last couple of days he's destroyed an entire oil industry, the biggest in the USA . . . sir, if there really is someone on the loose, we'd better find him real quick . . . I mean, strewth! Bin Laden was a fanatic, followed by fanatics who knew they were committing suicide in their attacks on us – this bastard is worse, because he's clever, and appears to have equipment to match our own, and he doesn't want to die. And so far he's making a fucking good job of it . . .'

Arnold Morgan looked thoughtful. And he turned back to the big computer screen. 'You see this point right here?' he said. 'The place where the pipeline blew off Graham Island, I think we might assume he was very close to that point when he unleashed his missiles at Valdez.'

'Well, I'd assumed he was out in the middle of the Gulf, sir. Down here somewhere, and then went over to the pipeline to place his explosive.'

'I don't think so, Jimmy. Because this character is as clever as us, and that's not what I would have done. I'd have positioned myself somewhere over here north of Graham Island, pre-programmed my missiles to swerve right around Valdez and then come in from the north. Then I'd have crept into the pipeline, done my business and left, knowing I'd be miles and miles away when the explosive went bang . . .

'So where is he, Jimmy? If he was right here somewhere near the pipeline at, say, midnight on Saturday . . . which way did he go?'

'Well, I would have headed for shallow water, probably back around the Gulf, very quietly. Not straight over the middle where the ocean depth is two miles . . . and SOSUS works.'

'Yeah . . . and then where?'

'Back across the Pacific – either running around the Great Pacific Plain, or just south of the Aleutian Islands.'

'He didn't come that way.'

'How do you know, sir?'

'Well, we have a permanent submarine patrol in the Aleutian Trench and they would have heard him, picked him up, and if the boat was Russian, probably sunk him.'

'Well he could have come in across that big deep Plain . . .'

'Doubtful. That's one of the most heavily surveilled SOSUS areas in the world. I would rate it just about impossible to bring a submarine right across the middle of the Pacific Plain without the United States Navy picking you up.'

'Well, how did he get here?'

'You tell me. I don't know.'

'Sir, could he have come north of the Aleutians? I don't think we have that patrolled, do we?'

'No, we don't. And yes he could have made passage along the north of the islands. But in order to get into his firing position, he'd have needed to come through the islands, back to the south. There's no other way into the Gulf of Alaska . . . probably three places he might have done it. But the water's pretty shallow, and it's swept by US Navy radar. If he did do it, I don't know how.'

'Well, if the bugger did get into the Gulf, he must have come through one of the three places. Otherwise he'd still be outside the Gulf, or sunk, right, sir?'

'Correct, Jimmy. But he did come through, didn't he? And he crept all the way over to Graham Island. And the little bastard's still creeping. And we have to find him.'

'Do you get the feeling, sir, we're dealing with a person,

someone who has so far outwitted us? Or does it seem like an impersonal situation – just a military opponent?'

'I feel it's a person, Jimmy. And I've had the feeling before. As if someone was taking me on . . .'

'You mean, like Admiral Rankov?'

'Christ, no. Someone a lot cleverer than that.'

0100 Tuesday, March 4
The Gulf of Alaska 48.OON 128W
The Barracuda was making only five knots through the water, 1,000 feet below the surface. There were still 8,000 feet below the keel, and their course had not changed since they pushed west out of the Dixon Entrance, and then swung south, seventy-two hours previously.

No-one aboard had any idea whether the bombs had detonated on the pipeline. And no-one certainly realized that right now, at 0900 Greenwich Mean Time, there was absolute pandemonium on the International Petroleum Exchange in the City of London. Only once, since the Gulf War, had there been anything remotely like the panic buying which now swept the London Exchange.

The issue, as ever, was Brent Crude Futures. The IPE had first heard of the giant oil slick near the Alaskan pipeline at around 3 p.m. (London) the previous afternoon. There was some disquiet, especially because the fires in Valdez were still burning, and the price of crude rocketed to thirty-five dollars a barrel by the close, up six dollars.

However on New York's NYMEX, operating five hours behind, the price of West Texas Intermediate climbed to thirty-nine dollars by late afternoon, and the oil business teetered on the brink of a major crisis. In the West, all-night service stations were starting to sell gas at five dollars a gallon.

Today, Tuesday, however, was an entirely different matter. The IPE in London, first of the major Western markets to open, saw Brent Crude explode to fifty dollars a barrel within one hour of the opening bell.

The traders had spent the night thinking, speculating and finally going into near-meltdown when the news broke that the massive Alaskan Pipeline feeding the west coast of the United States was incontrovertibly breached. It was clear even to the dimmest executives there would be no oil out of Alaska until a) the fires were out, b) new storage facilities were established, and c) they had mended the shattered undersea pipeline. One month minimum, maybe a lot more.

The trading floor in London resembled a madhouse. Dealers yelled and screamed, as an avalanche of orders for 'futures' came thundering in from the United States. This was beginning to look like the sellers' market to end them all. And it took the big oil corporations a matter of minutes to work out they could get what they asked for their product.

The main supplier of crude oil to the entire west coast of the USA, and beyond, was effectively out of business. Other producers, refiners, shippers, distributors and marketers were at the golden gates of hog-heaven. And brokers for the power generators, airlines, truck fleet operators and chemical companies were almost prostrate with worry.

At 9.14 a.m. in London there was an unmistakable power surge. The trader for Morgan Stanley suddenly bellowed, '*Plus five, plus five for three hundred thousand.*' And the price of Brent Crude was suddenly pegged at fifty-five dollars a barrel. Rumors swept the tiered trading pits that crude was going to eighty dollars, and the crowd seemed to sense the coming onslaught of Californian black-outs, dry-outs and cut-outs.

It was impossible to hear anything clearly except the shouts of *Plus Five! . . . Plus Two! . . . Plus Three!* And these were not calls of just cents, like they were last week. These were full-blooded dollars, and there were no minuses, no price drops. Just a stack of huge trades of 500,000 barrels and more.

Over at the London Stock Exchange the Footsie had no idea which way to turn – some oil shares were climbing, five and six percent every half hour as soon as brokers realized who would cash in on the west coast calamity and who would not.

But as rumors of burgeoning oil prices swept the trading floor, a whole raft of stocks crashed. Especially the oil giants whose businesses had a bedrock in the Alaskan Fields. Big oil consumers, especially airlines, took their worst hits since 2001.

The price of electricity in the American west hovered in a no man's land of doubt, and investors were uncertain whether the major power suppliers would somehow cash in on the disaster, or go bust. In one nerve-racking hour, shares in British Petroleum went up an astounding ten percent, then fell back to where they opened, and then crashed ten percent.

One broker who had shorted them on the bell, and then sold high before they rose again, was seen standing in shock, threatening suicide after a twelve million career-wrecking loss on behalf of a client.

Over at Lloyds of London, the insurance market had a collective heart attack, with grotesque visions of the crash of the 1990s standing once more, starkly, before the brokers. Losses in the little city of Valdez would be shuddering, but the breached pipeline with its colossal overtones of environmental damage, threatened to rival the gigantic claims which erupted after the *Exxon Valdez* catastrophe in Prince William Sound in 1992.

Cocooned in the control room of the Barracuda, 1,000 feet deep, 100 miles off the coast of California, General Rashood had not an inkling of the havoc he had wrought. He and Shakira, sharing their tiny office/bedroom, felt safe behind the slow, cautious driving of Ben Badr. And the submarine was in excellent shape, moving through the quiet, deep caverns of the oceans, with the minimum of stress on the turbines, the reactor running silkily, watched by a top-class team of newly-qualified Iranian nuclear engineers.

Captain Badr's navigator had them on a course of 180 degrees, running directly south through the Pacific, straight down the 128W line of longitude. The Dixon Entrance stands just north of the 54th parallel, and their next destination was slightly north of the 42nd. That gave them 12 degrees of latitude to cover, 720 nautical miles. They were making only 120 miles a day at their low speed of five knots, and Ravi and Ben estimated they would arrive on station in the small hours of Friday morning, March 7. They would be, predictably, 180 miles off the coast of the state of Oregon, but, unpredictably, almost 300 miles *south* of their target.

Meanwhile Lt. Commander Ramshawe scarcely slept, spending eighteen hours a day in his office, waiting for a SOSUS 'heads-up,' or that someone had heard something, somewhere, that there was a Russian submarine on the loose.

But there was only silence. Not a sound from the Barracuda. Indeed, on the international stage, the only loud and significant sound came from Admiral Arnold Morgan, personally railing at the Russian Navy HQ in Moscow, demanding to speak to the Admiral of the Fleet, Vitaly Rankov.

Admiral Rankov, a seasoned and wily operator, found himself

in a tight spot. He had already guessed the Barracuda had done its job on the far side of the Pacific, but he had much to protect. The culprit for these unprovoked atrocities on the American economy was a Russian-built, Russian-owned submarine, now based in the Pacific Fleet at Petropavlovsk.

But Vitaly had his story in disciplined order. He would reveal the submarine had been sold to the Chinese, and was believed to be making its way down to their Southern Fleet Headquarters in Zhanjiang, on the north-east corner of the great tropical island of Hainan. So far as he knew, there were no Russian personnel on board.

His policy was to duck and dive, avoiding a salvo of phone calls from the redoubtable Arnold Morgan, though he realized this would not work for long.

He actually kept it up for thirty-six hours until noon on Thursday March 6, by which time Admiral Morgan had yelled down the phone to Moscow at six different aides. Finally he had the President of the United States call the President of Russia and demand that Rankov speak to the White House immediately.

The instruction from the Great White Chief of all the Russians, to his Naval Supreme Commander was succinct: *Admiral Rankov: I have been asked by the US President to ensure you speak to his National Security Advisor on an important matter this day. Please do so.*

It was thus with a heavy heart that the Admiral of the Russian Fleet, at 1500 that afternoon, had his assistant call the White House and connect him to his oldest, and most dangerous nemesis, the most persistent, ill-tempered, gratingly powerful opponent in the world.

'Arnold! What a nice surprise to hear you again. It's been too long.'

'Thirty-six hours too long, insincere Soviet sailor.' Arnold was always delighted with alliteration of that music-hall quality. 'You are a devious sonofabitch. And you have deliberately not answered my calls, or my messages. I was just beginning to think you might be avoiding me.'

Admiral Rankov was unable to suppress a deep chuckle. Despite his uneasiness with Admiral Morgan, he was always amused by him, actually liked him very much. They had met on several occasions over the years, even dined together in Washington, London, and once in Moscow. 'I know . . . I know,' he said. 'I was avoiding you. Mainly because I sensed you were going to give me a very hard time, about matters over which I have no control.'

'I presume you are still head of that junkyard Navy of yours?'

At which point the two old Intelligence sparring partners both laughed, at the American's incorrigible rudeness, and the fact that the conversation had returned to its usual standard of wit.

'Arnold, look, seriously. I know what you are going to say . . . you know we made a Fleet Exchange, sending that old Barracuda to Petropavlovsk. You also know it left, and headed south. You also know, like we do, there is a large financial claim from a Japanese fishing boat which was snagged by a submarine just a few miles to the north. Same time. Same day. Am I correct?'

'You are.'

'And now you are going to ask me why our submarine dived after making course south, and then did an about turn underwater and went north? Right?'

'Right. There was no other submarine operational within a thousand miles. The goddamned *sushi* ship was hooked by the Barracuda.'

'Arnold, what you do not know . . . and why should you? . . . is that we sold the Barracuda to the Chinese. It was just too damned expensive for us to run.'

'Well, that's very interesting, Vitaly. Are there any Russians aboard?'

'None.'

'Well, where the hell's it going?'

'I was told Zhanjiang. But we have no way of knowing. The ship is no longer our property.'

'Vitaly, my main question is even more serious. And I am asking you to give me a straight answer.'

'If I can.'

'Did you guys ever complete the building of the second Barracuda, Hull K–240?'

'Arnold, I was up in the northern yard at Araguba just six months ago, and I saw that ship in its covered dock, with a number of plates missing from the casing. I believe we used it for spare parts for the *Tula*, the one we just sold. So far as I know, hull K–240 never went to sea. Why?'

'Is it still there . . . in Araguba?'

'I can't swear to it. But no-one has told me it has been

scrapped, or sold. If I can find out anything, do you want me to get back to you?'

'That would be good of you . . . and remember, I just want to know if you sold one Barracuda, or two, to the even–more-devious Chinese?'

'I understand, Arnold. Leave it with me.'

Arnold Morgan quietly said goodbye, and put down the phone. But he sensed a kind of edgy formality in the voice of the Russian Navy boss. Arnold had an actor's gift for recalling the rhythms and reactions of people and their speech. In his mind, he believed he should have heard something quite different from Admiral Rankov.

Something much more like . . . *Okay, Arnie. I'll check it right now. Hull K-240 . . . where is it? That's what you want to know. No problem. I'll be back to you in ten minutes.*

Instead it was, *If I can find out anything . . . do you want me to get back to you?*

'The actual *head* of the entire Russian Navy,' growled Arnold. '*If I can find out whether we still own a five hundred million dollar nuclear submarine!* Vitaly, you bastard, I think you are lying. I think you know full well whether your fucking rattletrap Navy still owns the second Barracuda. But, for whatever reason, you are not telling me.'

The Admiral was, however, still very nearly handcuffed by the situation. He could think of no other method by which any enemy could have done this much damage to the USA, except by using a nuclear submarine. A diesel-electric must have been detected already because of its need to snorkel and recharge batteries, and ultimately to refuel. In the electronic minefield of the North Pacific and the Gulf of Alaska, they could not have avoided being discovered.

But a nuclear boat: this was different. It did not need to surface or refuel. It could stay deep, unseen and unheard. If it was out there now, as Arnold was quite certain it was, that ship could be *anywhere*; lost in thousands of square miles of ocean. It could be on its way to China, or Russia. It could have turned back west, or south. Or it could have just meandered down the west coast of the USA looking for new targets.

Worse yet, it could hear any searching US surface ship, and then just slow right down, maybe 1,000 feet under the surface. And *never* be detected.

In his worst nightmares, Arnold Morgan had imagined the hopelessness of looking for a nuclear marauder off the US coast, and he had always felt the same terror and frustration everyone feels in dreams of running hard, without moving. Those nightmares had always given him the creeps. And right now he was in one.

To activate the Navy on a massive search-and-destroy mission would have been a) useless, and b) likely to alert and terrify the populace. But in his heart Arnold Morgan believed the USA was under similar threat to 9/11 – though he did not know how, or why, nor what to do. And he paced his office, fists clenched, head down, not for the first time, alone, at the front line of American defense.

He was afraid of what the marauder might do next. But he was powerless to stop him. He knew his best chance was to let his opponent move first, betray his position, or at least betray something, like he was on this side of the Pacific rather than the other. But he knew he must wait, and for a man of Admiral Morgan's temperament, this was very close to torture.

Meanwhile, in Valdez the flames were dying. Firefighters had contained the blaze to the operational storage areas only. The terminus was a write off, as was the giant tanker which had blown up at the bow on the night the missiles came in.

The fires in the storage area above the town had died a day earlier because the destruction of the main control center had cut off any incoming crude to the fuel-farm. What was already there burned, in an incinerating heat, but when it was spent the fires died.

Nonetheless the area around the town looked like Berlin in the aftermath of the Allied bombing in 1945. A pall of black smoke hung low over the landscape, helicopters clattered through the skies, searching for clues, searching for an enemy redoubt, searching for anything. FBI agents swarmed all over town, assisting the police, talking to anyone who might have seen anything. Under strict instructions from the National Security Agency in distant Maryland, not one word was released to the public about the observations of the late-night stargazers, Harry Roberts and Cal Foster.

Although the snow made everything in a sense more difficult, it also provided incontrovertible evidence that no enemy or terrorist force could possibly have gathered to the north of the town. The helicopters searched miles of perfect, unmolested snow, across hills and mountains, valleys and fields. They saw the tracks of bears and moose, but not the tracks of any vehicle, way off the beaten track, which could have launched a missile sufficiently powerful to wreak the damage which had been inflicted last Friday night.

Neither did they find any signs of a troop of at least eight people, who must have been scuffing the virgin snow, in an extremely remote area, in order to launch such an attack. And by Thursday night, March 6, there was no doubt in the minds of any of the investigators; whatever had slammed into the Valdez terminus had come in from the sea. Except that no surveillance system in the US coastguard, or Navy, heard one single squeak on that darkest of nights. The official record of shipping activity in the significant area read a great fat zilch.

0100 Friday, March 7
42.26N, 128.12W. The Pacific Ocean
The Barracuda cruised slowly, 1,000 feet below the surface, a little less than twenty miles south-west of the Jackson Seamount, a boomerang-shaped shoal which rises up from the two-miles-deep ocean floor. Since its highest point is still more than 5,000 feet below the surface, the Jackson is of little significance save as a landmark and a point of navigation.

Ben Badr had placed his ship in firing position, 175 miles off the coast of Oregon, twenty miles north of the Californian border. Directly east of them was the estuary of the Rogue River, a wide, often frenzied torrent which comes tumbling out of the Coastal Range, into the Pacific at Gold Beach.

General Rashood had specified no firm time for his next attack, except that he intended to carry it out in the dead of night. And the night could not get much more dead than it was right now, out here in the pitch-black, lonely waters of the world's largest ocean, miles from anywhere, hidden beneath the surface.

'Well, Ravi, do we fire or wait?' Captain Badr was calm but concerned. His crew was tired. The tension of the long journey and the two attacks had placed a strain upon them all. And, given his way, Ben Badr would have recommended a twenty-four-hour rest for everyone. But he guessed, correctly, that Ravi would opt for instant action, rather than any waiting around.

And he understood the urgency, because he knew the fourth

and final attack depended on split-second timing, and that the General would prefer to burn off time in the hours immediately before that last missile launch, than waste a day here in deep safe water.

'I intend to attack immediately,' said the General. 'Please order the crew to prayer, and then alert the missile launchers. Shakira reports pre-programmed navigation systems complete. Nothing has changed. Two salvos, three missiles each, initial course fifty-five degrees.'

'*Aye, sir . . . Missile Director to the Control Room.*'

'*Stand by tubes one to six . . .*'

Captain Badr offered a prayer on behalf of the crew, who, he was convinced, were attacking on behalf of Allah. He mentioned the oppressors who had caused so much hardship to his people, and who were especially cruel and brutal to the Palestinians, who had been unjustly robbed of everything. Except for their beliefs, their courage and their dignity.

And he prayed that Allah might speed on his missiles, and guide them towards the most heartless of enemies, whose arrogance had given strength to the evil hand of Israel. And who, even now, was supplying the Semites with weapons once more to murder the devout Muslims, who now cowered in their country.

Allah be praised, for you are great . . . and please grant us the power to wound the Great Satan.

'*Tube one launch!*' snapped General Rashood.

And the first of the mighty RADUGAS lifted off, out of the launcher, arrowing up through the black waters, and then howling vertically to around 200 feet and levelling off, its guidance systems swinging it around north-east to fifty-five degrees.

The gas turbines cut in, and the deadly missile accelerated to its cruise speed of 600 knots, racing above the water, neither losing nor gaining height, cleaving through the cold night air, on its twenty-minute journey to the coast of Oregon. Directly astern the second missile was under way, and the third was already under the control of the launch sequencer.

The RADUGAs would not cover identical courses, but they would be similar, and they would cross the US coastline approximately one mile apart, close to Yacquina Head, a great Pacific promontory which lies 120 miles due south of Grays Harbor.

At this stage the missiles were headed deep inland, on a 220-mile journey up towards the city of Yakima, still on a fifty-five degree heading. By the time the opening three-weapon salvo reached the Oregon coast they were undetected by any ship's radar and now they streaked in over near-deserted land, still maintaining their height of 200 metres.

They lasered through the dark skies, west of the city of Salem, and came rocketing over the border into Washington State, high above the mighty Columbia River, crossing it just west of the massive John Day Dam.

Straight above the vast Indian Reservation they flew, across some of the most beautiful, desolate land in the USA. The missiles awakened no-one in the sleeping river town of Wapato as they screamed into their long left-hand turn out by the Rattlesnake Hills, swerving around the City of Yakima, over the long timber-rich valleys.

At that point they had been running for a little over forty minutes, and Shakira had selected a wild and lonely landscape for the turn, out west of the city. On every map she had studied, this looked about as likely to contain an alert and watchful surveillance system as inland Siberia.

On a new bearing now, 260 degrees, the missiles headed into the high peaks of the Cascade Mountains, well south of the scarred and sculpted face of the 14,500-foot high Mount Rainier, but north of the half-as-high Mount St Helens, and still firmly in the heart of the Evergreen State.

The missiles had no dificulty with the terrain, despite the steep escarpments. They just kept racing forward, automatically climbing higher with each giant rockface, following Shakira's pre-set course. As the land began to fall away, when the Cascades began their sweep down to the coastal plain, those RADUGAs made the descent again on automatic, locked onto the primitive but serviceable brain in the nose cone.

Their flying height remained constant at 200 metres, their course just south of due east, again coming in the wrong way, from out of American land territory, rather than the ocean – from somewhere out in Idaho, rather than the Pacific.

Shakira had charted the mission brilliantly. Ravi's space-age broadside swept smoothly through the skies, above the forests, in the name of Allah, on behalf of the Islamic Fundamentalists, down towards the huge oil conversion station at the sheltered end of Grays Harbor, south shore, seventeen minutes and 170 miles from Yakima.

Fifty-seven minutes after launch-time, Ravi Rashood's first cruise missile was over the little town of Alder Grove, on its way into one of the refinery's three massive steel fractional distillation towers. Each of these is capable of colossal combustion, receiving a flow of blisteringly-hot crude oil, which has traveled through a 'furnace' at around 725F. The tower's steel walls contain a combination of gasses and liquids, heavy fuels condensing, lighter fuels like gasoline and kerosene rising into the middle and upper sections, with liquefied gas flashing off into the high vapor unit. All milli-second inflammable.

In the entire world of high-tech incendiary, these towers represent the nearest thing to a leashed tiger. And when Ravi's first cruise slammed into the first tower, at precisely 0219 on that Friday morning, March 7, the blast was not only seen and heard six miles along the shore in the slumbering boom city of Aberdeen, it woke up the entire town of Hoquiam, one mile directly opposite on the far side of the harbor.

The thunderous *K-e-r − b-a-a-a-a-m!* was much more an explosion than the pure fire of the Valdez destruction. And for the sleeping residents of Hoquiam, the searing white flash, which reached them before the sound, illuminated bedrooms, lit up the streets, and floodlit the entire town. Indeed that particular flash was seen by the bosun of a supertanker off Point Chehalis, thirteen miles away near the gateway to the long harbor.

The security staff at the quiet refinery, all of whom had been on a coffee break for the past couple of hours, came rushing out of the long, low building in which they made their headquarters, to investigate. They were just in time to see a second tower erupt like a volcano, not 600 yards away, as Ravi's second cruise blitzed its way into the most volatile section of the entire refinery.

They stood in awe of the monstrous explosion, gazing in horror at the wreckage, the flames, the black smoke and gushing spirals of sparks crackling up into the sky. There was no human death toll, but the scene was nevertheless oddly reminiscent of those pockets of early witnesses, shown on television, staring at the World Trade Center Towers on that shattering September morning six years previously.

But before anyone could mutter an expletive, far less issue a comment, Ravi's missile number three was in, narrowly missing the third fractioning tower, but roaring on into first one, then a second storage tank, both of which were filled to the brim with thousands of gallons of refined power-station oil.

Worse yet they headed up the pipeline which joins the storage system to the nearby railhead station, where lines of freight tanker cars wait to be loaded. When the third missile blew the two storage tanks, it also blew the other twenty. And the gigantic explosion blasted into the short pipeline, incinerated an entire forty-car train, and knocked down the station.

By some miracle no-one was killed, mainly because at 0230 no-one was working. The train was not scheduled to complete its loading until 0600, and the storage tank guards were essentially part of the same squad that was on its collective coffee break. And now they stood, all eight of them, dumbfounded by the magnitude of the explosion. No-one knew what to do, except get back to the Jeeps, and get on the mobile phones, fire, police and ambulance, and then get into the as yet unthreatened control and monitoring building and start switching off anything that might be releasing oil in any of its forms.

All three decisions were luckily made several seconds too late. General Rashood's second salvo of three RADUGA missiles was incoming fast. The first obliterated the control and monitoring building, killing the duty night operator, plus the night security guard who never left the building, and who at the time was watching television. The outer wall of the building collapsed and crushed all four of the security Jeeps.

The other two ploughed into the fuel-farm where the incoming crude from the Alaskan pipeline was stored in great holding tanks, forty of them on a hill behind the refinery on the eastern side. These burst into flames in precisely the same way as those in Valdez, burning fiercely without the massive explosion which accompanies the ignition of refined gasoline or fuel oil.

There was however one final, unforgettable blast to come. The heat of the fires finally began to melt the steel of the one remaining fractioning tower, which, seven minutes after the arrival of the first missile, exploded like a nuclear bomb, detonating upwards, entirely differently from the other two towers which had been flattened upon impact and exploded outwards.

Tower Three blew ferociously into the sky, steel, concrete, debris, pipes, gantries, stairways, roaring liquid gas, hundreds of feet, straight up into a billowing mushroom cloud of flames and swirling smoke. Never mind comparisons with an atomic bomb, they could very nearly have *seen* this in Hiroshima.

The astonishing thing was, none of it was identifiable as a missile hit. To the eight refinery security guards it was impossible to distinguish the missiles in a low sky which was already ablaze by the time they came charging out of the mess room. Each cruise flew its final half-mile in three seconds, mainly through black smoke, and the security men were down-range, on the west side of the refinery.

They could not even see the short fiery tail of the RADUGA as it speared into its target. Only if they had been somehow waiting for the first one, staring with binoculars directly into its approach path, could they possibly have suspected a guided missile.

No-one did. It just seemed like the end of the world, everything exploding, bursting into flames. The eight men on the ground, still 400 yards from the nearest fires, made their next decision in double quick time. The heat was bearing down on them, and growing hotter. Sweat poured down their faces, and like a slower, but just as determined start to an Olympic 100 meters, they turned tail and bolted out of the blocks, eight under-trained US sprinters, going for their lives, arms pumping, legs pounding, along the road to South Arbor, away from the burning air.

Meantime, over in Hoquiam the fire department was mobilizing, though most of the men, staring out across the gleaming, silver and orange harbor waters, to the blazing refinery, had no idea how to tackle such a task. The fire chief was yelling at them to activate all equipment and to be prepared to hold back the inferno from the city of Aberdeen.

The firemen were instructed to drench the entire area in water, expecially backyards to clapboard houses, containing trees and bushes. They would also instruct all residents to move their automobiles out of the area. There was, plainly, quite sufficient burning gas for one night.

The trouble was, the three little cities surrounding the head of Grays Harbor were joined together by a natural urban sprawl, and the homes of western Aberdeen were meandering along the road towards the refinery. Chief McFadden could not allow the fire to spread and take hold in that area, not in the gusty prevailing west wind off the Pacific, and if the heat would permit them, his men would make that prevention an absolute priority.

Right now McFadden was on the telephone to the Aberdeen Police Department, and they had already relayed news of the catastrophe to Washington State Police in Seattle. By 3 a.m. every late radio station in the state was alert to the disaster, and news of the fire was on the inter-state network to Washington, where FBI investigators were already on the case.

Everyone was putting two and two together. In the space of one week there had been gigantic oil fires in the Valdez terminus and the Grays Harbor refinery, the main cogwheels in the west coast energy industry. Plus there had been a massive breach in the pipeline carrying the crude oil from Yakutan Bay non-stop and directly to Grays Harbor itself. All three incidents occurring in the dead of night. This was no accident. This was a real live crisis. The USA was under attack, by unseen marauders, saboteurs, terrorists, lunatics, fascists, communists, fundamentalists or some other screwball activists.

Washington now knew that someone had it in for Uncle Sam. The President was awakened at 0310 and was in the Oval Office two minutes later in his pyjamas. In his opinion, 'That someone had better be found and stopped, real quick, before the goddamned lights go out for good.'

Admiral Morgan was in his car and headed for the Taft Bridge, driving himself at high speed to the White House, followed by three agents, who were trying and failing to stay with him in a light drizzle and a slick road surface.

By 0315, Lt. Commander Ramshawe was gunning his eleven-year-old black Jaguar up the Washington-Baltimore Parkway to Fort Meade. Admiral Morris was already in his office, with a phone call in to the Pentagon, to the busy-line of Admiral Alan Dickson, the ex-Atlantic Fleet Commander who now occupied the chair of the Chief of Naval Operations.

Admiral Dickson was also in his office, talking to Admiral Dick Greening, Commander-in-Chief of the Pacific Fleet, who was away from his Pearl Harbor office, visiting the giant San Diego Naval base. Stacked up waiting to speak to the CNO, in order, was Rear-Admiral Freddie Curran, Commander Submarines Pacific Fleet, General Tim Scannell, Chairman of the Joint Chiefs, and Arnold Morgan on encrypted speakerphone from his car.

The last call in was a raging priority for Alan Dickson, and he told Dick Greening he'd call him right back.

Admiral Morgan crossed DuPont Circle like a meteor across the face of the moon, astounding two Washington police officers parked on the north side, who nonetheless recognized a black White House staff car when they saw one, and elected to mind their own business.

'*Alan!*' yelled the President's National Security Advisor. 'Talk to George Morris or his assistant right now and get yourself up to speed. Then don't move, I'll be back in a half-hour.'

The line went dead, and Admiral Dickson who was already pretty well up to speed told a hovering young Lieutenant to call back Admiral Greening and tell him not to move from his desk. Then he hit the encrypted line to George Morris, who was in the call-waiting line anyway.

Finally the two men spoke, and Admiral Morris, who sometimes seemed slow of thought, and somewhat cumbersome in his assessments, was neither of those things this morning. He said immediately, 'Alan, this country is under attack . . .'

'I know,' said the CNO. 'And I haven't the slightest idea how to proceed . . .'

It was, they both understood, the modern military dread. The unseen enemy, lurking God knows where, planning God knows what, and answering to God knows who: colloquially known as Terrorists.

Both men were interrupted by the red light from the White House, and on both of their hotlines was the voice of Admiral Morgan, who was holding a phone in each ear, a feat of physical and mental dexterity of which he was relatively proud . . . '*Situation Room West Wing 0700. Don't be late.*' (Click). Small talk, blow out thy brains.

Admiral Morris hurried down to Lt. Commander Ramshawe's office, looking for a summary of submarine mystery sightings, possible routes into United States waters, and any other data his assistant could provide.

Both men were frantic with concern, all of it heightened because they had, in a sense, been on the case for more than a week. And now, suddenly, in the darkest hours of this night, all of their worst dreads had jumped into technicolor reality. The bastard had struck again, to deadly effect.

Admiral Morris gathered up every document his young Lt.

Commander could throw at him, all of it laid out in carefully written detail, from the flight of the Barracuda(s), to the landing of the missiles which had destroyed Valdez. From the obvious insertion of Special Forces to slam the pipeline north of Graham Island, to the sudden, shattering destruction of all the refined fuel oil on the west coast.

Someone was trying to put out the lights. And the President would be close to panic. Admiral Morris knew they would have to walk him carefully through this intricate and sinister scenario, but he was certain the Navy was on stream with cause, effect and remedy. Anyway the President rarely stepped out of line when the craggy face and glinting blues eyes of Admiral Morgan were facing him across the table. He might, however, be bolder this morning. Because the USA was essentially at war. With someone.

They gathered in President Reagan's old Situation Room in the West Wing shortly before 0700. The President, dressed now but not shaved, was the first to arrive in company with his Secretary of State Harcourt Travis and the Defense Secretary Bob MacPherson. General Scannell, Chairman of the Joint Chiefs, arrived with the CNO, Admiral Dickson, and the last man through the big soundproof double doors was Admiral Arnold Morgan, in company with Admiral Morris whose notes he was reading.

Four Marine guards were on guard in the corridor, and every White House security system was in place. As highly classified meetings go, this one ranked at the top level. The SWAT team which normally patrolled the roof of the building while the President was in residence had organized a team of four heavily-armed agents to seal the elevator which moved to and from the lower level where the Situation Room was located.

The subject was of course one which dare not speak its name beyond the four walls which now surrounded the most powerful men in the country. Admiral Morgan had placed at one end of the room a huge computer screen on which was an illuminated map, showing the Asian side of the North Pacific, all the way across to the west coast of Canada and the United States.

'Good morning, gentlemen,' said the President. 'Because this is about to develop into a military meeting, I am going to appoint my National Security Advisor to act as Chairman . . . Arnie, perhaps you'd take the seat at the head of the table . . . I'll sit here with my fellow politicos Bob and Travis next to me, opposite Admiral Alan, and General Tim . . . I imagine I'm kinda lagging in the most up-to-date information so maybe Arnie will brief me.'

Admiral Morgan who was unsmiling, still engrossed in Jimmy Ramshawe's notes, muttered, 'I'll be right there, sir . . . and I'll do it a lot better if someone can lay hands on a cup of coffee.'

Everyone chuckled and Bob MacPherson walked to a house phone and ordered coffee and English muffins since everyone present had been up half the night, most of them zigzagging around the city in the rain.

'Okay, sir,' said Admiral Morgan. 'I want to start with the first bang, up there in the oil terminus at Valdez in Alaska, early hours of last Friday morning, February twenty-ninth. Every report we have suggests two separate sets of detonations. One at the terminus itself and one minutes later at the fuel-farm. There is no evidence of any attack by land, there was nothing military or civilian in the immediate airspace, and no warship from anyone's Navy within a thousand miles.

'A massive search for clues has produced nothing. The only thing we know is the two areas did not go off bang all by themselves. And we have a coupla comedians who claim to have seen missiles coming overland south through central Alaska towards Valdez. We believe their evidence is sound, because their timing was accurate to within seconds and they could not have known that.'

The Admiral paused. 'Forty-eight hours later we have a massive breach in the new pipeline which carries the crude out of Yakutat Bay all the way down to the Grays Harbor Refinery. No evidence of skulduggery, but suspicious, to my mind, the breach happened at an obvious choke point, where the pipeline rises up to cross a shoal.'

'Why suspicious?' asked the President.

'You wanna blow a hole in a pipeline you need underwater guys to get down near it. Funny it happened in the near perfect place in the whole five hundred miles of undersea construction.'

'Okay,' said the President. 'Press on.'

'Sir, at this point we were already considering the possibility that the Valdez terminus was hit by maybe a half-dozen cruise missiles. Just because there can be no other explanation.

292

Something big hit the terminus, and it did not come from the land or air. There was no surface ship within reasonable range. Which leaves a submarine, submerged launch.'

'Jesus,' said the President. 'But whose submarine?'

'Well, that's where it becomes somewhat complicated,' said the Admiral. 'And if I may, I'd like just to continue to the next hit, which, as you know happened a few hours ago. Suddenly we got the same scenario. *Bam*! Up goes another huge oil installation, this time the biggest fucking refinery in the country. Grays Harbor.

'What did it? Don't know. Evidence? None. Except once more I'm hearing about two separate sets of detonations. One knocked out two fractioning towers, then something slammed into the fuel-farm . . . again no warships, again no aircraft, and again no possibilities over the land.

'Sir, whatever wiped out the refinery was big and powerful, and it must have been launched from a ship. Because there is no cruise missile in the world, so far as we know, with the range to get either Alaska or California from land. Unless it was ballistic, in which case we'd have tracked it, and shot it down.

'Right here we're talking about the fucking *Marie Celeste*. Because there was no ship. Again, sir, I come back to the likelihood of submerged launch missiles from a submarine. And I come back to it because I'm a devotee of Sherlock Holmes – *When you have eliminated the impossible, only the truth remains*.'

'Arnie, have we established, among everyone at this table, that the damage inflicted on Valdez, the pipeline and Grays Harbor, must have been military?'

'Well I haven't had time to ask everyone, sir. But there's no doubt in my mind. Whatever hit us packed an unbelievable wallop, and the delivery of such a device could scarcely have been achieved by a civilian.'

Everyone nodded in agreement. 'Which brings us to the next subject,' said Arnold. 'Timing. Which, as in all crimes, is critical. Okay, now the missiles were fired at Valdez a little after midnight on Friday morning. The pipeline blew probably just before midnight on Sunday. That's a gap of seventy-two hours, all day Friday, all day Saturday, pipeline busts late Sunday.

'We have to assume the pipeline was hit by a sticky bomb or sea-mine of some kind. And it was obviously primed around twenty-four hours before it exploded. Anyone with a lick of sense would be as far away as possible from the spot they inserted their frogmen.

'We're probably looking at maybe thirty-eight hours from the datum between firing and fixing the "stickies", right?'

Again everyone nodded in agreement. 'So, whoever fired at Valdez, fired from within a couple of hundred miles of the hit-point on the pipe, because, believe me, that submarine is moving real slow. And they had a lot of preparation for the insertion of the frogmen.

'So, gentlemen, we got a fucking interloper right near the west coast of Canada. At least, we know exactly where he was at midnight on Saturday, right near the Overfall Shoal. And next thing we know is a major hit at Grays Harbor this morning – that's a little over seven degrees of latitude south, four hundred and thirty nautical miles, plus eighty miles to get out of the Dixon Entrance . . . that's five hundred and ten miles.'

The Admiral rose to his feet and walked to the computerized chart. 'I'm talking right here,' he said, pointing to the shoal. 'And right here,' he added pointing to Grays Harbor. 'And the time difference between the pipe burst and the refinery hit is just about five days – at five knots, he makes one hundred and twenty nautical miles a day . . . that's four days and then some. But he's not stopping at latitude forty-seven, is he?'

'Why not?' asked the President. 'He wants to be near the target for his missiles, right?'

'Sir, his missiles can be accurately fired from one thousand miles away – so he'll almost certain go further south than he needs . . . just to get distance from the hit . . . no-one wants to be near an uproar zone . . . he's probably another hundred miles further south, which would take him almost exactly five days to the hour . . . down here somewhere . . .'

Arnold pointed further down the chart and added, 'He'll want to be well offshore maybe one hundred and fifty or two hundred miles, so my guess is, he was somewhere in here when he launched . . . from our point of view, right on time.'

He described a circle on the chart with his right hand. Then he stepped back and spread both hands apart, pausing for a moment, before saying, 'Christ knows where he is now. That was possibly accurate five hours ago . . . I'd guess he was still real slow . . . but I have not the slightest idea where he is now.'

'You mean he could have fired these things from the middle of the Pacific?' asked the President.

'Sure could, sir. But I don't think so. He came inshore for the Alaska attacks. And he came south for the refinery . . . my guess is he's now headed inshore to noisy water, staying as deep as he can, and as slow as he can.'

'What the hell's noisy water?' asked the Secretary of State.

'Oh, that part of the Pacific is very awkward, Harcourt,' replied Arnold. 'Cold currents from the north, warm currents from the south . . . produces some strange thermal effects, currents which "bend" the sonar rays. And it's always much more noisy near the shore. . . creates a kind of audio "fog" effect . . . hard to hear anything. He'll probably creep along the coast, with one hundred feet under his keel, and if he's slow enough no-one will detect him . . .

'Right now, gentlemen, we're kinda stuck with what I call the "flaming datum" – that means we cannot do a damn thing in the way of finding this bastard until he does something else. And those darned missiles of his allow him to stand right off, and hurl his punches long distance. It's the nightmare of submarine warfare . . . and remember, gentlemen, we've never had a terrorist in a nuclear boat before. But we got one now. I'm damn certain about that.'

'Jesus Christ,' said the President. 'You mean we're powerless?'

'Just about, sir, I'm afraid.'

'Well, we have a massive Navy which is always asking me for more money – why can't they organize a goddamned search or something?'

'Sir, I expect you've heard of a needle in a haystack,' said Arnold. 'We'd be goddamned lucky to find the haystack, never mind the needle. We're looking at an area of maybe three hundred miles by four hundred miles in which he could be anywhere . . . we don't even know whether he turned east, west, north or south. That's over one hundred thousand square miles . . . and we can't see him, nor hear him. He could pick a spot in deepish water, park his ship fifteen hundred feet below the surface and stay there for a fucking year . . . then go home, wherever the hell that might be . . .'

'Sir,' interjected Admiral Dickson. 'I have to say on behalf of our very expensive Navy that this kind of wide search is absolutely futile. A total waste of time, money, and effort. If we pulled out the entire Pacific fleet, their chances of finding an elusive nuclear submarine would be about a million to one. That's why we have so many of them ourselves . . . submarines are the single most dangerous weapon on earth . . . as the residents of Grays Harbor have just found out . . .'

'Okay, okay . . . I gottit.' The President was becoming visibly rattled. 'But, Arnie, you're always telling me we have a handle on every moving submarine in the world . . . and the first time we need real information . . . hell, we've got a damned great nuclear ship on the loose, smashing up the US of A – and no-one knows where it is, where it lives, or who owns the bastard . . . I mean, give me a break, willya? The Navy costs about a billion bucks an hour to run, and you're telling me we have to sit here like a bunch of cub scouts watching this fucking maniac beat us to death?'

'Sir,' said Admiral Morgan. 'In the end, we'll probably have to nail the archer not the arrow . . .'

'What kind of a goddamned riddle is that?' retorted the President.

'A pretty easy one,' replied the Admiral, grinning what he would have described on anyone else, as a shit-eating grin. 'Because right here we're looking at terrorism on the same scale as nine/eleven, except with hardly any death, but identical ramifications. And it's state sponsored. Which narrows the field down. I doubt if even the old al-Qaeda could have managed a nuclear submarine. Guys dressed in fucking bedsheets don't usually drive 'em. But somewhere at the back of all this is a foreign State or Republic, maybe even two. That's who we're after.'

'That might be who you're after, Arnie,' snapped the President, now visibly furious. 'But I'm after this fucking nutcase who's knocking down oil refineries . . .'

'Sir, we are not without a few clues here,' replied the Admiral. 'And it would be better if we could avoid all-out global war. But we suspect the submarine is Russian built, but flying the flag of a third party, very possibly China . . .'

'*China*!' yelled the President. 'Then you are talking global warfare! Jesus Christ!'

'Sir, so far as we can tell, there is only one submarine in all the world which could somehow have crept through arctic waters, across the Pacific and hit Alaska. It's a twenty-year-old Russian

Sierre I, Barracuda Class, Type nine-four-five. We've accounted for every other submarine ever built.'

The President hated playing cat-and-mouse with Arnold Morgan because he always ended up looking like a goddamned child. Especially in front of his top people. He wanted to say, 'Well go find it, smartass, right now, and stop bothering me with details.' But he knew better.

Instead, he muttered, 'Please go on, Admiral.'

'Well, they recently transferred this ship from their Northern Fleet to the Pacific Fleet and parked it in Petropavlovsk . . .'

'Where the hell's that?' asked the President, impatiently.

'Southern end of the Kamchatka Peninsula,' said Arnold. 'Big Russian Navy base in Eastern Siberia, ass-end of nowhere . . . we had already tracked that ship every mile of the way on its fleet transfer from the Murmansk area . . . but we now know it had been sold to the Chinese, because it was too expensive to run . . .'

'Well . . . where is it now?' Again the President seemed rattled.

'We watched it sail from the Russian base on Saturday morning, February ninth. Saw it turn south, and the Russians say it was almost certainly bound for Southern Fleet Headquarters in Zhanjiang. However we have reason to believe the Barracuda dived ten miles offshore and then turned north.'

'Why did it?'

'Sir, do you really want to know that detail?'

'No. I believe you. It turned north. Then what?'

'Big cruise missiles slam into Valdez twenty days later.'

'And all the priceless surveillance in our expensive Navy heard nothing?'

'Correct. Not a whisper.'

'Well, why the hell not?'

'Because it was creeping along like a sneaky little bastard, sir. When nuclear boats go very, very slowly no-one can hear them. 'Specially if they navigate away from obvious areas we might patrol.'

'Has anyone seen anything that could have been a submarine?'

'Not on this side of the Pacific, sir. But we know it was there. And in my opinion it still is. I imagine my colleagues around the table agree?'

'I don't think there's much doubt about it,' said the CNO, and General Scannell nodded, so did Admiral Morris and Bob MacPherson.

'Which leaves us with the option of the "flaming datum". We stay on high alert and wait for him to strike again.'

The President looked, felt and was, totally exasperated. 'Well, how many cruise missiles could he have?' he asked.

Admiral Morgan shook his head. 'We think a total of twenty-four.'

'And how many has he fired?'

'Don't know. At least accurately we don't know, because we are still investigating Alaska. But we think he could have fired a total of fourteen – possibly eight at Valdez, almost certainly six at Grays Harbor.'

'So we are looking at one more attack, at least?'

'I guess so.'

The coffee and muffins arrived at a timely moment, drawing the sting out of yet another Presidential riposte. But the Chief Executive now waited until it was served, waited until the man in the white coat had enquired formally of Admiral Morgan, 'Buckshot, sir?'

And then he demanded, 'But what about the Navy – there must be some kind of a protective barrier we can throw up?' He said it almost plaintively.

'It's a waste of time, sir,' said Admiral Dickson. 'By the time we put to sea, he could be anywhere.'

'I can see no option but to wait,' said Admiral Morgan. 'But I am worried about the Navy . . .'

'How do you mean?' asked the CNO.

'Well, it looks rather as if he is moving south, and there are a lot of ships in the San Diego base. It would be terrible if he fired a cruise missile, or even a torpedo at a carrier.'

'Are you kidding me or what?' said the President, eyebrows raised.

'Well, he just leveled an oil refinery which is a whole lot bigger than *six* carriers, and he didn't have much trouble doing that.'

'But surely there's some defense . . .'

'An incoming cruise,' said Admiral Dickson. 'launched from out of the sea, traveling at six hundred knots, ten miles a minute, two hundred feet above the surface, unexpected, in the middle of the night. The odds are heavily with the attacker.'

'The only defense is to keep moving the goddamned ships around,' said Admiral Morgan. 'Foreign countries have daily satellite pictures of all our bases, and this joker can very easily access and receive that data by sticking his mast a few feet out of the water for around seven seconds when he knows the ocean is deserted.

'Then he programs the GPS into the missile, and throws it straight at us, down the bearing, following the GPS data. It can't miss, and he's gone . . .'

'And moving the ships around would be a huge pain in the ass,' said Admiral Dickson. 'Sir, they are in the dockyard for several reasons, most of them to give the men some shore leave after months at sea, but also for refit and servicing. It takes about a thousand people to move a big aircraft carrier. It would cause havoc if we had to move them all every two days.'

'Hell, I guess so,' agreed the President. 'But there is one other thing I wanted to ask about the cruise missile . . . can it adjust its course during flight?'

'Sure,' said Arnold. 'You just feed in a few different numbers before you launch it. But you can't change the flight-plan after launch. Ultimately it homes in on the GPS data, the position it received from the satellite picture, accurate to three meters.'

'Smart little steel bastard,' said the President.

'Actually, sir,' said Arnold, 'I do hate to seem pedantic, but I am afraid the cruise missile is a particularly dumb little bastard. It's entire guidance system depends one hundred percent on the Global Positioning System which, as you know, is operated from one of our own military satellites. It allows everyone in the goddamned world to get an accurate fix to within three meters of accuracy . . .'

'*Well, what's everyone in the goddamned world doing on our satellites?*' said the President, literally shouting now.

'Because your esteemed left-wing asshole predecessor decided to make it available to everyone, in his usual devious, dishonest, know-nothing, liberal shithead manner.'

Even in moments of near paralyzing tension, Admiral Morgan's ability to bring the house down remained undiminished.

General Scannell and Admiral Morris simultaneously shot coffee down their noses, and Bob MacPherson burst into laughter. The President, chuckling, hesitated and then asked, 'No, seriously, how come everyone, even this lunatic hurling missiles at us, can have access to the satellite?'

'Sir, it used to be that the GPS was strictly military, for our use only. Then it was decided the system was such a navigational help, it would make all kinds of human activity much easier . . . you know, sailing, trekking, mountaineering, rallying, merchant marine, everything . . .

'So we opened it up. *But* . . . and this is a big *but*, the military insisted that while we retained the cutting edge of accuracy to three meters, everyone else could have accuracy to one hundred and fifty meters . . .'

'You mean,' said the President, 'if you were that far off course, you deserved to hit the beach in your brand new Chesapeake cabin cruiser?'

'Correct, sir. If one hundred and fifty meters wasn't good enough, go buy yourself a sextant and learn some navigation skills.'

'Well, then what?'

'I guess there was a whole lot of pressure from boat builders and navigational aid manufacturers,' said Arnold. 'And your predecessor gave in, and said he did not see anything wrong with providing accurate navigational aid to everyone.'

'Christ, the military must have objected?'

'They actually raised hell, sir, because of today's obvious reasons.'

'And?'

'Your predecessor ignored them, as he ignored everything they ever said, except if he needed them for some diversionary tactic.'

'You mean if we switched off the satellite that feeds the GPS, they could no longer guide those missiles long distance.'

'Yes. That's what I mean.'

'Well switch the fucker off then,' said the President.

'Okay,' said Arnold.

'Hold on,' said Harcourt. 'You can't just do that. There'd be about twenty shipwrecks on the first day, huge merchant freighters and tankers don't have the first idea how to navigate without GPS.'

'Tough,' replied the President.

'To whom shall I tell them to address the billions of dollars worth of law suits, all aimed at the man who turned off the navigation system that lights up the world?'

'Fuck,' said the President. 'I think you got me.'

'Sir, I know you can't cancel GPS worldwide for the reasons Harcourt just succinctly put forward. Couldn't even put it back to one hundred and fifty meters without due warning – there'd be people drowning all over the globe. But it is a problem. We should look at it. Because that's how this bastard in the submarine is finding his targets with such complete accuracy.'

'If he'd had only one hundred and fifty-meter accuracy, would he have missed the refinery?'

'Probably most of it,' replied Arnold Morgan. 'I doubt he would have nailed the big fractioning towers and that would have reduced the damage by around ninty percent.'

'I guess that's one more thing for which we have to thank my predecessor,' said the President thoughtfully.

'Absolutely,' said Arnold Morgan.

'Liberal shithead,' confirmed the President.

CHAPTER ELEVEN

By midnight on that Friday, Admiral Vitaly Rankov had not returned yet another call from Admiral Morgan. It was now plain that no-one was telling the United States of America whether or not the second Barracuda was operational, nor where it was, nor indeed whether Russia still owned it.

Arnold Morgan was not pleased. And in the small hours of the following morning he summoned to the encrypted telephone the sleeping Chief of the CIA's Russian desk.

'Tommy, hi. Morgan here. We still got that good guy in Murmansk?'

Tom Rayburn, an old friend of the Admiral's, was quickly into his stride. 'Hi, Arnie. Just. But he's about to retire . . . probably coming to live here.'

'Think he'd have time for one more mission? Nothing dangerous. Just enquiries.'

'Oh sure. Old Nikolai's always been expensive but cooperative.'

'Okay. I'm looking for a nuclear submarine. A Sierra I, Barracuda Class. Type 945. Hull K-240. We think it was never quite completed, never went to sea, and was subsequently laid up in the yards at Araguba, north of Severomorsk. I need to find out whether it's still there, in a covered dry dock. Apparently they were using it for spare parts for the one Barracuda which was operational. That's Hull K-239.'

Tom Rayburn took his notes carefully. 'Where's that one, just so we don't get confused?'

'I'm not sure,' replied the Admiral. 'But you may assume it's a fucking long way from Murmansk.'

The CIA man guffawed. Arnold Morgan's manner had not changed in the twenty years he had known him. 'Okay, boss,' he said. 'I'll get on it. You want to know whether the Barracuda's still in Araguba, and if not, where it is?'

'And especially whether they've sold it.'

'You gottit. Gimme twenty-four hours.'

At precisely the same time, 0100 in Fort Meade, Lt. Commander Jimmy Ramshawe was poring over a report from the office of the Energy Department detailing progress from the undersea repair team north of Graham Island.

The pipeline valves had been turned off, and after the tremendous crude oil leakage into the sea, they had successfully capped the breach in the line at the Overfall Shoal. It was difficult, but made easier by the shallowness of the water. The operation had entailed lifting both damaged sections of the pipe on cranes and making the repair on board a service ship, before lowering the entire section, using two ships, back onto the seabed.

It was then of course necessary to open several valves to make sure the repair, made on one of the major couplings, was tight. When the oil flowed again, the frogmen reported no leakage and everything seemed fine. However, to their horror, three hours later, another huge slick was seen developing about a half-mile to the north. And this was much more difficult to repair because the water, was much, much deeper.

All valves were turned off again, but this time they needed to send down an unmanned mini-submarine to inspect the further damage, which no-one had known about. And this was again terrible news, because the television photographs being relayed to the surface showed a shattering rupture in the pipe, nowhere near a coupling joint. This meant they would need to lift two entire sections off the floor of the ocean, using two giant 'camels'.

And this would be an immensely expensive and challenging operation. The Dixon Entrance is in a remote part of the world, and in early March, sea conditions can be very rough. They were looking at possibly six weeks to two months, when no oil would be carried down the pipeline from Yakutat Bay. And neither did it matter much whether the crude oil arrived in mainland USA or not, since the refinery at Grays Harbor was destroyed. And neither would there be any tankers heading south out of Prince William Sound where there were currently no crude supplies whatsoever.

If this fight between General Rashood's Fundamentalists and the American west coast's oil industry had been fought under Marquis of Queensberry Rules, the referee would have stopped it.

Jimmy Ramshawe stared at the report, and contemplated the colossal damage. He also pulled up and checked out the inflammatory words of Professor Jethro Flint of the University of Colorado . . . *they will never have tested that pipeline under real-life pressures . . . when you subject something to stresses it has never undergone before it can rupture . . . they've overloaded the pipeline, somewhat thoughtlessly, and it's come unraveled.*

'Wrong, Professor. Wrong,' muttered Jimmy. 'If you were right, the pipeline woud have ruptured at the joint, its weakest part, and that would have released the pressure instantly, with the bloody oil gushing out in a huge jet underwater. There would have been no second breach, 'specially right in the middle of the pipe away from the joints.

'I am afraid, old mate, your bloody academic theory is right up the chute. That wasn't pressure that bust the pipe, that was a couple of terrorist bombs, delivered by frogmen from a submarine.'

And he drafted off a hard-copy note to Admiral Morris, pointing out the obvious and fatal flaw in the argument of Professor Flint.

He ended with a flourish. 'Would you like me to circulate these findings on the e-mail to the FBI, CNO, Bob MacPherson and Admiral Morgan. Because they sure as hell just blew Fred Flintstone out of the water, right?'

Admiral Morris answered in the affirmative.

And now it was the weekend, and the markets were closed. Which left the media to run riot all over the world, piecing together the undeniable truth there there had been three massive 'accidents' in the Alaska oil industry. *Were they really accidents? Are they connected? Is this industrial sabotage on the grandest scale? If so, who? Is there someone out there trying to bring the USA to its knees?*

These were scare stories way up there on the Richter scale. And there were seismic shocks in every area of public life. Gas was already at six dollars a gallon at many west coast stations, and every newspaper and television screen from San Diego to the Alaskan coast was trumpeting about the fuel oil shortages which must begin to bite immediately.

The further north the city, the bigger the headlines, as the newspapers cited all of their usual sources of doom for maximum disquiet among the populace. They forecast . . . *power stations grinding to a halt . . . hospital emergency equipment without electricity (people may die)* . . . *no gasoline* . . . *senior citizens dying of cold and starvation* . . . *schools closed* . . . *government offices blacked out* . . . *no power* . . . *no computers* . . . *no social security pensions* . . . *no baseball games* . . . *floodlights* . . . *traffic lights* . . . *strobe lights* . . . *neon lights.*

The list was hysterical and endless. Hysterical, and accurate, bang on the money. This was a pending crisis the like of which no-one had ever imagined. Because not only was Grays Harbor, the largest refinery in the country, a) starved of product, and b) out of action, but there was no fuel oil running south to feed the biggest power station in California, Lompoc, custom-built to cope easily and exclusively with the power demands of the gigantic urban sprawls of both San Francisco and Los Angeles.

For once in their lives, the media had it absolutely right, putting two and two together to make a precise and pristine four; rather than five, or eighty-seven.

What they did not know, was a truth more chilling than anything in the imagination of even their most erratic editors. Out there, somewhere in the eastern Pacific was a seasoned, dazzling Special Forces battle commander, leading a group of highly-trained Islamic fanatics in a brilliantly-efficient nuclear submarine, which appeared capable of striking the US at will. And may not be finished yet.

At 9 a.m. on Saturday morning, Admiral Morgan read with equanimity Jimmy Ramshawe's note about the repairs on the pipeline. Every word confirmed what he already believed, *knew.* That there was someone out there, packing a serious wallop, with another 'X-minus' possible weapons in his magazine. And neither he, Arnold, nor any of the top military brains in the US armed forces, had the slightest idea how to proceed.

The Admiral was bewildered, along with the rest of them. He had never felt so vulnerable. In his mind, he knew that their enemy was virtually undetectable. The world was indeed his oyster. The bastard could do anything.

All previous run-ins with terrorists paled before this. Even when the massed maniacs of al-Qaeda had pranced about announcing they would fight to the death, they had at least presented a target somewhere in the remote hills of Afghanistan. It was difficult, but nonetheless tangible, and well within the massive capability of the US military, which proceeded to pulverize their foe.

'*But this,*' growled the Admiral. '*This is fucking preposterous* . . .

I don't know if our enemy is Russia, China, or one of the towelhead states. But I do know this is terrorism, the most modern terrorism, and there is no defense against it . . . because we don't know where it's coming from . . . nor who is committing it.'

He had of course entirely ignored the point that this was also his own favorite type of warfare, to slam an opponent to the ground, kick him to death if necessary, and then act as if it was nothing whatsoever to do with America. *Who me? Nah. Sorry, pal, don't know anything about it. Can't help this time. Stay in touch.*

Right now he had never been in such a dilemma. Alan Dickson had the Pacific Fleet on full alert. Two submarines coming in off patrol were watching and listening for any submarine from any nation which might be on the loose. But Arnold held out little hope. *If he's out there, and he's as goddamned brilliant as I think he is, the west coast needs a hard-hat and a goddamned lotta luck. I just hope to Christ he doesn't go for the Navy Base in San Diego.*

He knew it would be futile to try to gain any information on the movement of any Chinese warships. The Beijing military were not hostile, but they were not friendly to the USA either. And they seemed to operate independently from their own government.

Twice in the past few years there had been a major stand-off involving US servicemen being held in Chinese military confinement after sorties in the South China Sea. And the recent uproar over Taiwan had done nothing for Sino–US relations.

Alternately, Russia was saying nothing. And the US was, of course, unable, as ever, to have any proper rapport with the Islamic States, the atmosphere being altogether too fraught, too untrusting.

Admiral Morgan paced his office. A new communiqué from the Washington State Environmental Protection Agency suggested the still-leaking pipeline had at least been shut down, three miles back from the breach. But sea conditions were so bad it would be several days before they could begin their attempt to raise the fractured section and conduct the repairs.

In California, the Governor was conducting a day long, highly-classified meeting in Sacramento, the state capital, attended only by those officials who understood the razor's edge upon which their electricty supplies now rested. Jack Smith, the President's Energy Secretary, had flown in on *Air Force II* from Washington, and was listening intently as officials from the

Lompoc Power Station outlined the situation at the newest, most efficient electricity plant in the United States.

Built to take the heat off the rest of Californian's 1,023 major power stations (1/10th of a megawatt or larger), Lompoc operated solely on government-subsidized, inexpensive refined fuel oil coming out of Grays Harbor. Transportation to the power station was strictly railroad, straight out of Washington State, down the Union Pacific's permanent way to San Francisco, and then along the valley of the Salina River to the scenic peninsula, where the railroad starts to hug the coast.

Lompoc lies six miles inland, right in that triangle-shaped peninsula, 125 miles north-west of Los Angeles, 240 miles south of San Francisco. Its nearest coastline forms the northern shore of the Santa Barbara Channel.

The Union Pacific railroad runs all the way around that peninsula on its way down to Los Angeles, but there is a spur-line into Lompoc, expanded in the year 2007 to run into the new power station, and form the life-giving artery to virtually all the electric power for San Francisco and LA.

According to the best calculations, the Lompoc Power Station was sufficiently well supplied to keep pumping out electricity for three more weeks, possibly four. The problem was, it was not on a seaward terminus where tankers could bring in emergency supplies, if necessary from the Gulf of Mexico.

And it was simply not geared for road transportation to bring in refined fuel oil. Lompoc and the railroad were bound together, and right now the last two tanker freight trains were rumbling south, one just north of Monterey, the other west of San Luis Obispo, forty miles north of the station. Thanks to General Rashood, there would, of course, be no more deliveries in the forseeable future.

Right now it looked almost impossible to hook up the massive Lompoc outward power lines to the state-wide electricity grid. At least it looked impossible to achieve in under four months.

Lompoc had been built as a separate entity, to function alone, insuring that the state's two giant commercial centers could keep running, no matter how many black-outs and brown-outs afflicted the rest of the state. Equally, Lompoc's very existence considerably reduced the pressure on all of the other California power stations, which had been devoid of shortages for several weeks.

With no refined fuel oil from Alaska, the only solution had to be road transportation. The state of California could spare hardly anything itself, without putting the lights out in several cities, so it would have to come from the Gulf, through the Panama Canal, and up the west coast into the great artificial harbor of Los Angeles, a ponderous journey of close to 4,500 miles . . . assuming no delays in the canal, almost two weeks.

The Governor's emergency conference in Sacramento was racking its collective brain trying to find solutions. But there were no solutions, only ways to try and paper over the cracks, and to keep the lights on, more or less constantly, until the Alaska and Grays Harbor catastrophes were repaired. If the power station at Lompoc failed, and the great cities of San Francisco and Los Angeles went dark, it would be a national calamity of gigantic proportions.

It would certainly bring down the California Governor, and it could threaten the Republican Administration in Washington, where the GOP would be accused of pushing forward with vast money-making programs mostly beneficial to big oil companies, with no thought whatsoever to solutions if the grand schemes failed.

And there had been, of course, many citizens of Lompoc and its environs who had been vehemently opposed to the power station right from the start. The beautiful Lompoc Valley is known as the Valley of Flowers thanks to its century-old flower-seed industry, and the very idea of a power station bang in the middle of all that floral splendor had caused a political battle which raged for more than a year.

Only the intervention of the military, at nearby Vandenberg air base, had finally pushed the power plant through. Vandenberg was the first missile base of the US Air Force, and the lift-off site for the *Challenger* disaster in 1986. The immediate closing of the West Shuttle Program after the crash had caused a major recession in Lompoc, but now in 2008, more than twenty years later, they were preparing for the California Spaceport, and there were major advantages to having a huge power station close by. Not least the sharing of a big refined fuel terminal right on the Union Pacific Railroad.

The environtmental lobby still opposed it. All of it. And continued to hurl invective at 'money-grubbing industrialists and politicians,' hell bent on profits at all costs never mind the destruction of the Valley of Flowers.

Their objects had a plaintive ring of truth to them, but none of it was true, or justified. The President's entire energy program, masterminded by Jack Smith and his staff, was in fact a work of great brilliance, dispelling at a stroke America's reliance on Arab oil.

The unpalatable truth was, and is, a huge industrialized Western country like the United States happens to be vulnerable to grand-scale, state-sponsored terrorism. The senators in Washington did not yet know it, but they had much to be thankful for – namely that General Rashood did not approve of mass killing and would not indulge in it. However the senators did not know of the existence of General Rashood, nor the steely determination with which the HAMAS military chief intended to drive the USA, and the State of Israel, from the Middle East forever.

By Thursday morning, March 13, General Rashood and Captain Badr were creeping down the pristine central coast waters off some of the loneliest beaches in California. They were just beginning to move out into deeper water 130 miles off Los Angeles, and were making a quiet five-knot course to the south-west.

The Barracuda, now a month out of Petropavlovsk, was running perfectly, the reactor ticking along at low pressure, the turbines at cruising speed. The only discordant note in the entire submarine mechanism was the slightly arched conversation between General Rashood and Lt. Commander Shakira Rashood.

The world's first lady submarine officer was quite certain they should continue with the policy of sending in missiles on a roundabout route to the American mainland, disguising at all costs the true direction and launch-point of the RADUGAs. Shakira's point was simple . . . *it has worked well for us so far, no-one has come after us, and no-one knows we're here. We should continue with a successful policy.*

General Rashood held no such illusions. And he told his wife so in the gentlest possible terms.

'Shakira,' he said. 'The Americans will have been momentarily baffled by our opening attack in Prince William Sound. But someone will have seen something, and the Pentagon will by now know the oil terminus was hit by an incoming cruise missile. They will also have known we were very close indeed to the spot where the oil pipeline was breached on the Overfall Shoal.

'When we hit the refinery in Grays Harbor – if indeed we did hit the refinery – they will know of our existence. The big military brains will have worked out the missiles were most certainly fired from a submarine because there was nowhere else they could have come from.

'I would be surprised if they had not found out this Barracuda was missing from the Russian Naval base. They will know that someone dragged the fishing net off that Japanese trawler and it must have been the Barracuda . . .'

'Yes but what about the Chinese diversionary plan to help us . . . ?' she asked.

'Forget it. Because nothing will happen until tomorrow . . . and that's not important anyway. What is important is that the Americans will know for sure and certain that the total destruction of the refinery at Grays Harbor was the work of a terrorist firing missiles from a nuclear boat . . .'

'But how will . . .' she interrupted.

'Trust me, my darling,' he said. 'We are playing cat-and-mouse with some of the biggest brains in the world, particularly the US President's National Security Advisor. Believe me, they know what's happening. And it won't make one lick of difference whether the missiles come howling in to Lomboc from out of the San Rafael Mountains, or straight down the freeway from Santa Maria . . . it doesn't matter what we do, they'll know.'

'But surely they'd be better coming in from the east, the unexpected route . . . like the others?'

'Negative. Everywhere's unexpected. Our only advantage, and it's a big one, is that they have no idea, within say five hundred miles, where *we* are. My orders will be to fire a salvo of four RADUGAs straight at the Lompoc Power Station, straight out of the ocean, direct at the furnace and the turbines. From about two hundred miles out, a twenty-minute missile run, then hightail it south before the missiles even reach their target.'

'You mean fast?'

'Oh no, never fast. Just quietly offshore, in a million square miles of ocean, one thousand feet below the surface, chugging our way to safety. When the first of those missiles hits, every major military brain in the Pentagon is going to know what we've done. I just hope to spread enough confusion to allow us a clean getaway.'

310

'You mean my missile deception program is obsolete as from now?'

'Absolutely. This is our last throw, Shakira. And it's a punch which will come in straight and hard, at two of the most sensitive areas any great power has. Its competence and its pride. And the USA has a ton of both.'

'So have I. And I sense you have just fired me. Would you like me to leave?'

'No. But I might ask you to take off your uniform,' chuckled Ravi. 'Once we find somewhere private.'

Shakira punched her commanding officer playfully on the arm. 'That's my punch,' she said, laughing. 'Straight and hard. Did I ever mention how inappropriate you are?'

'I believe so. But right now I'd like you to be my wife rather than my missile planner. Hop below and organize a couple of cups of tea and some toast, would you? I've been here since two o'clock this morning.'

'My last humiliation. From Lt. Commander to steward. Right here in the middle of the Pacific. Demotion for the great mind that suggested Lompoc in the first place.'

General Rashood smiled, and watched his wife turn out of the control room. 'Just another couple of days,' he said. 'And we're on our way home.'

And the Barracuda moved slowly westwards into deep, silent waters, way off the coast of California, her great turbines moving her 8,000-ton weight effortlessly, under the deft guidance of Captain Ben Badr.

Meanwhile California went about its business. Aside from the endless tensions in the Governor's mansion, and the near-panic gripping the electric industry, life continued as normal.

The only other pressure-spot was around the junction of Hollywood Boulevard and Highland Avenue in north-west Los Angeles where streets were being closed and blocked off in preparation for the movie world's annual extravaganza on Sunday evening – the 80th Academy Awards ceremony, with its modest little worldwide audience of about a billion people. Shakira Rashood would have given almost anything to be there, dressed to kill, on the arm of her handsome, iron-man husband. Though, in a rather different sense, she would be. So would her iron-man husband.

For weeks now they had been preparing the spectacular $100

million Kodak Theater, the world's largest television studio, bang in the middle of one of the grandest new shopping malls on earth.

Right here in Hollywood, in the permanent twenty-first-century home of the Oscars, there were more electricians per square mile than would-be actors. The bustling Hollywood Boulevard was actually closed down for five days. On the night, they would block off Highland Avenue, Orange Drive, Franklin Avenue and a dozen other streets.

The fabulous shopping complex of the five-level Hollywood and Highland Mall, contains seventy upmarket retailers, restaurants, night clubs and the new 640-room Renaissance Hollywood hotel. On this Thursday afternoon, anything open was seething with sightseers, flocking into the custom-built H&H train-stop, directly off a fifteen-minute ride on Metro Rail's Red Line from Union Station in downtown LA.

The actual Kodak Theater, resplendent at the top of forty wide marble steps, is situated to the east of the six-screen, ornate Grauman's Chinese Theater. The Kodak stands at the head of Award Walk with its elegant plaques, mounted on pillars, commemorating eighty years of acting brilliance, an exclusive little garrison for the immortals of the screen.

Gregory Peck, Henry Fonda, Burt Lancaster, Sydney Poitier, Gene Hackman, Wayne, Newman, Pacino, Nicholson and Hanks; Susan Hayward, Kate Hepburn, Jane Fonda, Meryl Streep, and the rest. Their momentous achievements will once more pervade the complex on Sunday night, when this year's nominated make the 500 foot Sunday-night strut along a red-carpet, five boulevard traffic lanes wide, to the electronic wonderland of the Kodak Theater.

And there the 3,300 guests will assemble beneath the massive silver-leafed tiara of a ceiling, based on Michelangelo's Campidoglio Square in Rome. More than 100 television cameras, inside and out, earthbound and raised, on gantries and bridges, tucked into alcoves, would be zooming in on the main stage, zooming in on the audience, striving for the best pictures.

All through the theater, concealed cableways are hidden in the actual support beams and balcony fronts, ready to cope with the demands of television lighting and sound equipment on the big night. The theater's own sound system uses as much electric power as a space-shuttle launch. There is an entire catwalk for rigging and lights, even the orchestra pit is an electronic elevator.

There is every kind of lighting, designed to flood, flash, or pin-point. These searing theater lights can irradiate in white, red, purple, blue or any other hue. The Kodak will illuminate the hopes and dreams of every actor, director, producer, co-star or writer in the audience. When they hit the on-switch for this lot, the Lompoc Power Station shudders.

1900 Friday, March 14, 2008
South China Sea, east of Hainan
Barracuda II, under the command of Captain Ali Akbar Mohtaj, was almost at the end of her long, round-the-world journey. The brand new Russian-built submarine, which had left Araguba on January 31, had not been seen nor heard since the American SOSUS operators in Pembrokeshire, South Wales, picked her up south of the Rockall Trench off the Irish coast on the evening of February 7.

Since then she had traveled underwater, fast down the Atlantic coast of Africa, slower across the Indian Ocean, the long way around Indonesia and the islands, and then north up the Pacific, off the east coast of the Philippines.

Now she had made passage through the Luzon Strait which separates the northern headland of the islands from Taiwan. She was dawdling, waiting for the correct timing, early tomorrow morning, Saturday. Only then would she come to the surface at first light, right on longitude 111 degrees, cut her speed and move slowly across the sunlit surface of the South China Sea. She would head straight to the Zhanjiang headquarters of China's Southern Fleet, directly beneath the pass of the twice-daily Big Bird, America's silently-penetrating photographic satellite, 22,000 miles above.

She had been at sea for six weeks, all of it dived. No-one had seen the sun rise nor set. Captain Mohtaj's orders were unbending, to stay out of sight, out of contact all the way. And he had carried them out to the letter, except for that one carelessly-placed toolbox off the coast of Ireland.

And even then the American SOSUS operators had no time to make a positive identification. Like his co-conspirator Captain Ben Badr, the commanding officer of Barracuda II had made no contact with the outside world. Everyone was in the dark. And neither of them knew the extent or failure of the Iranian mission to the coastlines of Alaska and the United States.

313

At 0600 on Saturday morning, Barracuda II came up through the shining blue waters of the South China Sea, and burst onto the surface, blowing ballast. Ali Akbar Mohtaj was fifty miles from Zhanjiang, north of the sub-tropical beaches of Hainan, hoping fervently to have his photograph taken.

0900 (local) Saturday, March 15, 2008
Fort Meade, Maryland

Admiral Morris was awaiting the arrival of the Big Man, and he had already vacated his chair and desk in anticipation of the event. Dead on time the door swished open in a near-cyclone of air-current as Arnold Morgan made his entrance and strode across the office floor. The flag of the United States rippled in his slipstream.

'George, these bastards are up to something!'

'Sir?' said Admiral Morris.

'Don't sir me, for Christ's sake. I've got enough fucking trouble without my oldest friend going fucking obsequious on me!'

In Admiral Morris's view this was going to be a somewhat unpredictable meeting . . . 'You gottit, Arnie. I'm ready . . . what's new?'

'New? New? Nothing's new. The precise same crew of homicidal maniacs is still waiting off the shores of California trying to blow the fucking country up. Nothing's new. It's just the same old routine bullshit. Another death blow to Uncle Sam coming up, another chance the whole fucking place will be in the pitch dark before we're much older.'

'You want some coffee?'

'Damn right I want some coffee. I don't know how the hell I'm supposed to continue while you sit there not giving a shit, one way or another, whether I die of thirst.'

Enough. Both men burst into laughter. George Morris ordered the coffee, and Arnold moved into serious business. 'George, I heard back from the CIA's man in Murmansk. That second Barracuda, Hull-K-240, the one the Russians never put to sea, has gone. So far as we can tell it has not left the yards at Araguba for years, but one of our top naval observers in that part of the world says it's no longer there. But he was wary of the answers his contact was giving. Said he had a sense there was a lot more to it. But nothing he was going to be told.'

'Do we have evidence they did complete the ship? Our last report said it was in no state to become operational, may even have been used to provide spares for their other Barracuda?'

'In my experience, George, the only way submarines ever go anywhere is under their own steam. If the fucker was still in pieces it would still be in Araguba, right? Well, our man Nikolai says it's gone. And since even the Russians don't transport eight-thousand-ton nuclear submarines on trucks, my guess is the bastard's floating.

'And if it's floating, and not in the harbor, it's steaming somewhere. And since we can't locate it, and neither, it seems, can anyone else, it's being very secretive. And I want to know where it is, mainly because I'm afraid it might be bombarding US oil refineries.'

'What was the latest from Rankov?'

'He promised he'd find out for me if it was still in Araguba. But he didn't get back.'

'You think that proves it's out there?'

'Well it proves what I already know, that Rankov is a lying, devious, Russian prick. But I think it's *almost* decisive. Barracuda II, wherever it may be, is up to something.'

Just then two things happened. The waiter arrived with coffee, and Admiral Morris answered his internal line to hear Lt. Commander Ramshawe's voice asking to see him right away.

He replaced the receiver and said, 'Ramshawe's on his way, says he has two things – one of them hot.'

'That's gonna be a step up on this coffee,' Arnold grunted. 'Get that waiter back in here, and tell him to make it nuclear, steaming, the way I like it.'

Admiral Morris, the most important military Intelligence chief in the United States, apparently had no objection to being treated like a counter-clerk at McDonald's. But he did whistle up a secretary and had her deal with the matter. And then Lt. Commander Ramshawe arrived.

'Hello, sir . . . oh, g'day Admiral . . . didn't know you were here. But I'm glad you are. I've got a very interesting satellite picture right here.'

And he laid out on the desk of Admiral Morris a blow-up print of a shot taken that morning outside the Chinese naval base in Zhanjiang. And there, large as life, on the surface, was the Barracuda, thirty-five days and 3,500-miles out of Petropavlovsk.

In the South China Sea, exactly where the Russians had said it was going.

'Have the Navy guys confirmed this is definitely a Barracuda-Class Sierra? A genuine Type 945?' asked Admiral Morgan.

'Yessir. No doubts. One hundred percent. That's the Barracuda.'

'Well, we think it fired a salvo of missiles at Grays Harbor in the early morning of Friday, March 7,' said Arnold. 'That's eight days ago, and the Pacific ocean is damn nearly seven thousand miles across from our north-west coast to south China. So he must have made damn nearly forty knots all the way, which he can't. And he must have set off about seventy-three SOSUS alarms at that speed, which he didn't.

'That ship outside Zhanjiang, gentlemen, did not do the deed. That much is obvious. Which leaves our calculations in disarray.'

'Bloody oath, it does, Admiral,' said Jimmy. 'Where do we go from here?'

'Well, Lt. Commander, as you know, the Russians did build a second Barracuda, which spent all of its life in dry dock in Araguba. And I came here this morning to inform Admiral Morris that it had gone . . .'

'Gone, sir!'

'Gone. Vamoosed. Not there.'

'Christ. That puts a different light on it, wouldn't you say? I mean that ship outside Zhanjiang might be the second one, right? And the first one, the Barracuda that hooked the *sushi* net, might still be where we think it is. Off California.'

'That Jimmy, is what is causing me deep concern. And the more I think of it, the less I like it. You know why?'

'Sir?'

'Because the Chinese obviously do not wish us to know they have bought *two* Barracudas at three hundred million dollars each, or whatever. And in those circumstances they *should* have crept into Zhanjiang much more carefully, surfacing at the very last moment, and then crept into the jetties during the dark hours of the night, when they *know* we have no satellite pass.'

Jimmy Ramshawe was silent. He just sat there staring into space. He actually sat there for almost a minute without replying.

'Jimmy?' said Admiral Morris, concerned his Aussie assistant had gone into shock, or some kind of a trance.

But Jimmy ignored him. Just shook his head, and then exclaimed, '*H-o-l-e-e shit!*'

Admiral Morgan looked quizzical.

And then James Ramshawe punched the air. 'You just said three hundred million apiece, sir? The submarines China has plainly bought. *And that's it, sir. That's bloody it! Old Razormouth 600 confirmed* . . . that's the bloody message we picked up off the Chinese satellite. It was telling someone, Russia had accepted six hundred million dollars for *two* Barracudas. If you don't mind my saying so, sir, you're a bloody genius.'

Arnold Morgan, genuinely smiling for the first time for more than a week, replied, 'And if you don't mind my saying so, Lt. Commander, you're not so fucking dusty yourself.'

'And another thing, sir. What about that SOSUS detection last month, off the coast of Ireland – they thought it could have been a Russian nuke creeping down the Atlantic . . . does that make sense?'

'If that was the second Barracuda, and it was owned by China,' said Arnold. 'Almost every last piece of this jigsaw fits together. Including the possibility that Beijing is using the first one to cripple our west coast economy. By the way, the mystery submarine off the coast of Ireland, was on February 7 at 1935. The numbers are engraved on my mind. I think about it every day. Sneaky little bastard.'

'What bothers me, Arnie,' said George Morris, 'is why China should want to be involved in such a lunatic adventure. They must know stuff like this will provoke a colossal response from us.'

'Of course we don't know that China is responsible for anything,' replied Arnold. 'We only know for sure that Beijing bought one Barracuda Type 945, because the Russians told us. We also have Jimmy's razormouth message suggesting they bought two Barracudas. And we have seen one of them headed into Zhanjiang, and although we don't know which one, it does suggest a decoy. Because that little bastard headed into port in a way that suggested they *wanted* us to see it.'

'Okay, men, what do we do now, bomb the little pricks into oblivion?' Lt. Commander Ramshawe was only half-joking.

Admiral Morgan laughed. Nervously. 'I'm afraid there's more to this than meets the eye, Jimmy. And remember one thing. Russia is *never* going to admit the second Barracuda was sold. China is *never* going to admit anything . . . they may say a Barracuda submarine visited Zhanjiang under the flag of another country. They will also say that has absolutely nothing to do with the USA.

'As for our suspicions that someone is hitting our oil industry with cruise missiles, they will say that any suggestion that China is responsible is utterly preposterous, and would honorable President of USA like to have State visit to Beijing, and velly great welcome by Chinese people.'

Admiral Morris added, 'Remember also, that satellite picture Jimmy's just brought in. That's the only time we've seen either of those boats anywhere near a Chinese port of entry.'

'You're right,' said Arnold. 'And I am being driven to just one view . . . the only time this mystery gets solved is if we catch and nail whoever and whatever is out there off the coast of California. And I don't know how to do that. Yet.'

Ramshawe's reply sounded more Australian than Saltbox Bill, King of the Overland. 'Well, we'd better be right bloody sharp about it . . . before the shifty little mongrel bastard strikes again.'

'And one more thing, Jimmy,' said Admiral Morgan. 'I was informed you had two items of interest, when you arrived. What's the second one?'

'Sir, I've been scrolling through the SOSUS and radar surveillance reports on our internet for the past couple of weeks . . . naturally there's not a whole lot happening up in the Bering Sea to interest us. But I found one thing . . . happened on February 19, the Navy listening station at North Head, Akutan Island, picked up transient contact on radar, about thirty miles offshore, South Bering Sea fifty-four degrees forty-five minutes north, one-six-six degrees twenty-eight minutes west. No POSIDENT, but they got three sweeps on the radar. They thought it could be an intruder, but they never heard it again.'

'I guess it could have been anything,' replied Admiral Morgan.

'Well, yes, it could, sir. But those guys are used to tracking ships through the Unimak Pass, and whatever this was, it got their attention. Then it vanished.'

'It's a bit late to worry about it now,' said Arnold. 'But there's only one type of ship that can just vanish, right, George?'

'Only one, Arnie. Only one.'

1800 Sunday, March 16, 2008
The Pacific Ocean
The Barracuda was making a racetrack pattern 500 feet below the surface, 270 miles south-west of Lompoc, Valley of Flowers . . . 340 miles due west of Tijuana, on the Mexican border. Shakira

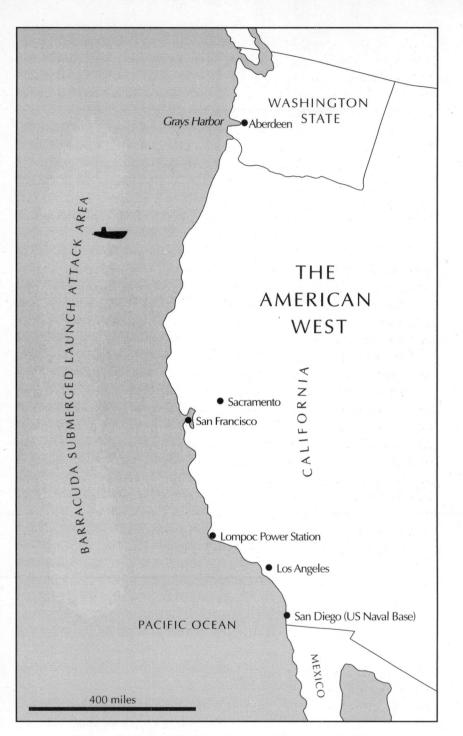

THE AMERICAN WEST COAST - OPS AREA BARRACUDA 945

had accepted, in principle, the concept of a straight hit and run. The final destination of the missiles was 34.39N, 120.27W. It was 120 minutes to launch.

Inside the Kodak Theater, the entertainment industry's biggest night was well under way. Members of the Academy of Motion Picture Arts and Sciences were seated with dozens of hopefuls, the short-listed nominees for the little golden statues.

They had already made the award for the best special effects to Bob Ferrer, Ray Ricken and Sydney Limberg for *Terminator XII*, and all three of them had thanked everyone they had ever met, with the possible exception of the studio cat. Oscars 2008 was already running ten minutes late.

Right now they were showing film clips for the Best Cinematography – for which Hiram Rothman was a hot favorite for his spectacular filming of the battle for the Gettysburg Heights in *Hope Not Glory*. The Civil War epic was also up for Best Director (Milt Brabazon) and Best Actor (Flint Carbury). And the entire row of Civil Warriors stood up and applauded the victory of Hiram, whose magic lenses had made them all look utterly wonderful.

Make your speed five knots and come to three hundred . . . Missile Director to the control room . . .

Hiram Rothman, who had won twice before in a long and perfectly brilliant career, was seasoned and dignified, and merely thanked everyone for being so helpful. A quick thank-you to twenty-seven relatives put the ceremony more or less back on track. But they'd never be finished by the scheduled 8.30 p.m. No way. It was already heading towards a 9 p.m. finish, just as Mrs Rashood had forecast.

Two more minor awards followed, and then, shortly before 7 p.m. one of the highlights of the evening occurred. Edna Casey, the Irish poet, won the award for Best Original Screenplay for *Timeshare*. The Oscar was not quite so interesting as the decision of the film's star, Troy Ramford, to unload his wife of eleven years last fall, plus their three children, in favor of the more exotic charms of the svelte Galway-born redhead, Miss Casey.

He had carried out this address-changing maneuver in the middle of the *Timeshare* production, and since he was nominated for Best Actor, it had been a world tabloid preoccupation whether Troy and Edna would show up for the Oscars together.

And right now, aided by about 500 megawatts of television

power, the world knew. Troy had the overjoyed Edna Casey in his arms, and Hollywood, ever anxious to accept and welcome a new regime, was on its feet applauding. The gifted Irish writer moved shyly to the podium, and told the audience, 'This means more to me than I can ever say. I'm sure Troy and I will both treasure it always.'

That was the confirmation of love the media had been awaiting for five months. And it probably caused an electronic surge at Lompoc as the pictures were beamed around the globe. Inside the Kodak, the audience erupted, as Edna waved her Oscar.

Conn-Captain . . . come to PD . . . Check surface picture visual . . . fifty-five minutes to launch . . .

The ceremony continued in glittering harmony. Best Musical Score was won by the ex-London busker, Bobby Beethoven (nee Schwartz) for *Ramraid,* a tacky but clever British low-life gangster drama, which was also up for best screenplay, written by the new Liverpool-based duo of Fred and Anna Zimmer.

The beautifully-filmed *Mary of Modena*, the story of the seventeenth-century Italian princess who became Queen of England, collected, predictably, the Oscar for Best Wardrobe (Ina Shinford). The movie, filmed in Ireland, was also up for Best Actress (Carrie Martin) and Best Supporting Actor (Charles Le Pen).

Ina Shinford had overcome the blow of her chief assistant, the full-breasted nineteen-year-old seamstress Tiggy Morova running off with the film's married director Craig Barstow, eighty-two. In her speech Ms. Shinford mentioned twenty-four-hour workdays, and her gratitude for the deep understanding of Mr Barstow. She ran eight minutes over her time.

Billy Cohn, picking up his fourth Oscar for a Best Adaptation, valiantly strove to be brief while praising the entire cast and crew of the 2007 'sleeper' *Free Agent*, a sports spoof which was too close to the truth to spoof anyone. He ignored his family in his thank-yous, but became overcome with grief when dedicating his Oscar to his late partner, an airline steward who had recently succumbed to AIDS. Billy had to be helped, in tears, from the podium by heartbroken executives from Provincetown International Airways.

Check all systems . . . nineteen minutes to launch . . . Lt. Commander Abbas Shafii to the control room . . .

The battle for Best Supporting Actress was now in full cry, and the clips were running. Hands were being held, clenched and placed over wide-open mouths. Inside the Kodak, the earth stood still . . . *and the winner is* – Maggee Donald, for *Free Agent*.

The spotlights searched and landed upon the slim, beautiful ex-Texan waitress and her unshaven country-western singer/husband Slack Brandiron. The music struck up and the world watched the girl who had played the Free Agent's lover make her way to the floodlit podium all alone. It had been only her second film role.

She accepted her gold statue from a black defensive lineman from the Oakland Raiders, who told her he had ambitions to play Othello when he retired from football. At which point Maggee just plain dissolved into laughter and tears, and kept saying over and over, 'I jest wish mah mommy could see me raht now.'

The audience was entranced as she began her speech at two minutes to 8 p.m. 'This is just . . . like the proudest moment . . .'

Prepare tubes one to four . . . final systems check . . . Lt. Commander Rashood to the missile control room . . .

'And I want to thank my late mommy who died only six months ago . . . and I know mah daddy's watchin' back home in Amarillo . . . and he's gonna be like so proud of me . . .'

Tube one – fire! . . . tube two – fire! . . . tube three – fire! . . . tube four – fire!

Maggee raised her Oscar high, and said, 'I'm liftin' this so high because no-one back home at mah high school's even gonna like believe this unless they see it, like personally. Thank you ladies and gentlemen, thank you from the bottom of mah heart . . .'

Make your course one-three-five . . . speed eight . . . bow down ten . . . go to eight hundred feet . . . we're going home, gentlemen.

The Academy of Motion Pictures, wary of putting their golden eggs at the very end of the program had now moved up the award for Best Actor to an estimated one hour from the conclusion of the ceremony. And the Kodak held its breath, as they announced the nominations and ran the clips, two minutes for each film, showing the shining moments of the best male acting performances of the year.

And the winner is (roll on the drums) . . . Troy Ramford for *Timeshare*. And again the spotlights raked the audience in search of the tall, Nebraska-born Oscar winner, who was currently kissing Edna, waving to well-wishers and trying to stand up.

In a maelstrom of backslapping, whooping and cheering, he walked up to receive his award, stepping out into the aisle and insisting that Ms. Casey accompany him. This caused a certain amount of disquiet among the stewards, and took a minute or two to sort out. Then it became clear that either Edna Casey went with him, or the Academy could present its Best Actor Oscar to the chief steward.

By the time the glorious pair were under way, Jake Milburn and Skip Farr, watching the security radar screen out on the western edge of the Lompoc Power Station, had spotted a line of four incoming flying objects screaming over the California coast. And they took longer to assemble their defenses than Troy and Edna.

Both men saw the first missile come arrowing in, directly over-head, low and fast, 600-knots plus. Incredulously they watched it dive and hit the massive generator building, which contained twenty-four 200-foot-long, 10-foot-high turbines, stacked in sets of three beneath the 80-foot high roof.

The entire structure was blown sky-high, the eight topmost turbines, weighing around 100 tons apiece, being hurled over 300 feet into the air, two of them intact. They had not yet crashed to the ground when the next missile hit the furnace room, blew the huge heating units assunder, and exploded in a 200-yard-wide fireball a half-million gallons of fuel oil, recently unloaded from Union Pacific freight car tankers.

The next missile vaporized the control room, and the last one blew up the entire fuel storage area, including its direct pipeline to the railroad terminus where every last barrel of fuel oil was pumped out and into the power station. Both terminus and the power station were history, and the fires rose hundreds of feet into the twilight skies, black oil smoke billowing on a west wind across the Valley of Flowers and engulfing the entire town of Lompoc.

It was impossible to see four yards on the freeway up to the Vandenberg Airbase, where the commanding officer ordered all aircraft to red alert. That was two minutes after the first missile hit. And that was when the lights went out in the Kodak Theater. Right out, that is. Not a glimmer, Troy and Edna stood in inky black darkness, film stars screamed, bimbos squealed, actors yelled, their minders cursed, and the management appealed for calm through microphones which no longer worked.

All over the world movie fans by the hundreds of millions were tuned to the Hollywood blackout. And it quickly became obvious that this was no ordinary blackout. There was nothing coming out of the Kodak whatsoever. Nothing out of Los Angeles. None of the television networks could fathom the complete shutdown of their west coast news operations.

And within moments there was complete chaos in the Kodak. The emergency generators kicked in five minutes after the power failure, but these were on a very small scale compared to the dimension of the lost wattage. There was sufficient light to provide a safe way out for a normal crowd in the electronic auditorium.

But this was no ordinary crowd. This was a gathering of people who were unused to inconvenience. Many had not been argued with for several years. Some of them could not recall the last time they were interrupted. And this. This total indignity practically sent them off their trolleys. The Kodak had become a world-convention of mass selfishness.

Screams rent the air. Self-important voices demanded an explanation. It was all the stewards could manage to prevent a riot, as more than 3,000 people stampeded for the exit, all of them demanding priority over everyone else.

If any of them had time to stop and think, they might have realized they were in by far the best place, a large auditorium with some lighting, in a complex with sufficient power to allow them access to the adjoining hotel which also had its own weak but useful generator system.

Outside was dangerous. The lights were out city wide, all the way to downtown LA and beyond, south to Santa Ana and east to San Bernadino. That included street lights, traffic lights, shop-lights, security cameras, millions of telephones, and televisions. Miraculously there were still lights in Malibu Canyon, which was operating off the San Gabriel South Mountain system. But Los Angeles was pitch black, grinding to a halt, the freeways already clogging as every street intersection began to experience crashes and permanent hold-ups.

More than 400 miles to the north, the city of San Francisco suffered a similar fate within eight minutes of Los Angeles. The lights suddenly dimmed and then failed completely on the Golden Gate Bridge which spans the narrow channel connecting the Pacific Ocean to San Francisco Bay. Within two more minutes every light on the entire peninsula was down. Nob Hill was nixed, Fisherman's Wharf wasted, and the cable cars kaput.

San Francisco just withered and died. The sensational night views over the city from its fabled 43 Hills, so vaunted in the tourist and hotel brochures, now permitted visitors only to stare down into a black abbys, lit only by distant car headlights and the occasional freighter on the bay. The mighty suspension bridge was a sinister black shadow in the night. In the same way, the heights of San Gabriel peered down into the ebony crater of the City of the Angels.

Beyond the coast of California no-one had the slightest idea what had happened. Jake Milburn and Skip Farr, still safe upwind of the fire in the security outpost west of the power station, were the only two people on earth who knew precisely what had happened. They had spotted General Rashood's missiles on their radar screens, then watched them swoop overhead and smash into the buildings.

And now they were running, terrified that more attacks were coming in. They made Jake's car and hurled themselves inside, then headed for the coast, grappling for mobile phones, trying to call the Lompoc police and fire departments. There was no use trying to get the power station's own emergency services. There was nothing left. Mercifully, there had been very few people on duty this Sunday night, maybe four, or at the most five, including the night patrol man whose jeep had been blown several hundred feet into the air.

Jake correctly assumed everyone else was dead and called his wife to tell her he was safe, and to let Mrs Farr know that Skip was fine too. All that Annie Milburn knew, at home in a valley east of the town, was that she never even got to see Troy Ramford get his Oscar because there'd been some kind of power cut in Hollywood.

The Lompoc police department was already fielding calls from the media, who were quickly on the case, the radio stations having been alerted by several listeners who were able to see the inferno raging in the power station. Exactly like Grays Harbor, exactly like Valdez, the Lompoc fire department was chiefly concerned with preventing the spread of the blaze outside the town.

Immediately Jake Milburn's call came in, the Police Chief notified the FBI in San Diego, which was standard procedure at the merest suspicion the USA had come under attack. Jake had recounted that both he and his partner Skip Farr, both trained security men, both ex-cops from Sacramento, had seen missiles, seen the attack, seen the cruises come in from the ocean, from the south-west, losing height as they homed in on the power station.

That rendered it a matter of national security. And within moments, the NSA at Fort Meade was informed. It was 11.30 p.m. in Maryland, but the duty officer nevertheless hit the wire for the Director, but Admiral Morris had just left. His assistant Lt. Commander Ramshawe was however still in his office and picked up the telephone, hearing, to his horror, what had happened at Lompoc.

Without missing a beat, he opened the Agency's hot line to the White House, and told the operator to get Admiral Arnold Morgan on the line, fast, wherever he was, and whatever the time. Then he left a message on Admiral Morris's answering service to call him as soon as possible. Jimmy knew the Admiral would get that message inside the next fifteen minutes.

The phone rang angrily. Admiral Morgan, who had been half-reading, half-watching the Oscars with Kathy, was on the line.

'Sir, our man just destroyed the Lompoc Power Station. San Francisco and Los Angeles are blacked right out. Two security men saw the missiles come in from the sea — fast and low, smashing straight into the main buildings. The flames right now are several hundred feet high. Place works on oil, as we know.'

'*Jesus Christ!*' yelled Arnold Morgan. 'This is the end of any kind of secrecy. Tomorrow the entire country is going to know we've been hit. It's gonna be like September 12. I'll have to organize a massive naval search . . . where's Admiral Morris?'

'Just left, sir. Around 11.15. Early night, right!'

'Lazy prick.'

'Okay, sir. What do I do?'

'Tell George to sit tight at his desk. You get to the Pentagon now. Meet me in Admiral Dickson's office in a half-hour. Bring everything that's relevant.'

'Yessir.'

Jimmy gathered up his charts, maps and e-mails, and headed for the parking lot, flung his packed briefcase onto the passenger seat and gunned the Jaguar through the empty rows of stationary cars towards the main gate. He flicked on the radio and headed for the Baltimore-Washington Parkway, racing down to the junction with the Beltway, but driving straight on, to the Anacostia Freeway.

From there he picked up 395 and charged straight across the bridges to the Pentagon. If he'd been stopped for speeding, he'd have asked for a police escort, and he was confident his NSA pass and Lt. Commander's rank would have done the trick. By now the entire world knew, not that the electric power supplier to LA and San Francisco had just been flattened by a terrorist, but that Troy Ramford's speech, about to be delivered with his arm around the lovely Edna Casey had been blacked out.

The late-night news programs were all saying the same thing, that the Oscars ceremony had been ruined by a power cut, the Kodak Theater blacked out just as Troy was going to collect the award for Best Actor and probably announce his forthcoming marriage to Edna Casey. In Jimmy Ramshawe's opinion this was like announcing there was still some unattended laundry in the *Titanic*.

He drove directly to security, and told them he was going straight to the CNO's elevator in the underground parking lot. And when he arrived, Admiral Morgan was just disembarking from his White House staff car. Two Marine guards on duty were about to ask for the Lt. Commander's identification, when Arnold Morgan barked, 'Get these two cars parked right away.'

The Marine, knowing full well with whom he was dealing, snapped, '*Yessir.*'

'No bullshit,' added the Admiral.

'*Nossir,*' confirmed the Marine, trying to suppress a smile.

Accompanied by a guard, they took the elevator to the fourth floor, emerging in corridor seven, right off E-Ring, the Pentagon's outer-throughway on all levels. A young naval lieutenant met them and mentioned that Admiral Dickson would be here in three minutes. He led them straight into the inner office and told them he'd have some coffee sent in immediately. It was a little after midnight.

'Hot, Lieutenant,' said Arnold.

'Aye, sir. With buckshot.'

Exactly three minutes later Admiral Dickson arrived, and before saying a word, he walked over to the wide computer screen on the wall and switched it on, punching in the numbers which would provide a broad view of the submarine roads into the San Diego base.

'Hello, sir,' he said, nodding. 'Lt. Commander . . . this is a very bad business. We're under attack, no doubt about it. And our chances of finding the culprit are still pretty remote. But we have made some progress . . . not, of course, where he is . . . but where we're pretty darn sure he isn't.'

'That's a kinda breakthrough, if accurate, Alan,' said Admiral Morgan. 'Because there is only one unassailable fact . . . after this character fired his goddamned missiles he did *not* head due east. Because that would have put him on the beach. All other options are open so far as I can tell.'

'I think the Navy will do a little better than that, sir,' replied the CNO.

'Okay, old buddy, shoot . . .'

'You'll remember I mentioned I had two submarines offshore, on their way in. Well, they're both LA Class boats, the *Santa Fe* and the *Tucson*, and we've had them patrolling 400 miles off San Diego for the past week, on high alert for any foreign submarine, especially a Russian Sierra I, Barracuda Class.

'They're around 200 miles apart which I realize is a pretty good distance. But between them we have a couple of guided missile frigates, Arleigh Burkes, the *Decatur* and the *Porter*. We have all four of them in a kind of crescent facing east. Behind them, maybe 300 miles, we have a cruiser coming in from Pearl, and it's watching for missiles. We've already checked. Whatever was fired at Lompoc did not sail over the masts of my ships. That means our quarry is very probably inshore . . .'

'I agree,' said Admiral Morgan. 'It's possible he may have given them the slip . . . but unlikely. Also I see from one of Jimmy's notes, right here, the security officers said the missiles came in directly out of the south-west. Which means they must have passed over the masts of your ships . . . that is, if he was further offshore than we think.'

'That's precisely what I'm getting at,' said Admiral Dickson. 'If we mark my crescent right here . . . and draw a straight line to the southwest from the Lomboc Power Station, it looks as though the submarine we seek was probably less than 300-miles offshore . . . somewhere here, in this area . . .'

'Can't argue with that,' said Arnold Morgan. 'Just one thing, though. The missiles did take a kinda circuitous route into Valdez and Grays Harbor, so why do you suppoose he fired 'em straight this time?'

'Mainly because there's no point ducking and diving with missiles over the water, when you must know beyond any doubt that the United States Navy is very much on your tail.'

'Correct,' said Arnold. 'Well observed. The two Lompoc guys both saw the damned thing incoming from the south-west, that's directly out of the Pacific. . . . hmmmmm . . . that circle you just put on the screen . . . the little bastard's in there, no doubt.'

'I've just talked to CINCPAC . . . they're diverting search aircraft, plus a couple of destroyers right in there ASAP. As you know, there's a ton of ASW kit on the frigates.'

'Plenty of torpedoes too, I hope,' rasped Arnold. 'What are their rules of engagement?'

'Shoot to kill. No questions asked.'

'That's my language, Alan. We find 'em. They die.'

'Of course, we still have a big problem, sir. We don't know which way he's headed.'

'No. And I guess our biggest worry is he heads slowly north-west, maybe eight hundred feet below the surface. That way he'd be near certain to get away. Unless he runs over a SOSUS hot-spot.'

'I know it, sir. But I don't think he can move to the west. We'd catch him if he did. Even if he was going pretty slowly. His options are really south-east, south, and south-west. In that ninety degree arc he has his back to the wall, but if he moves slowly, the odds are still in his favor.'

'Hmmmm. That's the trouble with oceans,' said Arnold. 'They're altogether too fucking big.'

'If you had to make an assessment, sir. If you were him, which way would you go?'

'Not westwards. Because that's where I'd be expecting trouble. Maybe due south. Because from where he is positioned, that's into very deep open ocean way off Central America. However I think he hugged the coast coming down from the Grays Harbor area, stayed in noisy water for maybe four days, and then headed further offshore for his attack.'

'You think he'll pull the same trick now, sir?'

'Dunno. But I would. I'd hug the coast of Mexico for a long time. I'd probably keep going at seven knots for two or three thousand miles, maybe three weeks. Then I'd angle off, come right to two-seven-oh degrees and charge for the south Pacific.

His chances of being caught in there are around zero. The area's just too big.'

'You mean if we're gonna get him, sir, we'd better get him real quick.'

'That's what I mean, Admiral.'

'If only he had to surface, or refuel, or snorkel, or any damn thing . . . life would be a lot easier.'

'That's been the trouble right from the start, Alan. In that ship he doesn't have to do any of those things. And that's why we might not find him.'

'What will you advise the President to say?'

'I guess he'll have to say we suspect terrorism. And that the oil installations were attacked, by persons unknown. But I think we'll leave it very open-ended for the moment. I'll have him refer to the possibility of land-launched missiles, or even planted bombs . . .

'But I cannot terrify the populace by admitting there's a foreign nuclear submarine, patrolling our shores, knocking down anything he fucking well pleases. That would cause mass panic. And worse, it would alert the controllers of our terrorists to be even more careful than usual.'

The CNO shook his head. And Lt. Commander Ramshawe climbed to his feet and walked closer to the big computer screen. He stared at it for a moment, then he turned back to the two Admirals.

'May I say something, sir?' he said, staring at Arnold Morgan.

'Sure, Jimmy. Go right ahead. Alan and I have exhausted our collective brains.'

'Okay. Let us assume our theories are correct. Somehow China agrees to purchase not one, but both Russian Barracudas. And sends one of them all the way around the Arctic Circle to Petropavlovsk, with a view to making an excursion into US waters, that's the relatively short passage across the northern Pacific past the Aleutian Islands.

'At around the same time, they pop out the bloody decoy and send the bastard round the world. Except no-one admits the decoy is floating, right? So when old razormouth starts banging out the refinery, then the power station, the decoy shows up, bold as brass, in Zhanjiang, proving beyond doubt it could not have been the Barracuda, because they know we think there is only one of 'em.

'However, they had two mishaps. One, the decoy 'cuda gets

heard off the coast of Ireland. Two, the other 'cuda hits the *sushi* boat, proving it's not where it ought to be, right?

'So now we are alerted to the possibilities of two Barracudas, not one. Although we can't prove it either way.'

'So far, well summed up,' said Arnold.

'Well, sir, I think we would all agree, that whoever came up with that scheme was one clever little bastard. And when you think about it, there was a kind of advantage in it for everyone. The Ruskies needed, and got, the six hundred mill, right? The Chinese, in my view, are not the principals in this, but they may have acquired the submarines for someone else. It's dollars to doughnuts if they get caught, there won't be a fucking Chinaman on board that submarine.

'*But*, a USA with a totally chronic shortage of oil, is fantastic for the Chinese. They've picked up a whole bunch of contracts in the Gulf, they own the main southern pipeline out of Kazakhstan, right across Iran to their terminus in the Strait of Hormuz. And crude's just hit seventy-five dollars a barrel. Not too bad, right?'

'So, for whom did they buy the submarine? Who could afford it? Had to be a State Government?' Admiral Morgan was pondering.

'In a sense, yes,' said Jimmy Ramshawe. 'But in another sense, no . . . because when you're dealing with international terrorism you've got all kinds of fucking maniacs involved. Not one country. The Islamic Jihad, which works against us and the Israelis, crosses borders. Look at that fucking nutcase Bin Laden, he had all kinds of nations involved, Saudi Arabia, Afghanistan, possibly Pakistan, Iran, Iraq, maybe Syria or even Jordan.

'I think that's what we're up against. Oh, sure, we can ask the Chinese what they did with their two Barracudas, but they will never provide a straight answer. And in the end, they'll say that if there is one, off California right now, it has never been within two thousand miles of China. Why not ask the Russians? And Admiral Rankov will say we don't even own the submarine, why not ask the Chinese?

'And where does that leave us? Nowhere. With options only to nuke Moscow or Beijing, which we are not about to do because public opinion will be heavily against us. Americans only get real cross when a lot of people die. And in this case there's hardly anyone.

'Trust me. The public will blame Washington for not being more careful, and making sure that asshole Troy Ramford got his stupid fucking statue.'

Both senior officers guffawed. 'Well, James,' said Admiral Dixon. 'What's your conclusion?'

'There is only one conclusion, sir.'

'And?'

'Whoever planned and carried out this program was nothing short of a fucking genius. Cleverer than any terrorist who's ever lived. That's my conclusion.'

Arnold Morgan was thoughtful.

'I believe you know what I'm thinking, sir.'

'Jimmy, I don't know what you're thinking. But I do know what you and I both are wondering.'

'Yessir. Where's that Major Ray bloody Kerman, right?'

'Yes, Jimmy. That's it. Where indeed?'

CHAPTER TWELVE

2315 Wednesday, March 19, 2008
The Pacific Ocean

The most powerful electricity generator within a few miles of the darkened city of Los Angeles was continuing steadily away to the south-east, its big turbines idling along at only five knots, 300 feet below the surface. The lights in the submarine were bright, the refrigeration system perfect, the air clean and fresh, the water pure, and the temperature steady.

However, the ultimate irony of the situation was somewhat lost on General Ravi and Captain Ben Badr's Barracuda crew. They had made the journey across the Pacific and successfully shattered the electric power system of the two biggest cities on the American west coast.

They were not, of course, aware of this, but they had left both San Francisco and LA in chaotic, dangerous darkness, with schools and shops closed, hospitals desperate, and thousands of tons of food rotting without refrigeration. All while Ravi and Ben casually accepted the benefits of their own private nuclear power cell, which, on its own, could have cheerfully restored full electricity to the entire district of Hollywood, and indeed most of north-west Los Angeles, without missing a beat.

The navigation officer had them at 28.15N, 117.00W, eighty miles south-east of Guadalupe Island, 130 miles off the coast of Mexico. Thus far they had found no need to avoid or in any way change course for searching US warships, or patrol aircraft. Their speed had been five knots all the way, and it was still five knots, leaving no tell-tale pattern on the surface.

There were of course several US Navy frigates and three LA Class submarines working off San Diego, listening for the engine beat of a rogue foreign submarine. And a couple of them had ventured south into international waters, but the ocean was too vast, and the Barracuda too slow for a positive detection, and both hunters and quarry knew it.

Captain Badr had no intention of altering his plans, his direction, or his speed for three weeks. And he and Ravi sat in the control room, moving slowly south-east, gleefully going over the plan of escape masterminded for them by the Chinese.

General Rashood had collected the instructions from the timed safe on board, way back in the Gulf of Alaska. And with Ben Badr had made a cursory study of the meticulous orders drafted by the Intelligence Command Center in Shanghai.

For the moment, it was simple to follow . . . *maintain submerged course one-three-five . . . speed five . . . then periscope depth into the Gulf of Panama. Surface the submarine 08.20 North, 78.30 West . . . proceed on surface maximum speed to Panama's Pacific Anchorage Expansion . . . course three-six-zero to latitude 08.51 North, 78.30 West − depth 10 fathoms − for rendezvous with PLAN patrol boat 1330 April 11 2008 . . .*

Well, it would be one hell of a long way at this slow speed to the Gulf of Panama, 3,000 miles and about twenty-six days, but at least they knew where they were going. And the Chinese had a plain desire for the utmost secrecy. In fact the Chinese had a greater desire than anyone: the Russians could always shrug everything off and claim they sold the boat. The Islamic terrorists did not in the end care who knew, as long as they had reached home safely. But the Chinese . . . if anyone even suspected they had been behind the monstrous attacks on the American mainland, that was very probably WWIII.

Silence, thy name is Zhang Yushu.

And it was with obvious satisfaction that General Rashood and Captain Badr now contemplated the escape route that lay before them. Both men knew the entire operation was predicated on the fact that China now controlled the Panama Canal, to the horror of many US military chiefs, and to the embarrassment of the more astute Democrats who somehow had allowed their party to be represented in the White House by the former Governor of Arkansas.

Nonetheless when the US finally handed over the Canal Zone to the Panamanian Government in 1999, they gave away a great deal more than anyone had bargained for. Because the wily, leftish rulers of that sweltering, tropical isthmus at the southern end of Central America, immediately began negotiations with the equally wily rulers of Communist China.

As a money-making scheme, this was a Golden Goose for the cash-strapped Panamanians. At either end of the canal was a huge US Naval dockyard/city: Cristobal on the port side of the Atlantic entrance, bordering the primitive and unsafe city of Colon; and Balboa on the port side of the Pacific exit, bordering Panama City. These two massive US strongholds dominated and controlled the canal for almost a century.

In addition, the sprawling Rodman Naval Base, exactly opposite Balboa Harbor, formed an impregnable US choke point. Since 1914, ships had transited the Panama Canal only when the United States authorities issued clearance, which was right and proper, since the US built the gigantic structure in the first place, supplied the manpower and bound the great concrete walls together with New York cement.

Without that Yankeee know-how there would *never* have been a Panama Canal. It is, to this day, regarded as probably the greatest feat of engineering ever achieved – a canal, eighty-five feet above sea level, into which every ship has to climb a gigantic set of locks to enter, and then negotiate another set of three towering locks which lower it to the exit. The entire process of flooding and emptying the locks is achieved by gravity alone, millions of tons of water gushing through fifteen-foot-wide tunnels. Ships almost 1,000 feet long have made the journey along this forty-four-mile-long-path between the seas, saving 7,872 miles against a voyage around Cape Horn.

The USA completed the building project in 1914, after taking over from the French who lost 22,000 men during a catastrophic attempt to build a canal without the help of America. If all the sand, shale, rock and mud excavated to build the canal were loaded into box cars, the resulting train would circle the earth four times at the nearby equator.

And in December of 1999, the entire operation, the engineering marvel of the canal, its locks, dockyards, controls, and great swathes of two cities, was handed over by the US Government to Panama, under President Carter's 1977 Treaty, which guaranteed at all times, *expeditious passage* for the United States Navy.

Within weeks of the new millennium it became clear what had really happened. Panama had effectively handed over control of the canal, plus its former US Navy and Army installations, to President Clinton's Most Favored Nation, Communist China.

The Panamanians had sold a fifty-year contract for the Cristobal and Balboa dockyards to Hong Kong shipping conglomerate, Hutchison Whampoa Ltd, a company which had inordinately strong links to the China Ocean Shipping Company (COSCO) which was totally controlled by the People's Liberation Army. That's the same COSCO which in 1999 came within a whisker of gaining control of the US Naval Shipyards at Long Beach California, which would have handed over that strategic corner of the Golden State to the Red Army.

Hutchison Whampoa ended up with the Rodman Naval Station, a portion of the US Air Station Albrook; Diablo and Balboa on the Pacific, Cristobal Dockyard on the Atlantic, and the island of Telfers.

The contract included 'Rights' to operate piloting and tug boat services for the canal, out of Cristobal and Balboa, and to deny access to ports and entrances to any ships deemed to be interfering with Hutchison's business. This later clause, secretly written into Panama's *Law Number Five*, was plainly in direct violation of Carter's Panama Canal Treaty. It allowed Hutchison Whampoa to determine which ships may enter the channel, and has effectively made Communist China the Gatekeeper of the Canal; thus enjoying total control of the great US-built waterway, at both ends.

The Panamanian contract with the Chinese could plainly have been severely obstructed, and then slammed into oblivion had there been a proper Republican President in the White House, rather than a self-serving left winger, who will always be remembered as the ideal President for China's ambitions. President Clinton was a man open to their attempts at bribery, tolerant of their transfer of weapons to questionable areas, helpful in modernizing China's military, and oblivious to a weakening of the US military, spread thin because of his own reckless humanitarian peacekeeping missions all over the globe.

Panama highlighted another side of that particular Democratic President, that of the weak and vacillating negotiator, utterly reluctant to follow through with hard-headed American threats, or even to act decisively, except against those powerless to resist. The snafu in Panama was precisely the kind of international disaster which invariably happens when a major power votes into office a President who dislikes the military, as Clinton, to his country's very great cost, most certainly did.

General Ravi Rashood, as a former serving commander in the SAS, knew the entire background to the Panama situation, and he had been able to explain to Ben Badr why they would be safe in the former Canal Zone.

'The Chinese can open and close the channels from either end, at will,' he said. 'My guess is that once we're in, they'll shut it off to all shipping on some pretext or other. And it's pretty clear we'll be flying home from somewhere in Panama. The US will probably catch sight of us, but by then it will be too late. The Chinese will just slam those lock gates shut. And that's one hell of a barrier, those doors weigh 800 tons each. It's the the one fact I remember about the canal . . .'

'But what about my ship, Ravi? What happens to that?'

'I don't know, but I understand all final instructions will be given when the Chinese pilot boards at Balboa before we move into the canal.'

'Did you make any recommendations before we left? It was your project in the first place.'

'Yes, I did. I told them the submarine would have to be dumped, in a place where it would never be found and from where it would tell no tales.'

'What! This beautiful ship which can strike against the Satan any time we sail it to the right place?'

'Ben, this ship is now poisonous. Its very presence is a threat not only to us, but to Russia and China, and world order. It certainly does not suit our purposes for China and the US to be at war. Because that way everyone would be caught up in the fallout.

'It would be in our best interests for this ship to vanish, leaving the Americans uncertain of what happened, the Chinese with their heads down, and the Russians denying anything and everything. That way we would have taken some very large steps towards an American exit from the Middle East, and made some very large profits for the Gulf states in the oil industry. Some of which will find its way into the coffers of HAMAS.'

'I see that, Ravi. But tell me one thing. How do you dump a nuclear submarine of this size without spilling radiation all over the place and alerting everyone on the planet to the submarine's location?'

'Not easily. You plainly cannot blow it up, nor even scuttle it, because of the nuclear reactor, and the terrible publicity surrounding radioactive material. An act like that would cause the West to come after any guilty State and maybe seize the entire country, or even flatten it. I don't think that's a good idea.'

'No. Neither do I,' said Captain Badr.

'However, I have recommended we shut the reactor down and just let the Barracuda sink into the mud in some totally inaccessible, uninhabited place with heavy rainforest cover. Seal it off and then abandon it. The Chinese could camouflage the sail, if it was still showing, and in a few months it would be completely gone.'

'Someone would probably find it in the end,' said Ben.

'Yes. But that might take fifty years. And who the hell cares?'

'Not I,' said Ben. 'But I regret we have only managed one operation in this superb ship.'

'I too. But remember, we do have another one.'

The late March temperature in the West Wing of the White House was hovering near the red zone. The President was absolutely furious, unable to comprehend the impotence of the United States Navy in finding the rogue submarine.

No amount of words by the CNO, no amount of logic from God knows how many admirals could convince him of the sheer impossibility of locating a nuclear submarine travelling at a very slow speed, in an unknown direction, in a million square miles of ocean.

Admiral Morgan, tired of the President's ranting and raving, ended up taking him aside and privately telling him not to be 'so fucking stupid, and to try to get a goddamned grip of yourself'.

'You got the best Navy brains in the country right here in the White House,' he growled. 'They are wrestling with the problem night and day. If it could be done we'da done it, so get ahold of yourself. And do some listening.'

The President had never been spoken to quite like that by anyone, except the unimpeachable, unsackable Arnold Morgan. And he did not much enjoy the experience. But a walkout by his revered National Security Advisor at a time like this would finish him, particularly as that might precipitate a further walkout by his Chiefs of Staff. Or even an unthinkable military takeover by the generals and admirals, who might judge him incompetent to lead the nation in a time of crisis, and obvious emergency.

Stranger things have happened. Commander-in-Chief the President might be, but that always presupposes the goodwill of the Armed Service Chiefs towards the White House. That goodwill had never been seriously tested, not even with Clinton. But equally there had never been a serious military threat to the US mainland, not by a foreign invader. Ever. But there was one now, and the military was edging into the inner circle of government, and the Chief Executive had to tread warily.

'Arnie, I'm sorry,' the President said. 'But to a layman like myself, it's unthinkable that the Navy of the USA cannot find a submarine which has been attacking our shores . . .'

'Sir, no-one can find a nuclear boat, which is travelling at five knots or under, three hundred feet below the surface. Not without tripping over the damn thing by accident. No terrorist has ever used a nuclear boat before, and we have to find out whose fingerprints are on it. Sooner or later he'll make a mistake, and we'll be waiting. Meanwhile we've got a lot to think about.'

The Admiral was correct about that. The price of oil had tripled to seventy-six dollars a barrel, and stayed there. The world's fuel markets were in an uproar. So were the Dow Jones Industrials, the Footsie, the CAC-40, the Nikkei, the DAX and the rest.

Stocks collapsed on a global scale. Shares in any public corporation which was dependent on oil or fuel, any transportation, were just about unsaleable. The two big California cities, unattached to the main state grid, were bereft of electricity. And the remnants of the power station at Lompoc were still burning. A mass exodus of millions from San Francisco and Los Angeles, to outlying districts, had caused chaos on the freeways, as drivers struggled to get into an electricity zone.

Every hotel, every motel, was packed with families who had fled the endless dark which surrounded night-time San Francisco Bay and Los Angeles. Thousands of people decamped with friends and relatives out in Concord, Livermore and Modesto; Ventura, Santa Clarita, Moreno Valley and Palm Springs. Many thousands more bought airline tickets at spiraling prices, from airlines with small emergency generators for computers, and battled their way out of the two international airports in the daylight hours. They had to be sharp, before the massive jet-fuel storage areas ran completely dry.

There was no question of key executives trying to commute their way into the city centers. Modern business runs on computers, and great office high-rises cannot function without electricity. There was no light, no elevators, and no security systems. There was a danger that law and order could break down. Every evening at twilight gangs of youths roamed the streets. Looting was becoming commonplace. The LA Polic Department, lit by three small generators, struggled to keep these mobs of amateur criminals under control. Emergency fuel was coming in by road in Exxon tankers to gas up the police cruisers.

The military were being called in, to mount street patrols and to guard the downtown buildings. Water supplies to both cities, dependent on electricity plant for purifying systems, were becoming stretched to the limit. Consumption was down, but the greater LA system still had to cope with the demands of a population cut by two-thirds, but still three million strong.

The Governor was safe in his Sacremento Mansion. But the mighty film studios were closed. All west coast television transmission was down, which hardly mattered since no-one could turn on their sets. If Troy Ramford was going to receive his Oscar publicly, any time soon, it would have to be somewhere out beyond San Bernadino, where the power was on. His Malibu home was dark, like the rest of the beachfront properties of the film and television 'talent'.

The President, guided and supported by his energy secretary Jack Smith was putting emergency measures into operation as fast as possible. The San Francisco and Los Angeles electricity supply companies were being connected to the main California grid, with massive powerline hook-ups out in Simmi Valley, north of LA, and to the west of San Jose, south of San Francisco. Jack Smith estimated power for the cities inside twelve days, which the President considered inordinate.

With the refinery gone at Grays Harbor, there was no further possibility of refined oil running south into the west coast states of Oregon and California, but there was a definite capability for US tanker fleets to start shipping refined oil through the Panama Canal and north to LA immediately. The fuel, colossally expensive, was subsequently government subsidized. And of course the huge diesel engines of the tankers themselves were sloshing back fuel which cost almost the same as cheap Scotch whisky.

Tanker fleets from the Midwest were already on the roads, barreling through the night, laden with gasoline from the big Chicago terminals, across Iowa, Nebraska, southern Wyoming, and Nevada, on what was virtually a mercy mission to the American west. Hundreds of fuel trucks were thundering out of Texas, west across the deserts of New Mexico and Arizona towards the stricken city of Los Angeles. Every one of them was laden with refined gasoline, which LA needed a lot more than it needed Oklahoma sweet crude.

And all the while the east coast media wanted to know what the hell the President was doing about 'this unprecedented crisis in the history of our country'? How was he proposing to solve it, find the culprits, and restore the power and dignity of the United States of America? Generally speaking it looked a lot easier from the offices of the *Washington Post* than it did from the Oval Office.

And through it all the US Navy wracked its brains, listening for the lonely bleep in the vast Pacific ocean, which would betray the presence of the murderous Barracuda Type 945, which Arnold Morgan swore was there.

The President had three times addressed the section of the nation which had working television sets, stressing the speed at which the emergency services were working to reconnnect the blackout cities. He admitted the likelihood of sabotage, even attack by terrorists, and swore US revenge on the perpetrators of these 'wicked and destructive crimes against our nation'.

He did not however point out the likelihood of a bunch of maniacs in a modern nuclear submarine creeping up and down the west coast, bombarding the most important oil installations with heavy Russian-built cruise missiles.

And nor could he envisage doing so, not before the Navy had detected and either captured or destroyed the enemy, whoever he might be.

The US diplomatic service was working at an unprecedented speed, demanding co-operation from every one of their international trading partners. They threatened the Russians and the Chinese, opened the lines to Tehran, Damascus, Cairo and Jordan, demanding to know if there was any connection to the west coast atrocities from any Arab Fundamentalist group.

The CIA called in favors, bribed, blackmailed and badgered agents all over the world. But no-one knew anything. Especially the Russians who would only say they had sold the Barracuda to the Chinese and knew nothing else.

The Chinese Navy merely asserted the only Barracuda they knew anything about was currently visiting the Southern Fleet HQ in Zhanjiang. Had been since before the Lompoc attack, and so far as they knew was still there in a covered dock. No other Barracuda had ever docked in a Chinese naval base. All true. Nearly.

Meanwhile the US satellites were adjusted to range along the west coast of Canada and the United States, from the Gulf of Alaska all the way to the 780-mile-long Mexican peninsula of Baja California. That was a total sea-and-air patrol distance of 3,000 miles, all of it essential, just in case the submarines turned north again, just in case it continued to head south.

CINCPAC reasoned the marauder was surely traveling slowly, otherwise it must surely have been heard, either by a patrolling submarine, which could have picked it up at 100 miles, or by SOSUS which is deadly sensitive all the way along the west coast. Only the lowest speed ensures near-total silence.

Which meant five knots maximum, and at that speed it would take more than eight days to cover 1,000 miles. Thus in the first week of the hunt, the Pacific branch of the US Navy was faced with a search-area of 3,000 miles by 1,000 miles . . . three million square miles, an area roughly the size of Australia, with nothing even resembling a submarine choke point.

All US satellites were adjusted to photograph the immense tract of ocean. The most modern observation systems of surface-disturbance were activated, all of them peering down through space, seeking the swirling patterns on the water which would betray the presence of a deep-running nuclear ship . . . unless it was moving at the pace of a basking Pacific turtle.

Everyone knew the task was probably impossible. But the Navy had to keep going, just in case the submarine made a mistake, and to prevent further embarrassment to the Presidency of the United States.

'The main trouble is,' Arnold Morgan privately raged, 'that no-one has the slightest idea which direction the goddamned ship is moving.'

He still believed it must be making some kind of a southerly course, but that only reduced the search area to 1.5 million square miles, half the size of Brazil.

By Thursday morning, March 27, four days after a hectic non-existent Easter break, the Navy still reported nothing. By now the Barracuda was more than 1,300 miles down the coast of Mexico, beyond the designated search-area for the US warships and aircraft, but not beyond the range of the satellites. It still had more than 1,800 miles to go before the Gulf of Panama, but with every turn of its fifteen-foot-high bronze screw, it pushed further away from danger.

In the White House, the President was at a level of frustration which he regarded as intolerable. He remained without comprehension where the Navy was concerned, muttering constantly about the billions of dollars he authorized every year for research and development in military surveillance; only to be told there was an 8,000-ton missile-hurling Russian submarine, fucking around somewhere off Laguna Beach, and no-one could find it, never mind zap it.

The situation was somewhat eased when the lights went on again in LA. On the Saturday afternoon of March 29, three-quarters of the city's electric power was restored, and though this would mean two-hour 'brown outs' in other parts of Southern California, it was sensationally good news for the residents of the city of angels.

The San Francisco hook-up took a day longer. But by Monday morning, March 31, both the big metropolitan areas were up and running again, despite chronic fuel shortages, and long lines at the gas pumps.

The President again went on television to explain that for the moment the USA was reliant on foreign oil, and that it would be several months before the Alaskan oil began to flow again. Work to rebuild the refinery at Grays Harbor was already under way, and the two breaches in the south-running undersea pipeline had been repaired. Right now the Energy Department was concentrating on refinery capacity, and routes were being established to run more and more crude oil into America's existing facilities.

'We should,' he told an expectant nation, 'be on top of the situation inside another two weeks. This will be a huge strain on our tanker facilities, but you have my word we're gonna be seeing the price of oil per barrel dropping firmly within a very few days.

'I have requested American tankers from all over the globe to bring crude oil into the Texas facilities on the Gulf of Mexico.

No matter the cost, no matter the effect on profits, now is the time for this nation to rally round, and get the fuel oil to the places where we need it.'

Again he took the greatest care to ensure no mention was made of the submarine the Pentagon believed had opened fire on the United States.

Meanwhile, deep in the lower level Situation Room in the West Wing, Admiral Morgan continued to preside over meeting after meeting with Security and Service Chiefs probing every last inch of the incoming data which might throw some light on the submarine.

Right now the Navy had two more Los Angeles-Class submarines, the *Boise* and the *Montpelier*, crossing the Caribbean towards the Panama Canal. Once clear of the pilots on the Pacific side, they would head north towards San Diego, at first 200 miles off the coast of Central America, and then as part of the Navy's search-line making sweep after sweep along the Mexico/California coast.

But nothing was shaking loose in this baffling jigsaw puzzle, and morale was suffering everywhere, especially in the Pentagon. All day and most of the night the surveillance officers checked the systems, checked to see whether the Barracuda had left Zhanjiang, checked on every submarine movement in the world, checked satellite pictures from Bandar Abbas to Beijing, and pored over the prints from the eastern reaches of the Pacific.

But the world seemed becalmed, and always there was nothing. Until April 11, when the *USS Boise*, on the surface now and clear of Panama's Chinese pilots, dived and headed for the deeper waters of the Pacific beyond the confines of the Gulf of Panama. At 1143 (local) her sonar room picked up a Russian nuclear boat heading slowly north at twelve knots, periscope depth, eight miles south of the main channel, in the Pacific Extension of the merchant ship anchorage.

Boise's CO had received no change to his standard COMSUBPAC rules of engagement – fire only in self-defense. And he knew the consequences of torpedoing a Russian nuclear submarine in Panamanian territorial waters . . . dire, especially if it turned out to be the wrong one. And anyway it was headed direct to the Canal where everyone would see it.

In accordance with his orders, he immediately put a signal on the satellite, which relayed it to Pacific Fleet Headquarters, Pearl

344

Harbor, and to the Base at San Diego simultaneously. From there it was beamed into the ops room of the 9,000-ton guided-missile destroyer, *USS Roosevelt*, Arleigh Burke Class, one of the most lethal fighting ships in the world. Heavily-gunned, bristling with missiles and torpedoes, she carried on her stern two Lamps-III combat helicopters, both equipped with Penguin and Hellfire missiles.

The *Roosevelt* was headed north having taken a swing along the northern coast of Columbia to keep the local drug barons on their mettle. She was now some three hours from the Merchant Ship Anchorage, clipping along at thirty knots. Her satellite orders from CINCPAC were clear . . . *locate Russian nuclear boat Sierra I Barracuda Class Type 945, detected by the submarine USS* Boise . . . *believed to be headed into the Panama Canal . . . track through canal to Atlantic Anchorage . . . rendezvous with two escorts . . . both LA Class ships, the* San Juan *and the* Key West *patrolling six miles north-west of Cristabel Harbor West Breakwater . . .*

The *Roosevelt* adjusted course to nor'nor'west and headed for the Gulf of Panama. Her commanding officer, Captain Butch Howarth ordered flank speed. Meanwhile Captain Ben Badr kept moving north towards his rendezvous with the Chinese fast patrol boat – the seventy-eight-foot twin-gunned *Gong Bian 4405* (Chinese Border Security Force – Maritime Command). The ships were, loosely, on a collision course.

By 1300 the Barracuda was on the surface, with the *Roosevelt* still making all speed, sixty miles to the south-east. Up ahead, silhouetted against the bright blue water, Ben Badr could see the buoy which marks the start of the dead-straight, six-mile dredged channel up to Balboa Harbor, and the gateway to the canal. The Chinese gateway.

There was often a small holding area 1,000 yards north-east of the buoy where ships, mostly merchantmen and tankers, lined up to make the journey through to the Atlantic. Today, there appeared to be no traffic, though Captain Badr could see three stationary tankers a mile away on the edge of the Anchorage.

The *Gong Bian* was waiting, and her captain pulled her alongside the Barracuda, offered a greeting and a welcome, then instructed the submarine to track the Chinese patrol slowly down the channel, red buoys to the right, and then to follow them into the harbor where the Chinese pilot would come on board to see her safely through the narrow waterway.

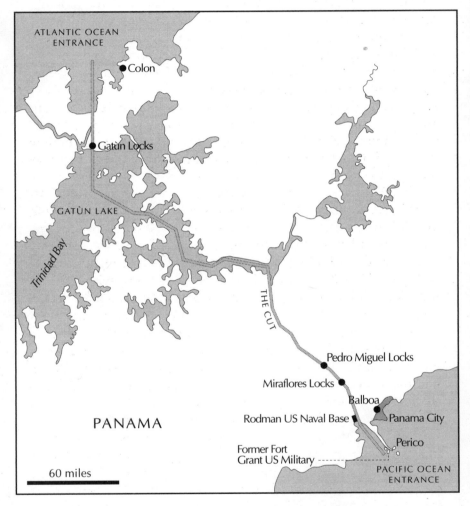

THE PANAMA CANAL PACIFIC ENTRANCE (BOTTOM RIGHT) - ACROSS THE
GATUN LAKE TO THE ATLANTIC LOCKS

Captain Badr, joined now by General Rashood and Lt. Commander Shakira, issued commands to his helmsman and navigator from the bridge. And together, the three most wanted terrorists in the world, stood and breathed their first fresh air, in the first warm sunlight any of them had seen for sixty-two days, since they left the freezing Russian Naval Base of Petropavlovsk. The Barracuda had almost 7,000-miles under its keel since then, and its commanders had not yet made a mistake.

Behind a light bow wave, and before a mild headwind, the jet-black 8,000-ton outlaw of the Eastern Pacific moved gently north-west, steering three-two-two, in the wake of the *Gong Bian*, leaving the treacherous San Jose rock to starboard. Four hundred yards further, at the end of a two-mile long causeway from Balboa, they passed the cluster of islands, Flamenco, Perico, Paos, and Culebra where the Panama Railway, all the way through the jungle from the Atlantic coast, finally ends.

The Americans constructed that as well, back in the mid-nineteenth century. The causeway itself was also American-built, in 1912, when the US established the fabled Fort Grant complex on all four islands. It was the most powerful military defensive fortress in the world, guarding the Pacific entrance to the canal, and once housing two massive fourteen-inch guns with a thirty-mile range, which could be swiftly transported through the jungle on their own railroad cars, in case of trouble at the Atlantic end.

All this crumbled history has today come under the control of the Chinese, with the historic old railroad joining China's two great Panamanian Dockyards at either end of the canal. All because of a President, who never much cared for America's achievements, especially the military ones, nor indeed for what America ought to stand for, in an often inferior world.

Two miles beyond the island railhead, the imposing span of the Thatcher Ferry Bridge sweeps the Inter-American highway straight over the canal from Panama City, and on to Mexico. The Barracuda chugged slowly beneath the bridge and on to the Balboa pilot station, where Ravi and Ben would hand over command of the submarine to the elite corps of Chinese canal navigators, employees of the Hutchison Whampoa Company.

The Panama Canal is the only place in the world where military commanders are required to hand over navigational control of warships to a foreign operator.

The Chinese pilot came on board and took over, issuing

347

instructions in English to the Islamic terrorists. Three and a half miles later they arrived at the towering Milaflore Locks, the first of the three on the Pacific side.

The waterway divides here, so the 1,000-foot-long lock chambers can operate independently to both incoming and outgoing traffic, quite often with one lock lowering, and the other raising, 80,000-ton ships, only yards apart, with fifty million gallons of water, emptying and flooding, every time.

The Milaflores Lock comprises two sets of chambers, which raise or lower ships, in two steps, fifty-four-feet to or from sea level. And as the Barracuda approached the first 800-ton lock gates, locomotives were attached to haul the submarine through. These engineering stalwarts represent another coup for the Orient. They cost $2 million each and are all made by Mitsubishi, and they help make Hutchison Whampoa many millions of dollars each year.

It took Captain Badr's ship a half-hour to make this first ascent, up to the short mile-and-half long Milaflore Lake which runs to the final Pacific side lock, the Pedro Miguel. And as the submarine eased its way through the narrow, flat waters, *USS Roosevelt* came thundering into the Merchant Ship Anchorage, almost ten miles in arrears and fifty-four feet lower.

Captain Howarth was ordered to halt, out alongside the three tankers which Ravi and Ben had seen, and to wait in line for entry to the canal. The US commanding officer hit the radio immediately, and demanded priority under the terms of the 1977 Treaty, which the Chinese Control room in Balboa affected not to understand.

Captain Howarth, like all US commanding officers working anywhere near the canal, had the wording of the Treaty on the ops room computer. 'EXPEDITIOUS PASSAGE!' he snapped. 'According to the Random House dictionary, that means prompt, or quick. And this Treaty was signed by the President of Panama and the President of the United States of America. So get buzzing . . .'

The Chinese controller understood neither expeditious, prompt nor buzzing. 'Control now run by Hutchison Whampoa,' he said. 'Not President of United States. Panama give us rights. And right now canal is closed for repairs. May take all day, all night. Sorry. You wait now.'

'*Closed!*' yelled Captain Howarth. '*What the hell do you mean, closed!*'

'Canal closed,' said the Chinese voice. 'That what I mean. Closed. No entry for you. Lock gates shut.'

'But you let a Russian submarine through there in the last hour,' said Captain Howarth, an edge to his voice.

'Canal not closed then. Canal closed now. Different.'

'Now listen to me,' said the American CO. 'If I have to, I'll have the President of the United States call the President of Panama . . . but first I shall need you to tell me your name, rank and number . . . since you appear unaware you may be causing an international incident right here.'

'No need for you to know my name,' said the Chinese voice blandly. 'I'm a civilian. No rank or number. Presidents of countries do not run this canal. Hutchison Whampoa run canal. And we say who goes through and who stays out. Right now canal closed. You stay out 'til we say you come in.'

Captain Howarth knew he was beaten. It requires the opening of six different sets of lock gates to make one complete transit of the canal. Three sets up. Three down. If these Chinese bastards elected to slam them shut and refuse to open them, there was not a whole lot anyone could do about it. At least not quickly, or expeditiously.

He slammed down the telephone. And dictated a satellite signal for immediate transmission to San Diego Base. '*Chinese gatekeepers closed Panama Canal at approximately 1435 (local) "for repairs". Barracuda entered 1345. Transit should take eight hours minimum. Stand by Atlantic exit 112230APR08. Roosevelt will stand guard Pacific End, Merchant Ship Anchorage, in case of Barracuda course change. Await further orders. Howarth.*'

Inside the canal, up on the two-third height level, leading to the Pedro Miguel Lock, Ravi and Ben stood with the pilots on the bridge, watching the shallow waters of the lake slip by on either side of the channel. Ahead they could see the great portals of the lock, and the huge gates that guard the entrance to the chamber, the one in which the water level would shortly rise, and lift the Barracuda the final thirty-one feet to the uppermost reaches of the canal.

And as they made their approach, the gates came slowly open. The pilots paused for the chains of the locomotives to be passed behind the sail, and then, engines cut, they were pulled into the chamber, for the ten-minute 'elevator ride' to the heights. Right here Captain Badr ordered the Barracuda's nuclear reactor shut down, the rods were dropped in, and for the first time since the Kamchatka Peninsula, the heat from the reactor began to die.

Reaching the top, the gates for'ard of the submarine's bow opened, and the great nuclear ship was now under tow. A waiting Chinese Navy tug was attached and pulled her out into the sunlit waterway of the Cukoracha Reach, which forms the Pacific end of the Gaillard Cut.

Brilliant engineering, and raw-boned United States muscle, had hacked a nine-and-a-half mile channel clean through here, through the Continental dividing range, the terrible mountainous spine of the isthmus, to send the waterway down to the Pacific.

The banks rise up steeply through here, and the channel makes a series of left–right zigzags, a testament to the near impossibility of cleaving a seaway through the jungle-foothills of the mountains, the landslides, the rockfalls, the murderous heat, rainforest fevers and disease. Thousands and thousands of Frenchmen died along here. And it was no picnic for the Americans, either.

The sight of the Chinese pilot on the bridge of the Barracuda, somehow in command of this thoroughly American enterprise, created one of the deepest enigmas in modern geopolitics. There was also an element of the surreal in the fact that former SAS Major Ray Kerman was right now trying to make a terrorist's getaway in a Russian submarine with Chinese help,

But that's what was happening, while Captain Howarth fumed out in the Merchant Anchorage, the Pentagon rumbled with fury upon receipt of his satellite signal, and Admiral Morgan was fit to be tied, as he paced his office in the West Wing.

'*Kathy*!' he bawled. 'Get the Chinese ambassador in here inside a half-hour. And have an ambulance parked in the Rose Garden in case I murder the little fucker.'

Kathy rolled her eyes heavenwards, but she did not consider her boss was overreacting. Rarely had she felt such tension in the White House as during the last half-hour, since the news came in, that China had closed the Panama Canal.

Harcourt Travis, the Secretary of State, was on the line to the Panamanian President who was secretly terrified of the USA – ever since December 20, 1989, when 26,000 United States troops landed in Panama with guns blazing, tanks rolling and aircraft strafing in *Operation Just Cause*. Their mission was to capture the corrupt drug czar and President, General Manuel Noriega, who had somewhat rashly declared war on the USA five days previously.

The President of Panama was quite prepared to accept Chinese cash, and more or less do their bidding over matters concerning the canal, so long as his country received a fair rake-off from the enormous profits. But he did not much envy General Noriega's present status in a Florida jail, and the thought of an angry USA was apt to strip him of his manhood.

He was occasionally nervous about the ruthless way the Chinese conducted their business. But he was cold-bloodedly scared of the USA, especially when they had a Republican President, surrounded by tough men, who could not give a damn for left-wing rhetoric, Third-World demands, and the empty rantings of various national leaders who threatened to 'fight the US to the death', but could not possibly match Washington's military might. At last count the number of world nations who could perhaps raise even five percent of Washington's military might, added up to one large fat zero.

The Panamanian President now had a smooth, teak-tough ex-Harvard law professor on the wire, telling him it would be a pity if the President of the United States were to get very cross with Panama, because that might prove unproductive to your 'unfortunate, sweating, largely poverty-stricken Central American country.'

The Panamanian was not fluent in the English language but the icy tone of Harcourt Travis left him in no doubt the Chinese were playing with fire, but the first ass that was going to get kicked was his.

'But Mr Travis,' he protested. 'You know full well we handed over control of the canal to the Chinese Hutchison Whampoa Corporation, and that we gave them a very free hand to run it efficiently, and as they wished. There is little I can do while that contract is in existence.'

Harcourt Travis sighed and said softly, 'The fact that your predecessor made the unhappy mistake of double-crossing a somewhat witless former President of my country, with an illegal agreement with Red China, is unlikely to cut much ice with the White House Administration of today. Might I simplify this for you . . . Mr President, we want that canal *open* within two hours, or else . . .'

'Or else what?' asked the President haplessly. But the line was already dead. And in the mind of the elected leader of the Panamanian nation there was but one thought . . . and it involved 26,000 troops landing and opening fire, American tanks rolling through the streets of Panama City, fighter-bombers screaming overhead, helicopter gunships clattering above the street.

He'd seen it before, run for his own life before the 1989 US onslaught. 'Holy shit,' breathed the Panamanian leader, in the unmistakable Spanish of south-Central America.

And with that, he summoned his ministers, and put in a call to the Chinese ambassador, on his direct embassy line, in the ritzy Punta Paitilla area of the city.

The connection took less than three minutes, and the ambassador was as helpful as the President knew he would be . . . *I understand there is some difficulty at the Milaflores Lock . . . yes, yes, I realize Americans may be displeased . . . I am afraid there is nothing I can do . . . the Hutchison Whampoa Company operates entirely independently of Chinese Government . . . their contract is with you, not China . . . our policy is never to intervene in matters of private companies . . . I am simply not authorized to utilize my country's embassy in that way . . . I'm sorry, Mr President, but I can't help . . .*

By now the Panamanian leader was becoming personally rattled. He knew, like everyone else in Panama, that Hutchison Whampoa *was* the Chinese Government, and they had plainly decided to close the canal for big reasons, and would continue to stonewall his own government until Li Ka-shing was good and ready to open it up.

Furthermore, he had not been warned, nor consulted, nor even advised. And there was this terrible bastard Travis on the phone from Washington, threatening God knows what. The Panamanian did not of course realize that Harcourt was one of the mildest mannered and deftest of diplomats in this Administration. And his own terror was nothing to the shuddering, sledgehammer blows currently being experienced in the White House West Wing by another Chinese ambassador, the one sitting opposite Admiral Arnold Morgan.

'Don't you dare lie to to me!

'I don't happen to care what your powers are, and nor do I give a goddamn what your tin-pot half-assed government thinks . . . Get that fucking canal open . . .

'Two days! I said two hours . . . and right now that's one hour and forty-two minutes . . . time might have stood still in fucking

Beijing or wherever the hell you live . . . but right here, in the US of A, it keeps marching forward, hear me?'

Kathy O'Brien had never heard Arnold more angry. In fact she was amazed the Chinese ambassador had not just stood up and left. It took only a few more seconds to understand why he was still there.

'You make any attempt to leave this place before I say you leave, you'll be on a one-way ticket to Shanghai this day . . . *deported* . . . understand?

'Whaddya mean, I wouldn't dare . . . stand up and try me!'

What Ms. O'Brien did not quite grasp was that Arnold Morgan was giving a performance; terrorizing the ambassador, no doubt. But preparing for a finale which would rock the visiting diplomat back on his heels.

It took the Admiral twenty minutes to deliver his punchline, and when he did so, the world of international relations momentarily stood still.

'Your Excellency,' said Arnold, silkily. 'If the Panama Canal remains closed for the rest of this day, the United States of America will retake it by military force. We'll knock down your stone-age dockyards at Cristabel and Balboa. We'll take both cities, and anyone who gets in the way, especially if he happens to be Chinese, will inevitably die.

'If the canal is damaged during our attack, we'll fix it, because by then we'll own it. Perhaps you would be good enough to relay those glad tidings to your crooked government. Now get out!'

It is doubtful if any ambassador in Washington in living memory had ever been spoken to quite like that. Kathy had to give the Chinese diplomat a glass of water before he was able to exit the West Wing.

And after that she took the boss some fresh coffee. With Buckshot Supreme, as he now called the new little golden sweetners that tasted just like sugar.

'I have never quite understood why you ignored a career in the diplomatic corps,' she said, sweetly. 'Such a subtle turn of phrase. So quietly persuasive . . .'

'Kathy,' he said. 'Do you know anything about the history of the Panama Canal? And why today it's finally in the mess I knew it would be nine years ago?'

'Well, I can't say I do really.'

'And I haven't got time to enlighten you right now,' he said.

'But I'll tell you this. Carter should never have permitted the Treaty. We should have flexed some muscle and hung on to control. The next Democratic President after him should have stopped those bastards in their tracks when they handed over control of the waterway to China . . .'

'Since it was then Panama's canal, how could he?' replied Kathy, who, being female, had always had a sneaking regard for Bill Clinton.

'Because it was all illegal. There were terms laid out, and bidding was organized on an international basis, for the right to run the canal. The USA put in a bid for control that was much, much higher than anyone else's. But the Chinese, offering a bribe the size of the Forbidden City, were given another chance, *and* told what the American bid was. A few days later the Panamanian Government handed it all over to that fraud corporation out of Hong Kong which is owned by Beijing.'

'Wow!'

'Wow, as it happens, is right. Though I wish you would desist from using the mindless, constipated speech of the young and goofy.'

Kathy, who ought to have been stung by his rudeness, burst out laughing as she always did, when her future husband handed out his customary grief. Let's face it, she had long ago decided, he talks to everyone like that. And anyway it was nothing like so bad as the battering he had just delivered to the Washington Ambassador of the largest country on earth.

'Well, what could the White House have done about it?'

'They should have told the Panamanian Government that the USA was going to run the canal. Anyone raises one finger to stop us, that would be regarded as an act of war, to which we would react appropriately.

'Then I'd have reminded them that canal was built with American engineering, American money, American muscle and American brains. And we never denied a ship passage, at least not in time of peace. We should have told them right away, if they think they're gonna trespass on the goodwill of the USA and hand the damn thing over to a totalitarian Communist country, with a human rights policy that would make Idi Amin look like the Good Fairy . . . and then give them the right to deny access to any ship they wished . . .

'Well, fuck it . . . they could try, but the USA would stop them

354

with whatever military force it might take. That's what should have happened.'

'And if Panama had called America's bluff?'

'Them? That half-assed bunch of gauchos? Kathy, I'm talking muscle right here. The same muscle and courage that built the canal. When the USA wants something that is quite obviously in the interest of the entire world, we should go out and take it, and tell the goddamned Panamanians to go feed their flea-ridden mules.'

'Nice analogy, Whitman,' she replied. 'And by the way, Gauchos are from South America . . .'

'Okay, so I made a one-stop mistake. From Panama, it's only about three hundred yards to the drug-crazed citizens of Colombia, right?'

Again Kathy laughed. 'Honestly,' she said. 'You are the most awful person . . .'

'Nothing like so awful as I'm going to be in a couple of hours, if those Chinamen don't open the canal.'

Meanwhile, the Barracuda was making stately progress through the breathtaking excavation of the Galliard Cut, steering three-two-five now, past the great mudslides that perpetually haunt the Culebra Reach on both banks.

The tug made another course adjustment fifteen degrees to starboard before running into Cascades Reach, which leads to the Gatun Lake, a 164-square-mile expanse of tropical water, patrolled by glowering crocodiles. The canal channel runs through the middle of it, still zigzagging, avoiding the islands

There are five course changes along the jagged twenty-four-mile route through the lake, past uninhabited rainforest and densely-wooded shores. The Gatun Lake is, of course, entirely man-made, created when they built the mighty Gatun Dam across the Chagres River, and flooded miles and miles of countryside, submerging twenty-nine villages, in order to start construction of the high canal.

The massive edifice of the Gatun Lock, with its gigantic three-step chambers from sea level to the upper lake, is one of the engineering marvels of the modern world, still regarded by academics as perhaps man's supreme building achievement.

General Rashood had told his wife all about it, this great concrete exit to the Atlantic, because he knew they were not going to see it. And just before 2100 that evening, still following the lighted beacons and buoys, the Chinese navigators ordered the submarine hard to port, off Pena Blanca Reach, two miles shy of the locks.

The tug hauled the submarine slowly into the desolate, western waters of the lake, which had been closed to tourists, fishermen and snorkellers for two days, pending the arrival of the Barracuda.

The temperature was cooling off to around seventy-eight degrees now, and there was a dampness in the sullen, tropical night, perhaps a harbinger of the first heavy rains of the season. In the distance they could hear howler monkeys not yet settled in the treetops, the occasional shriek of a macaw, and the high staccato clicking of cicadas.

In twelve fathoms of water they crept through the darkness. The navigators held big searchlights and demanded a course of first, two-seven-zero, then one-eight-zero, staying in the deepest water down the craggy shore of the lake. They moved by Trinidad Island in almost total silence, and then proceeded south, six more miles into lonely Trinidad Bay, a two-mile-wide dead end, still seven fathoms deep, but uninhabited to the eastern side.

The pilots called the navigation orders expertly, conning the submarine from the bridge behind the tug, until she was moving east. A half-mile later they rounded the jutting headland of Pelican Island, and the Chinese pathfinders ran the Barracuda right inshore, along a dead straight overgrown beach, through a dredged channel running beneath a dense overhang of rainforest.

With some alarm, Captain Badr called a depth warning, but it was too late. The bow of Barracuda 945 grounded to a near halt in soft mud, right on a yellow marker, left by the dredger the previous week. Her sail and casing was covered in tropical foliage, only fifteen feet from the shore. The tug now came alongside and edged the submarine into position, before casting off and vanishing north.

Almost immediately a Chinese patrol boat pulled alongside, instantly pushing a gangway between the two vessels in the flat calm, motionless water. Six engineers, normally based in the Yellow Sea submarine base at Huladao now came aboard, and almost immediately, General Rashood ordered the first twenty of his own crew to gather their possessions and disembark the submarine.

Everyone else was told to prepare to evacuate in the next two hours. Ravi and Shakira, plus the Captain, would be the last to go, on the second trip, way up to the north-east corner of the lake, close to the airport at Colon.

The round trip for the first half of the crew took almost two hours. The patrol boat returned just before midnight, and the remainder of the HAMAS mariners began to disembark. Ben Badr had by now ordered open the vents to the main ballast tanks, which had the effect of pushing the ship down, and the Barracuda was slowly sinking lower into the soft mud, settling hard on the bottom. Water was already washing over her upper casing.

Ben had the hatches open for'ard and aft. Most of the machinery was already shut down, but the emergency diesel motor was running, and the pumps were still working, forcing water to the compensation tanks, neutralizing any suggestion of buoyancy. All seawater lines were open.

The process of reducing the great underwater warship into a silent hulk would take possibly four more days, and the Chinese engineers would be working in a damp and gruesomely uncomfortable environment. But their orders were stark – *no-one must ever know that submarine existed . . . sink it into the mud, without trace.*

By midnight, only the sail remained in view, and by the time Ben had flooded the reactor room, she was inching even lower into the hole the Chinese dredger had dug for her. It was just a matter of time. Modern military camouflage, and a couple of 'DANGER' signs with an explosive motif, posted by the Chinese Navy, would keep the Barracuda, and her secrets, safe for decades.

Thus far, the plan was going forward without a hitch, until, from out of the dark, Shakira spotted a light, a bright searchlight flanked by a red and a green, an unmistakable motor launch, attracted by their own lights, and coming directly towards them. Fast.

'Jesus Christ,' said Ravi. 'Who the hell's this?'

And instantly his old SAS take-charge-right-now mentality kicked in. He called out to the helmsman of the Chinese patrol boat, 'Cast off and pull away, regular speed, no panic . . . hang around for a half-hour then come back.'

And as one boat left, the other came slowly, forward, a light bow wave phosphorescent in the dark water, as it pulled alongside. It was a thirty-one-foot Boston Whaler, and Ravi was astonished to hear an American voice.

'Hey guys, Joe Morris from Delaware . . . can you give us a hand here . . . we lost the goddamned chart . . . been camping down the bay for two or three days . . . beautiful fishing . . . are we headed up to the locks . . .? everything looks kinda the same around here . . .'

General Rashood answered in his best English officer's accent. 'Oh, good evening, Joe. We're British actually . . . organizing a World Wildlife meet here for next week . . . but you are right . . . keep heading north . . . you'll come right up to the locks on your port side.'

He realized he and Ben must have looked absolutely ridiculous, standing on the bridge of a submerged Russian submarine, jutting out of the water, but he hoped to God the American wouldn't notice in the pitch dark with only a flashlight.

But the American did notice. 'Hey, what the hell's that you're standing on . . . looks like a goddamned submarine . . . you guys smugglers or something?'

'Certainly not,' said the HAMAS General. 'This is the World Wildlife underwater vessel . . . we use it all over Central America . . . studying rare fish and stuff . . . very useful little toy . . .'

'Sure as hell looks like a submarine to me,' said Joe. 'And I used to be in the US Navy . . . Norfolk, Virginia. I seen a lot of submarines, believe me.'

'Not one quite like this,' replied Ravi. 'We've got a glass bottom . . . pretty amazing some of the things we see under the water . . .'

'Jeez. Sounds good. Hey, wait a minute I wanna get a photograph . . . just lemme find the flash. Wanna show it to some Navy buddies back home . . . they'll be real interested . . .'

The flashlight, which belonged to Joe Morris of Delaware, popped dazzlingly in the jungle light.

'Would you like to come aboard and I'll show you the underwater lights . . . some of those big crocodiles come right up close when we switch them on . . . bring your camera.'

'Hey, that'd be great . . . can my two buddies come over . . . just Skip and Ronnie? We're all from Wilmington.'

'Certainly . . . come round to the rope ladder on the other side of the bridge . . . we just hung it out . . . and watch how you go

. . . those crocodiles are mean little bastards . . . don't want you to get eaten alive . . .'

Ravi had a very quick word with Shakira, who left and went below. Five minutes later all three visitors were standing on the bridge of the Barracuda, and Ravi led the way down to the upper deck. He noticed Joe Morris had an automatic pistol jammed in his belt. The other two appeared to be unarmed.

The area below the steel stairway was, mercifully, still dry, and Joe Morris and his pals arrived cheerfully. When they were all gathered at the base of the stairwell, Ravi introduced himself for the first time . . . 'Welcome aboard, gentlemen . . . I'm Captain Mark Smyley, Irish Guards . . . working with the World Wildlife Commission, personal envoy of the Duke of Edinburgh . . .'

'Hey! How about that, guys? Stick with me, right? Never know who you're gonna meet!'

He smiled cheerfully, and was actually still smiling when Ravi slammed the head of a twelve-inch screwdriver bang into the space between his eyebrows, and then crashed the butt of his right hand with terrific force into the base of his nose, ramming the bone deep into the brain. Joe died instantly.

His companions never even reacted. They just stood there in amazement for about three seconds, the last three seconds of their lives, as it happened. Shakira Rashood, standing calmly below the periscope, blew them both away with four lethal bursts from an AK-47, obliterating both of their foreheads.

The Chinese engineers, now working one deck below, heard nothing, and Shakira and Ravi moved fast, dragging the bodies into a corner of the empty control center. Then he yelled for Ben Badr, and the two of them raced up the ladder to the bridge, climbed down into Joe Morris's boat and ransacked the luggage, finding wallets and passports.

They took those, started the twin outboard motors, and chugged away from the shore, around to the lakeward side of the submarine's sail. They made the Whaler fast, moving the bowline to the stern, set the steering for dead ahead, west, and opened the throttles slightly.

By now Shakira was up on the bridge moving the rope ladder to fall right behind the Whaler. They both climbed back onto the sail, Ben first, then Ravi.

The HAMAS General then cast the Whaler off, and watched it surge forward. Simultaneously, up on the bridge, Shakira ripped the pin out of a hand grenade and tossed it into the departing launch. Six seconds later, now nearly fifty yards away, the little vessel blew to smithereens, the wreckage sinking to the bottom of the Gatun Lake.

Shakira Rashood took the passports and wallets, and carefully shoved them into the appropriate pockets of the deceased fishermen, thus posing a fascinating problem for investigators, in the unlikely event the submarine should ever be found . . . *DELAWARE-BASED TERRORISTS BLAMED FOR OSCAR-NIGHT LIGHTS-OUT.*

For the next five minutes Ravi explained to the Chinese engineers precisely what he and Shakira had done, and why. The leader, a nuclear propulsion expert, spoke excellent English, and understood fully . . . 'Very good, General. My Admiral not want this ship found . . . if it is, I'll get blame . . . but I like Joe Mollis get real blame. Ha Ha Ha.'

Five minutes later, the patrol boat returned. General and Lt. Commander Rashood, in company with Captain Badr, said goodbye to the Chinese engineers, who were still busy flooding the submarine down. And then they joined their HAMAS colleagues for the run across the lake to the north-east shore.

Meanwhile, out in the Atlantic Anchorage, the comms room of the *San Juan* sent its third satellite signal to Pacific Fleet Headquarters '. . . *120046APR08. Panama Canal still closed. No sign of Barracuda exit through Gatun Locks. No ships entered, no ships left. Fourteen freighters and tankers in line close aboard awaiting entry.* San Juan.'

In Washington, where the local time was exactly the same as that in Panama, Admiral Morgan was still in his office, talking to Kathy, and on the line to the Pentagon and Fort Meade. Plainly the Chinese had ignored his dire warnings, and he had informed both the President and the Secretary of State that the Chinese Ambassador was to be sent back to Beijing first thing in the morning.

Lt. Commander Ramshawe had just called with firm photographic evidence the Barracuda had entered the Milaflore Lock shortly before 1530. The satellite picture showed it on its final approach along the narrow divided waterway on the Pacific side of the chambers. It was not under tow, yet, but its outline was the obvious shape of an old Russian Sierra I.

'Any other photographs, Jimmy?' the Admiral asked.

'Only one, sir. And it's a bloody awful print, taken just as it was getting dark, at the southern end of the Gatun Lake. It could very well be old razormouth, but there seems to be a much smaller ship right in front. Could be under tow, I suppose. But from this print, I don't think anyone could be sure. Funny thing is, I can't see one other ship anywhere along the entire length of the canal, in either direction. And it averages forty vessels a day.'

'Hmmmmm,' said the Admiral. 'I suppose the submarine couldn't have turned right around and headed back out into the Pacific?'

'If she did, sir, she'd run right into the *Roosevelt*. And they've told the Chinese Navy to get stuffed . . . and they moved real close in several hours ago, to guard that entrance.

'The water's much too shallow for the ole 'cuda to cross the Gulf of Panama anywhere except on the surface. And the bloody thing couldn't slide past, within a coupla hundred yards of a US destroyer, without being seen or heard.'

'No. Guess not. Which leaves us to wonder where the hell it is. We got the satellites adjusted to photograph every inch of the canal?'

'Yessir. And the fact is, the bloody thing has vanished – just like they scuttled her.'

'Not even the Chinese would dare to do that. Especially in an inland lake. They obviously would not sink her in the channel. And anyway, you can't scuttle nuclear boats, unless you want to become a pariah among the trading nations of the world. The pollution issue's enormous.'

'Yeah. I guess it is, sir. But it sure beats the hell out of me, the bastard's gone missing in the high canal. And I don't know where to start looking . . .'

'Nor me, Jimmy. Nor me. But it's gotta be in there some-where. Jesus Christ, this thing is three hundred and fifty feet long. It's like losing the Washington Monument in the Potomac.'

He replaced the receiver and pondered the time, and whether to go home or stay. He went over the problem again with Kathy, who told him quietly, 'That damn submarine has been missing for as long as I can remember. Wherever it is, it's always missing . . . and now it's missing in the Panama Canal . . . sounds nuts to me.'

'But things are hard to find if they're under the water.'

'I know that. But this has got to be shallow water, right?'

'Don't remind me.'

'Well, let me ask you this. If someone sinks a submarine in fairly shallow water, can it still be seen, detected by the satellites? I mean, if its reactor is still running . . .you know, infra-red and all that.'

'It could if its reactor was still running. But if you want to plonk a damned great submarine on the bottom of a lake, you'd turn the reactor off, shove the rods home, and flood it down with cold water, and just let it cool. In a few days the heat will be gone.'

'Then you couldn't see anything on the satellite photographs?'

'Not if the concealment crew had done their work properly. Got it buried good and deep in the mud, and shut down everything, maybe applied some camouflage . . . Christ, you'd never find it. And in time it would disappear, keep sinking further, 'til it was gone.'

Admiral Morgan looked pensive. And then he said thoughtfully, 'I gotta bad feeling . . . the only way we're ever gonna find that bastard, is for someone to drain the goddamned Gatun Lake, and solve the mystery.'

And even as he spoke, a chartered Boeing 747 bearing the livery of Air China, and bound for Damascus and Bandar Abbas, was hurtling off the runway at Colon, cleaving its way into the night sky above the Panamanian coastline.

It banked and headed east, towards the shifting sands of the Arabian desert, and there were just three passengers in the first-class cabin upstairs. Only one refueling stop was scheduled; Dakar airport, Senegal, the first Atlantic landfall on the great rounded coastline of north-west Africa.

As the American country singer, Arlo Guthrie, once poignantly observed – *halfway home, we'll be there by morning* . . .

CHAPTER THIRTEEN

The Chinese Ambassador to the United States of America, in company with his two Deputies, three First Secretaries, and two other officials Admiral Morgan said were plain and obvious spies, flew out of Dulles International Airport at 0900 the following morning.

Expelled from the country, they had been escorted to the airport by a detachment of twenty-four Marine Guards. A Boeing aircraft from Air China had flown down from New York to retrieve them in the face of threats by Admiral Morgan to throw 'the whole fucking lot of them in jail' by noon, to await trial in the year 2013 for crimes against the United States involving the completely illegal closure of the Panama Canal.

No member of either the Chinese Diplomatic Corps, or indeed of the American Government, even considered the possibility that the Admiral might not be serious.

There was a somewhat arched communiqué from Beijing mentioning that the Chinese Government had 'absolutely nothing' to do with the Panama Canal, or any of its operations. And that these expulsions of the lawfully appointed Chinese diplomats in Washington was a 'clear breach' of the international code of diplomacy. Furthermore the Beijing Government would be considering similar reprisals against American representatives in the People's Republic.

Nonetheless the Air China jet had arrived in Dulles Airport post-haste, and Beijing did not even attempt a dialogue with the White House. This was just as well since Admiral Morgan had read their communiqué, scrunched it into a ball, and hurled it across the room straight into the bin from about fifteen-feet range. Modestly pleased with his marksmanship, he pumped his right arm, turned towards the great portrait of General MacArthur on his east wall, and revealed his innermost thoughts. *Hit 'em hard, hit 'em fast, first time, right, Douglas? . . . Chinese pricks.*

The peal of laughter from Kathy O'Brien who was standing in the doorway awaiting instructions on some form of reply to Beijing, took him by surprise. But he was not even smiling.

'Get Tim Scannell and Alan Dickson in here right now,' he said. 'And George Morris, plus his sidekick Ramshawe. Harcourt's upstairs. Tell him thirty minutes, right here. And get a call into Admiral Bergstrom in Coronado.'

'I imagine you consider the time of six a.m. in California to be irrelevant,' replied Kathy, sweetly.

'Correct,' he confirmed.

Eight minutes later, at the precise time a US Navy staff car squealed up the ramp and out of the Pentagon garage, the phone rang in Admiral Morgan's office, and the crisp-sounding voice of the Emperor of all the US Navy SEALs, Rear Admiral John Bergstrom, said curtly, ''Morning, Admiral. Whaddya need?'

'Hi, John. You outta bed?'

'I'm in the factory. Been here for twenty minutes.'

'You must have sensed my feeling of urgency?'

'Well, sir. I'm only guessing. But rumor has it we got a boatload of fucking Islamic terrorists trapped in the Panama Canal like rats in a cage.'

'You're well informed, as usual. And you're right. They're in there. In a submarine. Trouble is the waterway is about forty miles wide, bolted and barred at both ends, with about seven billion places to hide under the surface for the next several years . . .'

'Not your average cage, eh? Guess you want my boys to go in and find 'em?'

'I don't think we can do that. The Gatun Lake is so goddamned big, and I don't think the satellites could give us much help. We'd want a force of about ten thousand guys with boats and heavy-duty sonar to have a prayer of locating the submarine. Plus we can't get even one ship in there. The goddamned Chinese, as you know, have closed it.'

'You want to bomb it?' asked Admiral Bergstrom. 'Or come straight at it with ground launched cruise missiles?' He was deadly serious, mindful always of the twin creeds of both the SAS and the SEALs – *the majority of the world's problems can be solved with high explosive.*

'I think in this case, John, bombs or missiles may be just too messy, cause too much havoc. Christ knows how many missiles we'd have to throw at it. Those damned canal locks are probably the most solid concrete structures ever built anywhere in the world. Also an attack like that would smack of the US bullying a defenseless Central American State. And that way we'd have to admit everything about the Chinese connection, even the tragic fact of the last Presidency. Most Americans have no idea we somehow allowed the Canal to be given to Red China.'

'Well, I guess you aren't planning to leave these Islamic bastards in there, are you?'

'Matter of fact, I don't think we're gonna catch 'em. But we are going to find the submarine, and we are going to kick some Chinese ass, *and* we are taking back the Panama Canal.'

Admiral Bergstrom exhaled with a low whistle. 'Lay it on me, sir,' he said.

'We're gonna blow up the locks on the Atlantic-side entrance.'

For a brief moment, the SEAL chief was silent. Then he said quietly, 'Did you not just say bombs were too messy?'

'I did. At least the kind of bombs we dropped on Kosovo and Afghanistan and Saddam are too messy. Right here I'm talking subtlety. Because our objectives have rigid guidelines. Because if these nutcases want to hide the submarine permanently, they're gonna have to turn off the nuclear reactor and then submerge. That of course will leave our satellites' infra-red just about blind to them.

'And if they do that, they have to disembark the ship because it won't have any power; no air, no water, no refrigeration, no light, nothing. Except for a few days' emergency supplies. There-fore they will almost certainly shut off the reactor, flood her down, and beat it, with Chinese help, to the nearest airstrip. I wouldn't be surprised if they were already out of there.'

'So you want to destroy one of the world's great international seaways in order to locate and examine the submerged hulk of an ageing, Russian-built submarine from which the crew has vanished?'

'Correct. That's what I want to do. Because if we take out the Atlantic-side locks, the entire Gatun High Lake is going to drain into the ocean. Millions and millions of tons of water. And that's going to leave that submarine high and dry. At least, high and wet. Somewhere.

'And when we find that wreck, it will have someone's finger-prints all over it. Which will give us the right to kick the Chinese right out of the Canal Zone for deliberately harboring terrorists. At the same time, we'll frighten the living shit out of the Panamanian government, and retake the canal unopposed.

'Remember that entire structure is American, and we're still the only guys on earth who could rebuild it. And that way we'll keep for ourselves every one of the millions of dollars it makes in toll charges every year. For a long time.'

'The Panamanians ain't going to like that.'

'The Panamanians can go stuff themselves . . . I'll teach those little bastards to tear up a contract they had with the United States and hand our goddamned property over to Red fucking China.'

'Well,' said Admiral Bergstrom, 'they did have the help of a US President. When push came to shove, Clinton never tried to enforce any of our rights down there . . .'

'Don't remind me,' said Arnold. 'But that moment yesterday, when a US warship was illegally denied access, was a moment both the Chinese and their half-assed Central American buddies will regret for many years to come.'

'Minor details, sir?'

'Of course.'

'Who's blowing up the canal? How? And when?'

'Your boys, John. Your fabulous boys. The gates on the upper Gatun lock, the ones that open into the lake itself. Forty-eight hours from now.'

Once more the veteran SEAL chief exhaled with a whistle. 'How big are the gates, sir?'

'Oh, quite manageable, really . . . 'bout seventy-seven feet high, sixty-five feet wide, seven feet thick. Not too hefty, eight hundred tons of course, because they're steel, riveted over iron girders. But they are hollow.'

'Oh. Thank God for that,' replied Admiral Bergstrom, a touch of irony in his voice. 'I was afraid they might be heavy.'

Arnold Morgan chuckled. 'John, I'm asking you to blow apart two of the heaviest gates ever built. But security is negligible. I don't anticipate a lot of opposition. And I forecast an unopposed landing.'

'By sea?'

'No. Helicopters, off a carrier. The *Dwight D. Eisenhower* has been in overhaul, Mayport, Florida. Right now she's in the Roosevelt Roads, east of Puerto Rico, on her way in. She's nearly twelve hundred miles nor'nor'west of Panama, thirty-six hours steaming. She'll be in the area by tomorrow night.'

'What's with her?'

'Usual battle group escorts . . . four frigates, coupla destroyers, the cruiser *Shiloh*, and two LA Class submarines. Ought to be enough to protect your precious SEALs.'

'Guess so. How do we get there?'

'Fly to Pensacola, then directly to the carrier.'

'Could I just ask when you worked all this out, sir? The damn submarine didn't even get into the canal until yesterday afternoon.'

'Mostly at around zero five hundred this morning. Alan Dickson and I have both been up all night. He'll be here in a few minutes.'

'Give him my best, willya. But I have one more question – if we blow the lakeward gates in the upper chamber – what happens if it just fills up the lock and the next gates hold. You want my guys to stay and hit them as well, or blow both sets at the same time?'

'John, I have had three guys from the Army Corps of Engineers in here in the small hours of this morning, and each one of them took about three minutes to make up his mind on one point . . . if the lakeward gates at the top are taken out suddenly, the force of the water crashing into the chamber will flatten the next gates. That chamber's a thousand feet long, a hundred ten feet wide and more than sixty feet high . . . you're talking around thirty thousand tons of water gathering speed and slamming into the second gates.

'Remember that chamber stood on its end is taller than the Eiffel Tower. It would be like hitting the second gates with the Eiffel Tower! And it's gonna be travelling at maybe sixty m.p.h. The engineers say chances of the second gates holding are a lot less than zero.'

'Works for me,' said Admiral Bergstrom. 'I'll be back on the line in two hours. Someone just told me there's all kinds of maps, charts and diagrams arriving on e-mail. I imagine that's from you guys.'

'Correct, sailor. Hop to it, now, and lemme know the size of the detachment going in . . .'

'I'll be back soon as my guys assess the amount of explosive we need to blow the gates. The more TNT, the more manpower.

That stuff's heavy, and we may have to carry it part way through the fucking jungle. Can't escape that, since we don't have any transport on the ground.'

'Okay, John. Talk to you soon . . .'

Just then Kathy pushed open the door and announced the arrival of the Chairman of the Joint Chiefs, General Scannell and the CNO Admiral Dickson. George Morris was about five minutes behind them in company with Lt. Commander Ramshawe who carried a heavy armload of papers and charts.

Harcourt Travis, whose office was located only about fifty yards away, was last to arrive strolling into Arnold's office somewhat languidly, wondering how quickly the Great Man intended to declare war on someone and whether he was planning to allow the President of the United States of America in on the secret.

'Maybe,' rasped Arnold. 'Just maybe. Though I never met a civilian yet who didn't get in the goddamned way when the military were about to move fast . . .'

'I never get in the goddamned way,' said Harcourt, agreeably.

'You know better,' said Arnold. 'In the end, I might even have you commissioned. Lieutenant Harcourt. Little precious. But I kinda like it.'

The Secretary of State smiled. 'Seriously,' he said. 'We have to tell the Boss about this pretty soon.'

'It's not a problem,' said Admiral Morgan. 'He's been ranting on about inaction for the past three weeks. In a coupla hours he's gonna get action.'

'I imagine so,' said Harcourt. 'This does not look like the kind of group which wants to write a letter, or order a Congressional Study.'

Admiral Morgan slammed his office door shut, retreated behind his desk, and then yelled through the solid oak barricade to the outside world, '*Kathy! Coffee for six . . . hot!*'

'Wouldn't that have been a tad easier if you'd placed the order when the door was still open?' asked Harcourt, mildly.

'Possibly,' growled Arnold. 'But it woulda lacked urgency. Right there you were looking at the operational difference between a diplomat and an ex-US Navy CO. You're trained to ease the pressure. I prefer to keep it on.'

'My sympathies, as ever, are with Saint Kathy,' replied Harcourt, smiling.

Everyone laughed at this somewhat elegant exchange between

two considerable minds, and Arnold told them to sit down anywhere, while he offered a few explanations.

'There are, obviously, several other people, political and military, who need debriefing,' he said. 'But right now I want the people in this room to be singing from the same hymn sheet. You will notice I included Lt. Commander Ramshawe, and that's because he's been tracking the situation for several months and knows more about it than anyone else.'

Everyone nodded, silently grateful for an apparent expert. The Admiral continued with the utmost brevity and care. 'As we all know, the United States has been under attack for several weeks. Somewhere along our Pacific coast, a Russian-built, but not necessarily Russian-manned, nuclear submarine has been firing missiles at our oil and power industrial installations.

'We never found 'em, couldn't stop 'em. And they knew precisely what they were doing. Gentlemen, we have been the victims of terrorism of the worst type since nine-eleven. Less death. Less outrage. But savage damage to our country. I suggest, more or less the way they planned it.

'Yesterday we located the submarine. An old Sierra I, Barracuda Class, Type 945. And right now it's trapped in the Panama Canal. I believe they've dumped it. Switched off the nuclear reactor and let it bury itself somewhere in the Gatun Lake, through which the canal runs, eighty-four feet above sea level, 'til it steps down again at the Pacific end.

'As you all know, the Panama Canal is currently under the stewardship of the Chinese. And they just closed it, presumably while they get rid of the evidence and help our enemies to escape.

'Naturally, we find that unacceptable, because it robs us of the chance for revenge, or even reprisals. However, the bigger picture is much, much more important. And the really unacceptable part is that China actually controls the Canal, illegally in my view, thanks to the fifth-rate fucking antics of a fourth-rate, lying Central American country, aided by a US President who kept his brains somewhere near the end of his pecker.'

'By all accounts that provided room for a considerable amount of brains,' interrupted Harcourt.

'None of 'em focused on the interests of this country and its global role,' growled Arnold. 'Which brings us to the crux of the problem – we wanna get the Chinese out of Panama, we'll have to throw 'em out. And for the sake of world opinion, we need a major reason to do so. We find that goddamned submarine, we have that reason.'

Again the five men in Arnold's West Wing office, nodded in agreement.

'Gentlemen, I am proposing we smash the lock gates on the Atlantic side which will drain Lake Gatun in short order, leaving our submarine exposed.'

The room went deadly silent.

'You mean bomb the locks, obliterate them?' asked General Scannell.

'No, General. I mean blow off the lakeward gates of the upper Gatun Lock, the entrance into the high chamber. The water will do the rest.'

'SEALs?'

'Precisely.'

'Well, it's feasible, I can tell you that. I made a study of the Canal at West Point, and I served in Panama in the 1989 invasion. Those top gates are critical. Knock them off, and it's all over.'

Arnold grinned, grimly. 'And I am quite sure gentlemen, it has not escaped you, that when the canal is effectively destroyed, the Chinese will have no further reason to remain. They will hear the thunder of Uncle Sam, bellowing, *Get out or else*. And they will likely vamoose of their own accord. In any event, we'll land a fighting force and clear the damn place out, both ends.'

'What about the Panamanian Government?' asked Harcourt.

'You mean before or after they change their pants?' asked Arnold – a question which caused Lt. Commander Ramshawe to laugh heartily.

'After,' said Harcourt, urbanely.

'We'll tell them we are reclaiming the canal we built because they have proved hopeless, treacherous custodians whose dumbness nearly caused a world war. We'll tell 'em we intend to rebuild the Gatun Lock, immediately, and to restore world order to the path between the oceans.'

'Who's paying?' asked Harcourt.

'We are. They're penniless. But we will assume total control of the entire Canal Zone, the railroad and all the territories which bound the waterway. That includes the dockyards. The towns at either end will essentially come under our control.'

'You mean we're going in there like Genghis Khan?' said General Scannell. 'Like conquerors?'

'Oh no,' said Admiral Morgan. 'Panama needs the money from that canal, and right now they have nothing. We are the only guys who can rebuild it. And for that we will require all revenues for five years, sixty percent thereafter. Panama can have the rest.'

'Neat,' said Alan Dickson. 'Very neat indeed. Two priceless naval bases, priceless dockyards, total control of the canal. And a damned kick in the ass for the Chinks. We just killed about two hundred birds with one stone.'

'One lock gate,' said Arnold.

'Two, actually,' said Jimmy Ramshawe. 'We need to blow two. They close folded, like a flattened V.'

'Thank you, Lieutenant Commander,' said General Scannell. 'Very informative.'

'Any time, Chief,' replied the junior officer in the room, grinning his lopsided Aussie grin.

Right now, there was that sort of mood in the lair of the National Security Advisor. No dissent. Everyone deeply grateful for the clarity of Admiral Morgan's discourse, his motives and conclusions, and the obvious merit of his plan.

'Do we intend this to be a public attack, with the entire world knowing who did what to whom?' asked Admiral Morris.

'Absolutely not,' said Arnold. 'It's dead secret. We admit nothing, and we rant on and on about the criminally negligent way the Panamanians and the Chinese have handled the upkeep and engineering inspections on the Canal locks. Within a dozen years of our leaving Panama, the entire thing caves in.'

'I suppose some people will guess what really happened,' said Admiral Morris.

'So they might. But they will prove nothing because we'll be in control. I suppose, sooner or later, the stupid media will work out the *Eisenhower* battle group was parked fifty miles off the Panamanian coast at the time of the lock disaster. But we'll be as mum as the goddamned Chinese would have been, if we did not find that submarine.'

At which point he lapsed into his best Shanghai brogue . . . *know nothing of it . . . did not see it enter canal . . . have no idea where it is . . . ask Russians . . . we buy Barracuda now in Zhangjiang . . . can't help . . . sorry your lights go out . . . Ha! Ha! Ha!*

Tim Scannell and Alan Dickson saved him the trouble of a sign-off. 'Chinese pricks!' they chorused.

Just then, Kathy O'Brien tapped lightly on the door and entered, gesturing a waiter to place the large coffee tray on the conference table. She carried with her an encrypted e-mail printout from SEAL HQ, Coronado, across the bay from San Diego.

Preliminary estimate TNT required take out lock gates — just less than one ton. We deploy detachment of thirty-six men, including command team of one Lt. Commander plus five officers. Each man to carry a thirty kg high-explosive satchel into the operational area. TWO Sikorsky Sea Stallion helos, repeat two, required for insert from carrier. Four inflatables. One ton explosive, plus lines and detcord, one heavy machine-gun, plus personal weapons and radios. Recce team of eight in tomorrow night (Sunday). Main force Monday night, utilize both helos. Ops time Monday forecast eight hours. Insert over Colon coast, tracking Chargres River. ETD San Diego-Pensacola 2100 tonight (Saturday). Bergstrom.

Admiral Morgan's heart jumped. It always did when the hard-nosed, hard-edged SEAL commanders went to work on a project. But for the moment he wished to say nothing of how far advanced his plans were. The plans he and Admiral Dickson had spent all night preparing.

Arnold handed the signal from Coronado to Admiral Dickson, who read carefully, scribbling notes in the margins as he did so. Then Admiral Morgan told the others to gather around the big table, where Lt. Commander Ramshawe would bring them right up to speed on the precise movements of the submarine and the area in which it was now believed to be.

Jimmy spread out a big chart of Panama, its coastal sea lanes and the lake which encloses the canal. He had marked times and positions all through yesterday, Friday, right until the moment the Barracuda slipped off the runway and seemed headed into the steaming rainforest islands which patchwork Lake Gatun.

Arnold waited a few moments, until they were each absorbed in the detail, and then told them he was headed to the Oval Office where the President, the Defense Secretary Bob MacPherson, and 'one or two other time-serving politicos' awaited him.

Like his first meeting of the day, Arnold's second one did not take long. It ended after six minutes when he pointed out to the Commander-in-Chief that it was political gold dust, that he alone, President John Clarke would be remembered in history as the man who took back the Panama Canal, had it rebuilt, and placed firmly under American control, denying no ship access in peacetime, just as the United States had always behaved in their long years of stewardship.

Whatever else President Clarke was, he was not stupid, and he did not need to be reminded that his speech announcing the canal takeover would contain all the right phrases . . . *this appalling negligence . . . saved, as it was built, by American muscle . . . American know-how . . . American money . . . and, perhaps above all, American fairness . . . cannot have this great international waterway in irresponsible hands . . . the appalling limitations of the Chinese . . . the incompetence of the Panamanians . . . the recklessness of the previous Administration . . . the whole world and all its ships can breathe a sigh of relief . . . thank God for mighty Uncle Sam.*

John Clarke loved it. And Arnold swept back into his office, stood aside, inside the door, and annouced, grandly, 'Gentlemen, the President of the United States . . .'

Lt. Commander Ramshawe stood to attention, and was greeted warmly by the Chief Exceutive, who addressed everyone in the room by their first names, thanking them for all they had done, and expressing his great confidence that the next couple of days would help sort out the very great problem which had been haunting the USA since the oil disaster in Alaska.

'You think the submarine's gonna yield all the information we need?' he asked.

'Maybe,' replied his National Security Advisor. 'It would be nice to find out precisely who our enemy is. But I do think we have a political victory, in that China, who may have helped them and then stood well back, will have done so at the cost of the Panama Canal, making the operation not worth the price, certainly not financially, definitely not strategically, and perhaps even less so in terms of prestige we will make them look like some Third World banana republic, which they hate worst of all.

'I like it,' said the President. 'I like it a lot.'

'Only we know how badly we came out of the whole thing,' said Admiral Morgan. 'The damage to our west coast oil and power industry was massive. They have caused us terrible pain and suffering for a few weeks and they proved we're damn nearly defenseless against attackers in a nuclear submarine. But that submarine gives us a sensational checkmate against the Chinese, and it will be a long time before anyone trusts them again.'

'Perfect,' replied the President. 'But, gentlemen, I hope you can reveal the identity of our real enemy, the little bastards who actually drove the damn thing and opened fire on us?'

'Sir, we have our theories. And of course we suspect the Middle East, as ever. And whether we find the culprits or not . . . that submarine will shed some serious light on the subject.'

'D'you think the Panamanians will be obstructive to our forces searching the lake for the ship?'

'Sir,' said the Admiral, all business now. 'When we *order* them to take us to that submarine *right now*, they'll jump right out of their fucking ponchos with fright. I'll tell them we want total co-operation. *No-one* is even to touch that submarine until our inspection is complete, and that might take several weeks. The general obedience of the Panamanian Government and its rabble of an army will not be a concern in the face of US authority.'

'Especially with the Chinese out of there,' said the President, smiling at the thought of it.

'Those little bastards will be gone by the end of the week,' said Admiral Morgan. 'Hightailing their asses back to Shanghai. For good.'

'Do you envision a precise sequence of events in the immediate aftermath of the collapse of the lock gates,' asked the President.

'Absolutely,' said the Admiral. 'The USA will announce, with a lot of outrage, that we are proceeding to the area to begin the work of repairing the Gatun Lock. We will inform the Chinese that an occupying force of ten thousand United States Marines is preparing to land in the Canal Zone and that all Chinese personnel living or working in the area will vacate the country immediately. We will advise the Chinese Government to assist with this evacuation since any remaining Chinese nationals will be incarcerated indefinitely until the canal is repaired. They'll protest. We'll ignore them.

'At the same time we will dispatch gunships to circle the presidential palace, while a force of one thousand marines, plus tanks, arrives at the main gates with the Treaty which will hand the entire Panama Canal Zone back to the USA.'

'How about the Panamanian President doesn't want to sign it?'

'In that utterly unlikely event, we may have to flatten the east wing of his fucking residence. But don't worry. He'll sign. First time. Fast.'

'And we'll be doing it all in the name of the world's free passage through one of its most important seaways?'

'Correct, sir. Plainly the Panamanians or the Chinese can no longer be trusted to undertake such a responsibility. And by that time there'll be about a hundred tankers turning south for the joys of Cape Horn, a seven thousand-mile journey in front of them. The entire world will be up and cheering us on.'

'I like it,' said President Clarke, using his favorite expression of approval. 'I like it a lot.'

'Sir, I will require you to sign this document giving formal permission for Operation Goodwill to begin . . . just authorizing the military to . . . er . . . observe the lock gates for a few days . . . and then to proceed to Panama to restore the Canal Zone to United States control, if our engineers deem it necessary.'

'Do I need to ask Congress?'

'No time, sir. Just pop the old John Hancock right here on the dotted line.'

President Clarke felt supremely safe with top naval and military people, either serving or non-serving. Guys who knew the real score, and made the least mistakes.

'Certainly, Arnie,' he said. 'Glad to.'

0400 Sunday, April 13, 2008
US Naval Air Base, Pensacola, Florida
The first of two US Navy CODS (Carrier On Delivery) thundered down the active runway at the sprawling Pensacola Air Station on this dark and humid night. The aircraft, a derivative of the mighty Grumman EC-2 Hawkeye, the largest and most expensive US aircraft able to land on carriers, banked left over Hovey Road, then proceeded out over the Big Lagoon, heading south-west over the Gulf of Mexico.

In the normal course of its duties the COD would be crammed with mail for the carrier's 6,000 crew, and spare parts. But tonight, the former combat fighter pilot Lt. Commander Steve Ghutzman was flying a very different cargo – sixteen armed US Navy SEALs plus thirty-six satchels each containing thirty kg of the most modern explosive in the US arsenal, a diabolical cocktail of RDX (Research Developed Explosive), TNT (Trinitrotoluene) and Aluminum to provide an ultra-heavy blast effect. The total weight of high-explosive contained in the satchels was a little over one ton.

To take the most recent instance of a massive warship being sunk by explosive, in 1982 when Admiral Sandy Woodward's force sank Argentina's cruiser, the *General Belgrano*, in the Falklands War . . . the torpedo that broke her back contained approximately one-tenth of the explosive currently flying over the Gulf of Mexico in the COD.

Tucked in the aircraft's hold were two of the four outboard inflatables which would be used in the operation, plus five radio transmitters.

The first two seats on the port side of the COD were occupied by the Commanding Officer of the operation, Lt. Commander Bill Peavey, a big, powerful former USC slugging third baseman. He was a remarkable physical presence, 6 feet 4 inches, 210 pounds of blue twisted steel. Came from San Francisco, where his father, the eminent attorney Bill Peavey Jr. ran a successful law practise.

The SEAL instructors at Coronado soon selected the former Trojan baseball star as a potential team leader. He had applied to join the SEALs at the age of twenty-seven after only five years in the Navy, and they saw him coming. He was a Lt. Commander at thirty-two and now, one year later, this was his first full command of a Special Forces operation.

He sat in that front seat surrounded by charts and maps of the jungle which surrounds the Gatun Lake. He spent most of the time dictating into the slim microphone connected to his computer, and making detailed pencil notes on a check list he was compiling for all four of his principal teams, the eight-man recce squad, the two bomb-lashing groups, and the protection wing.

Right now he was locked into the diagram of the upper lock gates, the lakeward pair which hold back several billion tons of deep-water stretching over a giant area of 164 square miles, through which runs the route of the canal. The gates which held back the lake from the lock chambers were seven feet thick with a railed walkway along the top. Each gate was attached by three colossal hinges, six hinges in total. It was the destruction of these cast-iron monsters, each one seven feet in height, which held the key to Bill's first operation.

And he read the Navy engineers' report with fascination – *the blast from the explosion will create severe oscillation of the water, and massive shock waves to the area of the hinges, precisely like a depth charge, but so powerful it will have repercussions for any ship in the immediate vicinity*. Lt. Commander Peavey's diver, Chief Petty Officer Chris O'Riordan, would go in with the recce party on the first night to measure accurate underwater distances, down from the top of the gates, from which each of the six bombs would hang, resting hard against their designated hinge.

Bill Peavey tried to imagine a force of ten times the power of that which put the 13,500-ton *Belgrano* on the bottom of the South Atlantic, and he thought, privately, that it might not be smart to get within two miles of that blast when the SEALs finally let it rip.

His 2 I/C Lieutenant Patrick Hogan Rougeau, a thirty-six-year-old former tennis professional from Massachusetts, was sitting right behind him in company with another member of the five-man command team, Lieutenant Brantley Jordan from Texas, who would lead the bomb-lashing team on the near side of the lock.

Lt. Rougeau, like the boss, Bill Peavey, had joined the Navy late, but he was a fitness fanatic, had applied to join the SEALs at the age of twenty-six, and sailed through the murderous BUDs indoctrination course with as much ease as was humanly possible – i.e. it damn nearly killed him, but not quite, and when the dust cleared he was still conscious, and still standing. Which was a whole lot more than could be said for most of the others.

Patrick Rougeau was not only a radio expert, he was also an underwater expert, who had immediately volunteered to make the first dive into the lake. However he was also an acknowledged expert with the heavy machine-gun and Lt. Commander Peavey refused to risk him being eaten by a crocodile.

'CPO O'Riordan can do that,' he had said. 'No crocodile in his right mind would risk breaking his teeth on that little sonofabitch.'

He referred to the legenday toughness of the ex-Chicago Southside street fighter, Navy boxing champion, and all-around professional hard-man. O'Riordan, who was as fast and as lethal with a combat knife as any SEAL who had ever lived.

At the age of twenty, he had fought on Saddam's oil rig, the one the SEALs ultimately blew up in the Gulf War. The one where not one of the Iraqi guard survived the SEALs savage opening assault from the water.

The three other young SEAL officers on the command team, Lieutenants Zane Green, Chris Hall and Brian Slocum, were riding out to the carrier in the second COD which had left

Pensacola thirty minutes in arrears. Right now both aircraft had reached their cruising height of 30,000 feet and were making 300-knots out towards the Cayman Trench, crossing high above the western end of Cuba. The lead COD expected to touch down on the *Eisenhower's* flight deck at 0830. Rendezvous point: 11.80N 81.50W, 1,320 miles south of Pensacola, 200 miles off the northern coast of Panama, 220 miles east of the coast of Nicaragua.

Every one of the SEALs carried a map of the northern Gatun Lake, and the Colon Coast, plus a diagram of the locks, showing how millions of tons of concrete form a sixty foot thick wall separating the inward and outward locks, two identical constructions, one for Pacific-bound ships going up, one for Atlantic-bound ships coming down.

By the time they landed, every one of the SEALs on this time-stressed operation, would understand with total clarity, the precise mission, the attack, and the exit. SEAL commanders do not approve of even the most junior member of an assault party being anything less than expert on the objectives.

And so they studied, high above the blue, deceptively deep and rough Caribbean, each man much within himself as they headed ever closer to the hot, scarcely populated northern jungles of the Republic of Panama. But first the landing on the carrier, always difficult, but especially so in this big, heavy aircraft, with its eighty foot wingspan, and famously difficult torque created by the turbo props.

In the clear skies, the pilot and his first officer picked up the *Eisenhower* some twenty miles out, steaming south-west, with a destroyer positioned a half-mile off her starboard bow.

Ears popped as the COD lost height, cutting its speed, keeping level, as it came under the control of the carrier's tower. Through the cockpit window, the landing space looked like a postage stamp and the sea was plainly rough. A one and a half degree motion in the center of a carrier represents a thirty-foot rise and fall on the stern, and it was all of that today.

Lt. Commander Ghutzman, sunglasses on, staring through the glare of the sub-tropical sun, throttled back, trying to judge the pitch of the deck. The speed of the aircraft dropped to 120 knots. They were about a half-mile short of the carrier now, and Steve throttled back some more.

With the great yawning expanse of the *Eisenhower's* stern now stark before him, he cut the speed to 100 m.p.h. right above the wake. The ship was making thirty knots, which made the COD seem even slower, and as they came in there was not a single passenger who did not believe they were going so slowly they must surely drop straight into the churning white water below.

But Steve had done this a few times before, 187 times to be precise, and, with the steel loop streaming out behind, he opened the throttles and rammed the wheels down onto the deck, engines howling, ready to scream down the runway and take-off instantly if they missed the hook. Anything to avoid flopping over the edge with no speed, and crashing under the keel of the carrier.

But they all felt the jolt, as the hook grabbed and held, and the aircraft went from seventy knots to dead-stopped in 2.9 seconds. In the back, sixteen hearts restarted.

The COD taxied to its normal parking space below the island for refueling, unloading through the stern ramp, and then re-loading with mail, and a few personnel returning to base.

And the flight-deck crews moved back to their allotted positions in readiness for the arrival of the second COD from Pensacola. There was always a heightened feeling of anticipation when a SEAL team was landing, and every one of the 6,000-strong crew knew that tonight the recce group was going into unknown jungle territory, perhaps to face a foreign enemy. Tomorrow, before dark, the rest. God help them.

The second flight came in with all the professionalism of the first. The SEALs were taken below to a special mess which had been oranized for them, and the carrier now turned due south into lonely seas for the five-hour run inshore to a point fifty miles north of Colon, from where the operation would begin.

Lt. Commander Peavey with Lieutenants Green and Slocum supervised the unloading and the loading of the big CH-53D Sikorsky forty-seven Navy helicopters, the Sea Stallions which would take the SEALs in, across the Panamanian coastline, and then onward to the lake, down the course of the Chagres River. They would fly over uninhabited rainforest, to a mainland point on the north-west shore of the lake, one mile south-west of the great dam which caused the lake to form in the first case, and almost two miles from the beginning of their target, the downward Gatun Locks.

The SEALs were all served an excellent breakfast of omelettes,

ham and hash-browns, with wholewheat toast – as much as anyone could eat – before they were led to separate sleeping quarters,
all of them having been traveling all night from California.

The recce party would eat again at 1730, before embarking the
Sea Stallion on the first step of the mission at 2030 just after dark.
They would take with them two inflatables, Zodiacs with
Yamaha 175 outboards, and compressed air-cylinders, six plastic
cans of gasoline, paddles, personal weapons, the big machine-
gun, two radio transmitters, food and water for thirty-six hours,
two 100-foot long steel tape measures, two wet suits, two
Draegers, the SEALs underwater breathing apparatus, a few hand
grenades, night binoculars, and a half-dozen cans of bug spray.

Those remaining on board the *Eisenhower* until the following
evening would attend briefings with the command team, and
then wait for the early recce report from the lake before turning
in for the rest of the night.

The second group would fly off the carrier in two waves, using
both Sea Stallions, departing at 1930. Same route. Same procedures. Objective: unchanged. Hopefully.

That Sunday passed swiftly. The eight-man recce team left the
mess hall having eaten salad, steak and eggs, followed by fruit
salad, then black coffee. They returned to their departure area as
the sun was setting, they blackened their faces, pulled on their
'drive on' caps and bandannas, picked up their heavy bags and
light machine-guns, and headed for the flight deck led by Patrick
Rougeau and CPO Chris O'Riordan.

They boarded the Sea Stallion, which took off immediately,
powering into the sky beneath its huge rotors, tipped south, and
thundered into the gathering night, straight at the north shore of
Panama, now only fifty miles distant.

Twenty minutes later the helicopter's young navigator picked
up the coastline through night binoculars, checked the GPS and
located the estuary of the Chagres River. It was only five miles to
the lake.

A bright moon lit the way as they came clattering over the
gleaming silver path of the river three miles west of the high
locks. They could see the lake now, way out in front, a vast
expanse of bright water. The pilot kept at least a mile distance
between the Sea Stallion and the Gatun dam, which may have
had an armed guardhouse, although the SEAL planners back in
Coronado said not.

In fact the planners back in Coronado considered this to be one of the slackest Third World countries on earth. The National Maritime Service, the Panamanian coastguard has only 600 personnel and maybe twenty patrol boats to police the entire country, half of them laid up in need of decent servicing.

The country is entirely linear, geographically, with coastlines hundreds of miles long on both the Atlantic and Pacific coasts. To the south lies Colombia and its crime-ridden borders featuring guerrilla incursions, cross-border drug villainy, refugees and asylum seekers.

Panama, now without American help was militarily useless, and certainly, if one of their creaking, lightly-gunned Vosper-type patrol crafts had stumbled accidentally upon the SEALs in action . . . well, if it had been a boxing match the referee would have stopped it before it started.

Nothing in all of the Panamanian military could possibly cope with the might of even a small number of America's Special Forces. The unknown factor was the Chinese, how many and how well armed, were their patrols which guarded the locks. Essentially, that's what the recce group was going in to find out.

The Sea Stallion put down unobserved on the shores of Lake Gatun, one mile west of the Guarapo Islands, a group of many such clusters all through the lake. They throttled back but did not cut the rotors, and disembarked, dragging their equipment out into the hot, damp jungle air.

It was dark now and intermittent cloud covered the face of the moon, for which everyone was grateful, as they began to haul the two inflatables out, six men taking the weight of the outboard engine, using specially constructed canvas handles.

They lowered the two boats to the ground, tested the radios, and instantly the big Sikorsky revved its engine to life, and lifted off, moving north as fast as possible, so as not to betray the position of the eight Americans working below.

With an inspired piece of navigation the pilot had landed on a clear stretch of shoreline, about thirty yards in from the edge of the water, running slightly uphill to a line of trees which sheltered the area from attack from the shore. For the moment they concentrated on inflating the Zodiacs, and carrying one of them to the water's edge.

Lieutenant Patrick Rougeau detailed two seamen, and a Petty Officer to man the new base, and again he tested the radios. Then he and CPO O'Riordan, in company with PO/2 Brian Ingram from North Carolina, and two other combat SEALs climbed immediately into the boat, filled the gas tanks and let the others push them out into the lake, paddling for 100 yards before they started the motor and began the quiet journey through the dark towards the Gatun locks.

There was not a sound on the lake as they chugged forward, steering north-east towards the point on the west corner of the lock's superstructure, where the gigantic concrete edifice met the rough shoreline of the lake.

They crossed the face of the silent Gatun dam, towering steep into the night to their port side, and they kept going, Lieutenant Rougeau watching the compass, watching for the great shadow of the locks to darken the water.

Up ahead they could see lights, not many, just a bulb every fifty feet, maybe thirty feet above the water level. They could discern no sign of life, which was more or less what they expected since the Panama Canal was formally closed to all shipping.

Patrick cut the motor and each of the five SEALs took up a paddle and they silently headed for the beach, tipped up the engine, and dragged the little gray craft into the shadows below the massive wall. CPO O'Riordan took one of the seamen and they cut brushwood and covered the Zodiac. It would be unrecognizeable unless you knew it was there.

Each man took his personal weapon, and binoculars and headed for the steel ladder which led up to the giant concrete jetties which bounded the lock gates. They carried with them two wet suits, flippers and two Draegers in case of an accident. The place was absolutely deserted, but they found a square gray building, which overlooked the upper chamber and offered a flight of stone steps to a second floor from which they could easily make the roof, and observe the entire downward lock system for all of the hours of darkness.

Five minutes later, they were all on the roof, scanning the complex, trying to discern any sign of life, the only disconcerting problem was the fact that the upper chamber was full, ready to receive a ship. And they wanted it empty.

But there were no ships. And there appeared to be no-one in sight. And the five SEALs just waited until 0100 on that Monday morning, scanning the area, looking for a sign of life.

There was an ops area on their map, and they could make it

out, over on the incoming side. But they could see only two lights burning in there, and no people.

At 0115 Patrick Rougeau gave the word, and young Brian Ingram assisted both him and Chief Chris O'Riordan into wet suits. They carried the flippers and the Draegers with them, and began the climb down from the flat roof and onto the jetty which bounded the right side of the giant lock gates (looking towards the lake).

Carefully the three jet black SEALs made their way across the walkway, crouching, but moving fast. Patrick Rougeau handed the end of the steel tape measure to Chris, while Brian fixed his flippers. And with that the veteran combat SEAL placed his fingers over the top of the gate and dropped almost soundlessly the eight feet into the black water on the lakeside.

Pulling the metallic tape with him, he kicked downwards, diagonally towards the huge girder which held the hinges, running his hand against it until he felt the top of the cast-iron fitting. He could feel the concrete wall make a sharp recess here and he calculated it three-feet deep by four-feet wide, presumably to give the hinges some 'breathing space' when the great doors were opened, and to allow the doors to settle at ninety degrees, flush against the jetty walls.

He kicked downwards until he reached the bottom of the hinge which the SEAL Intelligence Division had said was seven feet from the top. Then he came up three and a half feet searching for the center bolt. He found it, checked again that it was the exact middle of the hinge, then hooked the metal end of the tape into the center-groove and pulled down on the tape three times sharply.

Back on top of the gate, Lieutenant Rougeau lying flat, felt the tug, pulled the tape as taut as possible, and using a tiny pin-point flashlight, read the distance . . . *twelve feet exactly, Brian, that's the number.*

Chief O'Riordan kicked downwards again in the now pitch black water, breathing steadily, until his fingers brushed against the second hinge, some twenty-five-feet deeper. He pushed the tape into the same center groove, and tugged three times.

Thirty-seven feet, Brian, that's the number.

And again, Chief O'Riordan kicked deep, pushing down towards the bottom of the giant chamber, groping in the silent dark for the third hinge. He tried to judge twenty-five feet but in this pitch black it was near impossible and he just kept kicking down, sliding his fingers along the girder until he found what he was looking for.

And when he did so, he pulled the now heavy tape, more than sixty feet of it through the water until he could push the end into the groove. Three more tugs and the starboard hinges were well and truly located.

Sixty-two feet, Brian, that's the number.

The next part was trickier, because while they were nearly sure the opposite hinges would be identically placed, SEALs do not actually do *nearly sure*.

And they had agreed procedures. Chris O'Riordan did not wish to surface from more than sixty feet down, and then have to kick down again. Instead he hung on to the tape measure and set off across the bottom of the lock, kicking hard, and brushing the gates with the fingers of his right hand. Up above, Patrick Rougeau walked the tape across the top of the gates, back to the nearside, as if he was taking a willful pet seal for a walk, which, of course, in a sense, he was.

They both reached the jetty at the same time, and now they reversed the procedure, Chris slowly climbed the sixty-odd feet towards the surface, in the dark, jerking the tape measure to confirm the hinge positions. They were identical, sixty-two, thirty-seven and twelve feet.

And then, still well below the surface he turned his back on the gates, and kicked out into the lake, rounded the jetty, and swam quietly back to the beach where the others were waiting. He took off the wet suit, Draeger and flippers, drank some water, and took his turn resting in the boat, while the two junior seamen took up their MP-5s and made their way up to the roof above the jetty where the Lieutenant and Brian Ingram awaited them.

It was exactly 0238 and nothing happened until shortly before 0400, when a four-man patrol, obviously soldiers, shouldering weapons, strolled across the walkway of the upper gates and passed directly beneath them.

They were Chinese, chuckling and smoking, paying little attention to anything. The SEALs watched them through the glasses, saw them reach the end of the chamber, and then turn around and stroll back the way they had come. It would have been the work of moments to remove all four of them from the face of the earth. But the SEALs wanted no sound.

They waited until 0500 when dawn began to break and returned to the Zodiac under the bushes, climbed in, completed their notes and radioed their findings back to their little beachhead. They would take turns on watch until dark, calling in any movement whatsoever in the lock complex.

It was already plain the Chinese had no intention of opening the canal at least until later on Monday, presumably while they put last-minute concealment touches to the disappearing submarine over on Trinidad Bay.

0600 Monday, April 4, 2008
USS Eisenhower
09.07N 81.50W. Speed 10.
Lt. Commander Peavey watched the young SEALs manhandle six big reels of three-quarter-inch-thick, unbreakable, black parachute cord. He was running mathematical calculations in his head, working on the theory that each bomb was three feet long, and he thus wanted eighteen inches above and below center-hinge. Therefore it would be twelve feet less eighteen inches from meat-hook to the top of the gate – ten-feet six-inches, then thirty-five-feet six-inches, then sixty-feet six-inches.

'We need six lengths, two of thirteen-feet six inches, two of thirty-eight-feet six-inches, and two of sixty-three-feet six-inches – mark them all with tape exactly three feet from the end of each line . . . that's for lashing . . . splice the meat-hooks at the other end . . . take six inches for the splice . . . same length as those hooks . . . that way we'll be accurate . . . tape the splice point hard.'

His instructions were precise, and Mich Stetter, from Indiana, the NCO in charge of this area of the operation, the SEAL who would lower the bombs into place from the lock gates, watched every movement of his team as they prepared to destroy the Panama Canal. Normal SEAL procedures, slow, careful, no mistakes, a lot of checking, and even more double-checking.

The bomb satchels each had a metallic ring, top and bottom, and Mich wanted a trial run with regular parachute cord, black but thinner than the meat-hook lines, giving the men a chance to lash the satchels together in groups of six. Each group must include one of the six satchels with the thick, bright red band around it, the ones containing the arming devices.

This deadly package would total 180 kilos of high-explosive –

that's more than 400 pounds, but they always measure explosive in kilograms. It would then be further wrapped tight in detcord, the stuff that burns at five miles a second, before being placed in a waterproof black bag, attached to the meat-hook and lowered from the top of the gate, coming to rest right in the middle of the giant hinge.

When it blew, it would certainly be the most spectacular use of detcord since Major Ray Kerman liberated Islam's political prisoners on the other side of the world three years ago, almost to the day. It was hard to believe the two incidents would be so closely interconnected. And thus far, only Arnold Morgan, George Morris and Jimmy Ramshawe knew precisely how and why.

Meanwhile the SEALs on board the aircraft carrier practised and practised heaving the heavy satchels across the room and placing them in groups. Every one of them realized the next time they tried this it would be pitch dark in a confined space, and they would then have to haul each completed sack up to the lock using straps and handles. Bill Peavey considered it far too dangerous to assemble the bomb on top of the lock gate.

'It's always gonna be easier to assemble the sacks somewhere secluded, where we have time to get it right, then carry them to the walkway, hook 'em up and drop 'em straight in. Anyone gets in our way, they die.'

All morning they practiced, lashing, dragging and heaving, getting the satchels in the waterproof sacks, working by feel, trying to do it with their eyes shut, just in case there was no moon tonight. The youngest seamen would lift the satchels off the ground while the explosive men steered them into place. One seaman in each group would lash them together.

Lt. Patrick Rougeau would personally take charge of the detcord and detonating. Right now Mich Stetter was cutting thin, black electrical cord into approximate lengths of sixty-four feet, thirty-nine feet and fourteen feet. It was not possible to be accurate, but it couldn't be too short. Mich was allowing a couple of feet to connect to the arming device inside the red-banded satchels, and to the tiny float and whip-thin aerial which would bob silently on the surface, waiting for the electronic impulse which would detonate all six bombs simultaneously, with stupendous force, against the gates to the Gatun Lake.

They had a late breakfast at 1300, slept until 1730, and had their last food before departure at 1800 – roast chicken, salad and baked potatoes.

Just as they sat down in the private SEAL dining area, the message came in from the destroyer *USS Roosevelt*, whose commanding officer Captain Butch Howarth was still furious with the controllers of the canal. His message was simple . . . *Chinese reopened Panama Canal 141730APR08. . . . gave immediate priority to three Chinese ships in the holding area . . . first, the Luhu Class Type 052 destroyer* Qingdao, *then two freighters around 20,000 tons.* Roosevelt *still awaiting clearance. Howarth.*

Bill Peavey was immediately alerted, and someone brought his dinner to the comms room while he drafted a signal into the beach where the recce party's guards were manning the big machine gun and the radio . . . *Chinese reopened canal 1730 . . . Luhu Class destroyer* Qingdao *entered first . . . ETA Gatun lock midnight . . . stay alert . . . we arrive 2100. Peavey.*

Up on the flight deck the Sea Stallions were revved up, loaded and ready for take-off. Lt. Commander Peavey led his team out onto the hot, windy area high on the port side of the carrier.

One by one the SEALs boarded, each man's face blackened with camouflage cream, each of them carrying his personal weapon, the MP-5 machine-gun, combat knife, and binoculars. Some of them with hand grenades, all of them with small maps, charts and diagrams of the locks.

Two petty officers, the Texan Joe Little, and Tony McQuade from Georgia, sat with check-lists detailing the number of gasoline cans, compressed-air cylinders, paddles, the heavy reels of detcord, the ready-cut bomb lines, the satchels, the bags, the radios, the water canisters. The SEALs were to leave no trace of their existence. Every last piece of equipment had to be accounted for, both on the inward journey and the return. There was no food. This was to be a ten-hour round trip operation, door to door. Max.

They took off at 2030, following the route of the recce team, fifty miles into the Panamanian coastline, down the river and into the landing space on the narrow beach. Lt. Commander Peavey was silent for the whole journey, turning over in his mind the split-second timing they would now require – because that top chamber had to be empty when the gates blew, and that meant the first ship had to be completely out of it, and into the channel heading for the second lock, when the bombs were detonated.

Not too far, because with the heavy exiting traffic building up in the lake, the Chinese keepers would be refilling that chamber very fast.

The moment the first Sikorsky landed, the three SEALs manning the little beachhead rushed forward to help unload the inflatables, fill them with air, and gas them up in the shallows. One Zodiac was of course still there, ready to go. All of them had been fitted with twelve-gallon plastic tanks to give them a six-hour running time, ample for the stealthy four–mile round trip to the lock gates.

Everything was unloaded and the empty gas cans were stowed aboard the lead Sikorsky, which took off immediately after the second one landed. And still there was no sign of any patrol craft, nor indeed any indication that the control room up at the lock even knew there had been a landing.

In total silence, the twenty-eight SEALs pushed out into the black waters, huddled in the three boats. They kicked over the engines and began the short run up to the lock, past the great wall of the Gatun Dam, which was precisely where their luck ran out.

Up ahead they could hear the unmistakable sound of a powerful boat, about a half-mile north, traveling dirctly towards them, its red and green port and starboard lights easily visible in the clear tropical night.

The Zodiacs carried no lights, and their tactics were well rehearsed. All motors were cut and two of the inflatables peeled off, one left, one right heading back south. The lead boat carried on, four SEALs paddling straight towards the oncoming patrol, the rest flat down in the boat, all fingers on the trigger.

'Ahoy,' yelled Peavey, as a big searchlight settled on his boat. '*No es culpa suya!*' Which he hoped meant 'please help' in Spanish. '*Incapaz, indefenso,*' he added.

By now they could see the armed four-man crew up on the rail looking down in plain and obvious alarm. But not for long. Petty Officer Joe Little, from out of nowhere, blew all four of them away with a savage burst of machine-gun fire which riddled a grotesque pattern into the forehead of every one of them.

Tony McQuade boarded the ship, headed for the cockpit and blew away the radio. By which time, Lt. Commander Peavey was on board, stripped to the waist, boots off. He set the autopilot on 284, shoved Tony over the side back into the Zodiac, tossed his own machine-gun in right after him, and headed back to the control room.

He rammed the throttles wide open, sending the patrol boat straight for the dam wall at thirty unwavering knots. Then he jumped for his life, into the lake starboard side and waited for the Zodiac to come pick him up.

Wet pants, dead Chinese, and a wrecked boat, all in the first twenty minutes.

'Jesus Christ,' said Bill, as they hauled him out of the water.

And one minute later they all heard the dull crump of the patrol boat obliterating itself on the dam wall, the wreckage sliding down to the very deepest part of the lake, more or less as the CO had planned.

'Onward,' he said quietly. 'We got work to do.'

Five minutes later they were up level with their landing beach, paddling in, the other two Zodiacs now right behind them, two more SEALs standing in the shallows, ready to help them into the shadow of the towering Gatun lock jetty.

By now Lt. Rougeau was positioned close to the top of the steel ladder with Chris O'Riordan, ready to help haul in the satchels, as the SEAL assault group made the climb from the beach, the explosive strapped to their backs.

And one by one they made the killer ascent, each man with close to seventy pounds on his back, as well as his light machine-gun and ammunition clips fitted across his chest. The trouble was it was impossible for two men to carry the load. The task had to be achieved one by one, and there was no question of assembling the bombs and then maneuvering them somehow through the water.

The explosive had to be dropped in from the top of the gates, no ifs, ands or buts. And the SEALs had to get it up there from the beach. Failure, as ever, was unthinkable.

Their only recourse was for CPO O'Riordan to drop a heavy line with a meathook which could grab the metal clasp in the satchel and take some of the weight up the final steps. This was an option Lt. Commander Peavey laid out before they started. No-one took it. Each man fought his way up that ladder, carrying his huge burden all alone. None of them became US Navy SEALs by accident.

The last man reached the top at 2320. Time was running out. Patrick Rougeau steered them to a place in deep shadow where they split into their allotted groups. Two teams of six men took over the tying operation, lashing the satchels together in groups of six.

Two more teams descended the ladder and dragged two of the Zodiacs down the beach and back into the water, ready to round the jetty and provide protection for the men working on the high gates. Bill Peavey assessed that any danger or challenge would come from the lake rather than the somewhat slothful shore patrol up on the lock complex.

The two teams assigned to shore protection split to either side of the jetty, one group back up on the roof where Lt. Rougeau had started. The other on the far side of the lock, lying flat, looking back toward the control room. The men working close to the walkway were now covered by withering machine-gun fire, if necessary. But everyone hoped it would not be.

By 2340 the six bombs were ready, packed in their waterproof bags, the devices armed, the detcord wrapped hard and tight. Patrick Rougeau personally set the electronic wires, one end connected inside the red-banded satchel, the other end to the little floating radio aerial.

By now they could see the lights from the Chinese destroyer advancing across the lake, probably two miles away and making around six knots. And now the bomb teams faced the most difficult and delicate part of their operation. And they were short of time.

Lt. Commander Peavey grabbed the big handle on the first bag, and with three more SEALs on the other corners, they heaved it onto the walkway, half dragging, half carrying it the 110 feet across the lock where Lt. Rougeau awaited with the meat-hook line. Swiftly he inserted the hook, and Mich Stetter pushed the bag under the iron handrail.

They all took the weight as it slipped down eight feet and then became light as it submerged into the water on the lake side. Slowly they lowered it, feeling it bump down against the girder. As it reached its correct depth, some sixty feet below, Lt. Rougeau checked the marker tape was hard against the edge of the gate, and he lashed the remaining three feet to the base of the end strut. He used a bowline knot and cut the surplus line off. When the motorized handrail went down, when they opened the gates, that strut would slide through the line and the rail itself would hide it.

Twice more they repeated the exercise, dragging the huge weight across the lock, and lowering it into the water, fastening it off with the bowline, and feeling it swing gently against the giant hinges.

On the nearside of the gates, CPO O'Riordan was doing the same. But his men did not have that back-breaking journey across the lock, and it was as well that Bill Peavey, one of the strongest men in the US Navy was among the muscle present on that dark and treacherous night.

By midnight the SEALs had moved into position, Lt. Rougeau back on the roof of the original building, accompanied by three bodyguards, four MP-5s and powerful night binoculars. Lt. Commander Peavey was heading back out into the lake in one of the Zodiacs and everyone else was clearing up and preparing for the getaway.

The Commanding Officer was accompanied by Chief O'Riordan who was now speaking to Patrick Rougeau on the radio. They headed out into the lake more than a quarter of a mile from the gates, but still well within the range of the deadly transmitter which would flash its electronic signal simultaneously to the six bobbing little aerials outside the lock gates.

The plan was simple. Lt. Rougeau would give them clearance to detonate, when the Chinese destroyer was safely through the exit gates from the upper chamber, almost thirty feet lower, and being hauled along to the second chamber by the automatic locomotives. In various forms, these iron-horses have done the task for generations, like an old-fashioned carwash used to drag vehicles through the soap-suds.

The men on the lake would then wait six minutes for the SEALs to make their escape off the roof, back to the beach, and the last boat. At which point they would send in the fatal signal.

West of the destroyer's approach path, the SEALs watched from the Zodiacs, as it steamed slowly towards the lock gates. They could not see them slowly open, outwards into the lake, powered by no fewer than ninety-two electric motors, but they saw the great 470-foot-long hull of the warship slide between the jetties, at which point Chief O'Riordan knew the bombs would have eased back into the wide recesses in the walls.

Up on the roof Patrick Rougeau and his team watched the locomotives drag the warship into the chamber, and the giant gates shut behind it. And somewhere deep below them they heard the distant thunder of the water, millions of gallons, gushing through the tunnels, emptying the lock. The ship did not appear to be moving but after five minutes it was undoubtedly lower in the water.

For twenty more minutes they waited, until the superstructure of the ship had virtually disappeared. Then they saw the gates at the far end slowly open, and they could hear the revving of the locomotives as they dragged the ship out of the chamber into the narrow waterway towards the next set of gates, the entrance to the middle lock.

Over in the control room the entire procedure was being watched by four Chinese technicians on the sixty-four-foot-long electronic model, which demonstrates every progression, every step of the way for every ship that moves through the canal. It records the actions of every one of the 1,500 electric motors, and now it showed the Luhu Class destroyer at the beginning of its short run to the second pair of gates it would encounter.

'*H-hour! H minus six!*' called Patrick Rougeau. H for *hit* that is.

Out in the Zodiac, Bill Peavey hit the stop watch, which would count down the six minutes it would take Patrick and his boys to clear the rooftop, race down the stairway onto the jetty, down the long ladder to the beach and board the last inflatable waiting to ferry them away.

Chief O'Riordan working the radio, immediately summoned the Sea Stallions which were ready to take off from the carrier. They were all scheduled all to arrive at the landing beach together.

Five minutes went by, by which time Lt. Rougeau and his team were clambering into the boat, everyone scared to death the blast from the bombs might send the entire lock skywards, millions of tons of concrete. They fired up the engine, now careless of the noise, and travelling flat out, made 300 yards south, by the time Bill Peavey hit the button.

The electronic pulse flashed unseen across the dark water, hit the little aerials, and simultaneously detonated all six of the 400-pound bombs. They blew with staggering force, and with a deafening roar, which kicked a twenty-foot wave back into the lake, where the Zodiac carrying Bill, Chris and the boys was making forty knots, south-west.

The blast annihilated the great iron hinges and blew both lock gates fifty feet into the night air. At which point a wall of water, with a forward motion of zillions of tons, over sixty feet high, thundered into the empty chamber like the mother of all previously known tidal waves.

It slammed into the second gates with the kind of force which would have flattened the Pentagon. They gave way as if they were made of cardboard, and the thunderous torrent, now driven by another zillion tons of water surging in from the lake, reached the hapless 9,000-ton *Qingdao*, ripped it from the chains of the locomotive and hurled it forward.

The sharp pointed bow of the Chinese warship cleared the gates of the second chamber some thirty feet higher than it should have been and it was the keel and propellers which splintered the giant lock doors, smashing them off their hinges.

By now the torrent was gathering strength, and as the new water drove into the old, surging through the narrow reinforced concrete channel, it drove the destroyer's bow upwards, sending it through the second chamber at an angle of fifty degrees from the horizontal, the propellers tearing along the concrete bottom.

It hit the end gates like a gigantic battering ram, never even slowed as it ripped straight through the channel to the last chamber, slammed into those gates, cannoned off the sides, and then smashed its way forward through the last gates and crashed down the final twenty-eight feet into the Caribbean Sea.

Patrick Rougeau mentioned to his colleagues they had just watched the fastest transit in the entire ninety-four-year history of the Panama Canal, the final two chambers having been negotiated by the *Qingdao* in a little under forty-five seconds!

And it was by no means over. There was no way of stopping the tidal surge from Lake Gatun. The wall of water just kept coming, cascading through the locks, thundering downwards, picking up the *Qingdao* and hurling it clear of the channel out into deep water, holed, battered, many dead and injured, but still floating.

Meanwhile 164 square miles of deep lake water just kept roaring out through the world's biggest ever plughole. And it would continue to do so, for seven days until the lake was almost entirely drained.

The SEALs? They came racing into their landing beach, loaded up the helicopters, with everything except the far-too-heavy inflatables. These they sent out towards the middle of the lake, tossing a hand grenade into each one as it went. Then they all hit the beach and watched the little boats explode some sixty yards offshore, before scrambling aboard the Sea Stallions and heading back to the *Eisenhower*.

Lt. Commander Bill Peavey's signal was concise. '*Mission accomplished. Panama Canal destroyed. Casualties zero.*'

EPILOGUE

1800, Friday, April 25, 2008
The Karnak Bar, Damascus
Ravi and Shakira sat companionably with a couple of cold beers at their favorite corner table overlooking Martyrs' Square. Their short visit to the Librairie Avicenne bookstore had yielded two American film magazines, a copy of the London *Sunday Telegraph*, and Tuesday's *New York Times*.

Shakira was staring at a big cover photo of Troy Ramford, with the Irish writer Edna Casey, clasped in each other's arms, at a private ceremony at the Headquarters of the Screen Actors' Guild where Troy finally collected his Oscar for *Timeshare*.

The caption read: *Troy gets his statue one month after the lights went out. Edna gets her man.* Shakira was riveted.

She knew of course that the lights had gone out on the American west coast. They'd been home now for almost two weeks and the newspapers in the Middle East had been full of the story. But the Iranian Government had prudently forbidden HAMAS to claim responsibility.

It was her own stunning, precision timing that brought a huge smile to the face of Shakira Rashood now basking in the knowledge of her shocking impact on the climax to the 2008 Oscar ceremony. Here was old Troy picking up the statue in a private office, and all because of her.

Ravi, on the other hand, was equally riveted by the *New York Times*, which led its front page with the headline:

IT'S OFFICIAL – THE USA TAKES
OVER THE PANAMA CANAL
Bloodless Coup as Panamanian
President Signs 1,000-Year Treaty

What followed was an almost unheard-of interview with the

395

President's National Security Advisor, Admiral Arnold Morgan who declared in the third paragraph:

'*The International Seaway of the Panama Canal was built and financed by the United States almost one hundred years ago for the peaceful use of all the world's shipping. Between them, two Democratic Presidents, Carter and Clinton, managed not only to give it away to Panama, but to place it under the control of Red China.*

'*So now we had the great pathway between the seas in the hands of a backward Third World Republic, and a totalitarian Communist State who between them would find it impossible to build even a decent airliner, never mind service and maintain one of the great engineering marvels of the modern world.*

'*A couple of weeks ago we saw the disastrous consequences of allowing such people to take on a responsibility which was plainly too big for them. The giant high lock gates on Lake Gatun gave way after years of improper servicing and maintenance. As we all know the tidal wave which then swept down the outward locks on the Atlantic side completely destroyed the structure and indeed drained the Gatun Lake.*

'*The USA regarded this as a criminal act of negligence, and considered it incumbent upon ourselves to step forward to rebuild it in the interests of the international community. No-one else could rebuild it. But we were not about to rebuild someone else's canal.*

'*We thus sent in a military force of 10,000 United States Marines on a peaceful mission, to advise the Chinese personnel of the Hutchison Whampoa Corporation, which is controlled by the People's Liberation Army, that they must now vacate the entire Panama Canal Zone upon which they enjoyed the benefits of an illegal lease, and proved themselves inadequate custodians.*

'*Marine General Mo Sherman advised the Panamanian President of our views, and he agreed the Chinese must leave his country forthwith. The President understood our very real concern and thanked the USA for its generous offer to rebuild and run the canal.*

'*I am delighted to announce the Chinese have now evacuated the area, and that the USA is once more in sole control of the entire Canal Zone, including the dockyards situated on both the Atlantic and Pacific ends of the waterway. In addition we have reoccupied the old American Navy base at Rodman, and the railroad on the east bank, from the City of Colon all the way to the old Fort Grant causeway outside Balboa on the Pacific.*

'*Work will begin rebuilding the high lock gates in one month. We expect to complete the construction by the middle of 2009. The USA has offered a royalty contract to the Panamanian Government, payable from the tolls, after the cost of rebuilding has been recouped, probably coming into effect in the year 2013.*

'The Panamanians have indicated their intentions to accept those terms. And, mindful of the unstable nature of the country, the USA has agreed to keep a small peacekeeping Marine Garrison in Panama "for the foreseeable future".'

According to the *Times*, there were US army gunships seen circling the Presidential Palace last week, and a total news blackout was imposed throughout Panama City. The *Times* reporter, trying to operate from twenty miles away, claimed information has been extremely sketchy.

From the White House, Admiral Morgan would only say, 'I have no knowledge of any aggressive acts by the United States military in the Republic of Panama.'

General Rashid smiled. 'No, Admiral. I suppose not. You unprincipled, vicious bastard.'

Monday morning, April 8
The White House
Lt. Commander Jimmy Ramshawe sat before the Big Man while he read the latest CIA report of the highly-classified US investigation into the ruined Barracuda 945, eventually located in the Gatun Lake, half-sunk, its intakes choked with mud, its active days over. Soon the mud would suck it down completely, without trace.

The CIA report ran to forty-six pages, and the main good news was that the Panamanians had willingly led the Americans by helicopter to carry out their investigations on the shores of Pelican Island. The reason for the delay was the water was now too shallow for a boat and too much like a quicksand for a vehicle. The rainforest offered no clearing for a helicopter and they just had to wait for the mud to firm up.

When it did, the Americans swarmed all over the submarine for a week, finding practically nothing in the now silent hulk. No papers, no documents, no fingerprints, no clothing. There were six missiles left, Ravi and Shakira having fired eighteen of the twenty-four RADUGAs, and the boat contained no other weapons. Arnold guessed they had jettisoned everything out in the Pacific long before they entered the canal.

What, of course, they did find was the body of Joe Morris of

Wilmington, Delaware, with his two companions, Skip and Ronnie lying underwater near the base of the periscope, passports and documents still readable, the only papers left in the ship.

The report of their deaths was concise. Skip and Ronnie had half their heads blown away with bursts from a Russian-built AK-47 automatic. Joe Morris had died in a most unusual way. The skull bone between his eyes, an inch and a half above the bridge of his nose, had been smashed with a plainly round object. The central bone of his nose had been driven with incredible force into his brain.

Lt. Commander Ramshawe had highlighted that with a fluorescent green marker pen. And that was where Arnold Morgan stopped.

'Christ,' he breathed. 'It was him, eh, Jimmy? Our old buddy Major Ray Kerman, expert in unarmed combat.'

'Yessir. Yes it was. One SAS NCO, one British Member of Parliament, one unknown American visitor. All killed identically – unmistakable professionalism. Special Forces.'

'And we don't know where the hell he is.'

'Nossir. And we've been using that exact phrase for a damned long time . . . we don't know where he is.'

'I tell you what, though,' growled Arnold. 'We sure as hell know where he's been.'